Gold Coast Detective
Scotty Stephens

Book 4

INSEXT

ANDREW McDERMOTT

PRESS

INSEXT by ANDREW MᶜDERMOTT
www.andrewmcdermott.com.au

First published in Australia by X Press Publishing 2025
P.O. Box 395 Coolangatta
Queensland 4225 Australia
mail@andrewmcdermott.com.au

A catalogue record for this
book is available from the
National Library of Australia

ISBN: 978-1-7638597-2-2 (pbk)
ISBN: 978-1-7638597-3-9 (ebk)

Cover design by X Press Publishing © 2025
Cover background image: © KinoMaster (Shutterstock)

Typesetting and design by X Press Publishing © 2025

For Lucy

1

With the unfamiliar clarity of sober thought, Bobby Sexton's recollection of the last thirty years was gradually returning like gentle waves on an incoming tide. Wandering slowly through his Gold Coast mansion—as if for the first time—the gold and platinum discs, the Grammy awards and the priceless memorabilia acted as triggers, instigating memories of a rock star's life.

To the newly cleansed addict, fresh from rehab, the materialistic trappings surrounding him no longer had meaning. A promotional poster of the Sexton brothers fronting arguably the biggest band in the world, momentarily caught his eye, but not his attention.

As if oblivious to his surroundings, Bobby drifted towards the pool at the back of the house.

Like a slice of Manhattan, Surfers Paradise dominated the view, demoting the stars to an understudy status.

With the unfamiliar luxury of a rational mind, hidden memories materialised into visions of a murky past.

There was little force needed to hold down the comatose drummer. Lying face down in the pool, Jimmy Reggae was barely conscious after partying on a cocktail of drugs and alcohol.

Did that really happen? Racked with guilt, Bobby recited a mantra from his 12-step program: 'God, grant me the serenity to accept the things I cannot change, the courage to change the things I can, and the wisdom to know the difference.'

Guiding Bobby's thoughts, while calmly prioritising the tasks that lay ahead, the chant diminished to a whisper. The texts he'd composed in rehab were still in his phone. He would send them now. Only then could the healing begin.

After the familiar *schwoop* heralding the delivery of the last text, sounded, Bobby poured himself an iced tea and returned to the pool. Next, he would call the Queensland Police. *Should he dial 000?* Bobby had little knowledge of such day-to-day matters.

He lifted his drink, but before the liquid could reach his lips, the glass fell from his hand and shattered on the ground. A searing pain between his shoulder blades caused his back to arch, and his head to snap backwards. An involuntary gasp imploded as one of his lungs collapsed, increasing the pain tenfold. When he staggered forward, the pain allocation distributed from the knife in his back rendered a shard of crystal in his foot as undetectable.

Barely able to turn, Bobby showed no surprise when coming face to face with his attacker. Once described as one of the most original lyricists of the 20th century, Bobby Sexton's final words were of little significance. 'Of course ... it's *you*. I should have—'

Surfers Paradise suddenly turned on its side. The palm trees, the house and the world all followed suit. Then there was silence and an intense cold. The beautiful hair that was once sold in inch-long portions to his adoring fans, slowly swirled in a cloud of claret. As the pressure in Bobby's head intensified, he realised he wasn't alone. Jimmy Reggae was lying on the bottom of the pool, looking up at him. Jimmy smiled and reached out. Taking his hand, Bobby's pain immediately subsided. The cold became warm, and the perfect blue aura expanded into an infinite white light.

2

One hour earlier.

'I just wanted to say thank you, Mr Sexton—'

'Phil. Call me Phil.'

'Phil … for giving me this opportunity.' In contrast to the wild persona she portrayed from behind her drum kit, Zoey May relayed a polite shyness that was quite unexpected by her fellow bandmates.

'You're welcome. But you're not in yet. It's all down to Bobby.' Phil, avoiding the stare of Tommy Platt, his road manager and friend for over forty years, knocked on the door of his brother's Gold Coast home for the second time.

Tommy, angry that his suggestion was ignored, looked away.

'Bobby, are you here?' Phil knocked harder, using the side of his fist. He was pretty sure his younger brother was home. Since being discharged from rehab a week earlier, he'd been holed up, refusing to talk to anyone.

'This is a bad idea, Phil. You need to speak to him first … alone,' Tommy said.

'No. I think this will be a good tonic for him. He always loved a surprise.' Phil glanced around the small group of musicians as if rallying support.

Keeping their thoughts to themselves, Mick Mantle—the guitarist—and Jessie Flint—the bass player—nodded in that sycophantic way they'd honed over the years.

'Screw this,' Phil growled. Hoping the lock hadn't been reprogrammed, he punched in a four-digit code on the keypad in the centre of the double doors. The mechanism clicked. Phil tried the handle of the door on the right, and it opened. The same manoeuvre had already worked on the front gate.

'We can't just walk into his house,' Tommy said.

'Of course we can. He's my brother,' Phil said, stepping through the doorway.

Tommy reluctantly followed. Zoey entered next. Mick and Jessie's reluctance was on a par with Tommy's.

'Bobby ... you here?' Phil called out as he strutted through a marble-clad foyer.

All the lights were on, but the house was eerily quiet.

'Bobby?' With the entourage in his wake, Phil entered an expansive kitchen diner.

One side of the room was open to the pool area. Bobby was sitting cross-legged on the ground outside with his back to them. The only sounds were crickets in the night and the hum of Surfers Paradise in the distance.

'Bobby.' Phil marched over to his brother and rounded on him. 'Hey Bro, it's me.'

'Phil?' Bobby said, opening his eyes. His puzzled expression morphed into an angry scowl. 'What are you doing in my house?'

'Well, it's good to see you too, mate.' A patient tolerance laced Phil's grin.

When Bobby jumped to his feet, he turned and realised they weren't alone. 'What the hell is all this?'

'Uhm ... surprise!'

'You really are a dick, Phil!' Bobby growled.

Looking away once more, Tommy's expression mirrored Bobby's sentiment.

'Ah, come on,' Phil said, lurching forward, grabbing his younger brother by the shoulders and pulling him in for a hug. 'It's great to have you back.'

Bobby pulled back and almost pushed Phil into the pool. 'Don't touch me. How did you get in here?'

'You didn't change the code. 1994.'

'So, you thought you could just barge in? This is my home.'

'Bobby, I'm sorry. I just wanted to see you. Come on bro, what's going on?'

'What's going on?' Bobby's fists were clenched and ready.

'Okay, okay …' Phil raised his hands in surrender. 'I realise you're going to need some time—'

'Oh, I've had plenty of time. Plenty of time to think.' Bobby jabbed his right temple with his forefinger. 'Six months, in fact.'

'It's great to have you back. Isn't that right, Tommy? Mick, Jessie?'

The nods were non-committal.

'Well, you need to leave *now!* Bobby yelled. 'All of you.'

'Okay,' Phil said. 'But I want to leave you this at least.' He retrieved a memory stick from his pocket and forced it into Bobby's hand.

'What's this?'

'The new album.'

'What?'

'All recorded except for the lead vocals.'

'Are you fucking kidding me?'

'It's called "Resurrection". How do you feel about a world tour? Mick and Jessie are in. Oh, and this is Zoey, our new drummer.' Phil briefly gestured in Zoey's direction, but his eyes were fixed firmly on his brother. 'We're going to be back on top, Bobby!'

Bobby threw the memory stick into the pool. 'You're delusional, Phil … I was going to tell you later, but I may as well do it now, seeing as you're here …' He turned and eyed the rest of the group. 'Seeing as you're all here. I'm leaving the band … it's over. INSEXT is finished without me!'

'What do you mean?' Phil demanded.

'I can't make it any clearer than that, Phil. The band's finished. You're finished. It's time to move on, *bro!*'

Phil lurched forward and grabbed Bobby by the scruff of the neck. 'You listen to me, you little shit—'

From years of crowd control and holding back screaming fans, Tommy moved with an adept speed and skilfully pulled the siblings apart. 'Now then guys, come on.'

'Get out of my house, Phil,' Bobby yelled. 'And take your session musicians with you.'

'You ungrateful little bastard! You'd be nothing if it weren't for me,' Phil screamed.

'Well, we'll see about that, won't we?'

'Oh what, so you think you're gonna go solo, is that it?' Phil's patronising chuckle reeked of contempt.

'No mate, that part of my life's over. I'm going for what's rightfully mine.'

'*Phfff* … and what's that supposed to mean?'

'Like I said, I've had a lot of time to think.'

'Well, that's good. Means you've probably realised how lucky you are.'

'Not lucky. Ripped off!'

Phil's nonchalant manner suddenly hardened. 'Ripped off?'

Bobby stepped forward.

Tommy placed a muscular arm between him and his brother.

'Do you really think I didn't know what was going on?'

'Mate, you've been so out of it for the last thirty years, you couldn't even tie your own shoelaces without me.'

'You took advantage of me.'

'I protected you, looked after you. And that's what I'm still doing to this day.'

'I know what you *did*, Phil.'

3

Two years later.

I'll never get used to reading about myself. I'd been in the news quite a lot over the last couple of years. A rollercoaster of paradigm shifting stories beginning with the young detective who was plucked from obscurity and placed in charge of Australia's biggest murder case before becoming a hero after apprehending the Gold Coast serial killer known as *X*. To my embarrassment, the term "Saviour of the Gold Coast" still endured to this day.

The next big story was when I quit the police force and became a private detective, which was followed by a couple of high-profile cases—a five-year murder mystery in Tallebudgera Valley, and then the case of missing child star, Cory Evans, aka Freckles.

The stories were mostly positive, but for some reason, the *Gold Coast Bulletin* had adopted a negative stance against me. Unlike the love and gratitude showered on me by the people of the Gold Coast, the local journos were constantly writing articles tinged with sarcastic, patronising views questioning my character. Today's story on the front page, no less, had nothing to do with my achievements. It was about the loss of my home—the burning down of my recently purchased house in Kirra. I'd bought the old property from my childhood friend, Elvis. The same day, it burned to the ground. Instead of sticking to the facts and possibly offering a little sympathy, the local newspaper had taken a different viewpoint. Somehow, they'd gotten wind of the curse that was put on me by Moe Brennan, the mother of the notorious bikie gang leader, Mick Brennan. "Ya won't know where, ya won't know when, and ya won't know how … but ya can be sure it's coming," were the words of the fiery little Irish matriarch. A couple of days later, I lost my home and everything I owned to an electrical fire. *Curse or accident?* Of course, I'm going with the latter, but I have to admit, the way that woman leaned in and delivered the curse in the foyer of the Surfers Paradise Police Headquarters, did put the willies up me a bit. So, the *Gold Coast Bulletin* came at the story from two angles. One was the curse, the other was the possibility of insurance fraud, claiming that I had arranged for the house to be destroyed because the price I'd paid for it was a lot less than its actual value. Both claims were ridiculous.

Sitting at the desk in my office in Coolangatta, above what used to be the accountancy firm owned by my best mate, Elvis, I was between jobs and at a bit of a loose end. Elvis had returned to Melbourne to be with his parents after going through some kind of nervous breakdown. And with the loss of the house on Ruby Street, life really had changed. For the last twenty years, I'd been living the bachelor's dream. Sharing a house with my buddies, surfing every morning, following the footy, and partying like teenagers. The only problem was, we weren't kids anymore. Approaching my mid-forties, I had grown tired of the life and yearned for something different. "Be careful what you wish for, Scotty," was something my mother used to say. *Had I wished for this? Becoming successful, having money in the bank, had this only been possible by discarding or losing everything I knew?* Even my beloved VW Beetle was destroyed in the fire. *Was the old Scotty Stephens also gone?* And as if none of this were enough, my dog, Romeo, was killed at the hands of the Tallebudgera killer. At this moment in my life, I'd never felt so alone.

With the newspaper spread out across my desk, my phone rang. I didn't know the number but answered, hoping it wasn't one of those annoying telemarketing calls.

'Hello, is that Scotty Stephens?' It was a male's voice.

'Yes, it is.'

'Great. Hi … uhm … this is Ray Morris.'

'Ray Morris?' The only Ray Morris I knew was a well-known musician. Infamous rather than famous, his stake in rock 'n' roll history was for being the drummer who was dropped by Australia's most successful rock band, INSEXT, just before they hit the big time. But the infamy part was due to him being convicted of killing the lead singer, Bobby Sexton, thirty years later. That was two years ago. He was currently serving a life sentence in the Townsville Correctional Centre. '*Thee* Ray Morris?'

'The one and only. You're probably wondering how and why I'm calling you.'

'Uh, yeah.'

'I've been following your career over the last couple of years, Scott.'

'Rightio.'

'And I need your help.' There was a pause, which I purposely left open. 'I'm innocent, Scott. I never killed Bobby.'

'A jury tried and convicted you.'

'I know, but I can assure you I'm innocent. I would never have harmed Bobby. I loved him.'

'But he kicked you out of the band.'

'No, that was his brother, Phil; and Alex, their manager. I never saw eye to eye with them.'

'Have you got any proof?'

There was another pause. 'No … that's the problem. I was stitched up. Whoever did this planned it in advance. The knife, me arriving at the property when I did.'

'Do you have anything in your defence at all?'

'Just the facts and a few suspicions.'

'We're going to need a lot more than that, mate.' I could get the facts by reading the police reports and court transcripts. I only had a vague recollection of the case because it was going on at the same time as the *X* murders, but thanks to DI Jenny Radford, I still had limited access to certain police files if needed. The suspicions Ray mentioned obviously hadn't held up in court, so unless any new information came to light, there'd be very little to run with.

'I have money. I can pay your going rate.' His tone became rushed and almost desperate. 'Stella sold our story.'

'Stella?'

'My wife. She'll help you in any way she can.'

'I'll need to think about it, Ray.'

'Of course. All I can say, Scott, is that I'm innocent. I had absolutely no reason to kill Bobby. It was almost thirty years since I'd even seen him, but I suspect there are those that had reason to do him harm. There was a lot of money to be made from the band after Bobby's death.'

4

Seated at my desk, contemplating the call I'd just taken, for some reason, a reggae tune was playing in my mind. *Was it Bob Marley?* A gentle knock on the office door startled me. Normally, I'd hear the door at the bottom of the stairs open to the street, then listen for the *clunk clunk* sound on the linoleum floor growing louder as the visitor climbed the stairs. But there had been no such prelude. *Was I so deep in concentration that I had heard nothing, or had I been asleep at my desk?*

Through the opaque glass, I could see a short figure with dark hair on the other side of the door. 'Yes, come in.'

The door opened slowly, and a woman poked her head inside. 'Hello, Mr Stephens?'

Even without the over-the-top make-up and the sequined outfit, I recognised her straight away. 'Kea Chapman.'

She smiled and entered the room. 'Ahh, you remember me.'

'How could I forget you?' At times, having the ability of never forgetting a face could act as a curse rather than a blessing. Sometimes, ignorance was bliss. On this occasion, I had no such safe harbour in which to hide. The last time I'd seen the little middle-aged woman was in Tallebudgera Valley. Kea was a psychic medium. The agent of best-selling author, Ben Fisher, had hired her to assist with the Kathy Brown case by conducting a televised seance. I was having no part of it then, and wouldn't be now. But I was curious why she was here. 'What can I do for you, love?' I said, looking up from my desk.

She closed the door behind her and took the seat opposite my desk. 'It's more a case of what *I* can do for *you*.' She spoke with a cautious tone.

Uh-oh. I smiled patiently. 'Can I get you a cup of tea?'

'That would be lovely.' Above a warm smile, searching eyes were locked onto their target.

Moving to the small kitchenette in the corner came as a grateful distraction and an excuse to break eye contact.

'Your mum said to say hi.' The words rolled out as if she'd just bumped into my dead mother at the shops.

Water from the tap did little to drown out her words, but I continued my task with industrious preoccupation, as if I hadn't heard her. That was a mistake. I should have nipped it in the bud right away.

'Your father's very happy.'

'Milk and sugar?' I asked without turning.

'Milk. No sugar, please. I'm sweet enough.'

The time it took to make that cup of tea would have been worthy of an entry in the latest book of *Guinness World Records*. Those tea bags wouldn't jiggle themselves. That milk had to be poured just right—slowly and precisely. Reluctantly, when I could stretch the chore no longer, I handed her a not-too-hot mug of milky tea and returned to my seat.

'I see you're keeping the little fellow close.' She cocked her head toward Romeo's basket. 'He's always with you.'

'Look, Kea …' I moved uncomfortably to the front of my chair and leaned on the desk. 'You know I don't believe any of this, eh?'

She nodded enthusiastically, then took a precautionary sip of her tea. 'I do. That's why I'm here.'

'Are you here about a case or …? I have to say, my books are pretty full at the moment.'

Now it was her turn to deliver a patient smile. 'I am actually.'

'Oh, right? Has something happened?'

'Not yet …' *Was she deliberately being coy? All part of the act? Or was she choosing her next words carefully?* 'I don't expect you to become a believer, Scott. That's not why I'm here. I'm here about the drummer.'

Fuck me. It's a good job I didn't make myself a cup of tea because I would have dropped it right there and then. I'd only just received the phone call from Ray Morris. How could Kea know that? Thankfully, my little voice of common sense kicked in. She was a professional. It was her business to know what was going on. She was a master of research and an expert in reading people—or perhaps in this instance Ray or his wife had contacted her beforehand.

'Drummer?'

'Yes, the poor unfortunate soul who has yet to see justice.'

'I don't quite follow.' I wasn't about to encourage her, but I was curious to see what she knew.

'Take the case, Scott. Not for you, but for the drummer.'

'Ray Morris? Has he been in touch with you?'

She wasn't listening. And although her eyes were fixed on mine, she wasn't looking *at* me, more like *through* me. 'The killer is still out there.'

'So, you think Ray is innocent?'

'I know he is.'

'Do you know who the real killer is?' I wasn't encouraging her by any means. The question kind of slipped out.

She squinted as if trying to focus on small print. 'The killer is a shadow.'

'Male? Female?'

'I can't tell, but I know they're close.'

'Close to …?'

'To you. The killer will be watching and won't hesitate to strike again.'

'Well, this is all very—'

'I'm here to warn you, Scott. This case could be the biggest thing that's happened in your life or … it could be the last!'

'So why would I take it on if it's so dangerous?'

The smile that spread across her wrinkly face was the vehicle that guided her back into the room. 'Because you're Detective Scotty Stephens.'

'Who told you about the case? Ray? Or his wife?'

'It was the drummer.'

'Right. I thought as much. He's been in touch with me too.'

'He told me he'd been trying.'

'Well, he got me.' The 4/4 reggae strum of an electric guitar resounded in the back of my mind like a faint echo. *Why was I hearing this?*

Kea smiled. 'I thought as much.' She nodded and jabbed with her eyes as if I were missing something.

'I'm not following.'

'You see, we can tell …'

'Tell what?'

'For the poor soul to contact you means you have the ability to hear.'

'He rang me on the phone.' Bugger me, the bass and the drums kicked in, startling me into a slight jolt.

Kea narrowed her eyes and smiled knowingly. 'Will you be taking on the case?'

'I'm not sure if there is a case.'

'Oh, there is. And you must. That is, if you can find the time, what with all those other cases you have.' This time, the knowing smile was more of a mischievous smirk.

Still not intending to be rude, I said, 'You've done a bit of research, no doubt, but unless you can tell me who the real killer is, it's pointless you being here.'

'I'm afraid it doesn't work like that.'

"No shit!" I wanted to say, but didn't.

'I can only relay the information that comes through, but one thing is for sure. Once the investigation begins, there could be more deaths if you don't bring your A game.' She stood and placed the half-empty mug of tea on the desk. 'I'm not here for any other reason but to pass on what I've just shared with you.'

I couldn't help thinking there was an angle. There had to be something in this for her but remaining polite, I also stood and showed her to the door.

'There's just a couple more things, Scott. Nothing to do with the case, of course, but important to you nonetheless.'

'Okay.' I opened the door.

'Don't take her for granted. Realise what you've got and cherish it.' Her eyes burned into mine with a scrutinising intensity.

'Her?' I was confused, but although her next words were thinly cryptic, I knew exactly what she meant.

'And don't worry. The king will return to the throne!'

5

Completely cleared of debris, the block of land seemed small when trying to picture the house that once stood there. After walking across the dusty lot, I stood for a moment where my bedroom used to be, and trying to imagine where the kitchen and living room once was brought a lump to my throat. The charred remains of the dartboard that had dominated our Wednesday nights for so many years still hung on the scorched fence that was once one wall of the man shed. A blackened dart still protruded from the bull's eye, placed there by Tetley no doubt, our little Pommy mate, before he returned to the UK. Darts night had been right up there with footy nights, Poker Tuesdays and Domino Mondays (the game, not the pizza), although there were plenty of them too. The fact that the man shed that once stood across the back garden was no more, actually brought tears to my eyes. It meant so much more than just losing the structure—twenty years of my life, my memories, a life I was already beginning to miss, literally went up in flames.

A late model, red MINI Cooper pulled up at the kerb, and Jenny Radford climbed out. 'Hey sad sack,' she called over when she saw me blubbering.

'Ma'am.'

'You crying again?' she said, strolling onto the lot.

The jibes didn't hurt. In fact, I was more than grateful for them. Friendly banter had been a huge part of the relationship between the 'Four Amigos'—me, Elvis, Tetley, and Johno. We were best mates, which meant we could say just about anything, within reason, without one of us getting upset. Jenny had also become a practitioner of the art.

'I've got something that'll cheer you up.'

'Yeah?'

'Yep … the bank has approved my loan.'

'They have?'

Jenny nodded vigorously. Her cheeks flushed with excitement. 'We're gonna be neighbours, mate.' She jumped into my arms.

'Awesome. At last, some good news,' I said, burying my face in her neck and squeezing her tightly.

'Means we can finalise the plans with the architect and get them into Council.'

'Are we really doing this?'

'My bloody oath we are.' She pulled her phone from her pocket and tapped the screen. After more tapping and scrolling, she held it up so we could both see it. On the screen was a rendering of an ultra-modern, white, three-storey duplex. Each side was identical. Double garages occupied the ground floors, with balconies spanning the remaining two.

'Are you sure they're not too big?' I asked, struggling to comprehend how I could fill a four-bedroom house on my own.

'Future proof, Scotty. Remember? Who knows what you'll be doing in five years' time. Might be married with kids.'

For an experienced detective like me, Jenny was hard to read. Our relationship was a complicated one. We were lovers, had been since the *X* case, but we couldn't live together—we were too much alike. After the fire had left me homeless, I'd moved into her apartment in Burleigh, but it only lasted a couple of weeks. Not that we argued or anything like that. I guess we'd been single for so long, we'd become a bit set in our ways. I think we were both relieved when I found a rental in Kirra and moved out. But the suggestion of being married with kids threw me a little. *Was she suggesting we might be married? Or that I would find another partner?* It wasn't something we had discussed.

'Come on, let's go for a drink,' Jenny said.

It was early evening at the back end of summer. We'd both just finished work. Well, Jenny had. Her career had changed after her involvement in the *X* case. Being promoted to detective inspector meant her life was hectic. Me, on the other hand, I'd been sitting at my desk all day in my shabby little office, reading the newspaper, then finding out as much as I could about the Bobby Sexton killing. Compared to Jenny's day, mine was pretty cruisy.

The pub was walking distance, so we left our cars parked on Ruby Street.

'How's the new Dub?' Jenny asked as we strolled past the brand-new Volkswagen Golf GTI.

'Good. Well, more than good. It's bloody amazing.'

'Still can't believe they donated it to you.'

My shrug was the mischievous, nonchalant kind. 'Pretty usual for your average saint, apparently.'

Jenny laughed and playfully punched me on the arm which, as usual, bloody hurt.

When the people at Volkswagen heard about the loss of my beloved Beetle in the fire, they rallied local businesses and organised a fundraiser. I'd tried to protest, but they and the people of the Gold Coast were having none of it. Through a campaign called 'Give Back to Scotty', they actually raised ten times what the car was worth and donated the rest to charity. I was pretty chuffed, to say the least.

'What?'

'What?'

'What's that face?'

'What face?'

'You bloody know.' Yes, she was a damn good detective. 'You're missing the old girl?'

It was true. As much as the Golf was everything a bloke could want, I was still missing my dilapidated old 1967 Beetle. The shudder and the whine when you turned the key, the worn vinyl interior with the slight odour of petrol. She was gone forever. Another part of my wish I'd have to live with.

The new Kirra Hotel was only a few months old. I was already a regular and had agreed to help promote the place when it first opened. A couple of TV commercials featuring the pub and Kirra seemed to lift my profile even more.

As usual, my drinks were free. Jenny had a lemon, lime and bitters. I had a schooner of XXXX Gold.

'So, you'll never guess who rang me today,' I said after we parked ourselves on two stools.

'Who?' Jenny was far too impatient to play guessing games.

'Ray Morris.'

'Ray Morris. The drummer who—'

I nodded before taking a sip of beer.

'But he's behind bars.'

'Yep. Called me from the Townsville nick.'

'What for?'

'Reckons he's innocent.'

'Really? Why'd he call you?' She was hard to read. Was she being sarcastic or sincere?

'Cause he knows I'm the greatest Australian detective that ever lived. He wants me to help him prove his innocence.'

'Right, so he's what? Got new evidence or …? Why didn't he go to the police?'

'No. No. He's sticking by his original statement. Claims he never entered the property.'

'But he was tried and convicted. I'm not familiar with the case, but his version of the story would have been pulled apart. If he's got nothing new to add, it's a waste of time, surely?'

'Hmm, it would seem so, wouldn't it?'

'I know that look. You're going to take it on.'

As soon as I'd realised who I was talking to on the phone that afternoon, the case was mine.

6

The next morning, I hit the surf early. There wasn't too much happening in the way of waves, so I had time to think while bobbing around between sets. Until I got the police files from Jenny, I only had the archive media reports, so a little reading between the lines was required, and although I wasn't expecting to receive any sensitive details, at least I'd know it was factual.

How was I going to handle this case? From what I'd already read, Ray Morris was not only tried and convicted of the fatal stabbing of Bobby Sexton, but he'd also lost an appeal. The only thing I had to go on so far was Ray's insistence that he was innocent.

Regardless, my first job of the day, once I got in the office, was to initiate the request Ray had made just before he hung up the phone. 'Call Stella.'

Stella Morris was Ray's wife. They were married thirty-two years ago while Ray was still the drummer with INSEXT, and just before the band scored their first record deal.

'Scotty.'

'Chilly.' My barber, and good mate, paddled alongside me. 'You going somewhere else?'

'What?'

The first wave of a set rolled beneath us.

'Haven't seen you for a while. Got one of them posh hairdressers now, have ya?'

'No mate, just been busy.'

'Sporting the mullet, I see.'

'It's not a mullet.'

'See you this Friday arvo for a beer?'

We both caught the next wave.

Friday afternoon, once a month, saw me at the barbershop enjoying a coldie while getting a cut and catching up on all the local gossip. I'd missed last month. Chilly was probably worried he'd lost his famous customer.

My temporary home was a rental apartment in a building across the road from Kirra Beach, ironically called *X*. A two bedder with a pleasant view, expensive as all hell, but very handy.

Sitting out on the balcony eating a bowl of muesli with skim milk, long gone were the days of Rice Bubbles and Guinness, but I have to admit, physically, I felt better. A healthier lifestyle was working for me.

My phone rang. The photograph that filled the screen made me smile. 'Bradley.'

'Hi Scott.'

'How are you, mate?'

'I'm good.' Bradley was my assistant during my short time as a detective inspector in the Queensland Police Service. He's now a detective constable and keen to be working up the ranks. 'Jenny tells me you're going to be looking into the Bobby Sexton case.'

'That's right.'

'Interesting. I've got the report here, just had a quick squiz through it.'

'And?'

'At first it looks like an open and shut case. There was a witness that saw Morris leaving the scene around the same time as the killing. The murder weapon belonged to him. And then there was the text.'

'Text?'

'The records show Bobby sent Ray a text not long before he was killed.'

'What kind of text?'

'It was an apology for kicking him out of the band all those years ago.'

'Really? So, that would work in Ray's favour, surely. Why would he kill Bobby after he had apologised?'

'There's more. Bobby also claimed to be the father of Ray's son after having an affair with his wife.'

'Oh.'

'Oh indeed, and this all happened around the same time as the X killings. At that time, most of the police resources were being utilised for that case. I can't imagine what kind of resources, or lack of, the Sexton case received. And remember, Singleton was still the police commissioner then, and we both remember his partiality for closing cases quickly. It's a wild accusation and a long shot, but perhaps the case may have been rushed. It was a huge event, one of Australia's most famous entertainers slain in his home, sending shock waves around the world. A quick arrest would have assured that precious resources wouldn't be redistributed from the X case and attention would quickly fade.'

'You're going to make a fine detective, Bradders!' He hated being called anything other than Bradley, but seeing as I was the one that introduced him to the art of friendly banter, I sometimes got away with it.

'You better believe it. I'll email you the files now.'

After a takeaway coffee and a chat with The Good Old Boys, who congregated outside the Kirra Surf Club kiosk each morning after their early morning surf and swim, I always enjoyed the morning stroll around Kirra Point to my office in Coolangatta. I'd often stop halfway and watch the surfers that were still out there.

When passing the empty office that used to belong to Elvis' accountancy firm, I wondered if I'd ever get used to Elvis no longer being there. The entrance was at the bottom of the stairs below my office, which meant I had to pass it every time I entered or exited the building. Through the glass door, I could see the reception desk, the comfy couch and the water dispenser. The place hadn't been cleared out and a big part of me hoped that this was because Elvis might be back one day. He'd beat the depression that had suddenly taken over his life, pay off all his debts and be back in business. But then there was that little part of me, that voice that said, "*Well isn't this what you wished for Scotty?*"

Sitting down at my desk, I fired up my laptop and, good to his word, the Ray Morris case files were in my inbox. Good old Bradley.

7

At my fingertips, was the official report of how the sequence of events took place on that fatal night, and who was involved. The logical place to begin was with the witness testimony that put Ray Morris at the murder scene, around the time of Bobby Sexton's death. Mrs Yvonne Kennedy, whose house was directly adjacent to Bobby's property, was, in all accounts, it seemed, the unofficial neighbourhood watch. Over the years, there had been a history of complaints to the police regarding noise and disturbances coming from the enormous mansion across the street. However, during the week of Bobby's return prior to that fatal night, there had been no disturbances to report, which Mrs Kennedy found very odd. Reading between the lines, I suspected she was a little disappointed, being battle ready with no fight to contend.

Her report stated that although Bobby had returned from LA one week prior to his death, she had not seen him leave the house once. The only comings and goings were by the house staff—a Mrs Olivier Harris and her husband, George, who maintained the outside of the property; and an Indian gentleman who was later identified as Mr Amir Patel, the family butler who worked between the brothers' houses. It was the Harrises who called the alarm when they found Bobby's body in the pool, after arriving for work early on the Monday morning of February 25th.

At just after 7.00 pm on Sunday February 24th, Phil Sexton arrived at the property with the tall man Mrs Kennedy had seen often at the property in the past, and a group of three—two older men who Mrs Willis described as ageing hipsters, and a young woman who dressed like a punk rocker.

A triple garage took most of the property's street frontage, along with a double gateway. Built into the stucco wall to one side of the gate were an intercom and a security keypad. Mrs Kennedy observed Phil Sexton press the intercom and wait. After a minute or so, he tried again. After a third attempt, he punched in a security code and the gate opened. In order to maintain vigilance, when the group entered the front garden, Mrs Kennedy had to move to her second-storey, front bedroom window. From there, she had a good view of the group standing at the front door of the house. This time, instead of buzzing the intercom, Mr Sexton knocked on the door and waited three times before punching in the security code and entering the property. The group of four followed him into the house.

Alas, to Mrs Kennedy's bitter detriment, she did not have a view of the back of the house, but she maintained her vigilance nonetheless.

Fifteen minutes later, the group came out of the front door with Bobby Sexton behind them. It appeared as if he were throwing them out, but it wasn't until Mrs Kennedy opened her window that she heard the tirade of verbal abuse coming from the so-called rock star across the street. Her report stated that she clearly heard Bobby Sexton shout after his brother and the group, 'I'm gonna fucking sue you for every penny you ever stole from me.' Then he went back into the house and slammed the door behind him.

Hmm, interesting. The most important information from this report was that Bobby was still alive when the group—who were officially identified later as Phil Sexton; Tommy Platt, the group's long-time road manager; and musicians, Mick Mantle, Jessie Flint and Zoey May—had left.

Mrs Kennedy hadn't returned downstairs, instead she remained in the bedroom overlooking the street. From there, she could see the length of the exclusive close that ended in a cul-de-sac. To the left of Bobby's property were two vacant blocks—also owned by Bobby. And there was a further vacant block on the right side of the house, ensuring privacy from both sides. George Harris, the groundkeeper, fenced and maintained these blocks.

With one eye on the *Courier Mail* crossword and one ever vigilant on the street below, the spritely, middle-aged widow remained in the front bedroom, listening to the radio. Her attention was peaked when she noticed another figure approach the house around thirty minutes later. She didn't know who the person was, but the man she picked out later in a police line-up was Ray Morris, the former drummer with the band INSEXT.

Mrs Kennedy's report also stated that after numerous attempts to work the intercom, Mr Morris went to the side of the property and scaled the fence. She was about to call the police when the scheduled phone call from her daughter in Toronto Canada—which she'd completely forgotten about during all the excitement—came through.

After speaking to her daughter for around ninety minutes, engrossed in the news that she was to become a grandmother for the third time, the events across the street had slipped her mind, replaced instead with images of knitting patterns and plans of a trip to Canada. It came as a great shock when opening her curtains the next morning, to find an ambulance and four police cars blocking the street outside her house.

Mrs Kennedy was very precise, and I doubted I'd get any further information, but I'd talk to her anyway, just in case there was a chance of prizing out any tiny details that may have been missed.

In Ray Morris' testimony, he admitted to scaling the fence to the vacant block at the side of the property, but after discovering an eight-foot wall along the boundary, he'd headed back home. *Could anyone else have returned to the property that night without being seen?* The investigators estimated that the time of death was somewhere between 8.00 pm and 10.00 pm. According to Mrs Kennedy, Ray Morris arrived at 7.48 pm, which meant he either killed Bobby, or someone else returned shortly after.

A glance through the rest of the report confirmed that there was no evidence of anyone else arriving at the property until the Harrises turned up for work the next morning. Ray Morris was the last person to be seen on the street, but the most damning evidence was that the murder weapon was a Bowie knife that belonged to him. What made the situation more intriguing was that Bobby had given Ray the jewel-handled knife as a gift just before the band sacked him as their drummer.

Then there was the text that Bradley mentioned. Ray received the text at 7:36 pm on the evening of Bobby's death, which wouldn't have given him much time to write it, after Phil Sexton and his entourage had left. *Was it written earlier? If so, why did he wait to send it? And why then?* The report included a full transcription of the text:

> *Mate. I'm so sorry for waiting all these years to contact you. My biggest regret is standing back and doing nothing while Phil and Alex kicked you out of the band. I was wasted, man. You didn't deserve that, and I hope you can forgive me. I also need to take this opportunity to apologise for Jack. The thing with Stella was a very casual affair during a crazy period in my life. I'm sure you worked it out a long time ago, but Jack is my son, and I intend to fully amend for not being a part of his life.*

While reading an apology, I also couldn't help detecting the vindictive connotes in the short text. It was as if Bobby were unburdening himself of guilt. *And what if Ray hadn't known about the affair? Or that he wasn't the real father of his son?* For the prosecution, this just added credence towards Ray's motive for killing Bobby. *Hmm.* The final damning evidence was that Ray worked for the company who supplied and installed the security system on Bobby's house. Although he was only a forklift driver at the warehouse, the theory derived by the prosecution was that, even with limited knowledge, he could have deleted the recent footage from the security cameras.

No wonder the case moved through the system so quickly and the jury's decision was unanimous. If you'll pardon the cliché, this certainly looked like an open and shut case. *What evidence could Ray Morris have to prove his innocence?* I couldn't wait to find out.

8

From the official police report, I had a list of names. In my mind, I was strategising how to approach the case and concluded that the best course of action was to assume Ray Morris was innocent. Although the facts suggested the contrary, if I couldn't come around to a commitment to this belief, it would be a waste of time taking on the case. So, instead of bolstering what was already proven, I'd need to find new evidence to support Morris' innocence. A daunting task. *Was I up to it?* I would like to have said, "My bloody oath, I am!" but as in everything I did, the ongoing imposter syndrome wouldn't allow it. Part of me, the voice of little Scotty, was saying, "Don't even think about taking this on. You'll ruin your reputation, become a laughingstock!" While the other voice—big Scotty—the one I'd been working on recently, was relishing the challenge. There was something in Ray Morris' voice—a stolid confidence—that had resonated. So, with the absence of commitment, I decided to delve a little deeper.

One thing that Ray had insisted on was that I began the investigation by speaking to his wife, Stella. He'd given me her mobile phone number, a landline and an email address. Seated at my desk with a zillion files and numerous websites opened on the laptop, I rang the mobile number.

A woman answered after just a couple of rings. 'Hello.'

'Hi, is that Stella Morris?'

'Who wants to know?'

'It's Scotty Stephens …'

There was silence on the other end.

'I'm a private detective. Your husband contacted me. He said I should call you.' I'd grown accustomed to people on the Gold Coast recognising me, so it felt strange to have to introduce myself.

'Are you serious?' Her condescending tone came as a bit of a shock.

'He insisted that if I was to take on his case, I call you first.'

'His *case* …? There *is* no case!'

This certainly wasn't the reaction I'd expected. When Ray had mentioned his wife, I'd got the impression she would welcome a fresh investigation. He even hinted that she may have instigated it. But this wasn't the vibe I was getting.

'You know a jury convicted him and then he lost his appeal?'

'Yes, I am.'

'Then why are you wasting everyone's time? Looking for another show pony case, are you?'

Ha, so she did know me. 'Ray tells me that some compelling evidence has come to light.'

'What evidence?'

'Uhm, I don't know. He told me to ask you.'

'*Phhh*,' her laugh was the non-humorous, impatient kind. 'You don't want to get involved with this, Scott. Perhaps do another interview for *Woman's Own* instead. That would be more lucrative, I'm sure.'

"Ditto," I wanted to say, but didn't. During my brief initial research online into everything regarding the case, I'd come across an interview with Stella Morris in no other than *Woman's Own*. Wasn't this, as my mother used to say, the pot calling the kettle black? 'Have you given up on him?'

'How dare you?'

'I'm sorry, but I'm just finding your animosity a little confusing, that's all.'

'Have you any idea what I've been through over the last couple of years?'

'I can only imagine how hard it's been.'

'If there's nothing else?'

'Mrs Morris. I'm here to help.' I sensed a more formal address was required.

'Good, then help by leaving us alone.'

She was about to hang up, so I threw one last question at her. 'Do you believe your husband is guilty or innocent?'

There was a pause and a definite sigh. Then she hung up.

Hmm, interesting. I understood that being the wife of a convicted killer in such a high-profile case would attract a lot of negative attention, especially when the murder victim was a revered rockstar—the media, the fans, the crazies, even death threats perhaps. And I could understand her reluctance to bring all that up again. But if there was a chance that her husband was wrongly convicted, wouldn't she want to at least listen? Ray had, in fact, stated that she would be more than willing to help. That obviously wasn't the case. If I was going to take this case on, I'd need a face to face with Stella Morris. Speaking on the phone was one thing. My skill as a detective relied more on reading the facial expressions and body language of an interviewee.

With no cases on the books, the whiteboard was bare. Residues of faded lettering remained as imprints from previous scribblings. Using a felt cleaner, I scrubbed it clean and made my first list.

Ray Morris took centre stage. Not as the prime suspect, though, but as the wrongly convicted innocent man. Later, I would print off photographs and add them to the board, but for now, I just felt the need to make a start. Next came the victim, Bobby Sexton. I wasn't a hundred per cent sure why I had him on the list at this time, but it somehow felt right for his name to be up there. Next was his brother, Phil Sexton, and next to him was the band's manager, Alex Mercedes. At the time of his death, Bobby was married to his third wife, ex-international model, Sasha Coburn. The ex-wives were Jo Sexton, his first wife; and Angel

Sexton, his second. Both had retained the singer's name after the divorces. The brothers' parents were divorced. Maeve Sexton, a well know Gold Coast socialite, who still lived on the Coast. The father, Dave Sexton, lived in Byron Bay. As well as the long-time road manager, Tommy Platt, the two members of the original band: guitarist, Mick Mantle; bass player, Jessie Flint; and the new drummer, Zoey May; along with Phil, were the last people to see Bobby alive. The investigation and the court case later seemed to have rushed over their extremely important testaments. Their names were next. Although there were numerous band members over the years, session musicians mainly, I didn't add them to the board at this time, but I'd be giving them some thought. Sadly, the person who discovered Bobby's body, Mrs Harris, had since passed away. Then her husband, George, also passed away six months later after returning to his homeland, Scotland.

The list was crude, but it would give me a place to start. For the next hour, I memorised the names and verified with the police report why they were on the list. By the time I finished, I'd determined a starting point. To speak with Bobby's brother, Phil Sexton.

9

It was my homage to the famous James Bond scene when Sean Connery skimmed his hat across Miss Moneypenny's office, landing it on the hat rack. Except mine was a police constable's cap flying across the hallway of the house on Ruby Street. The outcome was usually the same—a perfect shot, but without the adoring accolade of M's secretary.

As I walked through the house, kicking off my shoes and relieving myself of certain articles of uniform, I could hear music and chatter coming from outside. The back garden and the man shed were as illuminated as The Gabba on game night. It was Friday evening, and not just any old match day. Tonight's game was Essendon versus Hawthorne.

'Hey, here he is, Officer Dibble,' said Tetley, swinging around on his barstool.

The man shed was permanently open on the front side and took up the full width and about a third of the garden. There was a bar in one corner with a fully stacked, glass-fronted bar fridge. A pool table took centre stage, and there was a large TV hanging on one wall, as well as a dartboard and footy memorabilia on the opposite wall. In front of the TV was a huge, well-worn leather couch. Tetley, my little Pommy mate, sat at the bar holding a bottle of beer in a Nottingham Forest stubby cooler. Behind the bar and vigorously shaking his latest cocktail recipe, was my best mate, Elvis.

'Hey bud, about time you showed up,' Elvis said, putting down the shaker. Throwing open the tall fridge door, he pulled out a bottle of Castlemaine XXXX Gold. On the bar top was a waiting Essendon stubby holder. Elvis twisted off the top and slammed the bottle down inside the holder, causing the cold beer inside to froth up and spill over. 'Get that down you, lad,' he yelled while Peter Garrett warned that the blue sky mining company won't save us. The TV was on with the sound down, but the game was yet to start. The usual panel of has-beens discussing the up-and-coming clash between our favourite and our least favourite teams.

'How was your day, mate?' Tetley asked with the sarcastic expression he'd honed over the years.

'Good.' Picking up the beer, I just about skulled half the bottle.

'How many old biddies did you help today, then? Rescued cats? Did you get little Timmy out of that hole?' It was the beginning of the evening's banter, to which Tetley was the king. Each of us had an area of weakness, and it was the others' duties to manipulate it by sticking in the knife and turning the blade almost to the point where any normal fellow would be on the brink of tears. Not so with us three. Under Tetley's skilful tutorage since our schooldays at Palm Beach Currumbin High, we'd grown thick skins and become pretty darn good at extracting the piss. My uneventful career in the police force was an ongoing joke, which Tetley and Elvis believed amounted to little more than me assisting old ladies across the street and handing out tickets to jay walkers.

'You must be knackered, lad.' It was a subtle start that would build through the evening with the increase of beer.

'Not as knackered as you. What is it you do again?' I offered in response to Tetley's recognisance. 'Oompa Loompa doompety-do.'

Since moving to Australia from the UK with his parents when he was around fourteen years old, Tetley, aka Sean Webster, hadn't lost his Pommy accent in the thirty years he'd lived here. Apparently, he had quite a good job with an engineering firm. Of short stature, and working in a factory, we often teased him for being one of Willy Wonka's Oompa Loompas. 'Did you bring any chocolate home?'

'Fuck off, Robo Cop.'

Elvis grinned as he poured an icy red liquid into a cocktail glass. A true connoisseur of the finer things in life, Elvis, aka Nicholadas Papageorgiou, was an accountant and had been my best friend since kindergarten in our hometown of Essendon, in Victoria. The black quiff may have long gone, but the swagger and presence of the coolest accountant in Coolangatta were still very much present.

'How's that team of yours doing? Booted out of the premier league yet?' I wasn't about to let Tetley off the hook. He'd made the first strike.

'Middle of the table, pal!' Straightening up, he raised his chin. 'We're talking about real football, though. The beautiful game.'

'Yeah, we've seen the ballerinas.' I was warming up nicely.

'Not like this stupid game,' Tetley offered, ignoring my jibe at the prima donna soccer players of the English Premier League. 'Poncin' around in them little shorts.'

'Shut the fuck up then, lad. Game's about to start,' Elvis said, making his way to the couch, arms laden with an enormous bowl of popcorn, a family-sized bag of chips under one arm, and his cocktail in the other hand.

Like the patriarch he was, Elvis sat in the middle of the couch and took control of the remote after dispensing the snacks to the coffee table that would also double as our footstool. Tetley and I sat one on either side.

The players were on the pitch and ready for the centre bounce. As it always did, my mind wandered to the days when I was one of Victoria's highest ranked schoolboy forwards, which inevitably brought back memories of the night I gave up the game for good. It was the night I was responsible for my mother's death.

Knowing the signs, Elvis squeezed my knee and offered a sympathetic smile. Then said, 'Cheer up you miserable bastard.'

God, I loved him.

'How long does this shite go on for again?' Tetley said with an exaggerated glance at his cheap watch. He wasn't a fan of Aussie Rules football.

'As long as always, mate,' Elvis said calmly.

'Too fucking long.' It was the beginning of an exchange that happened at this time every week.

Glancing to my left, I watched Elvis munching on popcorn while daintily sipping on his cocktail. Next to him, Tetley swigged on a bottle of Carlton Draft. We were living the dream, and I was loving every minute of the bachelor's life.

Tetley was the king of fart. The one he let go at that moment rattled through the couch and vibrated like the thump of a bass drum.

We laughed so hard I woke up still laughing. But the innocent pleasure turned to shivers of regret when I realised where I was—alone in a rented apartment. Had I really wished that life away? What I would have given at that moment to spend another night in that house watching the footy with my mates in the man shed. Was it possible that I caused all this change? As always, it was my mother's voice I heard as I drifted back to sleep.

'Be careful what you wish for, Scotty.'

10

The Getters Café was a cute, colonial style tearoom in a little hinterland township called Chillingham. The evening before, I'd received a call from Bradley, and during one of his regular *are-you-sure-you're-okay-Scott?* chats, I mentioned my intention of speaking to Phil Sexton. "But how do you get face time with a rockstar?" was my rhetorical question. Prior to entering the Cliffside Malibu drug rehabilitation centre in LA, Bobby used a company called Sunrise Security who monitored his movements. A team of bodyguards shadowed his every move, and his home was under twenty-four-hour surveillance. On his secret return to the Coast, he had cancelled the long-term contract and sent the firm packing. Luckily, the fans hadn't got wind of his return, believing him to still to be in the States, so they hadn't yet stormed the property in mass.

Phil, on the other hand, always had full security in place, except that is, apparently, when he regularly ate breakfast at The Getters. This was another secret held from the fans, and one, according to Bradley, that was fiercely guarded by the locals and the staff. The only information I had was that he was usually there between 8.00 and 9.00 am. Taking no chances, I decided to be there for 8.00 am.

The quickest way, and most picturesque route, to Chillingham from Kirra was to head out to Currumbin Valley, then double back into NSW via Tomewin. Then it was a matter of heading northwest and back into Queensland through the pristine hinterland countryside.

Chillingham was a tiny outpost that comprised a general store, a couple of shops, private properties and, of course, The Getters Café, which was hidden from the road.

An archway entrance, fashioned from bougainvillea and jasmine, led through to a quaint tea garden surrounding a white, heritage Queenslander. Wrought-iron tables with ceramic tiled tops and matching chairs were spread throughout the garden, offering diners a selection of private little areas in a relaxed garden setting.

Ducking my head as I entered the gate, avoiding the sharp thorns of the thick bougainvillea, I was relieved to find the establishment wasn't busy, but the first person I noticed was a large man wearing a leather jacket. With close cropped hair, he had a boxer's face and the angry scowl to match. Your clichéd bodyguard. At first, he eyed me warily as I passed through the magenta-coloured archway, then a familiar expression crossed his face when he recognised me. But this was quickly replaced by one of suspicion when he must have asked himself, "What's he doing here?"

With a nod, I said good morning as I passed.

'Alright?' he offered back. He was English, a little further north than Tetley, I surmised.

As with all original Queenslander style buildings, this magnificent specimen of a turn of the century wooden structure sat off the ground on wooden stumps. The café counter fronting the kitchen was underneath the house, but still had a vintage feel, so I guessed it had been operating as a café for quite some time.

Approaching the counter, I side glanced at my surroundings, scanning the area. And bingo! There he was, sitting alone, nursing a coffee and reading a newspaper. I suddenly sensed someone behind me and realised the bodyguard had followed. Fair play, it was his job to protect his client.

The face of the middle-aged woman behind the counter with a jolly disposition and a genuine smile suddenly flushed when she realised who I was. 'Oh, my goodness. It's Scotty Stephens,' she cried out. The chef and a young girl popped their heads around the kitchen door. Greeting them with a simple nod and glancing to my right, I noticed Phil Sexton was also looking my way.

'Fuck me,' he said. 'It is. It's Scotty Stephens.'

No way, you've got to be kidding. Phil Sexton knew who I was? Shut the f... ront door.

Standing, he beckoned me over to his table.

As I turned and strutted towards Phil's table, the bodyguard skilfully moved forward and placed himself, all be it to one side, in between us. Phil threw out his hand for me to shake. His grip was firm.

'Fuck me, Scotty Stephens,' he repeated.

I'd grown quite accustomed to this reaction since the *X* case. It's not surprising when you consider I was on the front of most Australian newspapers, and the subject of many a news bulletin for around a month. Unofficially, I was voted the most famous Australian of that time. Unbelievable. But never in my dreams would I have imagined that Phil Sexton would have known who I was. But more importantly, once again, my fame had opened a door. I was standing face to face with a famous rockstar, and he was beckoning me to join him at his table. *Get in.*

'Phil Sexton. It's great to meet you,' I said.

'*Phh*, mate. The pleasure's all mine. Take a seat, please, join me,' he said, gesturing to the vacant chair opposite him.

'No worries.' It was important to keep the situation under control and not become star-struck. I noticed glances between Phil and the bodyguard, which was followed by a single, knowing nod. The bodyguard stepped back but sat down at the nearest table.

As a fan, I had so many questions. "What's it like being one of the biggest rock stars in the world?" etc, etc, etc, but the truth was I couldn't get a word in. It was Phil who was questioning me. He asked me about the *X* case, of course, but was very interested in my career prior to being promoted to DI. For the next hour, over eggs, bacon and tea, shouted by Phil, I pretty much relayed my life story from growing up in Victoria, and moving to the Gold Coast, to my current life in Kirra. I got the impression he was enjoying being the fan and asking questions. We were getting on like we were best mates.

<h1 style="text-align:center">11</h1>

To be talking face to face with one of the most successful Australian rock stars of all time, for over an hour, was something I could never have imagined. I found Phil Sexton to be a warm, caring individual who, I suspected, spent most of his life surrounded by sycophants and hanger-ons. Although we hadn't discussed Bobby's death, as I drove back to Kirra, I couldn't help feeling as if I'd achieved a great deal. I'd made a new friend, but more importantly, I'd got my foot in the INSEXT door.

Instead of returning the way I'd come via Currumbin Valley, remaining on the NSW side of the border took me through the sugarcane fields surrounding the town of Murwillumbah. When I reached the banks of the Tweed River, with the charming little township of Tumbulgum on the opposite side, my phone rang. As always, the number on the screen made me smile. It belonged to Jenny.

'Hey you.'

'Hey Scotty. Where are you?' Her voice was loud through the car speakers, and I sensed a tinge of excitement in her tone.

'Just heading back to the office.'

'Cool ... guess what ...'

'What?'

'I've signed the papers. The loan's mine. We can go ahead with the build!'

'You bloody ripper!' I was as ecstatic as she was. 'Where are you? I think we need to celebrate.'

'Absolutely. I'm a … I'm a bit busy at the moment, but how about we meet up later at the block, then go for a drink?'

'Sounds like a plan. Congratulations, Jen.'

'See you later, neighbour.' She hung up.

Wow, this was great news indeed. It meant we could finally start the ball rolling with the build. The architect's plans had already passed through Council. Basically, all we'd been waiting on was for Jenny to come up with her side of the cash. Now we could move forward.

As I had a million times already, I went through the building plans in my mind. Two four-bedroom Palm Springs style townhouses side by side. Identical except that they were mirrored. With white rendered walls, straight lines and modern finishes, the cost was a shade under $1m each side. The post completion valuation for each was over $2m. But more than this, I found myself thinking about Jenny. This was happening quite a lot lately. It was becoming more apparent that Jenny Radford was the one consistent positive that had remained in my life since everything else went belly up. Our relationship was an open one, but I had seen no one else since meeting her during the *X* case and I was pretty sure she hadn't either. *Was the problem at my end? Were there still remnants of Bachelor Scotty fighting an inevitable future of domestic bliss?* I had to admit, when we weren't together, Jenny occupied a large percentage of my thoughts during my average day. A conversation I'd had with my brother, Josh, a couple of months ago, came to mind. We were having a drink at Kurrawa Surf Club near his home in Broadbeach.

'So, what the hell are you waiting for?'

'What do you mean?'

'Jenny, mate. Juliette reckons you two are the prince and princess who are going to ride off into the sunset and live happily ever after.'

Juliette was my eight-year-old niece.

'And Liz and I agree with her.'

'Ahh, mate, look we've tried—'

'Don't "ahh mate" me. She's the bloody one for you, Scotty. Everyone can see it, except you.'

'We love each other but—'

'You've got to learn to pull your head in and realise that life doesn't revolve around Scotty Stephens. A marriage is about give and take. You're not going to find the perfect partner who'll agree with everything you say and do.'

'Marriage? Who said anything about marriage?'

'What's holding you back? The clock's ticking.' His tone took on a serious edge. 'She's the love of your life, you stubborn shit. Don't fuck this up like everything else.'

'Whoa, that's harsh.'

'I'm your big brother. It's allowed. You're lucky I don't give you a slap.'

'Mate?'

He took a sip of his beer. 'We're worried about you, that's all. If you don't act soon, you'll lose her just like you've lost …' He stopped himself short, but I knew exactly what he was going to say. Just like I'd lost everything else in my life.

By the time I got back to Coolangatta, the remarkable morning with Phil Sexton was the farthest thing from my mind. One Miss Jenny Radford solely occupied my thoughts. The little pocket rocket with an infectious smile. The tough little glamour who could surf as well as me—if not better—could drink me under the table, match banter blows with even Tetley, and know exactly what I was thinking because we pretty much shared the same brain. *Had the answer I'd been searching for these last couple of years been right under my nose all the time?* Tetley was right, I was a twat. If I was honest with myself, I'd realise I'd be pretty hard to live with. Wanting change, but not really. Still the bachelor who cared and only had to think about himself. Jenny was perfect. Perfect for me. In the past she'd proved to be my confidant, my lover and my best mate, yet I'd pushed her away. I explained to my ego that we couldn't live together because I wasn't used to anyone telling me to put away the breakfast cereals when I'd finished with them or lower the toilet seat, or pick up the toe nail cuttings from the bathroom floor or, or, or …

As I climbed the stairs to my office, I'd decided I was going to call Jenny right that moment. I wasn't sure what I was going to say, but I just needed to hear her voice.

When I entered the office, however, a man studying the whiteboard immediately yanked my thoughts back to the present.

12

It was a large man wearing a leather sports jacket, jeans and tan suede boots. Sporting a ponytail, he stood with his back to me, studying the whiteboard. Although he must have heard me enter, he didn't turn.

'Can I help you?'

Still, he didn't move.

Marching towards him, I raised my voice, 'Excuse me.'

As if startled, he physically jumped. 'Jesus, you scared the shit out of me.'

'What are you doing in here?'

'Waiting for you.' He hadn't changed from the photograph of him on the whiteboard. 'I'm Tommy Platt ... but you already know that.' He pointed to his picture.

'How did you get up here?'

'Eh?'

'I said, how did you get up here?' Raising my voice as one normally would when addressing a person hard of hearing, my detective mind automatically putting two and two together. Long-time road manager of the band, roadie in the early years, driving the boys from gig to gig, and lugging around the equipment. Then later, overseeing the enormous operations at the international stadium shows, but always close to the speakers that grew in wattage with the band's popularity.

'The agent let me up.'

'The agent?'

'Yeah. The one that's selling the place.'

'Which place?'

Tommy exaggerated a glance around the room. 'This place. At first, she thought I was a potential buyer. When I explained I was meeting you, she let me up.'

'I wasn't aware we had a meeting scheduled.'

Tommy shrugged, grinned, then held out his hand. 'It's good to meet you, Scotty. Although I'm a bit surprised you have me down as a suspect.'

Before shaking his hand, I quickly turned the board over so that the scribbled list was facing the wall. 'It's good to meet you too, but you're not a suspect at this time.' I gestured for him to take a seat at my desk, which he did. 'I'm just getting together as much information as I can about everyone involved with the band.'

'I can see that.'

'Can I get you a drink?'

'No. I'm good … You're probably wondering why I'm here.'

Along with the information that my office was up for sale without my knowledge, this thought was up there.

'Stella Morris called me.'

'Right. Ray's wife.'

'That's right. She tells me you're looking into the murder case.'

My nod was the casual kind, inviting him to continue.

'It's probably not a good idea.'

'Why's that?'

'Well, it's done and dusted, mate. Why drag all that up again just to get the same result?'

'But if there is a chance that Ray was wrongly convicted, wouldn't you want to know about it?'

'The jury's decision was unanimous.'

I already knew all this, of course. However, one of the principal characters in the play had approached me. Whether he was willing to share information didn't matter. After years of experience as a detective, I knew how to squeeze the juice. But on this occasion, it seemed, none of my skills were required.

'I'm the one who was responsible for Bobby Sexton's death!'

'Excuse me?'

'You heard. I'm the reason Bobby is dead.'

'You killed him?'

Tommy leaned forward and interlaced his fingers on the desk. 'It was me who told Ray about the band meeting at Bobby's house that night. Me who persuaded him to go down there.'

'Why?'

'Because Phil was planning this big revival tour, getting together the original members of the band. Well, fuck me. You don't get more original than Ray Morris. He was there when it was just the four of us, travelling up and down between Byron and Harvey Bay from gig to gig in my old Kombi. It was bullshit when they sacked him for no reason.'

'Ray showed up at the meeting too?' I already knew the answer to this question. I'd read the case transcripts, but I wanted to hear it from Tommy to see if I could tease out that little bit of information that he may have withheld.

'Well, that was the idea. Mick and I had decided there couldn't be a reunion without Ray.'

'Mick the …?'

'Original guitarist. Ironically, he and Jessie, the bass player, were hired at the same time Ray was sacked, but Mick had kept in touch with him.'

'So, after Ray's departure, INSEXT was just the brothers and session musicians?'

'That's right.'

'Did Ray know they had a replacement drummer?'

'No, none of us did. Alex and Phil had only arranged that the night before.'

'Alex, the band's manager?'

'Yep.'

'So, you told Ray what time the meeting was taking place and that he should get himself down there?'

'Not exactly. I told him about the meeting, yes, where and when, but left it at that. I didn't tell him to go, but I hoped he would.'

'But he turned up late.'

'Yes.'

'What happened then?'

'He rang the intercom. When there was no answer, he scaled the wall at the side of the house and stabbed Bobby with the very knife that Bobby had gifted him all those years ago.'

'For what reason?' Once again, I was familiar with the official motive, but wanted to hear Tommy's take on it. Until now, he'd told me nothing new.

Tommy shrugged. 'Pent up jealousy, I guess. You got to remember he was booted out of the band just before they became one of the biggest acts in the world. While they were jetting around the globe, playing Wembley Stadium and Madison Square Gardens, he was working as a forklift driver at Mitre-10. Then there was the affair with Stella.'

'Do you really think Ray was capable of murder?'

'Not the Ray I used to know. But … I'd heard a few rumours. Apparently, he didn't take the dismissal too well. Hit the booze often as well as his missus and kid.'

'Did Stella tell you that?'

'No, she always stood by him. Blamed the brothers for what they did. Hated them, in fact.'

There was a low knock at the door.

'Come in,' I called out.

Tommy jumped again at my raised voice. He obviously hadn't heard the knock.

A young guy wearing a tight singlet, small shorts and runners entered the room. His face was flushed, like he'd been running.

'Hey,' Tommy said, rising to his feet. 'Scott, this is my boy, Lax.'

Lax approached the desk, and we shook hands.

'G'day mate. Cool name.'

'His real name's Larry,' Tommy interjected.

Lax blushed. 'It's good to meet you, Scott.'

There was something about Lax's manner. Something familiar. 'Scotty. Call me Scotty. Been for a run, mate?'

'Yeah, just a short one from Broadbeach.'

'Broadbeach to Coolangatta?' Must have been close to 30 kilometres. 'Hardly a short run.'

'He's a marathon runner,' Tommy said, placing a proud hand on his son's shoulder.

'I've got Brisbane in June, the Gold Coast in July, and Sydney in September.'

'Wow, so you're in training.'

Lax nodded and smiled. 'We've got to go, Dad.'

'Yes, we do.' He held out his hand once again. 'It was good to meet you, Scotty.'

We shook hands. 'Good to meet you too, but is there something you're not telling me, Tommy?' I had nothing. No cracks, no tell-tale body language, so the only choice I had was to just ask.

'Like what?'

'Well, you've come all this way to tell me what I already know. Did Stella ask you to speak with me?'

'She did. She just doesn't want to go through all this again, you know. The case was really hard on her.'

'Not as hard as on Ray. Surely, she wants to help him?'

'Just let it go, eh.' His demeanour changed instantly, and I could see why he would have been a good bloke for the band to have around in the early days. Roadie, bodyguard and mate.

'I'm afraid I can't do that. I'll be working for Ray, so if there is any information you can provide that will help me prove his innocence, it will be greatly appreciated.' That's it. I was officially in.

'Not such a smart bloke after all then.' Tommy made his way to the exit.

Lax shrugged and smiled. 'It was good to meet you, Scotty.' He followed Tommy out.

My spider senses tingled as I stood there, wondering where I knew that boy from.

13

I'd arranged to meet Jenny at the block on Ruby Street at 5.00 pm. During the short drive home, she was still on my mind. For some reason, I felt strangely excited yet anxious at the thought of seeing her. *What had changed in the last 24 hours since I last saw her?* I wasn't sure, but something very important had shifted in my life. *Heck. Was I thinking of asking her to marry me?*

We had planned nothing for the evening. Jenny was excited after signing the loan papers. Now it was time to celebrate.

Feeling the need to get dressed up, the only decent clothes I had after losing everything in the fire was a white shirt and a pair of trousers. Although we had no plans, normally we'd end up at the Kirra pub, I thought it might be nice to go somewhere different—Twin Towns perhaps, or that new Italian restaurant in Cooly.

The walk from Lord Street to Ruby Street took literally one minute. It was just around the corner. I was a bit early, so I stepped onto the block hoping I could spend some time imagining the buildings that would stand there in a year's time. But with the remnants of the man shed still present at the back of the block, the memory of the old place was still too vivid.

Behind me, I heard a car pull up. *Ahh, my saviour was here.* A car door opened and closed. 'Bloody hell, where are you going all dressed up?' There was a slur in her voice, followed by a mischievous giggle.

Hmm, seemed she'd been on the champers already. Jenny Radford could drink any bloke under the table when it came to beer and spirits, but her Achilles heel was Champagne, a weakness that I also shared. After only a couple of glasses, we'd be giggling like idiots, so we rarely drank it. This truly *was* a special occasion.

When I turned, she was already marching across the block towards me, a big grin on her face. There was a slight wobble in her walk, but I hardly noticed. The Jaguar parked near the kerb had my attention.

'Hey neighbour,' Jenny said, throwing her arms around my neck.

'Been on the bubbles already, love?' I asked playfully.

'My bloody oath. We've been celebrating.'

'We?'

As I spoke, the driver's side door of the Jag opened and a tall, well-built guy climbed out.

'Yep, been at the Burleigh Pavilion since lunchtime.'

I leaned in and lowered my voice. 'Who's the geezer?'

'Oh, this is Dorian.' Grabbing my hand and dragging me towards the street, she lowered her voice. 'He's my … uhm … architect … friend.' She giggled and my heart sank. I knew that giggle, it was *our* giggle. The one we used when we were taking the piss out of the world. 'Dorian, this is Scotty.'

When Dorian stepped forward, I immediately noticed he was wearing a white shirt and grey slacks similar to mine—only on him, they looked better. He was taller than me, wider. His short hair was a little dishevelled, but it still looked cool. 'Scotty, it's so good to meet you at last.'

We shook hands. And I can appreciate a firm grip, but what the hell? As well as squeezing my fingers excessively, he pulled me in towards him, knocking me off balance.

'Dorian's been helping me with my design decisions.' The giggle again and although her eyes were bubbly from the champers, when she looked at Dorian and grinned, it was the look and the grin that belonged to me.

I felt the sudden urge to punch Dorian in the head.

Dorian obviously hadn't been drinking. He was driving, inebriated or not. Jenny would never allow that. 'I'd like to get together and talk to you about the plans sometime soon, if possible, Scotty?'

Mister Stephens to you. 'Plans?'

'The house plans. We've decided we want to make some changes.'

We? Who the hell is this guy? 'Too late, I'm afraid. They've already been through council.'

'Not a problem, I can revise them. Do it all the time.'

'Well, you're not touching these plans, mate!' My voice rose automatically.

'Whoa, no need to get angry,' Dorian said, backing up a step.

Jenny laughed and slapped a hand across my shoulder. 'Scotty never gets angry. He hasn't got an angry bone in his body.'

Realising my fists were clenched, I *was* bloody angry.

'Maybe now isn't the time to talk about it,' Dorian said passively.

'There's nothing to talk about. We've already approved the plans.'

'So, where are you going all dressed up?' Jenny said, breaking the tension. 'Did someone die?' The giggle again, which was met by a patronising grin from Dorian.

'Nowhere … I was just … you know.'

'We've got to get going, Jen,' Dorian said, checking his watch.

'Yep … got some serious … planning to catch up on.'

I hadn't realised how annoying the giggle actually was until now.

Jenny threw her arms around me, but unlike the kisses we usually shared, this one was more like the one from the tipsy cousin you only saw at weddings and funerals.

When Dorian helped Jenny into his car, and I watched them drive away together, I hadn't felt this low since my mother died. *Was this all my making? Was I destined for a life of bad luck? Or was this still the effects of Moe Brennan's curse? And if so, would this be the end of it?* I wasn't thinking straight. The only thing on my mind at that moment was Jenny Radford.

14

There was no celebration that night. Not for me, anyway. I went straight home and almost threw the glads in the bin. If I was a proper drinking man, I probably would have hit the bottle, but although I often enjoyed a drink in a social setting, I never drank alone.

"You sad twat!" Tetley said as I lay tossing and turning in bed.

"This is what you wanted, bud," Elvis pipped in. "We're all out of your life now, just like you wished for."

"You won't know where and you won't know when, and that's the beauty of the curse." Moe Brennan's words morphed into a sickly laugh.

The next morning, as the sun came up, I lay awake listening to the lorikeets gradually stirring on Roughton Park, the sound of early morning traffic, and the gently tumbling surf. An advantage of living so close to the beach was that I didn't even need to get out of bed to know if the surf was up or not, and although a quick glance over the balcony would confirm my prediction, I'd grown accustomed to the sound of the waves. When the surf was pumping, it roared, but a gentle rumble like today meant I could stay in bed.

Staying in bed, however, was the last thing I wanted to do. My mind was still whizzing, so I got up, threw on a pair of shorts and a singlet, dug out the new runners from the bottom of the wardrobe, and did something I hadn't done in ages. I went for a run.

The air was cool and crisp as I made my way across Musgrave Street. The footpath that started in Rainbow Bay and went all the way to Currumbin was a popular place for the morning runners, walkers and bike riders.

Realising my legs were pretty stiff, I did some stretching on the grass before setting off.

'Good morning, Scott.'

Looking up from a hamstring stretch, I saw an attractive young woman smiling in my direction as she walked past. 'Good morning.' I had no idea who she was.

Slowly heading north towards Bilinga, I needed to get my head straight, and although my mind kept pulling me back to the situation with Jenny, I tried concentrating on the case. *Ray Morris, innocent or guilty? If guilty, why would he call me and why now? Was there any evidence? If so, was it really overlooked? Or was I wasting my time?* I hadn't given Ray a firm answer yet that I'd be taking on the case, but I'd decided I would, if for no other reason than keeping my mind active.

'Hi, Scotty.' This time it was two girls walking towards me outside North Kirra Surf Club.

'Hi, how's it going?'

'Good,' they said in unison, their smiles lingering as we passed.

Was I becoming nonchalant to the fact that so many people knew me and showed affection towards me? Was I in a self-made bubble of misery?

'G'day, Scotty,' said an old chap walking his dog. His smile was genuine and friendly, like he'd known me all his life.

'G'day.' How the hell could I feel so alone while still being so bloody popular? Lowering my head, I lifted the pace and forced my attention back on the investigation.

I needed to start speaking to witnesses and those involved with the case. Alex Mercedes was the manager of the band. If I could get to her, she would be a person of great interest.

Turning at North Bilinga Surf Club and heading back, my mind had inadvertently returned to Jenny. Bloody hell, I was pining. *Who was this Dorian bloke? What the hell did she see in him?* Being the detective with the analytical mind meant I could usually figure things out, but I was struggling with this. *Weren't we getting on really well? Wasn't our relationship about to move into a new phase by purchasing property together? Had I been ignoring the fact that I was in love with her and had I been taking her for granted?* Bloody oath I had.

By the time I got back to Kirra, I realised I needed some advice. And I knew exactly where to get it from.

'Morning fellas,' I said as I stopped outside the kiosk beneath Kirra Surf Club.

'Scotty,' The Good Old Boys said in unison.

Still wearing dick togs after their daily ocean swim, four of the gang had congregated, as they did this time every morning, waiting while Trish prepared their coffees.

'You been for a run, mate?' Dessie, the more vocal of the group, asked.

'I have. Needed to clear my head.'

'Coffee, Scotty?' Trish called over.

'Yeah, why not? Give me what these blokes are having.' I followed the gang to the retainer wall on the other side of the path.

'You look a bit down, mate.' Jerry was the shortest of the group, but the widest with an enormous belly that hung over a pair of canary Speedos.

'You know how it is,' I said with a self-sorry shrug.

'A new case?' Don asked, wiping his spectacles on his towel.

'Or personal problems?' asked Benny the fourth amigo.

'Where's Morris?' I asked, realising there was a member missing, and changing the subject.

'Bloody flu. Poor bugger can't shake it,' Dessie said. 'So, you were telling us what's up.'

'Was I?' I said, grinning as Trish brought over the takeaway coffees.

'Scotty, between us we have 320 years' experience,' Jerry said, smiling. 'There isn't a single situation we haven't experienced, trust me.'

They were all veterans of the Vietnam War. Dessie was a retired police officer. Don was once an established property developer. Jerry had owned a chain of fruit and veg shops. Benny used to be a bank manager. While Morris was an ex-pilot and a current committee member of the Currumbin RSL (Returned & Services League for Australia). Between them, they held a wealth of knowledge, which they shared and debated each morning after their swim. Putting the world to rights was the agenda.

'What's up, Scotty?' Jerry asked.

'Well, it's a bit personal.'

'Jenny,' Dessie said, side glancing at the group. 'You haven't let her slip away, have you, mate?'

Bloody hell, theses blokes were as sharp as tacks. 'I think I might have.'

'Tell us what happened.'

While I told them about the situation with the new houses and how I'd come to the realisation that I'd neglected our relationship, taken it for granted, the boys sat on the wall nursing their coffees with their heads down like judges deliberating over a testimony. Then I told them about Dorian.

'I think I've blown it, guys.'

A slow communal nod confirmed their thoughts.

'Tell us about this, Dorian,' Don said.

There was little to tell them.

After more nods and shared glances, the group seemed to reach a consensus.

'Scotty,' Dessie said. 'She loves you. We can all see that. The way you hold hands. The way you playfully put each other down. That annoying bloody giggle you both share. To a novice, it may appear as if you are both merely smitten, but to the experts ...' Once again, he glanced around the group to nods of agreement. 'It's obvious that you are *both* very much in love!'

'But she's got this other bloke now.'

They shook their heads in unison and looked up to the sky like they were on some telepathic wavelength. 'Can't you see what's happening, Scott?' Jerry said. 'She's a smart girl. She's sending you a message. She ain't gonna wait around forever while you get your shit together.'

'That's right,' Don chipped in. 'If you don't want me, I'll go elsewhere.'

'Really ... you reckon?'

The collective nod again followed by sipping of coffee.

'She's giving you the heads up, mate,' Dessie said.

'So, what should I do?'

'Tell her,' Don said. 'Tell her what an idiot you've been and that you love her and want to spend the rest of your life with her.'

'Hang on a minute, nobody said—'

'Scotty, Scotty, Scotty,' Dessie said, squeezing my shoulder. 'This is your problem. You've got to be honest with yourself.'

'But what about this other bloke?'

'*Phh*,' Dessie waved a hand as if he were swatting a fly. 'Do you want us to deal with him?'

The group chuckled.

'You know what you've got to do, mate,' Don said.

'Go get her, buddy,' Jerry said.

'Okay,' Dessie said. 'Now tell us about the case.'

15

Seated at my desk and with my mind fully on the case, or so I thought, I'd made a list of things to do for the day ahead. At the top of the list was Bradley's name. I wasn't sure why.

Bradley picked up after the first ring.

'Good morning, Scott. You're bright and early.'

'Hey, mate. Yeah, you know. Things to do.'

'What can I do for you?'

'Uhm … uh … just called to say G'day.'

'Really?'

'Yeah, how are you?'

'I'm good …'

There was a pause while I pondered over the reason I'd called him. He'd given me everything I needed for the case. *Why had I scribbled his name at the top of the list?*

'This has got nothing to do with Jenny, has it?' He'd lowered his voice.

'Jenny? No … why would it?'

'Dorian?'

'Who?'

'Come on, Scott. I know you met him yesterday.'

'Oh, him.' I reckon my nonchalant shrug would have travelled through the airwaves.

'Don't worry, Scotty. I'm on the case.'

'What do you mean?'

'I haven't met him, but Jenny has done nothing but talk about him.'

'How long has she been seeing him?'

'A couple of weeks.'

'Why didn't you tell me, mate?'

'Not my place, Scotty. She is my boss, after all. Look, everyone knows that you two are perfect for each other.'

'Do they?'

'Yes. And I will not let this Dorian get between you.'

'I think he already has.'

'She's just not thinking straight, that's all.'

'What are you proposing?'

'Oh, if there's anything on him, I'll find it. Don't you worry about that.'

'Then what?'

'We'll expose him for what he really is.'

'And if you can't find anything?'

'Then it'll be up to you to man the fuck up and pull your head out of your arse.'

Oh my God, I was shocked. I'd never heard such language from Bradley. His cussing usually comprised words like biscuits and fluff. 'What do you mean?'

'We both know what I mean, Scott. You need to put aside your little bullshit problems and step up. This is a wake-up call, mate.' He also rarely used the term 'mate'. Until now, I'd doubted it was part of his TSS vocabulary.

Crossing off the first name on the list, the next was Alex Mercedes, the long-time manager of INSEXT. Before signing up the Sexton Brothers, she'd made a fortune in property development. Due to the fact she was a mate of the ex-Gold Coast mayor, Julian Monroe, and I was the bloke who put him behind bars, it was doubtful that she would be a fan of mine. As high profile as she was, she'd be hard to get to, and it wasn't likely we'd be having a chance meeting in a hinterland café, so I'd need to come up with another way of getting to her.

We had actually met before, about fifteen years ago, but I doubted she'd remember it was me who'd arrested her. I hoped she didn't. I was still a young copper in uniform back then. There'd been a report of a woman allegedly causing a scene at one of Surfers' top restaurants. I was the closest officer available, literally just out the front of the building on Staghorn Avenue. When I entered the premises, she was holding centre stage like a crazed gunman with a room full of hostages. Instead of a gun, though, she branded a butter knife. The maître d' had a broken nose, and the manager was cowering behind the reception counter. The other diners sat in fear with their heads down.

'Do you fucking people know who you're dealing with?' Wearing a sequined dress, the woman of short stature but enormous presence, yelled while she scanned the room as if daring anyone to move. 'I'm Alex Mercedes. I own this fucking town! Now get out of my seat, bitch.' She directed her attention to a young couple seated at a table by the far window. The young woman seemed familiar. I later learned that she was an up-and-coming actress, famous from one of the soap operas, who'd just signed a Hollywood deal for her first movie. The table was the best in the house, the one Alex always patronised, but there'd been a mix up with the reservations.

'I said get the fuck away from my table.' She rushed towards the couple. The young man accompanying her did little to intervene.

'Whoa, whoa,' I called out, springing across the room.

Alex turned, and I found myself face to face with an angry tiger. She held up the knife.

'Hey, come on now. You don't want to be doing that.' Holding up my hands in surrender, I was relieved that her attention had shifted from the actress.

'I'm not doing anything. Get these people away from my table. NOW!'

'Put down the knife, and I'm sure these nice folks will be happy to move.' Glancing at the couple, they met my eyes with agreeable nods.

'Good. Get up then.' She turned back to the couple.

'Give me the knife and we'll sort this all out,' I said, moving in between Alex and the table.

'Get out of my way, you little shit,' Alex growled, holding up the knife once more. Then she lunged towards me.

I was no martial arts expert, but it was a simple textbook manoeuvre. A back hand to the knife wielding hand was enough to knock her off balance. Moving with the momentum, I grabbed her arm with one hand then wrapped my other arm around her neck from behind. Pulling her in close and exerting pressure on her wrist, caused her to drop the knife.

Like a rabid dog, Alex fought back. Elbowing me hard in the kidneys, she shot back her head butting me in the nose. 'You greasy little bastard,' she cussed as she struggled. 'I'll have your job for this.'

With blood pouring from my nose, I held on, bent her over the nearest table from which an elderly couple scurried away, and retrieved the handcuffs from my belt. While cuffing her, she stamped on my toes with her stilettoes and continued to yell and cuss. With pressure on her back, I held her there for a moment, restricting her movement until she calmed down some.

The diners and the staff all cheered as I read Alex her rights.

Suspecting that Alex would know of me, Scotty Stephens the detective, I hoped she wouldn't remember the young copper who arrested her that night. If I was going to get a chance to talk to her, I'd need to come from a different angle. Perhaps play to her ego. *Hmm* ... a plan began to hatch.

16

The photo on the whiteboard of Alex Mercedes was a recent one from the *Gold Coast Bulletin*. She was attending a high-profile fundraiser. Glamourous, wearing African diamonds, and a dress by Dion Lee—or so the article said—and with the latest beau on her arm, the heavy use of Botox gave the impression she'd had a head transplant with a Myers mannequin.

While spending some time that morning researching the infamous Gold Coast businesswoman, I came across her surprising beginnings. Real name Alexandria Petrof, she was the daughter of Czech migrants, Artyom and Polina Petrof. The family spent the first five years in Australia at the Bonegilla refugee camp in northern Victoria. On their release, they moved to Queensland. Artyom worked as a labourer for the Gold Coast City Council, while Polina found employment as a housemaid at the Surfers Paradise Hotel. There was little else information about the pair until their deaths in the 1980s.

Alex attended Nerang State School until leaving in 1966, at fifteen. There were no employment records for her until 1971, when she worked as a barmaid at one of the strip joints in Surfers Paradise. Ten years later, she opened a gentleman's club called *The Golden Touch*. From humble beginnings in a shabby little office over the club, she opened the *Alexia Talent Agency*. Within twelve months, most of the strippers and entertainers on the Gold Coast were signed to the agency. The company name changed to *Mercedes Media* five years later.

Her wealth and stature grew significantly when she invested in real estate: shops, office blocks and apartments. In the late seventies, she commissioned her first major building development, an eight-storey apartment block in Main Beach. Over the next twenty years, she was regularly in the news, but not always for the right reasons.

It was Alex who actually discovered the Sexton boys when they were strategically busking outside her offices.

'Good afternoon, Alexia Promotions, you're speaking to Tyler.' The smooth American voice reminded me of a chocolate ad.

'Oh hi, Tyler, would I be able to speak with Alex Mercedes please?'

'I'm afraid Miss Mercedes will be in meetings all day. Can I take a message?'

'Yeah … look it's … Scotty Stephens here—'

'Scotty Stephens? The detective?'

'One and the same.'

'Wow!' His vocal demeanour suddenly perked up. 'What can I do for you?'

'I was hoping to speak with Alex.'

'I'm afraid she doesn't take calls these days.' There was a pause then, 'Oh … you're not investigating her or anything like that, are you?'

'No, nothing like that. I wanted to discuss the possibility of her representing me.'

'Representing you …? Oh, I see. You're getting media work.'

'Yeah, lots of, but it's not just that. There's, uhm,' I paused before delivering the lie. 'I've been approached to make a movie about my life.'

'Oh yes, yes, of course. You *will* need representation, and Alex is the best. Look what she did for INSEXT.'

'I know. That's why I'm calling.'

'Right, right …'

I could hear him flicking through the pages of a diary.

'Okay, she can see you Thursday week at 3.00 pm. Would that suit?'

'No, not at all. I've got a meeting in two days with the Hemsworth boys. They're pretty keen to get a contract signed, apparently.'

'The Hemsworths?'

'Yep. Looks like I'll need to look elsewhere for management. No worries. Thanks anyway.' I hung up.

My phone rang instantly. It was Tyler. 'Scott, great news. Alex will see you tomorrow morning.'

'Really? That is great news.'

'My apologies. I'd forgotten she had a cancellation. How about I put you down for 10.00 am?'

'Perfect.'

'Do you know where we are?'

'I do indeed. See you tomorrow, Tyler.'

It was mid-afternoon. I didn't feel like finishing early. Keeping my mind on the case rather than pining over Jenny seemed a better option. Looking up at the faces on the whiteboard, one stuck out. He had the same eyes as Phil Sexton. I hadn't been down to Byron Bay in a while. It was Tuesday; the weekly evening craft markets would be on tonight. Perfect. Grabbing my car keys, I headed off, remembering to lock the office behind me.

My therapy session with The Good Old Boys hadn't just been about Jenny. They'd also enquired about the latest case. When I'd mentioned the Sextons, the mood of the boys changed somewhat.

Especially Dessie. 'That weak bastard, Sexton.'

My frown requested an explanation.

'We all did our duty. Fought for our country. But not him.'

'Phil?'

'No. The father. Dave Sexton. He was a consciences objector.' Dessie's face had turned a dark shade of red and his lips trembled.

'You knew him?'

Dessie nodded and pointed up to Kirra Hill. We went to school together.

He was pointing at the historical Kirra Community Centre that was once Coolangatta State School.

'What was he like?'

Dessie swirled a finger at the side of his head. 'Bloody fruit loop, even back then. A Beatnik, artist type, always protesting about something or other.'

'So, when the draft came through, what? He flat out refused to go?'

'Something like that. Kicked up a big stink. Called us all murderers.'

'Was he arrested?'

'Nah, claimed it was on religious grounds.'

'Even converted to Buddhism, I heard,' Don added.

'Do you know what happened to him?'

'I hadn't seen him for years, never even thought about him until his boys started appearing on the news,' Dessie said.

Jerry and Don sat on the wall listening as Dessie continued.

'I saw him last year in Byron Bay. He's got a market stall down there. Sells all that hippy shit, clothing and stuff. He didn't recognise me, not that I stopped for a chat or anything, but I recognised him. He'd hardly changed. Still spaced out, looked like he had one of them mail-order brides.'

'Do you know if he's still down there?'

Dessie shrugged. 'Wouldn't have a clue. Don't care.'

'If Bobby Sexton was anything like his father ...' Morris pipped in, '... I'd have bloody killed him myself.'

'So, what are you going to do, Scotty? The case is closed. Ray Morris is in jail. Do you think he's innocent?' Don asked.

'Too early to know.' Although the case was high profile and I had all the details at my disposal, the only things I really had to go on were the people. There was no additional evidence in Ray's favour. *Was there anything else to unearth?* Like an archaeologist sifting through the spoils of dirt, hoping to reveal something that was missed from the main dig, I'd need to check every little detail.

<h1 style="text-align:center">17</h1>

By teatime, I was pulling into the famous little town of Byron Bay. Architecturally, this placed had changed very little since I'd first visited in the early nineties. The local council had done a great job ensuring that all recent developments remained in keeping with the original layout—no high rises, no landmarks demolished just for the sake of progress. However, socially, economically and spiritually, Byron had seen some drastic changes. If there was ever a place designed for Timothy Leary's 1960s ideology, "Tune in, turn on and drop out", Byron Bay was that place. The Cape and its surrounding hinterland became the destination of hippies and those individuals who wanted to be free of society. Although the town still held a romantic essence of its former ethos, it was becoming harder to detect beneath the grasp of commercialism. Recently, every time I travelled there, I found myself missing the old Byron. Most of the dreadlock characters, the artists, the street performers, and the unique shops that sold locally made produce and goods were gone, replaced by familiar brands. Thankfully, though, the weekly craft market kept the era that we all missed alive on a Tuesday evening outside the old train station.

Although I could have parked closer to the venue, I left the car near the beach in the council car park. A trip to Byron would never be complete without standing for a few moments on the foreshore looking over the cape, with Julian Rocks in the distance, and the lighthouse sitting up high on Australia's most easterly point. Breathing in the fresh sea air, and enjoying the aroma of fish and chips from the kiosk by the public swimming pool, I watched the surfers for a few minutes, riding a not-too-shabby surf.

As always, the walk through town was a pleasant stroll. By the time I reached the Great Northern Hotel, the idea of dinner at the pub was quite appealing. Maybe later before heading back. The train station, reclaimed from the old Murwillumbah line, sat back from the road and also functioned as a pub. In front of it, there was a grassed area where the market was held. I was reasonably early, so the venders were still setting up when I arrived.

I had no idea what Dave was selling, but I spotted him right away.

With the help of a young Filipino woman, Dave's stall was just about set up. On the four internal walls of the brightly coloured gazebo hung tie-dye clothing, T-shirts, long baggy pants, dresses, and skirts. There was a trestle table on either side of the opening, angled as if leading browsers inside. Displayed on these were crystals of all colours and sizes, tarot cards, exotic bongs disguised as ornaments, and a range of bottled potions and oils.

The market was only small, perhaps twenty stalls. Scented candles, dream catchers and wind chimes, clothing made from hemp, crystals and natural health tonics and soaps seemed to be the principal theme. The familiar aromas triggered a feeling of nostalgia, while the natural friendly vibe of the seemingly carefree vendors became infectious.

So far, wearing a baseball cap and sunglasses, and with my head down, nobody seemed to recognise me as I strolled among the stores like an early punter. By the time I doubled back and arrived at Dave's stall, he was set up and ready for business.

'Welcome, friend, welcome,' he said as I approached. 'Feel free to enter and discover the world of tie.' With the sweep of an arm, his invitation to step inside the den of rainbow swirl seemed genuine and friendly.

'Thanks.' Familiar with, but not necessarily a fan of, the tie-dye concept of clothing, I'd never actually owned any. My aim was to be the inquisitive buyer. 'Wow, these are amazing!'

'Thank you.' Dave had followed me into the small area.

The woman sat on the edge of what looked like a massage chair in the corner, constantly smiling and enthusiastically nodding each time I glanced her way.

'This clothing is 100% locally made,' Dave added while I browsed the T-shirts hanging on the walls. 'All natural dyes, no chemicals.'

'Amazing. And what, you make them all yourself?' With my sunglasses still on, I turned to get a good look at him.

'Harmony makes the clothing.' He looked towards his partner, and when their eyes met, they grinned like school kids. 'I take care of the dying.'

'I've heard about you. You're quite famous.'

Dave blushed, but his piercing blue eyes remained firmly fixed on mine, as if tapping into my energy. Shirtless, his lean body was deeply tanned with grey chest hair. His skin was leatherlike, his face chiselled. His grey hair was long and tied back in a ponytail. He wore baggy tie-dye pants and had bare feet. 'Really? Where are you from?'

'The Gold Coast.' I held out my hand. 'I'm Scotty.'

'Hi Scotty. It's good to meet you.' He shook my hand. His smile was wide and infectious. 'I'm Dhani, and this is my wife, Harmony.'

Dhani? I thought your name was Dave. Removing my sunglasses, I mentally ducked. *Would he recognise me?*

'You've got the perfect body shape for this kind of clothing, Scotty. I'm guessing you surf?' So far, so good. He didn't appear to know who I was.

'Yep.'

He reached up to the nearest rack of T-shirts, checked the labels, and pulled one down. 'Here, try this one. Should be your size.'

Looking around, I noticed there was nowhere to change, so I took off my cap and pulled my Kirra Beach shirt over my head. When I put on the tie-dye shirt, it felt cheap and ill fitting.

'Wow, that looks amazing!' Dhani exclaimed.

There was no mirror. 'Awesome, feels great,' I said, adjusting the shoulders and lying through my teeth. 'How much is it?'

'For you, my friend, only $80, but if you wanted some matching pants too like these.' He grabbed the sides of his pants and opened them out. 'I'll be able to do you a special deal.'

80 bucks? 'Ah, no ... that's uhm ... I'll just take the shirt, thanks.'

'No worries.'

I took off the shirt and handed it back.

'We have a nice range of vegan sandals.' Dhani said, pointing to the row of footwear.

I nearly said, 'No worries, I don't eat shoes,' but remembered the company I was in.

'You're looking a bit tense, my friend,' Dhani said.

'I am?'

'Yes, I can see the rigours of daily life are taking their toll on your psyche.'

'They are?'

Like the magician's assistant, Harmony rose from the chair and swept her arm across it, inviting me to take a seat.

I was being played, but it was okay.

'I can help you with that, brother,' Dhani said. 'Take a seat.'

Reluctantly, I did as I was told.

It was like sitting on a chair backwards, and it was a bit tight with only enough room for Dhani to stand behind me, but instantly his fingers went to work on the muscles around the back of my neck.

Ouch, bloody hell. I cussed under my breath, flinching. I hadn't had a massage in a long time.

'Uhh, goodness me, there's a lot of tension there, Scotty.'

'Tell me about it.'

The idea was to gently question the man who was the father of two of the most famous people in Australia, but that was the furthest thing from my mind as I sat with my eyes clenched shut and my body in a tensed state of anxiety.

'Just try to relax, Scotty,' Dhani said. In normal circumstances, his calm voice would have been soothing, but at that moment, relaxation seemed like a past luxury that was no longer available. I wanted to yell out as his powerful hands and fingers probed, rolled and squeezed a layer of tight knots in my neck.

I wasn't exactly sure how long I was in that chair or if I'd even remained conscious through the massage, but I have to admit, when it was over, my neck and shoulders felt amazing—loose and free of the tension that I'd inadvertently gotten used to.

'I'd recommend a full body massage once a week, Scotty,' Dhani said, wiping his hands on a small towel. 'I have a salon in town, if you'd like to make a booking.'

'Thanks, I'll have a think about.'

'Okay.'

Harmony rang up the purchase and produced a credit card reader. 'Cash or card?'

'Uhm, card thanks.' Reaching into my pocket, I pulled out my credit card and tapped it on the little white square device. An extra $100 was added to the cost of the T-shirt.

So, I was already $180 in. Now I needed some information.

18

Although the transaction was complete, I lingered like an interested shopper. No doubt Dhani and Harmony were expecting me to move on.

'Where do I know you from, Dhani? You look very familiar.'

Dhani grinned. 'Of course you know me. I'm the tie-dye guy.'

'But I've seen you somewhere else.' It was the only angle I could think of without blowing my cover.

'Perhaps you've seen me on the other markets. We were at Coolangatta last week.'

'That's it. I've seen you at Cooly. You must be killing it with all this amazing gear.' Stroke his ego. Be friendly and involved.

'Yeah, we're doing all right.'

A small handwritten sign, like the kind created by a child using wax crayons, hung at the back of the stall. 'You're a yoga instructor too?'

'Yes, I am.' He put his hands together and lowered his head as if he were about to pray.

'I've always wanted to do yoga. Do you teach locally?'

'On the beach every morning at six.'

'Wow, can I come along?'

'It's a long way to come from the Gold Coast. Surely there are classes up there.'

A couple of young women entered the stall, and the space suddenly became very cramped. While Harmony tended to their needs, Dhani and I stepped outside the front.

'Can we grab a coffee or something, Dhani?' I picked up one of the crystals and appraised it in my hand. 'I'd really like to learn about adopting a more holistic lifestyle.'

'Sure.' He pointed to a small, brightly coloured, vintage caravan on the other side of the lot. The upper half of one side was open, and there were tables and chairs out front. 'I have a delivery for Denzel. We can chat there.'

'Cool.'

He picked up a dark bottle from one of the trestles, then called into the stall. 'Just going to see Denz, Hun.'

Harmony smiled and waved.

As we approached the Rasta-coloured caravan, the sound of reggae music grew louder. There was a black guy standing inside behind a counter. To the right of the open hatch was a painting of Bob Marley, and above this were the words, *Reggae Reggae Café*.

'Denzel, my friend,' Dhani said when we reached the van.

'Ahh me man Dhani, how goes it, brother?' Denzel was a big man with dreadlocks. Wearing a tie-dye T-shirt, and a wide ivory smile, he took up almost every inch of the van's interior.

Reaching up, Dhani placed the bottle on the counter.

'Me mon, me mon,' Denzel said, lifting the bottle and giving it a shake.

Dhani turned to me. 'Organic dreadlock oil, handmade. Denzel, this is Scotty. He's from the Gold Coast.'

'Scotty, good to meet ya, mon.' Denzel reached out of the van, and we shook hands.

As he did, I tensed a little, expecting him to recognise me and blow my cover. But he just smiled. News from the Gold Coast obviously didn't reach Byron Bay. Either that or the people down here just didn't care what was happening in the outside world. 'Good to meet you two, mate.'

'Can we get two green teas, please Denny?' Dhani said.

'Iri. Take a seat, and I'll be right dher.'

We made our way to one of a half dozen plastic tables with matching chairs. As I lowered into one of the chairs, it sunk into the grass slightly.

'So, Scotty,' Dhani said, sitting opposite me. 'What is it you really want to know?'

'Excuse me?'

Dhani smiled. 'Let's cut the pretence, eh? You're Scotty Stephens, the famous detective. I'm pretty sure you haven't come all the way down here to buy a T-shirt and talk about yoga.'

Bugger. He'd known who I was all this time. It was a double bugger when Denzel approached with two teas, and I pulled out some cash from my pocket.

'No way. Dis is on de house, mon.' His wide smile was warm and genuine. 'It ain't every day a famous detective comes to de *Reggae Reggae Café*.'

I was busted, even with my cap and sunnies on. I guess the folk of Byron Bay weren't as cut off from the world as I thought.

There was no use trying to deny who I was or why I was there, so after thanking Denzel for his kind gesture and waiting until he'd returned to the van, I was met by Dhani's piercing blue eyes. 'Okay, you got me.'

'This is obviously about Bobby.'

I nodded in defeat. 'It is, yes.' I attempted a sip of my tea, but it was too hot. 'I've been asked to look into the case by Ray Morris.'

Dhani nodded slowly. 'Makes sense.'

'Does it?'

'Yes. Ray's a good man.'

'Innocent?'

'Absolutely!' Dhani lifted his tea and had no problem sipping the hot, green liquid.

'What makes you say that?'

'History repeating itself. Ray was gravely wronged twice in his life. Once when he was kicked out of the band, and again when he was wrongfully convicted of Bobby's murder.'

'But the evidence against him was pretty damning.'

Dhani wafted his hand through invisible smoke. 'He was a patsy.'

'What do you mean?'

'I know who really killed him!' He sipped his tea again, and I wasn't sure if the pregnant pause was intentional or not.

Taking off my sunglasses was like moving a pawn one space forward. 'And who might that be?'

'Why Phil, of course!'

'Really? Your eldest son?'

'Yes.' He nursed the paper cup in his hands and gazed into it. 'Everyone who knows Phil knows he was capable of this. He'd been threatening to do it for years.'

'Threatening to kill Bobby?'

Dhani's chuckle harboured a nervous disposition. 'Did you know he almost beat his younger brother to death once?'

The shake of my head was enough of a reply.

'On more than one occasion, actually. Phil was a ... *is* a ... bully. He controlled the band with an iron fist, while Alex took care of business. 'I can't believe none of it came out in court. The amazing Alex Mercedes has friends in high places.'

'A cover up?'

Dhani leaned forward. 'Of the worst kind!'

'When was the last time you saw either of your sons?'

'Years ago.' He moved back in his chair and spent the next thirty minutes sharing anecdotes of his sons when they were boys. He seemed to have little recollection of them as adults. 'The last I heard from Bobby was from the text I received from him the night of his death.'

'Text?'

'Yes. In fact, I still have it.' He rummaged in a deep pocket and pulled out an ancient phone. After some serious squinting and tapping, he handed it to me. On the screen was the following text:

Dear Dad. I should have listened to you. You warned me about the traps of the music business and dealing with people like Alex Mercedes, but I didn't listen. My respect for you as a father has grown significantly since clearing my mind. Thank you. I hope you will forgive me for pushing you out of my life and I pray we can rebuild our relationship.

'And you received this on the night of Bobby's death?'

Dhani nodded and finished his tea. 'Maeve received one too.'

'Your ex-wife?'

'Yes … Well, I must get back. It's been good meeting you, Scotty.'

We stood and shook hands.

'It's been good meeting you too.'

Forgetting about dinner on the drive home, it was the text that now occupied my mind. Ray Morris had also received a text from Bobby on the night of his death. Although they were different, in a way they were the same because the sender seemed to be cleansing his soul in a way an addict or an alcoholic would when starting a 12-point program. *Hmm. Did that mean Bobby sent more texts out that evening?* It was likely. *And would some of the things he had to say cause a panic in certain people?* Maybe. Unfortunately, Bobby's phone was never found. The killer must have taken it.

19

During the drive home, I'd had time to contemplate my time with Dhani. The information he shared about his fatherhood days was candid and uninspiring. It was the story of a father with other things on his mind. He was a jazz musician back in the day—a saxophone player. His relationship with his first wife, Maeve, was on and off during the years they were together. Dhani, it seemed, was rarely at home and spent little time with his boys. The fact that Maeve was working two jobs and single-handedly bringing up the kids didn't seem to bother him. When I asked him about Vietnam, he'd brushed over it with a simple shrug and the passive statement, "War is murder".

So, his relationship with the boys was pretty much non-existent. Their fame meant nothing to him. He claimed he wouldn't even know one of their songs if he heard it, which I found hard to believe. Spanning a twenty-year period, INSEXT was arguably the biggest band in the world, their songs played over and over on most radio stations. *Was he jealous of the boys? Did he harbour a regret that he wasn't a part of their lives? Could he have shared in their wealth?* If he possessed any of those feelings, he certainly hid them well. Speaking with him, I got the impression that he was the one who had made it. He was the one who had discovered the answer to life. Dhani was living the dream.

The M1 in Northern NSW was quiet at that time of the evening, the odd freight truck making its way from Sydney to Brisbane or farther north, campervans heading to the Coast, a dribble of cars and motorbikes. I was in no hurry to get home, and I hadn't even realised that the car radio had somehow tuned into an obscure reggae station. By the time I reached Tweed Heads, the low steady beat had assisted me to mentally rearrange the list of things to do on the whiteboard.

A proper chat with Ray Morris was due. He knew the Sexton boys long before they were famous, and I think that was where I needed to begin my investigation—right at the beginning. What was the siblings' relationship really like? Although I didn't fancy travelling all the way to Townsville, hoping instead that a phone call would suffice, if the need arose to fly up there, I was willing to do it.

Another person who knew the boys well was their long-time road manager, Tommy Platt. He'd been around since their school days, and he'd worked with them until the time of Bobby's death, so not only did he know them from the beginning, but he would have witnessed first-hand their rise to stardom and how it would undoubtedly have changed them. If I could get him on side, Tommy would be a great asset.

By the time I rounded Kirra Point, the list of things to do was complete in my mind. I was mentally exhausted and looking forward to an early night. After entering my tiny apartment, I threw the keys on the kitchen bench, pulled out my phone, and dialled Jenny's number.

I was about to hang up after a dozen or so rings when she finally picked up. 'Hey Scotty, how's it going?' The background noise was loud, there was music and chatter like she was in a bar.

'I'm good. Where are you?'

'I'm in Noosa.'

'Noosa?'

'Managed to get a couple of days off. Dorian has a place up here.' The cheerful tone in her voice stabbed my heart like an icy blade.

'Dorian. Is he there too?'

'Listen, Scotty, I've got to go.' There was an explosion of laughter in the background, as if someone had just told the best joke ever. 'I'll be back on Friday. I need to talk to you about the house plans. I'll call you then, eh?' She hung up and my apartment returned to silence.

20

My appointment with Alex Mercedes was for 10.00 am. While at the northern end of the Coast, I'd also seized the opportunity to catchup with Bradley for lunch after the meeting.

Alex's office block was located in the prestigious Circle on Cavill at the far end of the avenue. I purposely arrived early so I could park near the beach and check on the surf. For all its faults, Surfers did still have that something that brought four million visitors to its shores each year.

Even at a steady stroll, it only took a few minutes to reach my destination. I was five minutes early, which was perfect. The words of my mother always played a part in my time management prior to an appointment. 'If you're on time, you're five minutes late!'

Mercedes Media took up the top floor of the exclusive thirty-storey building. When I stepped from the lift into a plush foyer, blue sky spilled into the area through the floor-to-ceiling glass windows. A black-and-white picture of INSEXT preforming on the Pyramid Stage at Glastonbury entirely covered the internal wall behind the reception desk. Alex Mercedes was standing at the side of the stage with her back to the band, looking out over an endless mass of fans.

A young man with an impressive afro was seated at the reception desk. He wore a tight-fitting suit, and the detail of the tattoo around his neck seemed to be lost somewhat on his coffee-coloured skin. Large, yellow-framed glasses gave the impression of an AI created being. The impossible white teeth from the perfect

81

smile only added to the illusion. A small golden name badge on his lapel read, 'Tyler'.

'Hi, I'm—'

'You're Scotty Stephens.'

'That's right.' My blush paled in comparison to the young man's, who rose to his feet.

'Oh, my God …' Fanning his face with both hands, his enormous hair wobbled with each movement. 'It's so good to meet you.' His Californian accent matched his handshake—warm and soft—and he smelled good too. 'Can I get you a coffee or …?'

'A tea would be nice.'

'No worries. If you'd like to take a seat, I'll let Alex know you're here.'

'Cool. Oh, and skinny milk, no sugar.'

When Tyler bowed his head, the fro swept forward and backwards like a wave of candy cotton.

As I sank into the leather couch by the window, a loud commotion coming from one of the offices suddenly startled me. I recognised the voice immediately.

'I COULDN'T GIVE A FUCK IF YOU WERE THE SULTAN OF FUCKING BRUNEI. IT'S SIXTY FORTY OR YOU CAN FUCK OFF BACK TO WAGGA WAGGA!'

Yep. That was Alex Mercedes.

Tyler glanced back at me warily from the coffee station in one corner and nodded reassuringly, as if apologising for his boss. Then I realised he was attempting to make tea with the coffeemaker. Not good. When he padded over with the tiny cup and saucer, the frothy, milky coloured liquid with tea leaves floating on the surface confirmed my fears.

'Cheers,' I said, taking the cup.

'Is that okay? I've never made tea before.'

'It's fine, thanks.' It looked terrible.

'Alex shouldn't be too long. Can I get you anything el—'

'I'LL HIT YOU SO HARD YOU'LL THINK YOU'VE BEEN RAMMED BY A FUCKING TRAIN!'

'Can I get you anything else?'

'No. I'm all good, thanks, mate.'

Speaking normally, I got the impression that Tyler and the staff at *Mercedes Media* were used to these kinds of outbursts from their boss, and probably lived in perpetual fear of the little woman. Suddenly, I felt like I was in the waiting room of my urologist preparing for a prostate examination. Alex had a reputation for being a hard businesswoman. The outburst I'd just witnessed did little to dispel the image. The only relief I felt when Tyler informed me that Alex would see me now was that I didn't get the chance to taste his tea.

The enormous office was exactly what you would expect of a high-profile rock 'n' roll manager, slash, talent agent, slash, property entrepreneur, slash businesswoman of the year more times than any other Australian woman. The internal walls were covered in framed gold and platinum discs. A glass, see-through desk elongated the legs of the tiny blonde-haired septuagenarian seated behind it, giving her a magnified appearance.

'Well, look who it isn't,' Alex said, rising from her desk. 'Detective Scotty Stephens.' Her ingenuine smile carried an air of authority. 'Take a seat.' She didn't offer her hand.

'G'day.' Trying to play it cool, I sat down on the matching transparent chair in front of her desk.

'So, you've hit the big time and you need some help, eh?'

'I spose.' Regardless of how successful, famous and intimidating she was, I wasn't about to piss in her pocket. I'd learned that she was good friends with Gladys Monroe, the wife of ex-Gold Coast Mayor and jailed felon, Julian Monroe. I wondered how much she actually knew about my history with the Gold Coast socialite. It was common knowledge that it was me who put Gladys' husband behind bars, but would Alex know about the fourteen-year-old upcoming AFL star who lost his virginity to the older cheerleader in a public toilet? I wasn't sure if the chilly reception I received was because of this or whether it was normal protocol.

'So, what are you up to? Why have you come here today?'

'Well, I'm constantly being approached by different media outlets for interviews and that. I've been asked to write a book and there's word of a movie.'

I knew a patronising grin when I saw one.

'You're a bachelor, right?'

I replied with a nod.

'Gay?'

'No.' A slight ruffle of the feathers.

'Would you ever consider reality TV?'

'What do you mean?' I knew exactly where she was going with this, but decided on playing dumb, allowing her to control the conversation—or so she thought.

'What if we dropped you on a desert island with a group of other losers and a handful of bimbos? Is that the kind of thing you're looking for?'

Other losers?

'Or assigned a film crew to follow you around twenty-four hours a day? There's big money in that shit.'

Although her suggestions horrified me, I went along with them as if I were interested. I needed to get her on side, while remaining equal to her authority. 'Never thought of it.'

'If I took you on as a client, I'll take you to the next level. I'm talking international super stardom. It'll be a long way from your current situation, the local has-been that never quite was, who'll probably end up a sad sack alchy trying to live off a mediocre past.'

Wow! Don't hold back, you old cow.

'The deal is sixty forty. Sixty for me and forty for you.'

I was trying my hardest not to laugh, attempting to play the dumb starstruck wanna-be. 'Sounds good. I'll need some time to think about it.'

'Sure, take as long as you want, discuss it with your partner, oh that's right, you don't have one. In the meantime, I'll get the papers drawn up.' There was a change in her smile, and an uncharacteristic warmth replaced the anger. As she blinked, I could have sworn I heard a *cha-ching!*

It was now or never. Glancing around the room, I parked my gaze on the wall of gold records. 'Wow! I didn't realise you were the manager of INSEXT.'

Alex leaned back in her chair and eyed me warily.

21

'You smug little bastard!'

'I'm sorry?'

Alex Mercedes sunk back into her chair. 'Geez, you actually had me there for a minute.'

'I'm not following you.'

'Who put you up to this? That bitch Stella Morris? Makes sense. I wondered what she'd do with all that money. *60 Minutes*. The *Sydney Morning Herald*.'

'Stella Morris has nothing to do with me being here—'

Like a traffic cop, Alex raised the palm of her right hand. 'Forget the bullshit. You're not here for representation. If it wasn't Stella ... then who ... not Ray?' She was asking the questions but not expecting answers. Then she laughed. 'Ray Morris has hired you to take on his case.' The laughter increased. 'And you agreed, ha! Do you realise how much hatred there is around the world for that man? He killed Bobby fucking Sexton, for God's sake.'

Realising it was a waste of time continuing with the charade, I came clean. 'Yes, I'm here on behalf of Ray—'

'So, you think you can just waltz in here anytime? What, you're coming for me now like you did Julian Monroe?'

I had no idea where this was going. I hadn't accused her of anything. In fact, I'd barely spoken a dozen or so words.

'Need to top up the popularity meter, do we, Scott? Fame wavering a bit, is it?'

'I'm not here to accuse you of anything, Alex.'

'Then why *are* you here?'

'I *am* looking for representation—' Now it was my turn to impersonate the traffic cop when she lurched forward in her seat. 'Hold on, hold on. Let me explain.'

Her scarlet, seething expression said, "Okay, take your best shot, but it better be a good one cause I'm gonna wipe the floor with you."

'Everything I've said so far is true—the offers, the deals. It's all a bit overwhelming and beyond my skill level, but I also wanted to talk to you about Bobby's death, and you're right, I have been asked to look into the case.'

A raised tattooed eyebrow accompanied a curious scowl. 'But why?'

'I'm not sure why. It's not like I've found any fresh evidence to prove his innocence or anything like that. It's just a gut feeling. But I'm here for two reasons, and I apologise for trying to deceive you. I should have known better.'

'Damn right.'

'I was hoping we could work together. You could be my manager, oversee my affairs for the book and that, but in return, I thought you might tell me what you know about what happened that night.'

'I know the same as anyone else—what I heard in court. On the night of Bobby's death, I was at a gala in Brisbane.'

'So, do you think Ray killed Bobby?'

'Of course he did! Who else would have?'

'How was Phil's relationship with his brother?'

'Whoa …' The traffic cop was back. 'Don't you be getting no ideas there. Those boys were tight. Always were.'

'That's not what I've heard. Apparently, Phil was a bully, even beat Bobby up on more than one occasion.'

'That's ridiculous.' She sunk back into her chair. 'Phil loved Bobby, looked out for him. I've never met siblings so close.'

'If that's the case, why did Bobby kick him out of his house on the night of his death?'

'They were brothers, they argued. Of course, they did.'

To my amazement, she appeared to be softening.

'When was the last time you saw Bobby?'

'Sixty, forty.' She was all business.

'Did you receive a text from him the night of his murder?'

There was a definite flinch. 'A text?'

As I sometimes did when trying to prize out a piece of new information, I delved into the realms of fiction. 'I know Bobby sent you a text not long before he was killed.'

The Botox didn't allow a frown, but the eyes did.

'Must have been a bit of a shock when he unloaded like that. How much was he going to sue you for? Everything?'

'Sixty forty, take it or leave it.'

'Fifty, fifty.'

While the rest of her face remained inanimate, slight movement at the corners of her mouth signalled a wry smile. 'A book and a movie?'

'And interviews, I've been offered a speaking tour, fundraisers, luncheons, that kind of thing.' This was all true, at least. The offers kept coming in, but in my pigheaded way, I'd been ignoring them.

'Sixty forty, take it or leave it.'

It may have appeared to be a crappy offer, but after some research, I was aware of the clout Alex Mercedes had in the entertainment industry and the heights her clients could achieve. Ex-soap stars transformed into Hollywood A-listers. Retired sports stars making a tidy living from a book deal and after-dinner speeches. Post fifteen minutes of fame, reality TV stars resurrected and rebranded. There was no doubting Alex's skill for nurturing and exploiting talent, but of course, I was having none of this. The offers would continue to be tossed in the bin, regardless of what

Alex offered, but she obviously didn't need to know that right now. I was slowly but surely working my way in. Or so I thought.

Alex rose from her desk.

I did the same, and we shook hands.

'Great. All you'll need to do now is forget any ideas about helping Ray Morris and we'll be good to go.'

Whoa, nobody said anything about dropping the case.

Like me, Alex, it appeared, was a master at reading other peoples' expressions.

'You hesitate?'

'Uhm …'

'Do you realise what I'm offering you here? Forget *60 Minutes* and morning television. I'm talking *Oprah* and *Piers Morgan*—and fucking God!'

'Yeah right … I'm … uhm … grateful and all. Just need a bit of time to think.'

'Sure, you do. But don't leave it too long. In the meantime, leave your details with Tyler on your way out.' She sat back down at her desk, opened up a laptop, and tapped the keyboard.

I'd been dismissed.

22

It was just after 11.00 am when I left Alex Mercedes' office. It was a cloudless, hot day, and the tourists were out in force. With an hour to kill before my lunch date with Bradley, I decided to have a stroll around the shops, see if I couldn't blend in. This bloody fifteen minutes of fame had to start fading soon, surely.

'Scotty Stephens, it's great to see you. Can we get a selfie?' It was a group of girls in brightly coloured bikinis.

I was barely three metres from the building. Once again, the baseball cap and sunnies did little to hide my identity. 'Sure.'

'We're up from Sydney,' the tall blonde spokesperson of the group said. 'Fancy coming out with us tonight?'

'I'd love to,' I said, grinning for the camera with sun-lotioned arms around my neck. 'But I can't, I'm afraid.'

There was a collective, 'Aaargh.'

'Sorry girls.' When the picture was taken, I untwined myself and headed off, leaving a wake of giggles.

Careful to avoid an oncoming tram, I crossed the junction of Surfers Paradise Boulevard and Cavill Avenue, along with a throng of tourists.

'Hey Scotty, how's it going?'

'Good.'

'Scotty my man. Give me five.'

'Scotty Stephens. Wow … hi.'

Then there were those that just looked, and those that peeked but pretended not to notice me. The ones that genuinely didn't

90

know me seemed far and few between, but I couldn't help wishing there were more of them.

Orchid Avenue was a little quieter. Strolling along to the end of the street, I noticed a new shop—a women's' boutique—but it was more the woman inside that caught my attention. She was sticking up a sign in the window that read, "Grand Opening This Saturday". At first, I wasn't sure. Perhaps there was just a passing resemblance, but as I got closer, I became more convinced it was her. When our eyes met through the window, I was a hundred per cent certain. The blush only added to the confirmation. It was Stella Morris. Although the door was closed and the shop clearly wasn't open for business, I knocked anyway.

Climbing down from a stepladder, Stella indicated with a nod that the door was unlocked, so I popped my head in.

'Hey Stella. I'm Sc—'

'Scott Stephens. I know who you are.'

'Mind if I come in?'

After an impatient, I-don't-really-have-time-for-this shrug, she said, 'If you must.' Reluctantly, she shook my hand.

'It's great to meet you at last. I've been meaning to get in touch again.'

'So how did you find out about this place?'

'I didn't. I was literally just passing.'

'Yeah right.' She turned and, negotiating her way through rows of empty racks and boxes of clothing, she headed to the counter at the back of the shop.

'It's true. Honestly,' I said, following her while removing my cap and sunnies. 'Do you mind if we have a chat?'

'As you can see, I'm really busy.'

'Shouldn't take too long.'

There was an intake of breath, followed by a prolonged sigh. 'Okay but make it quick. I've got to get all this hung and tagged.'

'Can I help?'

'No.'

'Right. Uhm …' There was a question I needed to ask, and I was pondering on the spot whether I should come right out and ask it or engage in a little preamble first. My brain decided on the latter but didn't seem to pass on the message to my mouth. 'So, I watched the *60 Minutes* interview.' After retiring to bed early the previous evening, I'd watched it on my iPad, courtesy of *ABC iview*. In the interview, Stella passionately exclaimed her drive to prove her husband's innocence at any cost, amidst the tears of the wife who was left behind. I didn't recall, however, any mention of her starting up an exclusive boutique in Surfers Paradise. 'It's awesome what you're doing. Trying to clear Ray's name. Your belief in his innocence was quite touching.'

She lowered her head and blushed. 'Thank you.'

'And using all the proceeds to fund a campaign to prove his innocence is quite admirable, and understandable.'

The nod again while avoiding eye contact.

'But there is something I don't understand.'

The slow shake of her head and the silent shrug could have meant two things—*pray continue*, or *what the hell's any of this got to do with you?*

'I'm here to help. When I spoke to Ray, he said you'd welcome my involvement, and help in any way you could …'

She was staring at a spot on the floor.

'But when I spoke to you on the phone, you pretty much told me to take a hike.'

'I did not.' Eye contact at last, but it was defensive and angry.

'Figuratively speaking, of course. But you don't seem to want my help.'

'I don't *need* your help.'

'Oh … right …? So, you've already hired someone?'

'No, not yet.'

'It's been two years since his conviction.'

'These things take time. You should know that.'

'What things?'

'Finances, mainly.'

'Of course.' Scanning the interior of the shop, I said, 'This place would be costing a pretty penny, I guess.'

'What the hell are you saying?'

'Nothing, well … not nothing. I mean … for two years you don't have the finances to help the husband who you believe is innocent of murder, and when you finally get some money, you buy a business, while he's rotting away in the Townsville nick.'

'I think it's time you left.'

'Did Ray already know Jack was Bobby's son, or did he only learn of the affair from the text?'

She moved forward in an attempt to usher me out of the shop.

'Did you get a text as well?'

'I want you to leave.' Her voice wobbled with anger.

'Sure, but can you answer me one question first?'

She was marching towards the door.

'Do you want help with Ray's case or not?'

She opened the door and swung around to face me. 'Like I said, I don't need *your* help!'

'Why?'

'I've got this under control. The last thing I need is some reality TV star getting in the way.'

Again with the reality TV stuff. I'd had this thrown at me twice in a day.

'Now get the hell out of my shop.'

After stepping outside, I turned so our eyes met once more. 'I'm really struggling to understand this, Stella. Ray reached out to me.'

'He should have spoken to me first.'

'The thing is, I'm a detective and I've decided to open a private investigation. If there's anything not quite right, I'll find it.'

She slammed the door in my face.

23

I'd arranged to meet Bradley for lunch at Andy's Café in Mariners Cove. It was a cool little joint Jenny and I often frequented when I was working for the Queensland Police. When I parked the car, I was still five minutes early, when my phone rang. It was Cassie Cooper, my architect. 'Hey, Cass. How's it going?'

'Not good, apparently.'

'Aye?'

'Couldn't you have just talked to me first?'

'What do you mean?'

'I thought you were happy with my work.'

'I am.' Turning off the car radio, I left the engine running for the air-conditioner.

'So why would you hire another architect to redo the plans?'

'I haven't.'

'That's not what Dorian Malloy is saying.'

'Dorian? What? He's called you?'

'Wants to meet up and discuss his taking over of the project.'

'Bullshit.'

'Are you saying you don't know anything about this?'

'My bloody oath I am. What did he say?'

'That the current plan wasn't right for the clients, and that he'd been commissioned to resubmit a revised design.'

'The cheeky bastard!'

'So, you haven't hired him?'

'No, I have not.'

'What's going on, Scotty?'

'I don't know but I'll bloody find out.'

'Would Jenny have hired him?'

'No …' *Would she?* 'No … not without discussing it with me first.'

'I'm so relieved. He's such an arrogant prick.'

'You know him?'

'Know *of* him. He's got a reputation in the industry. Thinks he's better than he actually is.'

'I'm so sorry, Cass. I'll sort it out.'

'Thing is, to change anything now would probably put back the project six months to a year.'

'Yeah, not gonna happen. If he calls you again, tell him to call me.'

'Will do. Listen, there is a small issue I need to discuss regarding the plans but it's not important.' Before she hung up, we arranged a time for her to come around to my apartment a few days later.

Bloody Dorian Malloy. Would Jenny really have put him up to this? It was hard to believe. Until a couple of days ago, the two of us discussed everything. I needed to call her, but I was a minute late for my luncheon now. Bradley would not be impressed.

By the time I arrived, he was already sitting at one of the tables out the front of the café, studying the menu.

'Hey mate. Sorry I'm late.'

He stood and we shook hands. Bradley's shrug was far from the nonchalant kind.

'Don't get bloody sulking. I was five minutes early but just got an unusual phone call.'

'Who from?'

'My architect.' We sat and I filled him in on the call while the waitress filled two glasses with water.

Bradley didn't seem too surprised by my tale. 'Dorian Malloy.'

'Have you met him yet?'

'No.'

'Did you find out anything about him?'

'Not yet … I only know what Jenny's told me.'

'Such as … ?'

He put down the menu. 'Well, at first, there was just mention of an architect friend. I didn't take too much notice, but then his name started popping up more. Then after a week or so, it was Dorian this and Dorian that.'

'Is she smitten?'

'I think so. She'd only booked a couple of days for a long weekend, but this morning she called in and requested an extension to a week.'

'Still in Noosa?'

'Noosa? She's on Hamilton Island!'

'Hammo?'

'Yep, on Dorian's yacht apparently.'

Hamilton Island in the Whitsunday Islands was a lot farther north than Noosa on the Sunshine Coast. Had Jenny lied to me, or had they travelled on from Noosa? 'Yacht?'

Bradley nodded, his eyes searching mine. 'Permanently moored up there.'

The waitress arrived and we ordered. Bradley had a vegan salad. I had my usual burger and chips. Although my mind was racing with a thousand questions, realising that Bradley wasn't the source of the answers I desired, I was relieved when he changed the subject.

'How are you getting on with the new case?'

My shoulders sunk. 'Not brilliant.'

'How come?'

Something had dawned on me during the short drive from Surfers to The Spit. When Ray Morris had contacted me by phone, he'd assured me that all my fees and expenses would be paid for by his wife, Stella. After meeting her, it quickly became apparent that this wouldn't be the case. Although I'd worked for free in the past, I wasn't planning on making a habit of it. 'I don't even know if there is a case, mate.'

'I've had a brief look through the files.' There was never anything brief about Bradley's actions, what he meant was he's studied it so was probably up to speed with me. 'Excuse the cliché, but it seems like an open and shut case.'

'I know. Ray's knife. The witness who saw him arrive at the property then scale the fence. The text.'

Bradley nodded. 'Around the same time as Bobby's death. No one else was seen entering or leaving.'

I shared with him an evolving theory surrounding the texts after learning that Dhani and possibly Maeve had received one.

'You think there was more than one text? The family, the exes, the band? A generic message or …?'

'No. Individual ones with specific meanings to each of the receivers. In some cases, apologies, perhaps an unburdening, or threats of revenge even.'

'They'd take him ages to write.'

'What if he'd already written them while he was in rehab?'

'As part of his therapy, the 12-Step program. Makes sense. Shame we never found his phone.'

The waitress arrived with our meals. We ate as we spoke.

'Have you spoken to everyone involved yet?' Bradley asked after taking a sip of iced tea.

'No …' I took a large swig of Coke then burped loudly. 'I've still got the band to speak with, and the witness across the street. Then there's Ray's son, Jack; and Bobby's wife, Sasha; and the exes; and of course, his mother.'

Unlike me, Bradley would never speak with a mouthful of food. He chewed slowly while pondering on my words. 'What will you do if no one steps forward to fund the investigation? Drop it?'

It was a question I'd been asking myself since leaving Stella's boutique. 'I need to speak with Ray again.' I had no idea how to do this. It wasn't like I could just call up the Townsville nick and ask to speak with Ray Morris. With a police detective credential, perhaps. But not a PI.

'Just use your charm. You're Scotty Stephens.'

'Yeah, but they wouldn't know who I am up there.'

'You might be surprised.'

'You reckon?'

'Worth a try.'

Later, after arriving home, I'd decided I'd make the call the next morning. In the meantime, I had another call to make. The phone rang three times then went to Detective Inspector Jenny Radford's voice message. Off duty or on, Jenny always answered her phone. But not this time. I left a message. 'Hey Jen, it's just Scotty. Give us a call back when you get the chance. Later.'

She didn't call back.

24

Apart from a minor conviction for disorderly behaviour in a Sydney Hotel after two days of drinking and partying, Bobby Sexton's record was clean. A dark area in the band's history, though, was the unfortunate death of Jimmy Reggae—one of their many drummers—ten years ago. Christened James Michael Hoff, the thirty-three year old was found drowned in Bobby's pool after another night of heavy partying. The cause of death was asphyxiation by drowning because of extensive intoxication. Jimmy's alcohol blood count showed 37 per cent. A verdict of death by misadventure was recorded. One thing I found interesting was that Phil Sexton was not present on either occasion.

At that time, I was in uniform—a constable patrolling the streets of Surfers Paradise. The only recollection I had of the case was the same as everyone else—information derived from the regular TV news reports. I remembered, though, that DI Des Williams, my old boss, was in charge of the investigation. Unfortunately, Des was no longer with us on the force for over thirty years. Two years ago, he took his own life when the force publicly replaced him as the detective in charge of the X case. Since then, feelings of guilt and sadness tarnish my fond recollections of Des because I was the detective who replaced him. But that's another story.

At the time of Jimmy Reggae's death, Des's right-hand man was Detective Sergeant Steven Cosonofski—or Cozzie, as everyone knew him as. Retired now for over four years, Cozzie lived in

Kingscliff, the delightful little seaside town just over the border in Northern New South Wales. A likeable bloke, and a mentor to most of us young guys entering the detective ranks, he was a hard-working detective with old school principals, who enjoyed nothing more than a drink with the boys. According to Bradley, since Cozzie's retirement, his hobbies were golf, fishing and watching the footy—NRL, a Gold Coast Titans fan—in the Kingscliff Beach Hotel over a quiet beer.

Thanks again to Bradley, I was able to obtain a copy of Cozzie's report. It was pretty straightforward. Documenting the scene as he found it on his arrival at 9.30 am, Jimmy Reggae was floating face down in the pool. Without the hindsight of the toxicology report and the post-mortem findings, Cozzie estimated the time of death according to the onset of rigor mortis as being at least two hours. *Would I be wasting my time following up on this? Maybe, maybe not.* I was desperate for information about the Sexton boys. If Cozzie could shed light on the band's mindset at that time, it would be a welcome difference of perspective instead of the garnished media reports. It would also be a good chance to catch up with an old mate.

Arriving unannounced wasn't much of a gamble. Kingscliff was only a fifteen-minute drive south from Kirra. It was Thursday evening. The televised game that night was the South Sydney Rabbitohs versus the Brisbane Broncos. According to DI Dale Mason, who regularly caught up with Cozzie for a drink, the old boy would be in the pub watching, regardless of who was playing. Arriving forty-five minutes before the game, I found him perched at one of the high tables with a good view of the enormous TV screen. Seeing him sitting alone reading the newspaper and nursing a schooner of beer, didn't stir any concerns, because I knew he was doing exactly what he wanted to do.

'Cozzie, you old bugger!'

When he looked up from the newspaper, his infectious, heart-warming smile brought back memories of Christmas parties and stag nights. 'Scotty. What the bloody hell are you doing down here?'

'Come to see me old mate.'

When he climbed down from the stool and we shook hands and hugged, I noticed he'd packed on a few kilos. 'You're looking good, mate.' I lied. He was overweight, his face was blotchy and a little bloated, and his eyes were watery and red.

'Ya lying bastard.' He was still the detective.

'You're right, you look like shit.'

'Thanks.' He skulled his beer. 'Can I get you one?'

'My shout.'

He didn't argue.

When I returned to the table carrying two fresh beers, Cozzie was chatting with an elderly couple who continued on their way towards the bar after I took my seat.

'There you go, Coz,' I said, sliding one of the beers over to him.

'Cheers, matey. It's good to see you.'

I suddenly felt guilty when I realised I hadn't seen him since Des Williams' funeral two years earlier. 'It's good to see you too.'

As two mates do who haven't seen each other in a while, we chatted casually, reminiscing and sharing a laugh or two. When I learned of Julie's—Cozzie's wife of forty-five years—new interest in Asian cooking, I realised the reason for her husband's weight gain. Cozzie talked fondly of his two grandchildren and how he was enjoying retirement. He also seemed to show a genuine interest in my life, especially since leaving the police force and becoming a private detective.

With the beers replenished, Cozzie checked his watch. 'So, we've got ten minutes until kick off. What can I do for you?'

There were no other words needed, no explanation, no apologies. We both knew I was there for a reason, and I'd been prompted to get to the point. 'I wanted to ask you about the Jimmy Reggae case.'

He frowned, then took a sip of his beer, and I imagined his mind sorting through a library of archive files until a mechanical hand retrieved the one marked 'Jimmy Reggae' and opened it. 'The guy who supposedly drowned in Bobby Sexton's pool.'

'Supposedly? You didn't agree with the verdict?'

'Nah …' He shook his head and took another sip of beer. 'You're a good detective, Scotty. You know people. You know when someone's lying, or when someone's got something to hide.'

'Bobby?'

'Yep, and his missus. They knew a lot more than he made out.'

I knew better than to question a good detective's intuition, and I understood exactly what he meant. Often when interviewing a suspect or a witness, you just knew when they were lying. You couldn't necessarily explain it and you certainly couldn't prove it without evidence, but it was a skill that a good detective needed to develop and hone. 'You think they were lying?'

'Bobby Sexton was totally out of it. It was hard to get a lucid response. Even when he'd sobered up later, he wasn't much better. Apart from the arrogance, that is. He acted as if it was okay for him to be inebriated, like it was normal behaviour for a rock star, and that everyone around him should understand that.'

'And the wife?'

'Jo Sexton. She was his first wife. Almost as bad as the husband, but I sensed something else in her. Fear. Like she was holding onto a secret.'

'Could either of them have killed Jimmy Reggae? And if so, why?'

Cozzie shrugged. 'Apparently, Jimmy was a reckless son of a bitch. Relatively new to the rock 'n' roll lifestyle, and not expecting it to last, he was taking advantage of the experience to the full.'

'Did he have anything over, Bobby?'

'It's purely speculation, of course, but I think Jimmy just stepped on too many toes. Indirectly or directly, I think Bobby knew something about the drowning. We just didn't have the proof.'

25

The surf was uninspiring the next morning. An overcast sky reflecting off the surface of the water turned the usually vibrant blue into a dishwater grey. My mind should have been focused solely on the case, but it was still Jenny who dominated my thoughts. You don't miss something until it's gone, or something like that was the old saying. This was certainly ringing true for me. I'd taken her for granted, loved her, and expected her to always be there for me without commitment. *What an idiot!*

I didn't stay in the water for too long. There was no sign of Chilly, which I was glad for. Not feeling much like talking to anyone, I was in a sulk.

After a hot shower and a bowl of muesli, I walked to work.

'Scotty.' Like a single-celled entity, The Good Old Boys greeted me in unison.

'Morning boys.' Purposely not stopping for a chat, I continued past them, hopefully giving them the impression I was in a hurry.

'See you later, Scotty,' Don called after me.

Raising an arm in acknowledgment, I lifted my pace. Of course, I knew I wasn't fooling them. Wise old buggers. No doubt I'd be the topic of today's debate.

When I entered my office, the whiteboard came as a welcome distraction. Until that is, I realised I still had very little to go on. Phil bullied his younger sibling. *So what?* Didn't mean he killed him. Stella Morris had spent the money she earned from

103

selling her story on launching a new business, instead of using it to prove her husband's innocence as she'd vowed to do. *Was this important?* Everyone I'd spoken to so far agreed with the verdict that Ray Morris was guilty, even though the case hung on the testimony of the witness across the street. It was like there was no thread to pull. The embroidery was so tight, so well stitched, I couldn't even pick at it.

I still had people to speak to, notably: Maeve Sexton, Phil and Bobby's mum; Jack Morris, Ray and Stella's son; Sasha Sexton, Bobby's wife; the members of the band who turned up at Bobby's house that night with Phil; and of course, Ray.

I was sitting at my desk pondering how I should approach calling up the Townsville Correctional Centre when my phone rang.

'Scotty, how's it going?' It was Ray.

'Good. I was just thinking of you.'

'Great minds, eh? How did you get on with Stella? Has she given you everything you need?'

'Hmm ...' I wondered if he knew about the boutique. 'She's been a bit busy, mate, so—'

'With the campaign, yeah, right. I don't know what I'd do without her, Scott. You'll just need to catch her between her appointments, perhaps arrange a meet with her.'

Should I have told him how I tried to do just that? And how she was damn right hostile towards me? And as for the campaign? What bloody campaign? 'Yeah, I will, mate.'

'Scotty, you *do* realise this is super important, don't you? I hope you're taking this seriously.'

'Of course ... when was the last time you spoke to your wife?'

'A week ago.'

'And did you tell her about me? You approaching me, I mean?'

'Yes, we discussed it. She was a little apprehensive at first, but I won her over.'

'Apprehensive in what way?'

There was a pause on the other end, and I could hear the echoes of prison life in the background. I pictured Ray wearing a blue overall standing at a pay phone on the wall of the communal recreation area, one hand cupped over the speaker so he could hear above the background noise.

'She doesn't think this is a good idea—or didn't until I persuaded her.'

'Why? Surely, she'd welcome any help and support she could get.'

'Yes, and she will. I'll speak to her next week. I just get the one call a week if I'm a good boy, although I can trade commissary, but I'm not that popular in here. The guy who killed the dream and all that.'

'Are you okay?'

'Yes, I'm … well, as well as an innocent man in a high security prison can be, I guess.'

'Ray, can I ask you about that night?'

'Yes, please do.'

'So, you went to Bobby's house. Why was that?' I'd read his testimony, but wanted to hear it from him.

'I got a call from Tommy Platt, saying that the band was reuniting with the original members. He told me that Phil and the musicians were going to Bobby's house for a meeting and suggested that I should be there too.'

'Had you and Tommy kept in touch over the years?'

'Yes. Tommy was a mate from way back. He was in the same class as me and Bobby at school.'

'Why would he suggest you turn up at the meeting unannounced?'

'Tommy was never happy with the decision to dump me from the band. He was angry, in fact, but he was just the roadie, with no influence. He knew only too well that Phil was running the show.'

'So, you went to the meeting but …?'

'I was late. Got held up at work.'

'And by the time you got there, the meeting was over.'

'Yes, but I didn't know that. I assumed everyone was still in the house. I knocked on the front door, but there was no reply. Assuming they may have been out the back, I went around the side of the property.'

'That's right, there were vacant lots on either side, but they were fenced.'

'Yes. I climbed over the fence. Big mistake.'

'And what happened next?'

'There was an eight-foot-high stucco wall along the boundary line between Bobby's house and the lot.'

I used my silence as a prompt to continue.

'The wall extended into the water. There was no way over it or around it. Not for an unfit old bugger like me, anyway.'

'So, what, you just gave up and left?'

'Yep. Exactly that. It wasn't meant to be.'

'Did you hear anything from over the wall?'

'No nothing. The house was illuminated, looked like every light in the place was on, but it was silent.'

'How did you get back to the street?'

'I went to the other side of the block and jumped back over the fence.'

'Hmm, and the witness didn't see that.'

'No, apparently she was distracted by a phone call from her daughter.'

I wasn't sure how long we had on the phone so decided to change tact. 'What was your relationship like with Bobby?'

'We were mates. Good mates. Until after the break.'

'So why did he kick you out of the band?' I'd asked him this question before, but wanted to test his reaction a second time.

'He didn't. That was all Phil and Alex Mercedes.'

'What was your relationship like with Phil?'

'Didn't really have one. Phil always looked down on me, like I was just a replaceable musician, which I guess I was in the end.'

'Was he jealous of your friendship with Bobby?'

'Absolutely. Bobby and I used to goof off a fair bit. We were still just kids, whereas Phil was older and took everything seriously. He was driven, so I can understand why he acted the way he did. I got the impression that I was in the way of his control over Bobby. Life would prove a lot easier without me.'

'So, he sacked you?'

'Yep. Well … he got Alex to do it. They'd flown out to Bali without me knowing. I was called into Alex's office. "Don't see this as the end, Ray," she said. "See it as a new beginning. We're going to form a band around you, give you full representation. You're going to be a star in your own right!"'

'And none of that happened.'

'That's right. I got a payout cheque for $2,000 and I never heard from them again.'

'Harsh.'

'Indeed.'

'I've heard reports of Phil being a bully. Even slapping his brother around on the odd occasion.'

There was an unexpected chuckle down the line. 'Phil thought he was the big man, but Bobby would have none of it. He gave as good as he got.'

'So, they'd what? Fight, physically or …?'

'Oh, yeah. They were always at it. Bobby was more the physical one. Phil's attacks were more the psychological kind.'

'Interesting. Until now, I'd thought it was all one sided. Phil the violent bully. Bobby the passive victim.'

'No, it was never like that. Phil provided the musical talent and drive, but Bobby wrote the songs and supplied the edge. Without his unique vocals and his seductive stage presence, INSEXT would have been nothing.'

'When you learned of Bobby's affair with Stella, did that change everything?'

'I didn't know about that until …' his voice lowered. 'Until … after.'

'So, you didn't know that Jack was Bobby's son?'

'There were never any tests done to prove it. Jack is my son. I know that.'

'Receiving the text must have stirred you up.'

'I didn't even see it until after I'd left the property.'

'Tell me about the knife.'

'Not much to tell. Ironically, Bobby gave it to me just before I was dumped.'

'Was it a parting gift or …?'

'Obviously at the time I didn't know it, but it certainly looks that way now.'

'You testified that you threw the knife away years ago, just after the band dropped you.'

'That's right. Threw it in the trash. Never saw it again.'

'Then how did it end up lodged between Bobby Sexton's shoulder blades?'

'I have no idea.'

There were a series of beeps on the line.

'Oops, time's up I'm afraid, Scotty. I'll call you next wee—'

The line went dead.

26

Frustration was setting in. Anxiety even. I had two dilemmas. First, there was little progress with the investigation, and second, it looked like there would be no funding, so it was likely I wouldn't be going any further. Until, that is, when both problems were potentially resolved from the call I received almost immediately after my chat with Ray Morris.

'Hello.' I didn't recognise the number.

'Scotty.'

There was only one American I knew. 'Tyler, how's it going?'

'I'm good my friend.' His assuasive accent was just as smooth as his coffee-coloured skin. 'Not as good as you, though.'

'How's that?'

'Alex would like to see you again.'

'Really? Geez, she's a pushy old thing.'

'This is Alex Mercedes, Scott. I don't think she even sleeps. Anyway, it's not about the book deal. It's much better.'

I was intrigued.

'How would you feel if I told you she wanted to fund the investigation into Bobby's death?'

'Aye …? Why would she want to do that?'

'This is Alex Mercedes, Scott.' His repetitive use of the term told me that there was more to the offer.

'Tell me more.'

'How would a million dollars sound?'

'What?'

'Have I piqued your interest?'

'Bloody oath you have.'

'Not only that, but you'll be privy to every single piece of information possible, including the stuff that wasn't mentioned in court. But more importantly, you'll have full access to everyone involved.'

'But how?'

'She wants to see you this afternoon. 4.00 pm. Don't be late.' He hung up.

Bloody hell. The universe works in mysterious ways. Full access to everyone involved, private information, and one million dollars? There was obviously a catch. "This is Alex Mercedes, Scott!" Boy was my mind whizzing.

My phone rang again. It was another number that I didn't recognise.

'Scotty. How's it going, Buddy?'

'Who's this?'

'It's Dorian.'

'Dorian?' I didn't mean to sound so surprised. *Buddy?*

'Dorian Malloy, Jenny's … uhm, friend. We met the other day.' His between-the-lines tone said, "Of course you remember me, *dick-squat*."

'Oh yeah, that's right, the architect chap.'

There was a chuckle on the other end of the line.

'I've been trying to get hold of Jenny for the last couple of days.'

'There's often little reception when we're out on the boat. You know how it is.'

Did I? 'Can I speak to her?'

'She's uhm, sleeping. A big night, if you know what I mean?' He clicked his lips, and I imagined him winking at the same time.

'What can I do for you?'

'I'm guessing you've probably seen the revised plans by now.'

'No. I haven't.'

'Oh, I'm sorry. I would have expected your architect, Candy is it—'

'Cassandra.'

'That's her. I would have thought she'd have contacted you by now.'

'She has.'

'Oh right, so she's explained the situation, no doubt. Have you looked at the plans?'

'I don't need to.'

There was a pause. 'Great, so you're happy to rely on my reputation of being the best architect on the Coast?'

'Nope.'

Another pause. 'What then?'

'There won't be any changes to the plans!'

'But … this is what Jenny wants.'

'Is it? I don't know that. I haven't been able to speak with her.'

'Oh, I can assure you, it's definitely what she wants. We both agree that the plans your … uhm .. Cathy supplied are substandard.'

'Substandard.' This wasn't a question. The jug was beginning to boil.

'Perfectly adequate out at Coomera or Logan, but not at the beach.' This guy had a way of passively insulting everyone. He'd not only affronted Cassie—my more than capable architect— and me for approving the plans, but also the entire population of Coomera and Logan, in a single sentence.

'Not gonna happen, *Buddy!*'

'But surely you want the best for Jenny?' His tone was passive aggressive and patronising at the same time.

The jug boiled over. 'I do, mate. That's why I'm gonna tell you to back the fuck off!'

'Excuse me?'

'You heard. Who the hell do you think you are waltzing in here and taking charge?'

'I'm just trying to help.' These were not words of sincerity, more sarcastic.

'What do you know about what Jenny wants? You've known her what? A couple of weeks?'

'Oh, I see … this is a personal thing …. you're jealous!'

'Jealous? What, of you?' Hard to believe, but I almost said, "I'm Scotty Stephen's, mate!"

'I understand what's going on now,' Dorian said, still calm, still in control.

My silence resulted from not being calm and not being in control.

'Did I steal your girl?'

I wasn't proud of my feelings towards him at that moment, but if we were in the same room, I probably would have decked him. Ignoring his jibe, I fought hard to quell the anger in my voice. 'Tell Jenny to ring me as soon as she wakes up.' Before he had a chance to answer, I terminated the call.

27

The house was enormous and a far cry from the little Queenslander at Budds Beach where Maeve Sexton almost single-handedly brought up her boys. I wasn't a connoisseur when it came to architecture, but even I knew a French château reproduction when I saw one. A wide, three-storey building with white stone walls, rows of bronzed coloured, ornate windows, and a curved turret at each end. The manicured lawns, precise topiary, the fountain, and perhaps the odd roaming peacock were left to the imagination, all hidden by an eight-foot perimeter wall. There was a large double gateway, also made from ornate bronze, and matching the style of the windows, the inside of which was covered with a flat opaque surface to stop prying eyes from seeing inside.

Leaving the car a little way down the street, I approached the gates after noticing there was an intercom built into the wall. At the bottom of a small, tarnished brass keyboard was a well-worn button with a bell icon. Next to this was a speaker. When I pressed the button, I heard a ring tone before someone answered. It was a woman's voice with a foreign accent, possibly Asian.

'Hello?'

'Oh hi, my name's Scotty Stephens. Would Maeve be at home by any chance?'

'No, she's gone out.'

'Do you know when she'll be back?'

'No.'

'Right. Would you know where she's gone?'

'No.'

'Okay. Could you tell her I called by and ask her to call me, please?'

'Okay.' She hung up before I could give her my number.

I pressed the button again.

'Hello?'

'You didn't get my number.'

'Okay.'

After I gave her the number, she abruptly hung up.

Bobby's house was only a couple of blocks away, so I left the car where it was and walked. Apart from the high wall that surrounded the property, his house was the complete opposite to his mother's—modern, minimalistic, straight lines, but just as big. The gate was to the left of a triple garage, with a similar intercom to the right of it.

Same dealio, but this time there was no answer. *Bugger.* As with Maeve, it was a bit of a stretch to expect Sasha Coburn, the ex-supermodel, to be at home and answer her door.

I now had a couple of hours to kill before my meeting with Alex Mercedes. There was one other person to speak to in the vicinity, but I didn't need to go looking for her. She found me.

'She's gone out.'

I turned to see an elderly lady wearing a face mask. She was standing in the driveway of the house across the street.

'About an hour ago … in her new car. The white one.'

Mrs Kennedy was the witness who testified that she saw Ray Morris scale the fence next to Bobby's house.

'Oh, goodness me. You're Scotty Stephens!' she said, clearly blushing as I strolled towards her.

'That's right and you are?' I already knew, of course, but didn't want to appear presumptuous.

'Yvonne. Yvonne Kennedy.'

We didn't shake hands. Because of the mask, I assumed she was still worried about the effects of COVID.

'Are you reopening the case?' There was excitement in her question.

'No, nothing like that. There wouldn't be much to open, would there?'

'Oh gosh, yes.'

'What makes you say that?'

'Well, as I kept telling the police and even the judge at the trial, I didn't actually see Mr Morris enter the house.'

'Right.' I knew this too, but I was happy to hear it in her words. 'So, what *did* you see?'

She told me how Phil and the band had arrived at the house earlier, but only stayed for a few minutes. Then how Ray had arrived later but hadn't gained entry to the building. She was very precise, and I realised she took her role in the Neighbourhood Watch very seriously.

'How long was he at the gate?'

'Around six minutes.'

'And then what?'

'He walked down the street a little and I saw him climb over the fence of the vacant lot adjacent to the house.'

'But you didn't see him enter Bobby's property?'

'No, he'd be hard pressed getting over that wall.'

'Did you see him again?'

'No, because it was then that my phone rang downstairs. I'd been expecting a call from my daughter in Canada.'

'What about from when Phil and the band left, and Ray arrived? Did you see anyone else during that time?'

'No, not a soul.'

'Did you ever meet Bobby Sexton?'

'No, never. Never even saw him on the street. He always arrived in black cars with darkened windows. They'd always drive straight into the garage.'

'What about his wife, Sasha?'

'I actually met her at a fundraiser not long before the murder. Introduced myself. Told her we were neighbours.'

'What was she like?'

'American!'

I waited for her to continue but she didn't, as if she thought this was enough of a description.

'Is there anything else you can think of? Something you may have forgotten to tell the police, or something you remembered later?'

'No, I told them everything. Not that they wanted to hear it all, though.'

'What do you mean?'

'Well, they weren't interested in the big bust up between Mr Sexton and his wife that afternoon.'

'They had an argument?'

'Did they what. When the wind blows in a certain direction across the canal, the sound carries and I get to hear a lot from the property, mostly loud music unfortunately, but on this night, I could hear them going at it as if they were in my garden.'

'Do you know what the argument was about?'

'He said he was going to divorce her!'

'Really?'

'Yes. But she said no. In fact, the words she used were, "I'll kill you first!"

Interesting.

'Then she stormed out. I didn't see her return until about a month after her husband's death.'

'Well thank you, Mrs Kennedy, you've been very helpful.'

'You're welcome and it's been lovely to meet you. And thank you for capturing that dreadful *X*. You'll always be loved by the people of the Gold Coast.'

'Thank you!'

While strolling back to the car, my phone rang. It was Bradley.

'Scott, where are you?'

'Not too far away from you as it happens.'

'Good, get yourself over to the Southport Watchhouse.'

'Why's that?'

'Ray Morris' son, Jack, was picked up last night for trying to rob a 7-Eleven in Robina. Might be a good opportunity for you to have a chat.'

'Cool. Thanks, mate. I'll be right there.'

28

A translucent complexion, dilated pupils, scabbing around the mouth, discoloured teeth, trembling hands, and a constant twitch. Jack Morris wasn't just a user, he was a full-blown addict.

Although protocol stated that I needed to be accompanied by a police detective, I got the impression I could have gotten in without Bradley's presence. Not because of the fame thing, but because the staff sergeant on duty that day was an old mate of mine, John Milton.

With the three of us peering through the brick-sized observation hatch, John said, 'I doubt you'll get much out of him, Scotty.'

'Withdrawal?'

'Yeah, big time. He was already coming down when he was picked up. That's why he was trying to rob the 7-Eleven.'

'How long has he been here?'

'A couple of hours.'

Glancing around the cell, I realised there was no one else being held. Most Friday and Saturday nights it would be chockers. On a mid-week afternoon, not so much. 'Can I go in?'

John glanced at Bradley as if to say, "Your call, mate."

'Is he violent?' Bradley asked.

'Could be. Desperation, anxiety, but you already know all that.'

'I'll be right.'

'I can't risk it, I'm afraid,' Bradley said.

'Fair enough.' And it was. I was asking too much.

'I need to interview the suspect, though,' Bradley said, sticking out his chest and raising his chin. 'There's been a spate of similar robberies up and down the Coast, but you can sit in and ask him some questions.'

'No worries. I'll put him in Interview Room 2,' Sergeant Milton said.

While Bradley got two coffees from the vending machine, I managed a bit of a catch-up chat with some of the other officers who were on duty. Being there, it felt strange no longer being a copper, a role I'd had since graduating from the academy over twenty years ago.

'So, do you miss it, Scotty?' asked constable Bernie Williams. She'd worked at the Watchhouse for as long as I could remember.

'Yeah, I do actually.'

'Any chance of coming back?'

'Nah … I don't miss it that much.'

'What's it like being a celebrity?'

'It has its ups and downs.'

Bradley returned carrying two paper cups. 'It looks awful. Don't drink it if you don't want to,' he said, handing me one of the cups.

John Milton returned. 'He's ready.'

The three of us entered the interview room. Bradley was in charge. Sergeant Milton was there for security.

'Jack, I'm Detective Constable Bradley Foster, and this is Private Detective Scott Stephens.'

Like a baby bird fallen from its nest, Jack's frightened eyes flicked between us as if we were feral cats eyeing up our next meal. 'Scotty Stephens, that detective guy?' He spoke through painfully dry lips.

As if anticipating this, Bradley slid over a plastic bottle of water.

Jack grabbed it, had a little difficulty unscrewing the lid, but then almost drank it all in one go.

'Scott would like to ask you a few questions if that's okay, Jack?'

The next words were crucial. If he'd said he wanted to see his brief, the interview would be terminated immediately. Thankfully, he didn't. 'What's this about?' His eyes rested on me. 'I didn't do them robberies.'

'We know that, mate.' My tone was soothing and sympathetic. 'I just wanted to talk to you about your dad if that's okay.'

'My dad?' He frowned, and I noticed a resemblance to his mother.

'Yeah, he's asked me to look into the case. Reckons he's innocent.'

Jack lowered his gaze, his eyes searching the surface of the table.

'What do you reckon?'

He looked up. 'About what?'

'About your dad, sitting up there in prison for the rest of his life for a crime he didn't commit.'

'What did he tell you?'

'Not a lot, just that you could help us?'

'How? What could I do?' He sat up straight and the ever-present twitch intensified.

'He said you had some important information to share with me.' I had no idea where I was going with this. Ray had said nothing of the kind.

'He said that?'

'What was it that you didn't share with the police at the time, Jack?'

'Nothing.' Like a school kid being wrongly accused of nicking bikes from the bike shed, his head shook rapidly.

'Do you know who really killed Bobby Sexton?' I'd come here today just hoping to get an insight into the relationship between the father and son, in an attempt to build on the collage I was creating of Ray Morris. Call it intuition, a sixth sense, but the detective inside me was telling me this young man was hiding something.

'No, why would I?'

'Don't know, you tell me.'

'I didn't steal it. That was a lie!' He'd raised his voice considerably.

I had no idea what he was talking about, but he obviously didn't know that. 'Then who did?'

'Not me?'

'Look mate. We know you had it. Nobody's saying you stole it. You're not going to get in trouble for that. We just need to know what happened to it.' I couldn't resist a glance in Bradley's direction. His frown said, "What the hell are you talking about?"

I didn't know either, but whatever *it* was that had stirred up the sudden emotion in Jack Morris, it was extremely important. 'So, what happened to it?'

He shuffled in his seat, sat on his hands and glanced towards the door as if considering his escape.

'Come on, mate. I can help you.'

'I sold it.'

'Right. Do you remember who to?'

He shook his head violently. It had been two years since the death of Bobby Sexton, and I wondered how many items Jack had stolen and sold for drugs during that time.

'Okay, tell me how you got it and why.'

There was a brief smile. 'He didn't know he had it … he'd thrown it away, but she got it out the bin and kept it.'

'*She*?'

'My mother.' There was no sign of affection in his tone.

'Can you describe it to me?' I still had no idea what *it* was.

Lifting his hands from under his butt, he held them apart about six inches. 'It was about this long. Sharp as fuck. The handle was covered in opal chips. It was beautiful. Valuable.'

'A knife? I mean … *the* knife, right?'

Caution and suspicion manifested in his expression.

'You didn't steal it, because your dad had thrown it away.' I was back peddling. 'It wasn't your mum's, so you had every right to take it.'

This seemed to work, and he visually calmed down by sinking into his seat.

'Who did you sell it to, Jack?'

He shrugged and his eyes returned to the tabletop.

'Think, Jack. Please. This is really important.'

'I don't know. Some muso.'

'A musician? One of the band members?'

The shrug again. 'It was a long time ago, man.'

I guess two years to a drug-fucked zombie was a lifetime.

Although it seemed like I still had very little to go on, a sinew of information was forming. Knowing now that the murder weapon was possibly sold to the killer was a huge breakthrough. However, as much as I tried, I couldn't find out who Jack sold the knife to. The fact that he may have forgotten was certainly a possibility, but there was also a chance that he was covering up. With pending release from the Watchhouse later that day, another chat with him was definitely on the cards.

29

There was still a bit of time to kill before my meeting with Alex Mercedes, so I decided to try Maeve and Sasha again. It was a bummer that I didn't have their phone numbers, so the only way of communication was by paying them a visit. While I was up this end of the Coast anyway, it made sense to call back.

After climbing into my car, I was just about to turn the ignition when my phone rang. Looking at the screen made my heart skip. On it was a picture of Jenny standing underneath a beach shower at Burleigh Heads, wearing a half wetsuit pulled down to her waist, and a yellow bikini top. She was looking back over her shoulder. The look of surprise and mischief on her face when she realised I was taking her picture, was priceless. I remembered the morning well. We'd just had a great surf, the weather was perfect and so was everything else.

'Hey Jen, how's it going?'

'Good, mate. You?'

'Not too shabby.'

'Sorry I missed your call this morning. Was having a bit of a lie in.'

'Yeah, so I heard.'

'So, I hear there's a problem with the house plans?'

'Uhh … *yeah*. These changes are gonna put things back about six months, possibly more.'

'Changes?'

'And as you can imagine, Cassie's not too happy.'

'I haven't got a clue what you're on about, Scott. Has there been changes to the plans?'

Was Dorian just winding me up? Asserting his manhood, perhaps? Discussing this over the phone probably wasn't the best idea. 'When do you get back?'

There was a slightly blissful sigh. 'I'm not sure. Absolutely loving it up here.'

'Well, let's talk about this when you get home.'

'Okay …' There was a pause. 'Listen, while I've got you, I've been meaning to ask. Are you okay with me being up here with Dorian?'

'Me?' *Of course I wasn't okay. That arrogant prick had taken away the last thing that mattered in my life.* 'Yeah, I'm fine. Why wouldn't I be?'

'Oh, that's good. I was a bit worried.'

'Why?'

'Well, we're mates.'

Mates? Is that all we are?

'I didn't think about it until later, but just upping and going like that was a bit selfish, I guess.'

It was more than that, but I remained quiet.

'I've never been swept off my feet like this before, Scott …'

Since when did she call me Scott?

'It feels pretty darn good, I can tell you.'

'Okay, look, I've gotta go,' I said, inadvertently glancing at my watch. 'Call us when you get back, eh, and we'll meet up.'

'Yeah, no worries. See ya.' She hung up.

It was a hot day. Without thinking, I'd been sitting in the car with the windows and doors closed. Sweat was dripping off my chin. After turning on the ignition and cranking up the aircon, I sat there for a few moments, enjoying the blast of cold air.

Seeing as Bobby's house was marginally closer, I went there first. After pulling up at the kerb outside the property, climbing from my car and delivering a quick wave to Mrs Kennedy, who was peering over the gate at the side of her garage, I approached the intercom. After three rings, a woman with an American accent answered.

'Hello?'

'Oh hi, my name's Scotty Stephens. I'm a private detective. I wondered if I could—'

'Scotty Stephens?' It was a different voice to the first—female but more mature and Aussie. 'Is that really you?'

'Uhh, yes it is. Who's this?'

The line went dead, but the gate clicked, and I realised someone had released the lock from inside the house. With Mrs Kennedy's eyes burning into my back, I entered the gate and closed it behind me.

There was a short path leading to a large front door that seemed to be made of a single piece of slate. When the door opened, the smiling face of Maeve Sexton met me.

'Well, I never. It really *is* you!'

Sasha Coburn appeared over her shoulder. Her expression wasn't as welcoming—more suspicious, defensive.

Wearing white shorts, a white top and white Reebok shoes, Maeve skipped towards me, then hugged me as if she'd known me all her life.

Hoping the squirt of deodorant I'd applied that morning was enough to combat the effects of the car sauna, I reciprocated.

'It's great to meet you. Come on in.'

Sasha was standing in the doorway. She was tall and slim and wore a similar outfit.

'This is my daughter-in-law, Sasha,' Maeve said, guiding me towards the front door.

Sasha's handshake was inanimate and limp. She didn't smile.

'We've just got back from our weekly tennis class,' Maeve continued, 'and was about to have a gin. Would you like to join us?'

'Yeah, that'd be great.'

Sasha turned and entered the house. With Maeve's arm entwined in mine, I followed.

The inside of the house wasn't what I expected. Minimal. Polished concrete floor. The smell of fresh paint told me it had recently been redecorated.

On an enormous kitchen island there was a bottle of Isle of Harris gin, two glasses and a granite mortar and pestle with some kind of green herbs at the ready.

'Get another glass for our guest, Sasha, dear,' Maeve said after directing me to one of the bar stools then taking up the pestle. 'Do you like a gin, Scott?'

'I don't mind the odd one now and again.'

'Scotty Stephens. Do you know who this is, Sasha?'

With her back to us while reaching up into an overhead cupboard, Sasha shrugged and shook her head. 'No. should I?'

'He's only the man who saved every single woman's life on the Gold Coast.'

Sasha didn't seem too impressed as she continued to search the cupboard.

Maeve, on the other hand, couldn't hide her excitement. 'Scotty Stephens. It's so good to meet you.'

'Why are you here?' Sasha asked abruptly after finding another glass and placing it on the counter.

I half expected Maeve to chastise her for being rude, but she didn't. Instead, she watched my reaction while grinding the herbs.

'I've been asked to look into the case.'

As if someone had pressed the pause button, Maeve stopped grinding and stood motionless, looking down into the mortar.

'Why the hell would you want to do that?' Sasha said.

My shrug wasn't meant to come across as casually as it did. 'I'm a private detective. That's my job.'

'But who asked you to do this?'

'Stella Morris, I bet,' Maeve threw in, her wrist slowly coming back to life.

'Is that true?' Sasha asked, folding her arms and concentrating her blue eyes on me. She'd make a good cross examiner if this modelling gig didn't work out.

'I'm not at liberty to discuss my client's details.'

'Then get out of my house.'

'Now then, now then, there's no need for that Sasha, dear,' Maeve said, the grinding increasing considerably in tempo. 'Let's just have a drink and let Scotty tell us what's going on, eh?'

Sasha raised her voice. 'But why?'

'I'm sure Scotty's got a good reason for coming to see us. Isn't that right, Scott?'

'Absolutely. First, I just wanted to say how sorry I am for your loss—'

'It was two years ago!' Sasha's reaction even seemed to take Maeve by surprise. 'What good is it going to do dragging all this up again?' Scarlet blooms appeared across Sasha's cheeks and her jaw trembled with a simmering anger.

'If it means I can prove an innocent man was wrongly committed, then I think that will be a lot of good.'

Maeve lifted out a fork from a drawer in the counter and administered a measure of ground herbs and spices to each glass. 'It will cause a lot of pain, Scott. I hope you can understand that.'

I did and acknowledged this by offering a sympathetic nod. 'I know and I'm really sorry, but you also have to remember that if Ray Morris is innocent, it means the killer is still out there.'

'Oh my God. You're enjoying this, aren't you?' Sasha spat.

Maeve put down the fork and stroked her daughter-in-law's arm.

Sasha brushed away her hand. 'How much are you being paid for this?'

Shaking my head, I looked away.

'I'll double it. Triple. Whatever you want. Just tell me a number.' With each word, she seemed to grow in height, as if stepping up to an opponent.

'That won't be necessary.' As had become a habit of late, I ventured once again into the whelms of fiction. 'So, tell me about the text you received from Bobby on the night of his death. Must have been a bit of a shock.'

Sasha froze, and I got to witness why she'd been a successful model. The high cheekbones, the chiselled nose and full lips, made me think of a Grecian goddess.

Maeve's reaction was the opposite. She seemed to shrink like a child after being caught telling a fib. My scanners were on full bore.

'Did you compare them?' My eyes shifted to Maeve.

Maeve frowned and her mouth hung ajar. 'I'm not sure what——?'

'The texts that you *both* received. The Bobby Sexton who came out of rehab was very different to the guy who went in, wasn't he?' I wasn't sure if my nonchalant attempt at the you-know-I-know game was working, but I'd definitely stirred up a reaction in them both.

'Get out!' Sasha growled.

When Maeve showed me to the door, she whispered, 'Ray Morris killed my son, Scott. *That* is what's important!'

<h1 style="text-align:center">30</h1>

I was still a little early when I reached Alex Mercedes' office. Tyler's smile was wide and genuine as I entered the reception area.

'Scott.' He jumped up from his desk and thrust out his hand. 'It's good to see you again, man.' Unlike Sasha Coburn's transatlantic accent, his slow, Southern California intonations came across as friendly and ultra cool.

We shook hands.

'You're early, buddy. Alex likes that. Can I get you a coffee?'

Remembering his attempt at making tea, I said with a grin, 'Sure, that'd be great.'

'Cool. Take a seat. I'll be right back.'

The coffee was good. So was the entertainment. To a bona fide people watcher who enjoyed nothing more than just sitting in a public place and watching the passers-by, Alex Mercedes' office reception was like the Grand Central Station for the weird and wonderful, the beautiful and the bold. A steady flow of entertainment types approached Tyler's desk, there to leave their details in consideration for representation by Australia's most famous agent, but none were allowed past the gatekeeper.

'Scott, Alex will see you know.'

Leaving my half-empty coffee on a small table by the couch, I followed Tyler into Alex's office.

Unlike before, Alex was standing in front of her desk. When I entered the room, she rushed towards me with her hand held

129

out. 'Scott. It's great to see you again.' With a Mike Tyson grip, she shook my hand vigorously. 'Come in, come in, take a seat.' While still gripping my hand, she placed her other arm on my shoulder and guided me to the vacant seat at her desk.

I was surprised that Tyler didn't leave the room. Instead, he sat down casually on the arm of a leather sofa to my left.

Alex rounded her desk and dropped into her chair. 'So ... do you know why I've asked you back so soon?'

'Uhm, something about you wanting to finance the investigation?'

Alex wobbled her head and nodded at the same time as if she were agreeing and disagreeing, to which she then acknowledged that that was exactly what she was doing. 'Well, yes and no.'

When she glanced towards her assistant, Tyler sat up straight as if he were about to be summoned.

'I hear you've become quite the celebrity around the Coast,' Alex said. 'How are you finding that?'

'Good. Free carrot cake.'

It was obvious by Alex's focused expression that the question was rhetorical—a preamble for what was about to come. 'How would you feel about taking it to the next level?'

'What do you mean?'

'Superstardom. Not only on the Gold Coast, or Australia even, but internationally?'

My shrug relayed the fact that I hadn't given it much thought.

'Okay, let's stop fucking around. I'll get to the point.' There was another glance in Tyler's direction, and I got the impression that he was more than just the receptionist. 'We *do* want to finance the investigation,' Alex continued. 'But there's more. Much more ...'

I wasn't sure if the pause was for effect or if she was gathering her thoughts. I suspected the former.

'We're going to document it.'

A quizzical frown was my only reply.

'We're going to televise it.'

'What?'

'I'll set you up with a film crew and a production team. We'll film every moment of the investigation. *Channel 9* has already agreed to air it. You're going to be a superstar, Scott!'

In an attempt to digest Alex's words, I shuffled uncomfortably in my seat and exhaled loudly, allowing my lips to flap.

This time, it was more than a glance in Tyler's direction. Alex nodded, as if handing him the podium.

Without standing, Tyler said, 'It's going to be more than just a documentary about the investigation. In fact, in the beginning, this will hardly be mentioned. The main attraction will be the reformation of the band.' He paused, as if expecting the obvious question, which I obliged. 'But how can you reform the band without the lead singer?'

'We've been auditioning replacements for Bobby for the last year.'

'Really?'

'Oh, yeah, this isn't a new thing. Phil's in, and the original band members have all agreed to take part. This was the initial concept, and shooting was about to begin next week. But ... there was a problem, and it looked like it wouldn't go ahead until ...' He shot Alex a look and I wasn't sure if his smile was respectful, sycophantic or rhetoric. 'Until Alex had the brilliant idea last night of bringing you in.'

'I'm not getting it.'

'Okay, let me explain.' Tyler stood and moved so that he was behind Alex. 'Phil agreed to allow us to film the recording of a new album. He has a shit load of new songs, apparently. All except for Ray Morris, of course; we've assembled the original band. And we had Damian Casey. You might remember him from *The Voice*, season before last?'

I replied once again with a shrug and a shake of the head.

'You haven't heard of Damian, or you haven't heard of *The Voice*?'

I hadn't heard of Damian, and the only thing I knew about *The Voice* was that it was one of those talent shows that Elvis loved to watch. I wasn't familiar and relayed this with another non-committal shrug. I was aware that Alex was watching my every move. 'You said *had*.'

'That's right. It was to be a nostalgic biopic while recording and releasing a new album, with Damian taking on the vocals. It was all to be in the memory of Bobby Sexton.'

'Was?'

Tyler's constant glances towards his boss gave me the impression that he was checking in with her before continuing. 'Phil decided he didn't need a replacement singer. Instead, he decided he was going to take on the vocals himself.'

'Great. So, what's the problem?'

Alex's smile reminded me of a patient parent. 'Phil can't sing.'

'Phil Sexton, one half of the Sexton brothers, can't sing. Are you serious?'

'Deadly serious.'

'So, what do you need me for?'

'Your participation will take the focus away from the music and add a whole new level. No one has ever attempted this concept before. Imagine Scott, not only will you have full access to all the suspects, but you'll be getting paid a massive amount of money. At first, you'll just seem to be a part of the entourage, a hanger-on perhaps.' Her eyes widened with excitement as if she were discovering new ideas as she spoke. 'But as the story unfolds, it will slowly reveal you as the true star of the show. Especially if you solve the case and expose the real killer.' She turned in her chair towards Tyler. 'My God, this is going to be epic!'

Grinning, Tyler nodded, sending his afro swaying in all directions.

'Hang on, hang on,' I said. 'What on earth would make you think I would want to be a part of this?'

The smile that only occupied the bottom half of Alex's face tightened, and I suspected that if she'd had control over her brow, it would have knitted into a scowl. 'A one-million-dollar fee, with 2% of future earnings. If ...' she corrected herself. '... *When* this show goes to syndication, you'll become a very wealthy and a very famous man!'

31

I didn't actually remember walking back to the car, and even the drive back to Kirra was an automated blur. *Was this really happening?* Of course, my initial reaction was to turn down the offer, and although Alex and Tyler were very persuasive, I didn't give them an answer. I did, however, leave the office with an invitation to a dinner party at Phil's house for that evening. *Couldn't hurt to go, I suppose.*

What did hurt, though, was that I didn't have a date to go with. Jenny was my girl, and she would be the one to accompany me at times like this. My chest suddenly felt tight. I'd be going alone.

As I often did, I drove down Ruby Street on my way home. Sometimes I'd walk around to the block and just stand on it, contemplating, reminiscing. Slowing down as I passed the spot where the house once stood, I noticed there was someone there, a man standing with his back to the road. Once again, my heart skipped. I knew who it was. Pulling into a parking spot just down the street a little, I left the car and rushed back.

I didn't speak, just came up alongside him.

He didn't react, wasn't startled. He knew I was there before he saw me; I was sure of that. We were brothers. We'd shared just about every experience in life.

'Hey mate.'

'Scotty.'

'When did you get in?'

'About five minutes ago.'

We were both staring at the back fence, the spot where the man shed had been.

'I can't believe it's all gone.'

Taking a step forward, I turned to face him. 'It's good to see you, old buddy.'

'It's good to see you too, mate,' Elvis replied. He'd lost some weight, and his face was more relaxed since the last time I'd seen him in Melbourne. He looked younger, fitter too. Dressed in a black sports jacket, white open shirt, jeans, and tan coloured boots, he stood tall with an air of authority. By his feet was a leather overnight bag.

'How long are you here for?'

'A day or so.'

Normally we would have hugged by now. But there was hardly even a greeting.

I didn't like this. 'What's going on, mate?'

'You tell me.' At last, his eyes met mine.

'Why didn't you tell me you were coming up?'

He shrugged. 'Thought you'd be too busy.'

I grabbed him by the shoulders and pulled him in. 'I'm never too busy for you. You should know that.'

He stayed there for a moment.

When I let him go, he stepped back and said, 'So, what happened?'

'To the house?'

His expression said, "Dah!"

'The dodgy water heater, apparently.'

His nod was solemn and understanding. He'd been aware of the faulty tank that once stood in the laundry cupboard. 'You had insurance?'

'Yep. Just.'

'I can't bear to see it like this,' Elvis said, his stare returning to the back fence.

'I know. It breaks my heart every time I go past.'

'Does it though? You've done alright out of it.'

'What do you mean?'

'Cassie tells me you're putting two houses on it.'

'She told you that?' I guess, unlike a doctor, there was no client confidentiality clause with an architect.

'She's my friend, remember?'

'I do, but I thought I was your friend too?'

At first, I wasn't sure if his nod was agreeing to the fact that we were friends or that he'd also thought we *were* friends. Until he said, 'But this is exactly what you wanted, isn't it?'

'What do you mean?'

'This is what you wished for.' He turned to face me again. 'You were sick of me, sick of Tetley, Johno, the house, sick of the life we had.'

'Who told you that?'

'You did, mate, every single day since you took on the *X* case. Every beer you turned down, every disapproving glance when the banter between the boys was getting heated, every moment that you chose not to spend with us in the man shed.'

God, he really did know me as well as I knew myself. It was no good denying it. 'Is that why you went away?'

'Among other things.'

'I'm really sorry, Elv. You know I love you like a brother.'

'So, how's Jenny?' There was disdain in his tone when he changed the subject.

'Good.'

'I expect she'll be moving in with you. Sell the other side and you'll have a nice little set up, eh?'

'No, she's not moving in. Well, not with me.'

He could still read me like the sports page of the *Bulletin*. 'A falling out?'

'Nah, nothing like that.'

'Mate, you haven't fucked that up as well, have you?'

'No.'

'You have!'

Now it was my turn to avert my eyes towards the back fence. 'Why would you care?'

'It's irrelevant whether I care or not, mate. But you two were meant to be together.'

'She's bought the house next door. The new one.'

'Oh, I see. Cosy.'

'No, you don't see. She's got somebody else.'

'Bullshit!'

'It's true.'

'No, I don't believe it.'

There was a need for me to change the subject. 'So how ya been? You're looking bloody good.' And he was.

'Getting there. Seeing a therapist twice a week.' Not too long ago, this would have been prime fodder for a banter theme. But not anymore.

'That's good.'

'What about you?'

I told him about the case.

'What? You've met Phil Sexton?'

'Yeah.' My attempt to play down the situation was as transparent as the five o'clock shadow on Elvis' chin. 'I'm actually seeing him tonight.'

A flicker of the old Elvis appeared from nowhere. His eyes darted with excitement. 'What's he like?'

'He's alright.'

'Alright? It's Phil Sexton, Scotty, the greatest Australian songwriter ever.'

I had him back on side. 'Where are you staying tonight?'

'Ridges at the airport.'

'I've got a spare room.'

There was a hesitation before his expression hardened.

'I can tell you all about Phil and the case.' I suddenly had an idea. 'In fact, I can do better than that. How would you like to meet him?'

Elvis' eyes almost popped out of his head, and I got another glimpse of my old mate.

'At his house tonight?'

I thought he was going to drop to his knees and beg like an excited puppy.

It was completely superficial, of course, but for now, Elvis was back in the building.

32

'What's he like?' Elvis asked as we climbed into my car. He didn't seem to notice that I no longer had the Dub.

'Phil? Seems like a nice enough bloke.' We headed back towards my apartment.

'And will anyone else famous be there?'

'Don't know. Maybe.' The invite was for two. As I no longer had a partner, it was perfect timing for Elvis to show up.

By the time we reached the entrance to the X building on Lord Street, he seemed to have forgotten all about his troubles. 'What time have we gotta be there? Shit, what shall I wear? How will we get there? Will you be driving or—'

'Limo's picking us up at 7.00 pm.'

'Limo?' He turned in his seat to face me.

'Not just any old limo, not the dodgy kind we used to hire. It'll be the INSEXT car!'

After parking in my allocated spot beneath the building, we walked towards the lifts, and I pressed the up button.

'Do you realise the significance, Scotty?' He dropped his bag and ran his hands over his face. 'Bloody hell. I can't believe this is happening. It's like something compelled me to come to Queensland.'

The lift arrived, and we stepped in.

Elvis didn't speak again until we reached the third floor, but I could tell his mind was racing. By the time we stepped into my apartment, his mood had changed. He was solemn again. 'I always knew I'd come back, but it's just …' There were tears in his eyes. 'It's just that I always thought I'd be coming back to the house on Ruby Street.'

After throwing my key on the kitchen bench, I took him by the shoulders and pulled him in for a hug. 'I know, mate. I'm just really glad to see you.'

'Ditto, buddy. I'm sorry I've been such a dick. Just went to a bad place, that's all.'

'You've got nothing to be sorry for.' Pushing him back playfully and, as if subconsciously testing the depths of the revised banter regulations, I said, 'Now toughen the fuck up, you soft twat, and stop your crying.'

This made him smile, but it was a different reaction to the one I'd been used to all these years. Cautious. Fragile. Uncertain.

'So, this is it, eh? The new abode,' Elvis said, glancing around the tiny apartment.

'Temporarily yes.' I opened the sliding door, and we moved out onto the balcony.

'Nice view.' He said, staring at the beach to our left.

'So, you're booked in at Ridges?' I asked as we leaned on the glass balustrade.

'No, not yet. There are plenty of rooms available, though.'

'Well, you're stopping here then.'

'No, no … I can't—'

'I insist!' Luckily, the rented apartment came fully furnished, which was ideal because after the fire, I had nothing. There was a tiny spare room with a trundle bed until I took it over. The place had been a holiday rental.

'Are you sure?' Elvis seemed a little uncomfortable.

'Of course. Mate, it's me, Scotty.'

'Okay cool.'

We stood for a moment in silence, enjoying a cool ocean breeze. I couldn't resist a wave to the old chuck who sat on her balcony each day across the street.

'So, what are you wearing tonight?' Elvis asked.

'Hmm, that's the only problem. I've only got one pair of half decent trousers and a shirt.'

'What happened to the flash suits?'

'Gone, mate. Up in smoke—literally.'

'Bloody hell, I've only bought shorts and T-shirts so I can't lend you anything. I'll have to wear what I've got on.'

'Don't worry, I've got it covered.' At that very moment, the intercom on the wall by the front door beeped. Leaving Elvis on the balcony, I marched across the living room and checked the tiny screen.

Two minutes later, there was a knock at the door.

Elvis had followed me back inside. When I opened the door, his face lit up for the second time that day. 'Johno!'

Our old Kiwi mate, the Happy Ranga, came bounding into the room. Over each shoulder he had several suit bags. 'Elvis?' He threw the bags onto the couch, grabbed Elvis, and bear hugged him. 'Fuck me. When did you get in?'

'This arvo.'

'It's great to see you, bro.'

'It's good to see you too, mate.'

While the boys caught up, I got three beers from the fridge, twisted off the tops, and handed them out. 'Here's to the return of los amigos.'

'Los Amigos,' we said in unison, clinking together our bottles before taking a hearty swill of cold beer.

'Shame Tetley's not here,' Johno said.

His words mirrored my thoughts exactly.

'Still in Pommy land?' Johno asked.

'Not for much longer,' Elvis said. 'He's coming back soon.'

'You've spoken to him?' I asked.

'Yeah, once a week, at least.'

Strange, on only the couple of occasions I'd spoken to Tetley, he'd never once mentioned that he'd been in contact with Elvis, even during our recent call when I'd told him all about Elvis returning to Melbourne.

As if sensing tension, Johno changed the subject. 'INSEXT, eh? How the hell do you do it, Scotty?'

'Do what?'

'He's a celebrity now, Johno. Mixes with the rich and famous. Hasn't got time for his old mates,' Elvis said.

Shit, I was losing him again. Thank God for Johno.

'Well, he's always been a pretentious twat. We know that, Elv. Anyway, let's have a look at what I've brought. There's a selection, so there's something for you too, mate, if you see anything you fancy.'

The sideways glance between Elvis and myself told us both that we remembered only too well Johno's dress sense. Our fears were confirmed when he opened the first of the bags to reveal a green checked suit.

'Fuckin hell, Johno,' was my natural reaction.

'What?'

'You actually bought this?' I asked, feeling a sleeve with my fingertips.

'Yeah, it's me best suit.'

'Be alright for St Patrick's Day,' Elvis said.

'Exactly,' Johno replied, as if not picking up on the banter. He thrust the suit into my arms. Luckily there were two more, not so leery. Elvis picked a not-too-bad two-tone number. Mine was a blue pin striped, which would have looked great if it weren't for the wide lapels.

'I suppose these'll do,' I said, appraising the outfits.

'What do you mean, they'll do? It's rock'n'roll, mate!'

Unfortunately, Johno couldn't stay long. He was a busy dad these days and a loving husband. Before he left, though, the three of us vowed to catch up at the weekend for a session.

At five to seven, we made our way down to the foyer. Elvis didn't look too bad. Losing the excess weight that he'd carried since leaving school, really enhanced his good looks. The retro suit with four buttons and narrow lapels made him look like one of the English Mods that Tetley used to tell us about. Me, on the other hand, I looked like I was heading out to a 1980s business meeting. But when the Rolls Royce Spectre pulled up outside the entrance to X, we forgot all about our fashion woes.

33

Frank Mallard had been Phil Sexton's bodyguard and chauffeur for almost twenty-five years. Apparently, the need for a personal driver had become warranted after Phil lost his driver's licence due to a number of road infringements, namely speeding. Phil's only defence was that he believed it was impossible to drive a Lamborghini Countach or a Ferrari Portofino at the speed limit, and that special considerations should be allowed for such cars. Of course, Queensland Main Roads was having none of it and suspended his licence for three years. Realising that it would be impossible to maintain a clean licence, even when the ban was lifted, his bodyguard also became his chauffeur and although his collection of supercars continued to grow, he only drove them on the track at the Norwell Motorplex every chance he got. Yes, I'd been doing my research.

Frank was no more talkative than the last time we'd met at the café in Chillingham. Sitting in the back of the most luxurious car imaginable and sipping Champagne, while half listening to Elvis' chatter, I was going over the information I'd learned partly from Bradley and partly from the internet.

An ex-marine, Mallard was originally hired by Tommy Platt as a roadie during the band's first English tour. He caught Phil's attention one night when a bunch of kids breached the stage at the London Hippodrome. Frank was the closest, and when he easily swept them up and away from the band, Phil was so impressed, he hired him as head of security the next day. After travelling the world as a part of the INSEXT machine, the Englishman ended up moving to Australia. Then when Phil lost his licence for the first time, Frank also took over the role as his private chauffeur. Of course, it was pure speculation due to a lack of evidence, but there were also rumours that Frank Mallard became the band's unofficial drug runner. I needed to open him up a bit, if possible.

'Geez, you'd know the boys pretty well, Frank,' I said, draining the first glass of Champagne and reaching for the ice bucket.

'Would I?'

'What was the relationship like between Phil and Bobby?'

Two large shoulders rose into a non-committal shrug.

'I've heard Phil could get a bit violent.' The Champagne was kicking in already.

Frank eyed me warily through the rear mirror. 'You're that detective.'

'That's right. Alex has hired me to look into the case.' This wasn't entirely true. I hadn't agreed to Alex's offer yet, but I thought dropping her name rather than Ray Morris' would have more clout. And it did.

'Alex hired you?'

'Yeah, I'm gonna be sticking around for a bit.' I topped mine and Elvis' glasses up and returned the bottle to the ice.

'What does Phil think about that?'

'I guess we'll find out tonight. What did you think about the verdict? Do you believe Ray killed Bobby?'

There was a silent pause. 'I suppose.'

Noting a lack of conviction in his answer, I asked, 'Did you know, Ray?'

'No, that was before my time. The band was at its peak when I showed up on the scene.'

'Did you work for Bobby as well?'

'Yes. I've been head dogsbody for them both over the years.'

'What was he like?'

'Your typical rockstar.'

Deciding to stay clear of the drugs topic, I asked, 'Was *he* ever violent?'

'Bobby? *Nah.* Annoying, maybe. Unpredictable. Tardy. You could never rely on him to be at the studio on time. I always had to pick him up and deliver him. Used to piss Phil off no end.'

'Was Phil ever violent towards his brother?'

'Is this line of questioning confidential?' Through the mirror, his eyes flicked from me to Elvis and back. 'I mean, I know you used to be a copper and all, but not anymore. And who's this bloke?'

'Sorry, this is a good mate of mine, Elvis.'

'Elvis?'

'Long story,' Elvis said. 'Good to meet you, Frank.'

'This is totally confidential,' I continued. 'I'm going to be asking a lot of questions over the next few weeks, I'm afraid. So, you were telling me about Phil.'

'Phil's a perfectionist and his frustration with everyone around him who doesn't share his genius can spill over into fits of rage at times.'

'Physical?'

'Yeah. This is one reason why there was never a permanent backing group. He'd be firing musicians all the time.'

'And Bobby, I guess he couldn't fire him so …?'

'Bobby was practiced in the art of winding up his brother. He knew when Phil was in one of his moods and he'd just keep going at him.'

'Did you ever see Phil hit Bobby?'

'Yeah.' Frank chuckled, as if he were recalling fond memories. 'But Bobby could give as good as he took. They were both fiery little buggers.'

We were approaching Surfers, so I cut to the chase. 'Were you driving Phil the night of Bobby's murder?'

'I was. We picked Tommy and the band up along the way. I drove them to Bobby's place, then I waited down the street.'

'Do you know what happened inside the house?'

'No.'

'Phil must have been livid when he got back in the car.'

'No, not at all. He was the opposite, in fact.'

'Did he say anything on the way back?'

'Yeah, didn't shut up, seemed excited. "We don't need him. INSEXT is bigger than Bobby Sexton. For all I'm concerned, he can rot in hell."'

After passing through an electric gate, the Rolls travelled along a tree-lined driveway towards what I could only describe as my impression of an exclusive Beverley Hills country club.

'Did Phil return to Bobby's house that night?'

'If he did, I didn't take him.'

I couldn't help but notice the lack of defence for his employer.

'Although he doesn't drive much nowadays, he's got a full licence and lots of cars.'

'So, he could have driven himself back.'

The car cruised around a circular driveway and stopped outside a lavish front door. 'I'd dropped him and Tommy back here, then I took the band back to their hotel in Surfers. After that, I was off duty.' He turned off the ignition, jumped out of the car, and opened the back door. 'There you go, sir,' he said as I climbed out. 'Enjoy your evening!'

34

Standing to one side of the front door was a tall, well-built Indian gentleman wearing an immaculate traditional costume, including a golden turban.

'This is Mr Patel,' Frank said after opening the car door for Elvis. 'He's the house manager.'

I wasn't sure how to interact with the impeccable man. *Do you shake a butler's hand? Do you say G'day?*

'This is Mr Scott Stephens and …'

'Elvis,' Elvis and I said in unison.

Mr Patel bowed his head and with only a hint of an accent, he said, 'This way, please, the party is awaiting your arrival.' When he turned and opened the door, a familiar face appeared from inside the house.

'Tyler.'

'Hey Scotty.' Bounding towards us, he thrust out his hand.

Any worries regarding our apparel became insignificant. Tyler wore a black and white cow design suit, a bright yellow shirt, purple tie, shiny green Doc Marten boots, and a pair of orange framed spectacles. He should have looked like a clown, but he didn't. He looked bloody cool.

'Tyler, this is a good friend of mine, Elvis.'

'Elvis, my man. Welcome to the Gold Coast's very own Graceland!'

'Hi.' Elvis seemed somewhat overwhelmed by the flamboyant figure as they shook hands.

'Come, come,' Tyler said, guiding us into the building. 'They're all waiting for you. Mr Patel, if you'd like to announce the guests, please.'

Mr Patel bowed and led the way into the house.

'Just one thing, Scotty,' Tyler said, lowering his voice as we followed. 'Nobody knows who you are.'

'Huh?'

'I mean, they'll know who you are as soon as they see you, but it will be a surprise. All Alex has told them is that there'll be a special guest joining us.'

'Right.'

'Just thought I'd give you the heads up. I'm not sure what kind of reception you're going to receive.'

'I hope they're not disappointed.'

'Well, I overheard whispers. "Elton John Perhaps?" "Taylor Swift?" "Springsteen?"'

'Bugger.'

'They wouldn't have been expecting Elvis,' Elvis said, grinning. I could see he was excited, and I suddenly felt exhilarated by the fact that he was here.

We followed Mr Patel through a large two-storey atrium. The place certainly gave off a resort feel, and I wondered if someone had purposely designed it this way or if it was once an exclusive hotel.

Mr Patel approached a closed double doorway and turned to face us. 'If you would like to wait here, please. I'll make the announcement.'

When the Indian gentleman opened one of the doors, the sound of chatter above background music instantly died. 'Ladies and gentlemen, I'd like to introduce Mr Scott Stephens and Mr ... Elvis.'

Tyler gently nudged us from behind.

Upon entering, the number of people present surprised me. They were all seated at a long dining table. With heads turned our way and mouths agape, it wasn't hard to gauge their reactions. I became the centre of attention as everyone focused their gaze towards me.

It was Maeve Sexton who broke the awkward silence when she sprung from her chair and breezed towards us. 'Scotty, it's so good to see you again.' Throwing her arms around my shoulders, she hugged me tightly. As she did so, she whispered in my ear, 'What on earth are you doing here?' I could tell from her mischievous smile that she wasn't expecting an answer.

Scanning the room as quickly as possible, I recognised a few of the people present. Phil Sexton sat at one end of the table. To his right was his wife, Dee. On either side of them was two of the band members, facing each other. I recognised them from the photographs I'd found on the net as Mick Mantle, the guitarist; and Jessie Flint, the bass player. I didn't recognise the young woman sitting next to Dee. Then there was Tommy Platt and his son, Lax. At the far end of the table sat Alex Mercedes. Without looking at her, I could feel her eyes burning into my skin. To her right sat Sasha Coburn. Next was the empty chair where Maeve had sat. People I didn't know occupied the rest of the table. A couple of geeky guys wearing T-shirts, and a young woman in a khaki shirt and a New York Yankees baseball cap, looked somewhat out of place next to a group of executive types wearing tuxedos and ball gowns. The arrangement of three vacant chairs in the middle, down one side of the table, clearly indicated that they were reserved for Tyler and the mystery guests.

Phil Sexton stood, and all heads turned towards him. His expression was hard to read—a mixture of confusion, disappointment and excitement perhaps. 'Scotty Stephens?' His gaze moved from me to Alex. Heads followed automatically.

Alex stood. 'Come on in, Scotty. Take a seat.' She gestured towards the empty chairs with an open hand.

'What's going on, Alex?' Phil asked, as Tyler guided us to our seats.

'This is our special guest. I'm hoping that he's going to be joining us for the recording.'

'But why?' Phil quizzed.

'It's good to see you again, Phil.' Not wanting to appear like the deer in the headlights, I approached the end of the table and held out my hand.

Reluctantly, he shook it.

'Scotty is my latest signing,' Alex said. 'I'm sure most of you already know who he is. This project will not only be documenting the recording of the new INSEXT album and the reformation of the original band, but it will also be a launch pad for Scotty's celebrity career.'

Phil frowned and, focusing his eyes on a spot in front of him, I realised he was analysing the information. After a few awkward moments, he turned to me … then he smiled and said, 'Bloody great idea!'

35

The people who I didn't know were introduced as record executive Bruno Hinman and his wife Cherry, and Pedro (Titto) Javez—an extremely handsome Mexican—and his wife, Maryke. I learned too that Phil and Alex were to be the executive producers of the doco that was to be called *The INSEXT Revival*. The two geeky guys, Chris and Tim, were camera and sound, and the khaki chick, Margo Mills, was the producer. None of these people interested me too much. They were new players and hadn't been around at the time of Bobby's death. Apart from Phil's wife, Dee, the only other players I hadn't met yet were the band members. Mick and Jessie appeared friendly enough when they were introduced to me. The young woman I'd noticed earlier was Zoey May, the new drummer. Dressed somewhere between punk and gothic, she stood out as much as the khaki chick.

'Emo!' Elvis whispered into my ear.

After we had taken our seats at the table, Alex tapped the side of her glass with a silver fork and stood. 'First, I'd like to thank everyone for coming. You all know why you're here tonight.' She glanced at me. 'In one week's time, filming will begin, but not here as you all expected.' When she paused for a moment, as if gauging the reaction, I couldn't help but notice the executives' puzzled frowns. 'We've acquired a facility in Byron Bay. A full recording studio, and a private compound with living quarters for you all. It's the perfect location.' She seemed to be taunting the execs with her eyes, as if expecting retaliation. 'Together we're going to make history … and have a wonderful time while doing it.'

There was some light applause. When it died down, Sasha Coburn said, 'Yeah, but what's this detective doing here?' She squinted in my direction.

'As I said, Sasha, Scotty will be present as an observer, he'll be—'

'He'll be snooping around again, I bet.'

Mr Patel rescued the awkward moment when he reappeared, followed by a host of catering staff carrying plates of food.

Alex sat down, but I didn't miss the cautious scowl she directed first at Sasha and then at Phil.

We ate a vegetarian meal of Asian cuisine, and there was an awful lot of it. I was a little concerned because from first-hand experience I knew exactly how Elvis' gastro system reacted to this kind of food. Let's just say there was a likelihood of severe winds later. My concern only increased when I noticed him shovelling it in.

'So, are you onboard, Scott?' Margo Mills, the director, whispered. She was attractive with a friendly smile, and slight greying around the temples told me she was around my age, possibly a little older.

'Scotty … uhm, not sure yet.'

'Really? I thought you'd jump at the chance.'

'Yeah? Why's that?'

She grinned. 'Come on, mate. You're the detective. You don't get any closer to a perfect scenario than this.' She'd obviously been briefed on Alex's real reason for asking me there. 'The brash young detective investigating a murder. All the suspects together in a single place. You don't get more Agatha Christie than that!'

I hadn't thought of it this way. Until now, I'd been dead set against the idea, certain that I was going to turn down Alex's offer. My main reasoning had been why the hell would I get involved with something like this? What would be the purpose? And did I really want the fame that would likely disrupt my life even more? Although there *had* been those little niggling voices, "But what if, Scotty? And what life do you have anyway? You've lost everything! Perhaps this is exactly what you need."

'Please think it over at least, Scotty. We'd love to have you onboard.'

'Thanks Margo. I will.'

More time to speak with Phil would have been good, but he spent most of the evening in heated conversation with the execs. Towards the end of the night, though, when we finally got together, I got the impression he felt the same way. I was pleased when he invited me to meet him for breakfast the next morning at his café in Chillingham. 'I think we need to have a proper talk, Scotty. Don't you?'

My sentiments exactly. 'That'll be great. By the way, this is my mate, Elvis. He's a big fan.'

Elvis blushed and shook Phil's hand.

'Elvis, eh? It's good to meet you, man.'

'Good to meet you too.' And that's all he had. Star struck, overwhelmed perhaps, terrified that he might say the wrong thing, Elvis lowered his head like a shy schoolgirl.

'I'll see you there, 7.15,' Phil said, turning back towards me before mingling with the rest of the guests.

Maeve was an absolute legend, guiding us around the room, introducing us personally to each of the guests.

The band was courteous, and I was glad for the chance to speak with them. Mick Mantle, the lead guitarist, reminisced about their time on the road with the brothers with no prompting. Jessie, the bass player, nodded and threw in his own anecdotes. Each of them painted a rosy picture from their recollections.

'Didn't either of you feel a bit unappreciated?' I asked.

"Nah," was the unanimous reply. 'INSEXT was always about Bobby and Phil,' Jessie said.

All this time, Elvis had been following me around the room. From the corner of my eye, I saw him approach the young drummer. When they began to chat, I automatically engaged my detective antenna, allowing me to listen in on two conversations at once.

'How's it going? I'm Elvis.'

'Zoey.'

'It's good to meet you.'

'Same.'

'But surely you guys could have received more acknowledgement?' I was gently stirring up the musos while gauging their reaction.

Heads shaking and nonchalant shrugs told me they didn't feel that way, but I wasn't completely convinced.

Elvis and Zoey moved away to replenish their drinks, and they were soon out of earshot.

'Why would any of this interest you, Scotty?' Mick asked.

'To be honest, mate, it doesn't.'

'So, this isn't an investigation or anything like that?'

Subconsciously, I must have decided not to lie to these people. Instead, like a politician, I skirted around the question. 'The detective's mind is always active, mate. You guys would have been good mates with Ray?'

'Not really,' Jessie said. 'He wasn't around long after we arrived on the scene.'

'Ray and I were mates,' Mick said.

Jessie frowned as if he were learning this for the first time.

'What was he like?'

'Phil used to treat Ray like shit,' Mick said. 'He could get away with talking to us musos like that because we were never really a part of the band. But Ray saw himself as one of the founding members.'

'Did they used to fight?'

'All the time. That's why Ray had to go.'

'That doesn't explain why he killed Bobby … and all those years later.'

'There were other factors,' Jessie said.

I was about to invite him to expand on his comment when Mick continued.

'After his stint in rehab, Bobby was about to turn everyone's world upside down.'

'Everyone? Surely just Ray?' I wasn't about to let on that I knew about Dhani's text, but then a new question popped into my mind. Did these guys also receive texts from Bobby? 'What did it say in your text?'

Mick blushed and his searching eyes told me I'd captured him off guard. Glancing at Jessie's paling complexion told me I'd touched a nerve there too.

'You both received one, right?'

Side glancing at each other, they shook their heads as if I'd just asked which one of them farted.

'I never received a text from Bobby,' Mick said causally.

Jessie's shake of the head said the same.

Maeve took me by the arm and guided me away. Whispering in my ear, she said, 'I want to introduce you to Dee.'

Dee Sexton was surprisingly down to earth for the wife of a famous rockstar. Of indigenous ancestry, she was a Gold Coast girl from Palm Beach.

'It's so good to meet you, Scotty.'

'Likewise.'

'You know we were at school together.'

'What?'

'Well, you would have been in Grade 10 when I was in Year 12, but I went to Palm Beach Currumbin State High too.'

'No way.'

'Yep, I don't remember you, of course,' she giggled. 'You would have been just a little kid.'

'Still am.'

As if determined to make sure I got to chat with everyone in the room, Maeve pulled me away once more. 'I want you to get to know Sasha,' she said. 'I don't think you started off on the right foot. She's a lovely girl when you get to know her. Sasha dear.'

Sasha seemed more interested in the execs than anyone else in the room. When she turned in reaction to Maeve's call, I noticed her expression harden.

'You remember, Scotty.'

'I never forget a mullet.'

I wasn't sure if this was an attempt at humour or not. She didn't smile, so I tested the waters. 'It's not a mullet.'

'It *so* is.'

'*Nah,* just ready for a cut, that's all.'

'Right.'

'I have to say, *you've* got beautiful hair.' I didn't know what else to say.

'Thanks.'

'Listen, I'm sorry if I upset you the last time we met. None of this is my idea.'

'Good, so you'll be turning Alex's offer down, then.'

'Ahh, I wouldn't say that.'

'Why? What else would there be here for you? You're a detective.'

'That's true, but—'

Maeve, God bless her, rescued me. 'Scotty's a friend of Phil's.'

Was I?

'Phil's asked him as a guest.'

Did he?

'Yeah right. I've got to go,' Sasha said. She leaned over, kissed Maeve on the cheek and swanned towards Dee.

'It's okay,' Maeve said. 'She'll come around.'

At that moment, Tommy Platt, the road manager, made a beeline for me and tapped me on the shoulder.

'G'day Tommy,' I said, offering my hand.

'Scott.' His handshake was firm and threatening. 'You remember Lax.'

His son, who I remembered as familiar the first time I'd met him, also shook my hand. 'It's good to see you again, Scotty.'

Maeve's face lit up and, moving from my side, she squeezed the young man's arm. 'And how have you been, Larry?'

With the antenna still on automatic, I noticed reactions from both Phil and his wife, who were on the opposite sides of the room when Maeve and the young man hugged. And then it hit me where I knew him from. *Bugger me*. He was the spitting image of his father ... Bobby Sexton.

36

Frank took us back in the Rolls. Elvis and I polished off another bottle of Champagne during the journey, so by the time we got back to Kirra, we were a bit merry. Elvis chatted nonstop, and I could tell he was excited. Just like the old Elvis. I was so happy to have him back.

Frank said very little. Staring straight ahead, our eyes met a couple of times in the rear mirror, but that was it. After dropping us home, he bowed his head and said, 'See you in the morning. Good night.'

It was late, but Elvis and I fancied another drink, so we took a couple of beers out on the balcony.

'So, what do you reckon?' Elvis said, leaning against the balustrade and staring at a fishing boat on the horizon.

'About what?'

'Will you go?'

'To Byron?'

Elvis nodded and took another swig of beer.

'Before we went tonight, there was no way I'd be getting involved in a publicity stunt. Reality TV. Not my bag, man.'

'Something changed your mind?'

'It was something Margo said, the producer. She pointed out how it would be the one and only chance to solve the case once and for all—all the players, all the suspects in the same place at the same time.'

Elvis stood and straightened his back. 'It's Agatha-bloody-Christie, mate!'

'That's pretty much what she said, and I must admit, this is probably a great opportunity. A one-off.'

'Of course it is. The perfect storm.'

'I'm not interested in the fame or launching a new career as a TV star. In fact, that's the reason I was going to turn it down.'

'You're such a knob, sometimes.' Elvis ruffled his shoulders and stuck out his neck before asking the next question. 'Have you thought about who you're gonna take with you?'

'Eh?'

'Your partner? Looks like the invite's open to loved ones too.'

'Hmm ... well Jenny's gone and shacked up with some bloke in the Whitsundays. There isn't anyone else I can think of.'

'What about me, ya poof?'

'You?' It honestly hadn't dawned on me that Elvis would be interested, but that was because I was thinking about the new Elvis, the guy I felt I hardly new. It hadn't sunk in yet that the old Elvis was back. Of course, he'd be interested in this. He'd sell his left testicle to be able to hang out with Phil Sexton and the original members of INSEXT. 'I thought you were going back to Melbourne?'

Elvis finished his beer then bounded back into the apartment, only to appear moments later carrying two fresh ones. After handing me one of the bottles, he dropped into one of the outdoor chairs. He was serious now, frowning slightly as if choosing the words he was about to speak. 'That's what I thought too.' He took a long swig of his beer. 'I thought I was just coming up here to put the demons to rest once and for all. You see I've been ... improving over the last few weeks, maybe it's the medication, maybe not, but I've been able to think again. A big part of this, no doubt, is ... *was* ... the problems with the business. I thought Pacific Holdings was going to sue me for millions. I was going to lose everything.'

'Has that situation changed?' I gently sat down on the other chair facing him.

Elvis nodded. 'Looks like it might. I've known Ted Lister, the CEO of Pacific, for years. No one's denying that there was a discrepancy in the accounting, but after learning of what I'd been going through, he's agreed to work with me.'

'Can you fix it?'

The nod again, more enthusiastic. 'I think so, in fact, already have. That was the reason for the sale of the house. The Porsche has gone, the record collection, and just about everything else I own. I still owe them a fair bit, so I'll be working off the debt for some time, but … it's doable.'

'Geez mate, I didn't realise how serious it was, but it's not like you stole their money. It was a genuine mistake.'

'Yep. And Ted sees that now. Thank goodness!'

It was a double-edged sword—on the one hand it was great that Elvis wouldn't be sued for an error in judgement, but it was hard to except that he'd had to discard everything he owned to make the problem go away. But although the outcome seemed the same, I realised that the stress factor had been minimalised greatly, if not completely, after arriving at the current arrangement. Then something else dawned on me, something that bonded us. When the house on Ruby Street burned down, with everything I owned inside, I was also left with nothing. The house was also the one last link Elvis and I had to our past life, but now that was gone too. There was no going back.

Elvis leaned forward and sat on the front edge of his chair. 'The thing is … this was going to be the last hoo-rah. I just needed to see the place again—Kirra, Ruby Street … you. I'm heading back to Victoria tomorrow. I've got a job interview lined up for later in the week. I've got it all mapped out. Get a job, gradually pay back the debt, meet a nice Greek girl, there's plenty of second cousins down there. That would make Mum and Dad very happy. Then I'll settle down and get married, have a couple of kids, a mortgage, a Toyota Camry, and a labradoodle.'

I was resisting the urge to shake my head and dismiss his words as bullshit, but it wasn't my opinion that was important here; it was what was right for Elvis' current state of mind that mattered. 'But none of that's going to happen, right?' I couldn't help myself.

Elvis threw himself back into the chair, crossed one leg over the other and his foot began to shake nervously. 'No, not now. I'll be paying back the debt of course, but ...'

'Are you coming back up here?'

He smiled. 'If you'll have me.'

Jumping to my feet, I thrust out my hand. 'My bloody oath, mate.'

Elvis stood and we hugged.

'And yes, you old poof ...' I whispered in his ear. 'You can come to Byron with me.'

<h1 style="text-align:center">37</h1>

We didn't retire until around 2.00 am. At daybreak, I was lying awake with my eyes closed. While still in that unconscious moment between sleep and awareness, I was in my old bedroom at the Ruby Street house with the doona over my head. In my mind's eye, I could clearly see the room, last night's clothes slung on the only chair. The wooden wardrobe, hand painted with light blue gloss paint. The tallboy, its top piled high with knick-knack junk. The old beige carpet stained and worn. White panelled walls well overdue for a lick of paint. But as my consciousness slowly returned, the reason for the image and its amazing clarity was down to one thing, something that I'd woken to every morning for over twenty years—Elvis' snoring. Yes, the boy was back.

A glance from the balcony confirmed the conclusion of today's brief surf report, supporting the belief that whenever there was no time, the surf was pumping. *Bugger!*

I'd arranged to meet Phil for breakfast in Chillingham at 7.00 am. Excuse the cliché, but now that the cat was out of the bag, I was hoping we'd be able to have a more indepth discussion surrounding Bobby's death. This was something I'd hoped for the previous evening at his house, but there were just too many people around. Elvis and I did get a guided tour of the place, but the production crew and the execs joined us. Leaving with the impression that Phil wanted to talk as much as I did, I was glad for the invite to meet the next morning. The highlight of the tour for both Elvis and I was Phil's collection of cars. And although the line-up of classic supercars was very impressive, there was only one girl that caught my eye: a 1967 VW Beetle. Exactly the same as my beloved and much missed Dub—she was the same year and even the same colour, only in pristine condition. Phil explained proudly how she'd been his first car when he was at high school, and how he'd tracked her down years later, purchased and restored her.

Reluctantly, I followed the group as they moved away and into the next room that Phil described as his memorabilia room. It was a man cave, not unlike the man shed we once shared at Ruby Street, but on a much grander scale. Come to think of it, it was nothing like the man shed, more like a private Planet Hollywood. The bar on one side of the room was from the original Surfers Paradise Hotel. The Wurlitzer jukebox was from Memphis. The pool table was made from transparent crystal with neon veins. Inside a large glass display case on another wall hung a pink feathered cape. In the bottom, right corner was a photograph of Elton John wearing it at a Madison Square Garden concert in the 70s. There were various outfits worn by Bobby and Phil throughout their career. Guitars and gold discs. A handwritten lyric of an unreleased George Michael song, a bejewelled handgun that once belonged to Elvis. But pride of place, and also in a glass case, hung a somewhat battered old black and white electric guitar. On the head was the word 'Rickenbacker'. The photograph in the bottom, left corner showed John Lennon playing the guitar on stage at Festival Hall in Brisbane in 1964. There was no mistaking the pride in Phil's voice as he talked about the origin of the instrument and his acknowledgement of owning such a valuable relic. Another piece of Beatles memorabilia was a Ludwig bass drum with the band's famous logo, the skin signed by Ringo Starr.

After we entered the next room, which contained a fully operational recording studio, Phil's love for the Fab Four was evident when one of the execs asked, 'Why will you be recording in Byron Bay instead of here in the house?'

'Rishikesh!' Phil replied.

A collective and puzzled frown among the small group invited him to explain what he meant.

'In 1968, The Beatles were invited to attend a meditation retreat as guests of the trans-meditation guru, Maharishi Yogi in Rishikesh, India.' Phil scanned the group as he spoke. 'Although Paul and Ringo left after eleven days, John and George, stayed for six weeks. It was a very creative experience for the band. They wrote many songs during that time.'

'But the Maharishi was later accused of being a fraud, even The Beatles disowned him,' Margo, the producer, said.

'That's right,' Phil said. 'But that's irrelevant … what I'm hoping to do is recreate the same creative atmosphere.'

'Can you really do that without Bobby?' The exec asked.

Phil's face flushed with a sudden anger, and he raised his voice. 'Of course I ca … *we* can.' He scanned the group once more, this time with an apologetic smile. *Were we witnessing one of the anger outbursts that Ray had warned me about?*

'Bobby's going to be there, not just in spirit.' He lowered his voice. 'I still have the last recordings we made together.'

'So … hang on …' Margo interrupted. 'This resort in Byron—'
Phil's laugh cut her off. 'Who said anything about a resort?'

I watched keenly as the production crew and execs glanced at each other.

'Well, it *is* … a resort, isn't it?'

'It will be whatever you want it to be.'

'Where are we actually going to be staying, Phil?' the exec said with growing concern.

'There's a little farm I purchased recently between Mullumbimby and Byron Bay.'

'A farm, oh right,' Margo said enthusiastically, and I sensed us all sharing the same image of a stone cottage, lambs frolicking in the paddocks, milking cows, an endless supply of freshly baked bread, and free-range eggs.

'You're going to love it. Trust me,' Phil added, once again managing to meet the eyes of each of us as he spoke. But there was something in his tone of voice and the slight grin that told me this wasn't all what we thought it was. I was vaguely aware of seeing archive footage of The Beatles stay in India. I'd need to do some research. The best place to start would be with Elvis. He was a mind of rock 'n' roll information.

38

The drive out to Chillingham was just as pleasant as the first time. A warm summer mist welcomed me as I headed deeper into the hinterland. Until now, I hadn't realised how much I'd grown used to the comforts of a modern car. The old Dub had been my baby for most of my adult life, but she'd also been a bit of a bone shaker. Seeing the old girl's pristine twin sister last night parked in Phil Sexton's underground car garage made me a little nostalgic.

Getting used to no longer having to change gear, the new VW Golf glided along the slippery country roads with ease and allowed me time to think. The evening before was basically the latest in a series of distractions and I realised that none of them were helping me with the case. *Oh, that's right, there was the matter of a murder case, wasn't there?* So far, besides my suspicions that Bobby sent more texts, I still had nothing to support Ray Morris' claims of innocence. No suspects, no motives, no evidence to make me think the jury got it wrong. *What the hell was I doing?*

Unlike before, I immediately noticed the black Range Rover parked at the side of the Chillingham Café. Like a nightclub bouncer, Frank Mallard stood just inside the Bougainvillea archway to the tea garden.

'Good morning, Frank,' I said warmly, holding out my hand while falling into line with the underage teenage metaphor, hoping to be allowed into the club.

Reluctantly and without words, the big man's bone-crushing handshake was a reminder that he could snap my neck like a popsicle if I stepped out of line. A flick of his head was the signal it was okay to enter.

Phil was sitting at the same table as before, reading the *Gold Coast Bulletin*. Hardly recognisable in a Gold Coast Titans baseball cap and large sunglasses, he wore a white T-shirt adorning the famous Beatles Abbey Road album cover. 'Scotty,' he said, standing.

'Phil.'

We shook hands, and he gestured for me to take the seat opposite him.

'Beautiful day.' With minimal resources in my social toolbox worthy of interest to a world famous rockstar, it's all I had.

'My oath, mate.' When he raised a hand and peered towards the old Queenslander, Jen, the middle-aged waitress appeared with a pen and pad. As before, he ordered two full Aussie breakfasts, orange juice and coffee. 'That alright, mate?'

'Bloody ripper!'

'So, Scotty boy ...' He took off his sunglasses and regarded me with narrowed eyes. 'Sorry I didn't get a chance to talk to you much last night.'

'That's alright.'

Jen returned with a bottle of water and filled two glasses.

'Was a bit of a shock seeing you there, to be honest.'

'Alex didn't tell you?'

'Nope.'

I'd assumed Alex had discussed the situation with Phil. Obviously, she hadn't. 'What do you reckon ... to me tagging along?'

Phil shrugged, closed the newspaper, and rolled it up. 'I don't know what to think, to be honest.' He paused, as if considering his next words. 'There's something that's bugging me.'

'What's that?'

'I've got a couple of questions.'

Sitting up in my seat, I realised Frank was watching us from the shadows.

'The other day when you stumbled in here. Was it by accident that we met, or did you plan it?'

Whoa. Should I be honest and come clean, or should I lie?

'And second, are you opening an investigation into my brother's death?'

Jen reappeared carrying two large glasses of freshly squeezed orange juice. It was a welcomed distraction that allowed me a little time to think. Phil was an intelligent guy. There was only one option. The food also arrived super quick, and I realised the staff were most likely pre-prepared.

Over breakfast, I told him about Ray Morris contacting me. 'As for the case, there doesn't even appear to be one.'

'Well, what have you found so far?'

'Uhm … nothing!' The fact that Jack Morris may have sold the murder weapon to the killer was sensitive information that I wasn't about to share.

There was a pause as we continued to eat.

'Listen, I'm really sorry for deceiving you, Phil. I don't actually know what I'm going to do yet.'

'It's obvious, isn't it?'

'Is it?'

Phil put down his knife and fork, leaned forward and lowered his voice. 'Sounds like you know exactly what you're going to do. How much did the scheming old bag offer you?'

'Huh?'

'Alex.'

'Oh right … a substantial amount.' Heat spread across my cheeks.

'I bet she did.'

'I haven't agreed to anything yet. Not with Ray or Alex. I don't have to take it on.'

'Bullshit! This could be exactly what we need.' Phil straightened his back and laughed. 'Bloody Alex, a fucking genius!'

'So, you don't mind?'

'Mind? Of course, I don't mind. The more publicity surrounding the launch of the next album, the better. Regardless of the outcome, I mean we all know Ray is guilty. This could be bloody huge!'

Washing down a mouthful of cool orange juice, I couldn't help analysing Phil's unexpected reaction.

'You *are* going to do it, right?'

My uncertain shrug was a genuine answer.

'You've got to. How much is she paying you?' He didn't wait for a reply. 'I'll match it!'

<h1 style="text-align:center">39</h1>

My phone rang and interrupted our meeting. Glancing at the screen, I was surprised to see whose number it was. It was Ray and Stella Morris' estranged son, Jack.

I was about to flick the phone to silent and ignore the call, but as if sensing from my puzzled expression that something was amiss, Phil said, 'Take it if it's important.'

The call intrigued me enough to do as Phil asked. 'Hello Jack.'

As if startled, Phil immediately raised his chin when he heard the name of the caller.

'Scott …' His voice was low and spacey. 'We need to meet.'

'Sure, has something happened, mate?'

'We need to meet now.'

'Okay.' I glanced at Phil and, like a dog with his head cocked to one side, I could tell he was trying to listen in.

As if sensing that his boss was suddenly under stress, Frank appeared at the side of the table. 'Is everything okay, Mr Sexton?'

Phil waved him away.

'You wanted to know who I sold the knife to?' Jack continued.

'I did. Have you remembered?'

'I never forgot. How could I?'

'Where are you?' I was confident by Phil's frustrated expression that he couldn't hear the other side of the conversation.

'I'll meet you at your office.'

'I can come to your place.'

'No … it's too dangerous … they know!'

'Who knows what?' I hadn't meant for my eyes to lock on to Phil's at that moment.

Phil frowned, and he leaned in.

'I'll need 20k,' Jack continued.

'What?'

'That's what it's going to cost you to find who really killed Bobby Sexton.'

I wanted to continue with the line of questioning but realised I needed to speak with Jack in private. 'Where are you know?'

'That doesn't matter. I'll be in Coolangatta at two o'clock this afternoon. Make sure you've got the money.' He hung up.

'Everything okay, Scott?' Phil asked as I returned the phone to my pocket.

'Yeah, all good, mate.'

'Anything to do with the investigation?'

So far, this case had been like an impenetrable slab of concrete. There were three ways to break through such a barrier— chipping away with a hammer and chisel, as I'd been doing for the last few days, upgrading to a sledgehammer, and swinging harder, or going at it with a jack hammer. And it wasn't the obvious pun that swayed me to the latter, or even the sudden interest that Phil took when he heard the name of the caller. It was the fact that so far; the case was going nowhere. The curious, mischievous kid who hid inside the detective needed to stir things up a bit. 'It was Jack Morris.'

'Jack?' Phil's faux nonchalant expression was the first piece of the slab to fall.

'Ray Morris' son—'

'I know who Jack Morris is.'

'Says he knows who killed Bobby.'

Phil shuffled in his seat. 'That's hardly a secret. The killer's behind bars in Townsville.'

'Not according to Jack.'

'Jack Morris is a desperate drug addict and a thief. I'm guessing he asked you for money?'

How far could I go with this? Should I really be sharing this information? 'Yep. Wants to meet up.'

'Scott, over the years, Jack Morris has used every angle to get money from the family to finance his habit. I'm sure with your experience in the police force, I don't have to tell you what that's like.' He took a sip of his juice. 'Don't you think that if he had information like this, he would have approached someone before now?'

It was a fair point. Addicts of Jack's calibre were smart and desperate. They'll do anything they can to get money, including stealing and, in some cases, physical violence. Why would he hold on to this important information until now, when there was money to be made?

'Don't let him play you.' Phil rotated his glass in one hand.

'How well do you know him?'

Phil smiled without humour. 'Let's just say I'm not the doting uncle. Have you got the contract yet?' he asked, changing the subject.

'Not yet, no.'

'Have you decided to join us?' He anxiously checked his watch.

My nod began slowly, then increased in tempo. 'Yeah ... why not?'

Phil shook my hand. 'Good man.'

Using the car's voice activated speed dial as I drove, I called Jack's number. There was no answer. I hardly noticed the drive back to Kirra. Normally, when working on a case, I could focus fully on the investigation, but my mind was far from sharp on this occasion. I still wasn't sure if there *was* a case. *Did Jack really know who the real killer was? Or did he just suddenly remember who he'd sold the knife to? Or – the more likely scenario – was he about to spin me a yawn in an attempt to extort money to fuel his drug habit?* From my experience working on the streets of the Gold Coast, both in uniform and as a police detective, I suspected the latter and wasn't expecting too much of an outcome from our meeting. However, there was something he said that warranted some deliberation. Five words that Jack had said when I'd suggested we meet at his apartment. "It's too dangerous. They know!" The obvious questions were: Who were they? And what did they know?

Before going to the office, I swung in home to check on Elvis. I'd left him sleeping that morning. Although he was back, there was still doubt that our lives could be the same as before. This feeling was reinforced when I entered the apartment to find a Post-It note stuck on the fridge. He'd returned to Melbourne.

40

It had only been a couple of days, but it seemed like forever since I'd stood in front of the whiteboard in my office. Normally, this would be a daily occurrence, adding the names of suspects and photographs, shuffling them around as the investigation evolved. There had been none of this since starting the initial setup of the new board. But for the first time since kind of taking on this case, I had a couple of leads.

Jack Morris' confession that he stole the murder weapon from his parent's home prior to the killing was a biggie. Then add to this the fact that he claimed to have sold it was also of huge importance, and although his recollection of who he sold it to was unclear, I got the impression that he was hiding something. This was confirmed during the latest phone conversation that morning when he said, "They know."

My attention shifted to the women involved in the story. Finding pictures of them was easy; pretty much anything to do with INSEXT was archived on the internet. In no time at all, I had printed off pictures of Maeve Sexton, Sasha Coburn, Alex Mercedes, Dee Sexton, and Stella Morris, as well as Bobby's ex-wives, Jo and Angel Sexton.

I was open to exploring a range of scenarios. Could any of these women have harboured a motive to kill Bobby Sexton? The wives possibly, but surely not Maeve, the doting mother?

To Alex Mercedes, the band's manager, INSEXT was the golden goose. Why would she want to destroy that? Did Bobby have something over her he felt the need to absolve in his new era of sobriety? Did she receive a text, perhaps?

Apart from the tabloid reports and the accusation by Mrs Kennedy, I had very little to go on regarding the state of Bobby and Sasha's marriage. There was lots of information though regarding her numerous failed business ventures attempted after her modelling career had ended—her own clothing label, a fragrance line, and even a line of Sasha Coburn handbags—but it was the high-profile court case that brought her modelling career to an end when Chanel sued her for breach of contract. That was of the most interest. Apparently, she had been moonlighting while still under contract with the fashion conglomerate. The court case ended with Sasha, unable to defend the accusations, being sued for $60 million. *Wow!* Although it had dragged on for some years, the high-profile case ended only a couple of weeks prior to Bobby entering rehab. Was this the thing that finally pushed him over the edge? Since Bobby's death, there was no record of Sasha having worked as a model or continuing with her entrepreneurial quests. Bearing in mind there was a pre-nuptial agreement in place, *would she have been left broke if Bobby divorced her?* A quick search confirmed that after his death, she received a large portion of her husband's estate.

I'd need to also look into the mindsets of the ex-wives. *What were their relationships like with the singer after the divorces?* There were no children involved, but did they keep in touch with the family, *or did they part with animosity?*

Jo Sexton, Bobby's first wife, had been very much the socialite during the peak of the band's fame. With her petite appearance and a carefree personality, the only real news about her was during the divorce when, with no prenuptial in place, she was awarded 50% of Bobby's assets and a substantial allowance derived from a percentage of Bobby's future earnings.

Angel Sexton, Bobby's second wife, was an interesting character, an athlete at the time of their brief marriage. She narrowly missed out on winning a bronze medal in the 1996 Olympics for Judo. After the divorce, she retired from the sport and disappeared for a couple of years, only to re-emerge as the figurehead for a martial arts and fitness franchise called SexTone. The venture quickly grew into one of the biggest brands of its kind in the world, incorporating a unique form of self-defence, as well as the manufacture and supply of supplements and gym wear. As in Sasha's case, there was a pre-nuptial agreement, which meant she walked away from the marriage with nothing. With little evidence or record to show where the financing came from to even start such a venture and nurture its success in such a shot matter of time, building a business would be hard enough. But then setting it up as a national franchise would be impossible without a hefty amount of time and investment. Digging further into her business history, I also found no record of backers or investors in her business. *Could she have been stealing from Bobby when they were together?* Skimming off a few assets, perhaps? *Would she have had access to her husband's bank account? If so, and if Bobby was so out of it as everyone suggests, would he have known or cared about what was going on?* This was pure speculation, of course, my detective mind exploring all scenarios. It was a long shot, but worth exploring all the same.

Then there was Stella Morris. My interest in her had grown substantially after meeting her. *Why wouldn't she welcome the extra help if she were running a campaign to prove her husband's innocence? Was there more to her relationship with Bobby?*

Dee Sexton came across as a genuine, friendly person, but did she also harbour resentment towards Bobby in any way?

With the metaphor of the concrete slab still firmly in mind, I realised there'd be a lot of jack hammering to do. Adding to the credence that Ray was innocent, the possibility that each of the players received a text from Bobby that night was totally feasible. *If only I could find Bobby's phone.* The next best thing would be to check the phones of the receivers. An impossible task.

My phone rang. The screen displayed the name Alex Mercedes.
'Hello, Alex.'

'Yeah right, fella, as if the great Ms Mercedes would be calling a bum like you.'

The smooth accent was unmistakable. 'Tyler.'

'Scotty, my man. Alex asked me to give you a call.'

'Right.'

'Have you made your decision yet?'

'About what?'

There was a slow *tut* followed by an intake of air. 'Scotty, Scotty, Scotty. How many other offers of a lifetime have you received this week?'

'Oh, you mean have I thought about being a part of the boy scout camp in Byron?'

Even Tyler's chuckle emanated a soulful aura, and I wondered if he had any aspirations of being a singer. 'Dib, dib, dib. Is that an Aussie thing or British?'

'Both ... I think.'

'So, are you coming?'

I'd been giving it a lot of thought. My initial response of flat out refusing the offer wavered somewhat, mostly because without it, the investigation would be near impossible to continue with. All the suspects in one place would be hard to ignore. The fame aspect of which I'd sampled over the last couple of years was a double-edged sword. While it provided advantages like freebies and an ego boost, it also hindered me because people recognised me wherever I went, which isn't ideal for a detective trying to remain inconspicuous. The recording of the event as an international TV series could change my life forever. *For better? Or for worse?* This was the dilemma that was hindering my decision. But Alex needed an answer, and I understood that. This was also a door of opportunity that was only open for a short time. If I didn't step inside, I'd be locked out forever. And if that was the case, I may as well end the investigation now. Then, of course, there was the money. A possible $2 million. Presently, I was flat broke. Every penny I had was tied up in the new build. I was approaching middle age, no wife, no kids. 'Okay … tell her I'm in.'

'Yes, bruh. That's awesome news. I'll let Alex know and get the contract over to you.'

'Uh, mate … would it be possible to get a small advance?' I hated to ask.

'I don't see why not.'

'I'll just need some new clobber and stuff, you know.'

'Yes, yes, absolutely. I'll get back to you asap.' He hung up in that American way without saying goodbye.

Checking my watch, it was 2.30 pm. Jack was supposed to have arrived thirty minutes ago. I guess punctuality was low on his skill set. An hour later, he still hadn't arrived, so I gave Bradley a call. After some initial chat, I told him about the planned meeting with Jack.

'What if he's the killer?' Bradley asked.

It was an obvious scenario that I'd also contemplated. After living in self-imposed poverty for all his adult life as a drug addict, *what if he'd found out who his real father was? Would he have received a similar text as Ray?* When I'd spoken to Jack, it was obvious he was in a desperate place. Once this level was reached, an addict would do anything to get money to fuel the habit. *Did he show up at Bobby's house that night?*

'How about you meet me at Jack's unit?' I said. Sharing the information I'd harvested with the police was not only the right thing to do, but it kept me on the right side of the law. It was also important for me to keep an open and honest working relationship with Jenny and Bradley, regardless of the fact that they were my friends.

'Okay.'

I gave him the address, and we arranged to meet at the property in an hour's time.

41

Winterburn Gardens was well-known to the police as a haven for drug addicts, prostitution and domestic crime. It amazed me how in this time of sky-high property valuations in one of the most sought after postcodes in Australia, that this 1970s sixteen-unit block of brick and tile units at the Southern end of Surfers Paradise hadn't been snapped up by a developer, demolished and replaced by a multi-million-dollar high-rise.

Bradley was already there when I arrived, sitting outside in a Queensland Police unmarked BMW. After parking up in a space, a couple of cars behind him, I climbed into the passenger seat, startling him from his thoughts.

'Hey, mate.'

'Hi, Scott.' He turned down the radio.

'Thanks for meeting me.'

'That's okay. Bit quiet at the station at the moment.'

'Really?' This would have been very rare.

Bradley turned somewhat awkwardly in his seat to face me. 'So, do you believe him?'

'I'm not sure yet. The thing is it's the only lead I've got so far.'

Bradley nodded with interested enthusiasm. 'Let's go in.'

We climbed from the car and like the experienced coppers we were, we instinctively scanned the area. The block of units in question was like the last stronghold against the encroaching gentrification. The developers were certainly closing in. There were two new projects in different stages of construction on the street, as well as trendy new apartments and villas. In complete contrast, Winterburn Gardens was a dilapidated, dirty remnant of the Gold Coast of yesteryear.

There was a chest-high wall between the street and the rectangular block of brick and tile units. A row of wheelie bins sat along the inside edge. Cream coloured, honeycomb security screens covered bronze framed windows and doors. I had been here many times in the past as a uniformed police officer, following up on a disturbance or reports of domestic violence.

Walking cautiously over the boundary, Bradley and I immediately noticed a familiar face. Sitting at a cheap outdoor setting in front of the first unit was a skinny, middle-aged man wearing a singlet that was two sizes too big, and shorts that were two sizes too small. His greying hair was pulled back into a ponytail and his feet were bare. His sundried tomato skin was loose and winkled over his skinny arms and legs. While keenly watching our approach through squinted eyes, he skilfully rolled a cigarette from a tin of tobacco.

'Bloody hell! It's the great man himself,' he said before licking along the edge of the rolled-up cigarette. 'Scotty-fuckin-Stephens. Didn't think I'd see you around here again.'

'Billy the Bong. You still living here, mate?'

The skinny little man lit his cigarette then raised his chin. 'My bloody oath. Why wouldn't I be?' He spoke while inhaling. 'Millionaires' row this is.'

I'd known Billy (aka William Cardell) for years. He was a police informant of my old boss, Detective Inspector Des Williams. His rap sheet was nothing more than petty crime, a bit of receiving in the early days, a couple of accounts of possession, but as far I know he'd been clean for quite some time.

There was a half full stubby on the table next to a yellow Castlemaine XXXX ash tray that was piled high with cigarette stubs. After exhaling a cloud of smoke, he took a sip of beer. 'And Detective Constable Foster. Gosh. And where might Ms Radford be today?' The brown-stained broken smile was the remnant of a barbiturate habit.

'We're not here to see you, Billy,' Bradley said, ignoring the question.

'Oh, what a blow.'

I'd already picked out unit number 5 where Jack Morris lived. It was only two doors down from Billy. 'We're here to see Jack … know if he's home?'

Billy shrugged and took another drag of his cigarette. 'You just missed the big bloke, though.'

'The big bloke?'

'Yeah, about ten minutes ago.'

'Somebody's been to Jack's place?'

With the cigarette in one hand and the stubby in the other, Billy alternated between the two as if with mechanical arms. 'I didn't see him arrive. I'd just got back from Coles, looked out and saw him leaving.'

'Do you know who it was?' Bradley asked, producing his notepad and pen.

'Nah, didn't get to see his face, just an outline through the window. A big bugger, though.'

He could have been describing Phil Sexton's security guard, Frank Mallard, or Tommy Platt.

'How did he seem?' Bradley asked. 'In a hurry or—?'

'Is there uhm …' He put down the stubby and rubbed his fingers together. 'Is there anything in this for me Mr Foster?'

'Maybe.'

Billy's eyes flicked from Bradley's to mine.

I offered a small reassuring nod.

'He was in a hurry to leave. That's all I know really.'

'What sort of car was he driving?'

Billy shrugged and shook his head.

'Would you know if Jack's home?'

Billy frowned. 'Wouldn't know. Couldn't care.'

'You don't get on with him?'

'Nobody does around here. That bastard would rob you blind and fuck ya granny over.'

'Alright, well we'll see you later, Billy,' I said, moving away from the table.

'Don't forget me uhm …' He rubbed his fingers together once more in Bradley's direction.

Ignoring the gesture, Bradley went to follow me, so I stopped, turned, pulled out my wallet, and threw Billy a ten dollar note.

'Thanks, Scotty,' Billy said, catching the note and scooping it into the pocket of his shorts.

'What did you give him that for?' Bradley asked as we continued towards unit 5.

'You've got to keep your informants sweet, Bradders. Even though he didn't have much to offer this time, he's come through for us in the past and will again,' I said over my shoulder.

Bradley's expression hardened and his cheeks flushed red. 'Maybe, but we don't have the resources these days, Scott … and don't call me Bradders. You know I hate that.'

'Sorry, bud.'

When a rap on the frame of the security screen of Jack's unit didn't solicit a response, I tried the small catch with my thumb and forefinger to find it was unlocked. The screen squeaked and groaned when I opened it. A louder knock followed by the old policeman hammer still didn't bring anyone to the door. After first, glancing at Bradley, I tried the handle and it was also unlocked.

'Hello, Jack. Are you home?'

There was no reply. Opening the door wider, my senses were met with the stench of a squatter's nest—decaying food, stale smoke, alcohol, and marijuana. The place was quiet, so with Bradley close behind, I entered the property.

42

The scenario that revealed itself to us as we entered the property was very much the clichéd type portrayed on the detective TV shows, mostly stemming from the UK or US. A dimly lit, filthy apartment littered with half eaten take-away meals, garbage and the stench one would expect to accompany such a place. In my mind's eye, I'd seen the body before we even entered the living room. I guess you could say it was a kind of premonition, but more likely a product of years of experience of entering squats and drug addicts' lairs. Sprawled out on the sofa, empty eyes staring at the ceiling, vomit around a crusty mouth. But that's not what confronted us. Yes, we found a body, and yes, it was Jack Morris, but this certainly wasn't a death by misadventure. The deep open wound in his neck confirmed this. Bradley rushed to the body, but I could tell even from across the room that it was too late. The main artery was severed, there was blood everywhere. The eyes were definitely empty, but instead of looking up, they were fixed on a point on the other side of the room. It looked as if he'd died clutching desperately at his throat. His hands were stained red, his clothes were drenched and still wet.

While Bradley checked his vital signs, I focused my attention on the young woman, perhaps in her mid-twenties, sitting on the floor on the other side of the room with her back against the wall. Like Jack, she was skinny and deathly pale. Her hair was a shade of yellow, and blonde with black roots. Her eye sockets were deep and ringed with dark shadows. Scabs caked her nostrils and the corners of her mouth. There were bruises and track marks on her arms, as well as random homemade tattoos. She wore a discoloured pink *Barbie* singlet and a pair of men's boardshorts. Her filthy feet were bare and knobbly. She too, was covered in blood, especially her hands. Between her open legs lay a knife. Like a discarded doll, her inanimate eyes also looked straight ahead, meeting the stare of the dead man across the room. Then I noticed a discarded syringe next to her on the floor.

'Bradley,' I whispered.

When Bradley turned away from the corpse, I gestured with my eyes towards the girl. He obviously hadn't noticed her when we entered, which was understandable. The only light in the room was through a missing blade in a closed Venation blind that covered the single window. Ironically, a ray of sunshine lay across the face of Jack, leaving the rest of the room in shadows.

'Easy,' I continued in a low voice. Then, directing my attention to the girl, 'Are you okay, love?'

Her eyes suddenly rolled towards the top of her head, and she began to shake uncontrollably.

'Shit. She's OD'd,' I yelled, 'Call an ambulance, Bradley.' Acting quickly, I laid her down on the floor and administered CPR.

The ambulance arrived around fifteen minutes after the first squad car. My old mate, Dale Mason, was the first police detective to arrive. While the paramedics took over with the CPR, I joined Dale and Bradley as they were looking over Jack's corpse.

I was proud to see how Bradley, the young rookie, stayed in control, dishing out orders to the uniformed personnel. Dale's assuring glances in my direction told me he was also impressed. The paramedics continued to work on the girl as they moved her on a gurney to the ambulance. We quickly cordoned off the area and awaited forensics.

'Do we know who the deceased is?' Dale asked.

'His name's Jack Morris,' I said. 'He's the son of Ray Morris.'

'No shit,' Dale said, suddenly becoming interested.

'Didn't you work on the Bobby Sexton case, Dale?'

'Only briefly. If you remember, we were all otherwise occupied.'

'With the *X* case,' Bradley said.

'That's right. There wasn't much to investigate with the Sexton killing. Within 24 hours, the police apprehended and charged Morris, allowing all the resources to remain focused on capturing *X*.'

'Do you think Ray got a fair go?'

'Nobody really cared, mate, to be honest. Bobby Sexton was an Australian icon. Justice was swift for his millions of fans. Do we know who the girl is?'

'No, not yet. No ID that I could see,' Bradley said.

The forensics arrived, and while Bradley remained to brief them, Dale and I were ushered from the building. The ambulance had already left.

Once outside, Dale lit up a cigarette. 'So, this is obviously no coincidence.'

'What do you mean?'

'Is it true you're looking into the Bobby Sexton case?'

I nodded.

'Well, you start snooping around in a high-profile cold case and the son of the killer is suddenly found murdered.'

I had to admit, it would be a bit of a stretch to peg this as merely a coincidence, especially in light of the fact that Jack had called me that morning to tell me he knew who the real killer was. Then something dawned on me. The only other person who knew about the call I'd received from Jack was Phil Sexton. *Hmm … interesting.* Billy the Bong mentioned seeing a big man leaving the property earlier. Could that have been Phil's security guard, Frank Mallard?

Along with a rag-tag group of onlookers, Billy was standing on the other side of the crime tape across the driveway.

'Can we let Billy through for a minute?' I asked Dale.

'Billy the Bong? Yeah, sure. If anyone saw anything, it'd be him, eyes like a hawk, that bloke.'

Unfortunately, Billy had little other information to offer about the person he'd seen leaving earlier.

'Who's the girl?' I asked.

Billy shrugged. 'Just another lost waif. They come and go.'

I remembered the one thing that Jack had said during his call to me that morning—"They know ..."

'Has there been any incidents just lately—shouting, comings and goings?'

Billy chuckled and opened his tin of tobacco. 'Uh, yeah. All the time. But that's perfectly normal for this little part of paradise.'

'Do you know if Jack was ever violent?' I was grateful for Dale allowing me to ask a few questions.

'Oh shit, yes. A nasty piece of work. Hard to believe his dad was once the drummer of the best rock band in the world, eh?'

Bradley joined us. 'You'll both need to accompany us to the station for questioning,' he said, gesturing with his eyes in mine and Billy's direction. 'And we'll need signed statements.' This information was obviously more for Billy's sake. I was well aware of the procedure.

'Would you be able to take them in your car, please sir?' Bradley asked Dale. 'I'll need to follow up at the hospital.'

Dale turned his nose up. 'When was the last time you had a shower, Billy?'

Offended and hurt, Billy barked, 'Cheeky bastard!'

43

I had my appointment with Alex Mercedes at 4.00 pm to keep. Thankfully, it didn't take long for Dale to take my statement at the Surfers Paradise Police Headquarters. While I was checking my details, he asked, 'So you didn't go away with Jenny?'

'Nah,' I said without looking up from the sheet of paper. 'She's gone with that new bloke.'

'New bloke? What new bloke?'

'Dorian, or whatever his name is.' I added my signature with a final sweep of the pen.

'She's got another bloke? I thought you guys were tight?'

Sliding the form across the table, I shrugged dispassionately.

'Bugger me, mate. What happened?'

'Nothing, as far as I know.' *Perhaps that was the problem.*

'You didn't fuck it up, did you, Scotty? You guys were made for each other.'

This seemed to be a growing theme. 'I don't know … maybe.'

Bradley returned from the hospital with some grim news. The girl didn't make it. A postmortem scheduled for that evening would likely confirm that she'd died from an overdose.

'Do we know who she was?'

'Not yet,' Bradley said.

'Do you think she did it?'

'Of course. Her prints are all over the knife. She was the only other person there.'

'What about the big guy Billy the Bong mentioned?'

'Not much of a description. He only saw a silhouette through a filthy flyscreen, and he couldn't be sure if he was coming from Jack's apartment or one of the others.'

I checked my watch; it was 3.30 pm. My car was still outside Jack's apartment. The distance to it was about the same as the distance to Alex Mercedes' office, so I decided to walk there first, then I'd walk back to the car after our meeting. Thirty minutes would give me plenty of time to get to Circle on Cavill.

'Jenny's on her way back,' Bradley said, as he accompanied me out of the station.

'Really?'

'Yes, flying back to Brisbane tonight. She'll be back in the office bright and early tomorrow.'

'Was she due back anyway or—?'

'No, she's cut her holiday short.'

'You rang her?'

'No, she's been calling me every day.'

'So, you told her about Jack Morris?'

'Of course. And your involvement.'

'Did she ask about me?'

'No.'

Surfers Paradise was busy with holiday makers at that time of the year. If I was going to make my appointment with Alex on time, I needed to slip through the crowds without being noticed. That was easier said than done these days. I had my sunnies on, but had left my cap in the car, so I ducked into the nearest souvenir shop on Surfers Paradise Boulevard and purchased an *Aussie, Aussie, Aussie*, yellow and green bucket hat. Looking into the tiny square mirror on the hatstand, I doubted anyone would recognise me wearing this. Keeping it on while paying for it, I felt my spirits lift when the shopkeeper paid me no attention.

The clock was ticking, so my trek through Surfers was more of a march than a stroll—and thank goodness. For the first time in two years, I made it through the thrall without having to stop for selfies and autographs. That ten-dollar hat was my best investment by far.

'What the hell are you wearing?' Tyler said, peering over a bright purple pair of glasses.

I quickly pulled off the hat and rolled it up in my hands. 'Sun smart, mate. It's bloody hot out there.'

Tyler leaned over the desk and pressed a button on the intercom. 'Our boy's here.'

I didn't hear the reply, but couldn't miss the sway of the afro when Tyler nodded. Standing up straight, he gestured with an arm for me to lead the way. 'She's ready for you.'

When I entered Alex's office with Tyler close behind me, I found Alex standing in front of her desk like before.

'And here he is, the next Aussie superstar!'

The thought of popping on the *Aussie, Aussie, Aussie* hat and doing a kind of Irish jig suddenly entered my mind, but thankfully it passed as quickly as it came.

'Tyler. Do the honours.'

Tyler disappeared back towards the reception area.

'Come in, Scott, come in.'

I doubted she'd ever call me Scotty. Perhaps the extra syllable was just too much for her enhanced lips.

For a moment, I thought I was going to get a hug, but instead she grabbed my arm and lead me to the couch on the opposite wall.

Tyler returned carrying what I guessed was the contract. He passed it to Alex, who remained standing. With them both staring down at me, I suddenly felt like a little boy.

Alex handed me the bound document. 'Have a quick read through. If you're happy, sign at the bottom of the last page.' She produced a pen and held it out.

'Thanks. Will do,' I said, taking the pen.

The contract was for one million dollars. It stated that I was free to conduct my investigation while remaining at Camp Sadie for as long as the recording might take.

'Camp Sadie?'

Tyler smiled. 'At first, Phil was going to simply call it the Ashram, indirectly referencing The Beatles' meditation camp in the 1960s, but then he came up with the idea to blend the name of the song John Lennon wrote about the Maharishi Mahesh Yogi after becoming disillusioned.'

My confused frown must have offered the same effect as, "Huh?"

"Sexy Sadie.' It's a Beatles song from *The White Album* ... Camp Sadie. Do you see?'

'Right ... How long does it usually take to record an album?' I asked without looking up.

'Depends,' Alex said. 'INSEXT's last album took six months—'

'Six months?' Now the frown said something entirely different.

'Yes, but that was down to Bobby,' Alex said. 'He always held up the process with his ... his ways.' She blushed.

'Didn't that also include all the final production and stuff?' Tyler said.

'It did,' Alex agreed. 'The final touches will be added later in a studio in Sydney.' She turned and headed back to her desk.

'Phil is very motivated,' Tyler said reassuringly. 'He already has the songs, and he's producing the album himself. I've seen how he works. The man's a machine.'

'It was always a cause of friction between the brothers,' Alex added, now seated at her desk. 'Well, Phil ... most of the time, Bobby couldn't care less if he showed up at the studio or not. Especially on the last album.'

'Did that make Phil angry?'

Alex smiled. 'Sign that contract and I'll tell you everything you need to know about the Sexton family.'

Reading through the rest of the document, it seemed pretty straightforward. There was one part, however, that I found interesting. Clause 33 caught my attention as it stated that regardless of my findings from my investigation, Alex Mercedes and her company could not be held liable in any way or form. I was about to quiz her but decided against it. If Alex had anything to do with the death of Bobby Sexton, me signing this contract would have no bearing on the outcome of the law.

With the same scrawling signature I'd used earlier that afternoon to sign the police statement, I swept the expensive pen across the dotted line at the bottom of the contract.

Tyler clapped his hands together and gave a little jump for joy before disappearing once more, only to return moments later, pushing a silver trolley laden with an ice bucket and a bottle of Champagne.

'Welcome to the family, Scott!' Alex said. 'The Golden Detective. Your life is about to change forever!'

44

The next morning, I woke early and went for a surf. Turning down a second glass of Champagne the night before was mostly because I was driving but also because I didn't really feel comfortable in the presence of Alex Mercedes. Far from the bubbly, friendly, girl-next-door type, she was more like a calculating mannequin with the agenda of world masculine domination. Thank goodness for Tyler, keeping the spirits high with his transatlantic millennial wit. I was surprised to learn that the camp would begin the following weekend, which meant I had only a few days to prepare. Also, receiving an advance cheque of $250,000 was a lifesaver. Because of the new build and the recent hold-ups, I was literally down to my last couple of hundred dollars.

'Get some new clothes and smarten yourself up,' Alex said, after handing me the cheque.

The surf was good. As usual, Chilly, my barber, was out there off Kirra Point. Sitting side by side on our boards, bobbing up and down between sets, I briefly mentioned the up-and-coming camp with Phil Sexton.

The response wasn't exactly what I'd expected. No 'Wow', or 'You're kidding me', just an indifferent shrug. 'INSEXT, the band that never was.'

'What do you mean?'

'Well, let's face it. They were no INXS, were they? I never rated them.'

'They had a few good hits.' I wasn't sure why I was defending them; I can't say I was a fan, either.

'Exactly. A couple of dodgy records. And that's it.'

I knew Chilly was a bit of a muso in his spare time. He had a black Les Paul guitar hanging on the wall of his barbershop. 'You didn't know them back in the day, did you?'

'Yeah, of course. We did a couple of gigs at the Playroom around the same time they were starting out.'

'*We*?'

'My band, The Stingers.' The first wave of the next set rolled beneath us. 'Heavy metal. Not like that shit Phil Sexton was pumping out.'

'Did you know, Phil?'

'Not really, nobody did. He was an arrogant prick—even then.' The next wave came through, but it was smaller and not worth going for.

'Fancy a coffee?' I asked.

'Sure. I've had enough anyway.'

We rode the next wave into shore, then trundled up the beach with our boards under our arms. After a quick, cold shower, I ordered two coffees from the kiosk beneath the surf club while Chilly showered. The Good Old Boys were already in deliberation.

'Hey Scotty,' Dessie said. 'How's the case going?'

'Good.' I had little to tell them and obviously wasn't about to share the news about Jack Morris. I needn't have worried.

'I see Ray Morris' son was found dead yesterday. Stabbed!' Don said. 'It was on the news this morning.'

'Yeah. I'm not sure of the details yet.'

'Did the girlfriend do it? Or has it got anything to do with your investigation?' Dessie asked. Like a band of speedo-wearing inquisitors, four pairs of eyes scrutinised my response.

'Drug related, I reckon. Nothing to do with the case.'

Four nodding heads.

Trish handed me two large take-away coffees from the kiosk just as Chilly joined us.

After a brief discussion about Chilly rising the rate of a senior haircut, we tore ourselves away from the group of teenage pensioners. Leaving our boards leaning up against the wall of the kiosk, we planted our butts on the low retainer wall on the other side of the esplanade.

'So, you were telling me about Phil Sexton?'

'Was I?'

'You said he was an arrogant prick.'

'Yeah, he was.' Chilly sipped his coffee. 'Bobby was all right, but you never got a chance to hang with him without Phil being there.'

'What? Protective of his younger brother?'

'Nah, jealous more like. I could never understand why Bobby put up with him.'

'Agro?'

'My oath. Bobby would often turn up at gigs with a black eye or a bust lip.'

'From Phil?'

'Yep.'

'Is there anything else you can tell me about them?'

'Well, it was common knowledge that Bobby was shaggin' Phil's girl.'

'Dee?'

Chilly nodded and grinned. 'He was into everyone apparently, even the roadie. What was his name?'

'Tommy Platt?'

'That's him. He used to follow the band around lugging their gear. Had an old van.'

I was aware of Tommy's history with the band, but I didn't know he and Bobby had a thing going.

'Then, of course, there was the old manager chook.'

'Alex Mercedes?'

Chilly's grin widened, and I got the impression he was enjoying the moment.

'Bobby and Alex?' I couldn't imagine it, but I guess thirty years ago, things were a little different.

We sipped our coffees in silence for a few moments until Chilly said, 'So what about you and Jenny? What's happening there?'

Hoping my casual shrug would be enough to steer the conversation in another direction, I was wrong.

'You need to pull your bloody head in, mate!'

'What do you mean?'

'Do you love her?'

Chilly's candid question took me by surprise. Our conversations were usually about surfing, the footy and music. Our friendship wasn't the kind where we shared intimate details. The shrug again was the only reply I could muster.

'Mate, don't let her slip away. You'll bloody regret it for the rest of your life if you do.'

Peering across the path, I could see the eyes of justice focused on my words. For a combined age of around 300, the old buggers didn't seem to have a problem with their hearing.

The coffee had cooled so, finishing it in one gulp, I rose to my feet. 'I've got to go.' Without making eye contact, I retrieved my board, bid everyone good morning and strolled home.

45

Two days later, I still hadn't heard from Jenny. *Were we still mates even though she had a new bloke in her life?* If not, it was going to be very awkward once we became neighbours. *Bloody hell, mate, pull yourself together.* I'd just signed a million-dollar contract to investigate Bobby Sexton's death as part of a reality TV show, I had a client serving a life's sentence in Townsville for the killing he claims he didn't commit, and his son had just been murdered. And all I could think about was Jenny Radford. A self-imposed slap around the head was administered to regain focus.

Standing in front of the whiteboard in my office, my phone rang. It was Bradley. Straight to business, he had the post-mortem results for the girl found dead in Jack Morris' unit.

'She died of a heroin overdose. It looks like she shot up a lethal dose just before we got there.'

'And she fatally stabbed Jack before killing herself?'

'Looks that way.'

'Sounds a bit suss, mate.'

'Hmm.'

'Is her ladyship back?' *Why was I asking this now?*

'She is.'

'And?'

'And what?'

'Has she said anything?'

'About what?'

'Bradley!'

'Okay …' He paused for a moment. 'She said she had a pleasant time in the Whitsundays.'

'Come on, mate.'

'She's looking good. Tanned. Letting her hair grow.'

As long as I'd known Jenny, she'd always had short hair.

'She seems kind of … happy.'

This wasn't what I wanted to hear, so I changed the subject. 'How did you get on with Ray and Stella Morris?'

'I broke the news to Ray over the phone. He basically just went quiet for a moment, then thanked me and hung up.'

'And Stella?'

'Not as upset as you would have expected, to say Jack was her only child.'

'Did she say anything?'

'Only that she had a massage booked, and she'd be late.'

Hmm, had Jack been giving his mother a hard time? In a lot of cases, it was the parents who felt the brunt of an addicted child's actions, and without Ray on the scene, Stella would have been it. 'Did forensics find anything?'

'There were no signs of a forced entry or even a struggle. Apart from the obvious cause of death, there was also heroin found in Jack's bloodstream.'

'What about the girl? Do we know anything about her?'

'Her name was Katie Lawrence. Twenty-two years old. She ran away from her home in Sydney at sixteen, lived in squats ever since. The only police record of her was for vagrancy.'

'Is Dale on the case?'

'He is.'

'Good. At least he's thorough. What does he reckon?'

There was another pause before Bradley answered. 'He's pretty much declared the case closed.'

'Really?'

'Yes. Two drug addicts get into an argument. One kills the other, then overdoses. Case closed and good riddance.'

We ended the call with Bradley promising to let me know if any new information arose, but we both knew that was unlikely. Jack Morris' unit was already cleared out, scrubbed clean and was being redecorated. A thought suddenly occurred to me. It was a long shot, but worth following up on. Then, as often was the case since leaving the police force, I cussed at no longer having the resources available at my fingertips. It was a cheeky move, but wasn't I that cheeky larrikin who everyone loved?

'Hey Suzie, how's it going my darlin'?' I asked down the phone.

'Is that you, Scott?'

'The one and only.'

We chatted casually for quite some time, catching up on each other's lives. Suzanne Roberts had worked in admin for the Queensland Police for the last twenty years. She was the go-to person on anything to do with domestic information.

'Long service leave, eh? You bloody deserve it! Will you be going anywhere nice?'

'Just about everywhere. John and I are going on a world cruise.'

'Wow!'

I listened respectfully as she reeled off a long list of destinations.

'And what about you? Any plans for making that girl an honest woman yet?'

'Uhm ... Jenny you mean?'

'Of course.'

'Nah ...'

'You better hurry, Romeo. She won't wait around forever!'

Did Suzie know something I didn't? Changing the subject, I tentatively moved onto the real reason for my call. 'While I've got you, Suzz.'

'Ahh, here we go. The real reason for your call.' She could see right through me.

'I wondered if you'd mind doing me a favour.'

'What do you need?'

'I need to know who owns a unit in Surfers Paradise. It's a rental.' I gave her the address.

'That shouldn't be too hard to find. I'll call you back.'

'Thanks, dahl, you're an angel.'

'Call me dahl again and I'll come down to Kirra and give you a public flogging.' She hung up. But good to her word, she called me back fifteen minutes later. 'Hey Scotty. You'll never guess who owns the unit you enquired about—'

'Hmm, let me see now … it wouldn't be a Mr Phil Sexton, would it?'

'Oh, okay, mister clever clogs. I bet you don't know who owned it before him.'

I really didn't want to appear as being smug but there was no chance of avoiding it. 'His brother, Bobby?'

'Smart arse!'

I'd developed the habit of standing motionless in front of the whiteboard, gently massaging my temples. It seemed to help me focus. However, my concentration broke when someone opened and closed the door to the street below. There was some huffing and puffing, followed by a moment of silence. Listening, and without turning, I was trying to imagine who would stand in the small foyer at the bottom of the stairs. After a couple of minutes, the mystery person ascended the stairs heavily, and the door to my office burst open.

'How's it goin' Big Balls?'

Turning, a familiar face welcomed me. 'Elvis.'

'Yep, I'm back.'

The silent moment at the bottom of the stairs suddenly made sense. He'd been peering through the glass door of what used to be his office on the ground floor. Marching across the room, I threw my arms around him. Looking over his shoulder, another mystery revealed itself, the reason for the huffing and puffing. There were three large suitcases at the foot of the stairs. 'Shit, you really are back.'

'Absolutely. I want to take you up on your offer.' He pulled back and eyed me with a cautious frown. 'If you'll still have me?'

Before he'd returned to Melbourne, I'd thrown it out there that he was more than welcome to stay with me if planning a return to Queensland.

'Of course, mate.'

'Just until I get myself back on my feet.' His serious expression betrayed his embarrassment.

'You're more than welcome to stay for as long as it takes.'

'Cool. Thanks Bud.'

We entered the office, and I was just about to flick on the jug when ... bugger me, the street door opened again. This time there was a loud cuss when whoever it was must have tripped over the suitcases.

'Fuck!'

Elvis and I rushed to the door at the top of the stairs. There appeared to be a mannequin lying face down at the bottom of the stairs, the head buried beneath a mass of hair, two gangly legs sticking up in the air over the cases. The head moved with a swish of candyfloss. Angry eyes looked up at us through a crooked pair of bright yellow glasses.

'Tyler ... you alright mate?'

'What idiot left these fucking suitcases here?'

When our eyes met briefly, Elvis winced.

Rushing down the stairs, I helped the beanpole to his feet. 'What are you doing here, mate?'

Awkwardly unravelling his spindly legs, he stood and patted down the tight, calf length, paisley trousers. 'Can I come in?'

'Sure. Come on up.'

His shiny brogues clonked heavily on the linoleum as he followed me up the stairs.

'I was just making a cuppa. Want one?'

'A what a?'

'Tea.'

After acknowledging Elvis with a nod, he declined the offer of tea.

'So, what can I do for you?'

'Day one, mate.' His attempt at an Aussie accent made me smile.

'Day one?'

'Yep. You're the property of Alex Mercedes now.'

Elvis' eyes opened wide. 'You signed the contract?'

'I did.'

'Awesome. So, you're going to Byron?'

'Apparently.'

Elvis fidgeted like a schoolboy bursting to answer the teacher's next question.

'Yes mate, you can.'

His face displayed a composite expression of fear and disbelief as he listened.

'You can come with me.'

Grabbing me, he jumped up and down on the spot.

'Alright, mate. Calm down.' I said, gently pushing him away.

I hadn't noticed before, but Tyler was carrying a leather satchel over his shoulder. Opening it, he pulled out a plastic Flight Centre wallet and handed it to me.

'What's this?' I'd been led to believe the camp was in Byron Bay. Australia's most easterly point was only a forty-five-minute drive south from here.

'A return ticket to Townsville.'

'Townsville?'

'Margo and the team will meet us at the airport in ...' He checked the enormous watch on his skinny wrist. 'In about an hour's time.'

The confusion in my expression prompted an explanation.

'We've arranged for you to interview Ray Morris.'

Tyler followed us back to my apartment in his black Mercedes. As I drove the short distance from Coolangatta to Kirra, Elvis—obviously excited at the prospect of accompanying me to Camp Sadie—chatted nonstop like a rainbow lorikeet at dusk.

'Who else do you think'll be going? Kylie? Barry Gibb? Molly Meldrum, perhaps?'

'We'll have to wait and see. You don't mind me leaving you here while I go up to Townsville?'

'No, not at all. I'll catch up with Johno and a few of the boys.'

'There's not many of the boys left, I'm afraid, mate.'

'It's all good.'

'I'll only be away for one day.'

'It's all good.'

When reverting my eyes to look at him, he quickly turned his head and peered out the window, and I couldn't help but notice the instant change of expression from happy curiosity to the sad clown. Realising that he was still far from okay, at least I'd have him with me for the next few weeks. If my buddy needed help, I'd be there for him.

46

I'd arranged to meet Tyler at Gold Coast Airport in the Virgin lounge an hour later. Margo Mills and the production team would also be flying to Townsville with us.

Elvis agreed to drop me off in my car. 'So, will they be filming the interview?' he asked as we pulled out onto Musgrave Street.

'Looks like it. Why else would they fly all the way up there?'

'Are you nervous?'

'About what?'

'About, you know, being filmed?'

I hadn't given it much thought. *Was I nervous?* 'No, I don't think so.'

It took literally four minutes to drive from my place to the airport. When we pulled up outside the busy departures terminal, I was surprised to see Margo waiting for us. Behind her was Chris, the cameraman, with the large camera on his shoulder ready to roll, and Tim, the sound engineer, holding a microphone on a boom overhead. Just before I stepped out of the car, the camera started rolling.

'Scotty, it's great to see you,' Margo said, approaching with her hand held out.

'Good to see you too.' I couldn't help but look straight into the camera. 'What's all this?'

Margo turned side-on, remaining out of the shot. 'This is what it's going to be like from now on, Scott. We'll be filming your every move.'

'Really? I didn't expect—'

Elvis jumped out of the driver's side, rounded the car, and joined us.

An elderly couple came over and the man, wearing a Hawaiian shirt, patted me on the shoulder. 'Scotty Stephen's. It *is* you, isn't it?'

'Hi, yes, it is—'

'I told you, Betty. I told you it was him.'

'Oh, Mr Stephens,' the woman said, 'it's such an honour to meet you.'

'Thank you.' I warmly shook both their hands. Meanwhile, a crowd had formed around us.

'Does this happen a lot?' Margo asked.

The cameraman pulled back and stepped out of the crowd to get a wider shot.

'Uhm, sometimes, yes.'

Someone thrusted a travel brochure into my hand and asked me to sign it, while two young women pushed in either side and took a selfie.

'Excuse me, do you mind me asking how you know this man?' Margo asked the elderly lady.

'Are you kidding? This is Scotty Stephens. He saved us all from that dreadful killer.'

'*X*?'

'Yes. This man's a saint!'

After a few more autographs and selfies, Margo took me by the arm and led me into the airport terminal. Over the mayhem, I didn't get a chance to say goodbye to Elvis, but I was sure he was okay. He'd have the car and a free rein of the apartment for the day and night while I was away.

Margo stayed out of shot while the cameraman filmed me going through security. It wasn't until I'd passed through the body scanner that the camera went off.

Margo joined me while Chris and Tim loaded their equipment onto the conveyer belt. 'How was that? Realistic enough?'

'What do you mean?'

'Our little fan club out front.'

'You staged that?'

'Of course.' She turned to look at me with a quizzical frown. 'That doesn't *really* happen, does it?'

It was a habit I'd picked up from my little Pommy mate, Tetley. Whenever he got a little rattled, he'd fluff up and stick out his chest like a pigeon. I didn't realise I was doing it until Margo giggled. 'Yeah. All the time.'

'Cool, that makes it even more authentic. But we didn't want to take any chances, so we slipped them $100 each before you got here.'

When the camera crew joined us in the departures hall, filming resumed.

As if I had a point to prove, I purposely made eye contact and nodded at everyone I passed while making our way to the Virgin lounge. To my embarrassment, nobody approached or even acknowledged me, distracted by the camera, perhaps, but not me.

I'd never been in an airport lounge before. The need to stock up on free food and drink whenever the occasion should arise was a primal instinct of a forty-something-year-old teenage boy from Kirra. This worked out great too because in all the hurry to be at the airport on time, I'd skipped lunch. The burgers looked good. I took two. The hot chips were fried to a crispy perfection. *Be rude not to.* A bit of salad to keep it healthy. Oh, battered fish, *why not?* A dollop of barbeque sauce. *Yum, garlic bread. Two? Nah, three slices. Should I get dessert now or come back later?*

'Get it now, lad,' the voices of Elvis and Tetley spoke in unison.

Sticky date pudding with ice cream. Chocolate sprinkles? *Well, thank you very much.* And to top it all off, a schooner of XXXX Gold. 'Is this all really for free?' I whispered in Margo's ear, joining her at one of the tables and forgetting about the microphone boom overhead. I'd also been too distracted to notice that Chris, the cameraman, was filming the buffet rampage.

'It certainly is. Get used to it. You're a star now,' Margo said, stirring a mug of coffee. I noticed she didn't have any food.

At that moment, Tyler appeared flushed and out of breath. 'Sorry I'm late.' Plonking his satchel on the vacant chair between us, he went to get himself a coffee. When he returned, my mouth was crammed full of burger.

'Did I miss anything?' he asked.

Unable to speak, I shook my head, while Margo nodded and said, 'Ohhh, yes. This is going to be very interesting.'

When we boarded the plane, I was surprised to learn that Margo and I were sitting at the front. 'Business Class?'

'If you can call it that,' Margo said, glancing at the seats that were just a little wider than those in economy. She threw her bag in the overhead locker, then stepped to one side. I did the same with the overnight backpack that Elvis had loaned me. Then, pushing past her, I took the window seat.

Although Chris was a big bloke, he somehow kept the camera rolling while remaining out of the way of the boarding passengers. Tim, the soundman, now used a handheld woolly microphone instead of the boom.

Looking a bit sulky, Tyler kept moving towards Economy Class and disappeared somewhere near the middle of the plane. Looking over my shoulder, I had to smile when I noticed his afro sticking up a good foot above the seat in front of him.

When all the passengers were onboard, and the head flight attendant asked the camera crew to take their seats, it felt good to be off camera.

'How are you holding up?' Margo asked.

'Alright. Are they uhm ...' I flicked my head towards the back of the plane. 'Are they going to be filming everything?'

Margo rested a hand over mine, and with a twinkle in her eye, she said, 'Not everything.'

47

During my time in the police force, I'd visited most of the nicks in Southeast Queensland, but this was the first time I'd been to the Townsville Correction Centre. Originally built in 1893, with more modern wings added over the years, the place is your typical penal facility.

Like sheep herded into a cattle pen, the five of us waited until a buzzer sounded, and the heavy barred door in front of us slid to one side. With the camera rolling, a tall, stocky prison guard called Greg Kanofski showed us to one of the octagonal tables in the centre of a windowless hall. 'Wait here,' he said, then went and stood by another barred entrance at the other side of the room.

Margo remained standing just behind the camera while I took a seat. Chris angled himself so he had a view of both me and the entrance. Tim stood further back, holding the microphone boom overhead. Tyler remained behind the group.

Another buzzer rang out, and the entrance guarded by Kanofski clanged and slid open. Wearing a green overall, a shackled figure appeared, and although he looked different from the photographs—older, thinner—I recognised him right away.

Before entering the hall, we'd been briefed on the prison protocol. After a bombardment of the rules and the signing of a declaration, there was to be no physical contact with the prisoner.

Ray Morris was guided to the seat opposite me at the table and told to sit, which he did. At first, he eyed Margo and the camera crew warily.

'G'day, Ray.' *I was a poet and didn't know it.*

'Scotty. It's good to meet you at last. What's all this?' The handcuffs he wore rattled when he lifted a hand towards the crew.

'Didn't anybody tell you about these guys?' I said, shooting Margo a questioning glance.

'No.'

'I'm sorry about that, mate. And I'm really sorry for your loss. Jack, I mean.'

Ray shuffled his shoulders and looked away.

'I've decided to take on the investigation.'

This news caused a positive reaction. His face brightened and his eyes met mine once more. 'Really?'

'Yes. And these guys are going to help me.' I waved a hand towards the team behind me. 'If you really are innocent, Ray, the entire world's going to know about it.'

Ray let out a burst of relief. 'Oh, thank God, thank *you!*'

Aware that we had little time, an hour tops, I cut right to the chase. 'Why don't we start by you telling us what happened that night?'

Ray gave an enthusiastic nod, straightened his back and moved forward in his seat. His recollection was pretty much word for word, the same as the statement he'd made to the police. He'd arrived late for a meeting with Bobby, Phil and the band. When he got to Bobby's house, there was no answer at the intercom, so he left.

'Did you go around the back of the house?' I suddenly wondered what the hell I was doing there. What on earth was to be achieved by asking the same questions that had been asked a zillion times already, Ray shook his head. 'I went over the fence of the joining block, but didn't climb the wall surrounding Bobby's place.'

'Why's that?'

'It was far too high. So I went home.'

'Were you angry when you found out that Jack was Bobby's son?'

'Of course, but at that time I knew nothing about that.' His expression instantly hardened.

'That's right,' I squinted, as if recalling the police statement in my head. 'You claimed you didn't read the text until later.'

The phone was in my pocket. My wife used to go crazy at me all the time for keeping it on silent.

'But surely you already knew?' I wasn't there to pussy foot about. He'd hired me to find out the truth.

'It's a lie. Jack was my son!' Ray hammered his fists onto the steel table, sending an echo through the hall.

Kanofski rushed over, reaching for something from his belt.

I stood and raised a hand. 'It's okay, my fault ... I'm sorry.'

The guard glanced cautiously between me and Ray, but then backed off.

Taking my seat, I looked into Ray's eyes. In them, I saw the genuine anger of the type I'd witnessed many times during my time on the police force. 'I'm sorry, mate. I didn't mean to—'

'To do what? Make up stupid lies about my son who just lost his life?'

I suddenly felt like shit.

Ray stood, glanced at the guard, then leaned forward. 'You're off the case, you cunt!'

'Ray, mate. Listen. I need to explore all the avenues.' The clichés were coming out thick and fast, but I could tell I'd lost him so I had nothing else to lose. 'Were you angry when you found out, Ray? Was that the real reason you went to Bobby's house that night? Did you climb over the side wall and stab Bobby with the knife he gave you?'

As Kanofski put his hand on the prisoner's shoulder, Ray said calmly, 'You stupid, stupid bastard. Jack was *my* son. That's never been at question. I thought you were better than this, Scott. That's why I wanted to hire you ... but look.' He gestured towards Margo and the crew. 'This is what you've become. A monkey in a circus!'

We watched in silence as Kanofski led Ray through the exit. Aware that the camera was still filming, I turned to Margo.

'That went well.' Her sarcasm was justified.

We were all tired when we returned to the hotel in the centre of Townsville. After dinner, Tyler disappeared, so we retired to the hotel bar for a drink. The camera crew was still shadowing my every move. Margo had suggested it would be a good opportunity to conduct an interview so, facing each other, we sat at a high table by the window. Margo made it clear to Chris that she wasn't to be included in any of the shots, so the camera was focused solely on me, which was quite uncomfortable.

For the next hour, I was questioned about my childhood, my time in the police force, the X investigation, quitting my career and becoming a private detective, the Kathy Brown and the Freckles cases, surfing and footy. I reckon she would have gone on all night if I hadn't finally said, 'Can we go to bed now?'

'I thought you'd never ask,' she said with a mischievous grin.

'No, I didn't mean—'

Chris and Tim looked at one another and shared a smirk. When Margo gave them a nod, the camera finally went off. Neither of them needed further prompting.

'Good night,' Chris said, and the pair disappeared into the lobby.

I was about to follow them when Margo stopped me. 'One last drink?'

'Ah, I'm a bit knackered.'

'Come on. We've worked hard today.' She raised her hand to get the bar staff's attention, then pointed at the empty drinks on the table in front of us.

'Just one then.' Like I had a choice.

'I was thinking of going for an early paddle tomorrow morning before we head home.'

'Paddle boarding?'

'Yes, do you paddle?'

As a laugh, the boys and I used to hire paddle boards every now and again at Currumbin Creek, but I hadn't done it for a while. 'Sometimes.'

'I love it. I never got the hang of surfing, but I live on the canals behind Surfers, so I like to paddle around there.'

'I might give it a miss.'

'Okay. How are you finding all this?'

'The filming, you mean?'

She nodded.

'Strange. Awkward. Do the cameras have to be on me all the time?'

'For now, yes. It won't be as bad when we get to the ashram or whatever it is. You'll no longer be the centre of attention then.'

'Still going to be there, though, following the investigation.'

'That's what you signed up for. Don't worry, you'll get used to it.'

A waiter arrived with two more drinks. When he'd cleared away the empty glasses and returned to the bar, Margo leaned forward and placed her hand on mine.

'We could always take these back to my room.'

At first, I wasn't sure if it was intuition or just a bloke's egotistic wishful thinking, but she'd been flirting with me all night. The suggestive glances, the cheeky grins, constant grasping of my hand in reassurance.

'Uhm ... no better not.'

Her hand clamped a little tighter. 'Why not? It's still early.'

I'm not sure why I said it. *I was a single guy, wasn't I?* And Margo was an attractive girl. 'I'm in a relationship.' Averting my eyes, I picked up my beer with my free hand and took a mouthful.

'Oh.' She pulled her hand away. 'I'm sorry. I didn't realise ... Elvis?'

Like a scene from a Richard Pryor movie, the fine spray of beer coated Margo's face and hair. The heads of the bar staff and a few remaining patrons turned in my direction as I coughed uncontrollably. 'No,' I eventually said through my fist.

'Tyler?'

'What?' the coughing abated, and I took another swig of beer. 'Do you reckon I'm gay, do you?'

Margo nodded, as if appraising the question. 'That was half the attraction.'

'I can assure you I'm not. I've got a girl.'

'Oh, right, sorry. It's just that … during our interview, you talked about everything but a girl. It was all Elvis and Johno and Titley?'

'Tetley, and they're me mates.'

'Scott, if you're not interested, you don't have to invent an imaginary girlfriend.'

'I'm not!' *Was I?*

'Okay,' Margo stood. 'My apologies. I misread the situation. It won't happen again.'

The heavy stool scraped loudly across the floor when I stood.

'I'll see you in the morning,' Margo said. We shook hands. 'I'm looking forward to meeting this …?'

'Jenny.'

'Jenny, right. No doubt she'll be accompanying you to Camp Sadie.' Before I could answer, she bid me good night and breezed off towards the foyer.

48

We flew back the next morning. Elvis picked me up from the airport. By crikey, my old mate was definitely back.

'Two more sleeps, bud!' He danced in the driver's seat as he drove.

It was Wednesday. We were due to travel down to Byron that Friday morning. 'You're excited, aren't you?'

'My bloody oath, I am. Locked down in a resort for God knows how long, with Phil Sexton and the band.'

Realising that Camp Sadie would be no holiday for me, I'd be pretty much working 24/7 starting tomorrow, with a film crew following my every move, today would be my last day of freedom, so I decided to relax at home and do nothing. A bit of TV, sunning on the balcony, catching up with the local news. Elvis had things to do, so he didn't mind.

We had planned an evening at the pub, but by the time Elvis got home, I no longer felt like going out. My decision to have an early night didn't go down too well, but Elvis understood when I told him how the Townsville trip had taken its toll.

Lying in bed in the tiny apartment listening to the TV on full blast in the next room, I drifted off to sleep, wondering if I really did miss Ruby Street that much.

The next morning, I was up at 4.30 am. The familiar sound of Elvis snoring from the spare bedroom brought back a welcome burst of nostalgia.

Wearing only a pair of boardshorts and thongs, and with Chilly's dinged surfboard under my arm, the film crew, Chris and Tim, greeted me outside the *X* building. They were both wearing half wetsuits.

'What's going on, boys?'

'Margo said you hit the surf around this time,' Chris said.

'And so it begins.'

'Indeed.'

'Margo not coming?'

'Nah,' Chris said, smiling. 'Too early for her.' He checked his watch. 'I've got to text her when we get out of the water.'

During the flight home from Townsville the day before, Margo had handed me a written itinerary.

'We want to film a normal day in the life of Scotty Stephens.'

'Oookay.'

The itemised list was thorough and precise. The day would begin with a surf off Kirra point. After a cold beach shower and a brief chat with The Good Old Boys, I was to meet Jenny for breakfast at Haig St Café. Margo would be both disappointed and suspicious, no doubt, when Elvis rocked up instead.

Tim took my board and put it in the back of a Landcruiser.

'Do you blokes surf?' I asked, climbing into the backseat.

They both nodded from the front while clicking on their seatbelts, and I realised I hadn't actually heard Tim speak. Ironic for a guy whose life revolved around sound.

'I've also done a fair bit of surf photography,' Chris said from the driver's seat.

'Cool!' And it was. Surf photographers not only had to be skilled at their craft but to get the shots we see in the magazines and on TV, they had to be right there, among the action, paddling in sometimes monstrous surf.

With bugger all traffic and a fiercely red shimmering orb peeping over the horizon, we were pulling into the surf club car park in little more than a minute.

'Fuckin' ell, what now?' Chilly said from his board when he saw me paddling out with my little entourage. 'He thinks he's fucking Mick Fanning.' He yelled over his shoulder towards a couple of the other lads.

A cheesy grin was the only reply I was willing to extend.

We paddled away from the little group and for the next hour, I just surfed as if there was no one else there. There was certainly nothing spectacular about my technique. Luckily, the waves were pretty good. Chris and Tim, using nothing more than a GoPro and a hand-held microphone, were true professionals. They didn't get in my way once.

Keeping to plan, and as if prompted, The Good Old Boys were all present in their usual spot. Drinking coffee, they watched on as Chris and Tim returned from the Landcruiser with the larger equipment, and filmed me taking a shower. And when I joined them at the kiosk, they acted as if having a camera crew filming their morning chats was a regular occurrence.

Later, when Elvis and I showed up at the café for breakfast, wearing casual T-shirts and shorts, the crew, plus Margo, were already set up and waiting.

'Oh, no Jenny then?' It was more of a statement than a question.

'No, she's working.' My glance in Elvis' direction was sign language for, "Keep it shut!"

'That's a shame. I was looking forward to meeting her.'

Over scrambled eggs, Elvis chatted with a tireless enthusiasm about the up-and-coming camp.

'According to Phil, it's going to be an ashram,' Margo said.

'What's that?'

'An Indian spiritual hermitage.'

'What's that?'

'Uhm … basically a camp.'

After breakfast, Elvis and I parted ways and, following Margo's instructions, the crew and I headed to my office. What will no doubt look seamless and effortless once the footage is edited, the actual process of casually walking down Griffith Street in Coolangatta, entering my office building, then climbing the stairs, seemed to take forever. Each shot was filmed, then refilmed from a different angle. By the time we reached the office, I was bored shitless and a little cranky. *Was this how it was going to be every day from now on?* Footage was taken of me sitting at my desk working on my laptop, taking an imaginary phone call, standing in front of the whiteboard. After that I was filmed having a pub lunch at the Kirra Hotel, then the afternoon was spent shopping for clothes at Pacific Fair. The last item on Margo's list was drinks at home with friends. Underneath the last typed line, she'd added the handwritten words 'and Jenny'.

It wasn't much of a get together. Apart from Elvis, the only people I invited were our old mates, Johno and Chilly. Normally, I would have asked my brother, Todd, and his family, but they were away on holiday in Tasmania. I asked Bradley too, but he had something else going on. The thought of asking Jenny also crossed my mind, but the fear of rejection sustained.

I couldn't tell if Margo was disappointed or just smug when I told her Jenny wouldn't be joining us.

'So, is this it? Your body of friends.'

For some reason, the question hurt. Two years ago, we would regularly fill the man shed with mates. *Where did they all go?* I was about to answer when my phone rang. Looking at the screen, my stomach muscles tightened. It was Jenny.

As if making it her business to miss nothing, Margo leaned over and also looked at the screen. 'Ahh, the elusive Jenny.' This time, her expression wasn't so smug.

'I need to take this,' I said, heading for the balcony.

'Of course you do.'

Closing the sliding door behind me, I answered the phone. 'Hey Jen.'

'Scott, how's it going?' *Again with the Scott.* She only called me that when she was pissed off with me.

'Good. So, you're back?'

'Yes. Sorry I didn't call earlier. I've been kind of busy, as you can imagine.'

'Of course …' I was just about to ask her about her holiday when she took charge.

'I've been speaking to Bradley this afternoon. He's filled me in with the Jack Morris case, but he also tells me you've decided to go ahead with the Bobby Sexton investigation.'

'That's right.'

'And something about an ashram?'

'Yep.'

'You know what an ashram is, don't you?'

'Yeah, it's an Indian spiritual hermitage.'

'Sounds more like a camp to me.'

'Yes.'

'Right … well, listen, the likely outcome of the Jack Morris case is that the girl will be posthumously charged with his killing over a drug deal that went sour.'

'Open and shut case!'

'You don't believe that, and neither do I.'

That's my girl. We still shared the same detective instincts.

'Bradley tells me your invite is for two people.'

Oh crikey. Was she about to ask if she could accompany me? Had I been worrying about her and this bloke Dorian all this time for nothing?

'I need a favour, Scott, and it's a biggie.'

Of course you can come. Elvis won't mind when I explain it to him. It'll be like old times.

'I want you to take Bradley with you.'

'What?'

'He'll be undercover. I've read through the case and there's something that's just not sitting right with me. Ray Morris contacts you to plead his innocence, then his son, who recently admitted to stealing and selling the murder weapon before Bobby's death, is then killed. Are we really to believe this is all a coincidence?'

'My thinking exactly.'

'I already knew that.'

'I know you did … the only thing is, though, Jen. I've already told Elvis he can come, and it's given him a massive boost.'

'I'm sorry to hear that, but this is important.' Her words were firm and final. 'I've instructed Bradley to be at your place by mid-morning. I really appreciate this, Scott.' She hung up.

Fuck! A light ocean breeze caused a slight shiver as I peered into the apartment at Elvis holding court in front of the camera. *How the hell was I going to break this to him?*

49

There was no way I could have told him that night. Although there was only a small group of us, Elvis was his old self again—the joker, the blokes' bloke, my best mate. *Had he been storing away jokes in readiness for this moment when the black cloud finally lifted?* He was on form, that was for sure. Deciding to tell him the next morning was probably the reason why I couldn't sleep. Instead, I lay awake thinking about the case and the up-and-coming camp. From experience, I was adept at reading body language and unless Ray Morris was a bloody good actor, I was certain he didn't believe that Jack was Bobby's son. Or was it something he'd denied and suppressed all these years? Unlike Lax, Jack looked more like his mother, so it wasn't like anyone would have guessed. If Ray *knew* before receiving the text, it was one of those dark secrets that was stored away in the archived minds of a broken family with a secret. However, if he *didn't* know and if he didn't read the text until later, like he claimed, gone was the motive. Ray Morris was convicted purely on the evidence of the witness across the street. There were no fingerprints or DNA found at the scene. Ray was the only person seen arriving at the house since Bobby threw out Phil and the band. Ray owned the murder weapon, and even though both he and his wife testified the knife was discarded some years prior, the prosecution had skilfully reconstructed a range of events that possibly saw Ray secretly retrieve the knife from the trash and hide it away without Stella's knowledge. Of course, this was all speculation, but the highly paid prosecution team did a good job of convincing the jury—and it was enough for a conviction.

Although I had my doubts, I stuck with the standpoint that Ray Morris was innocent, so it was my job to find out who the real killer was. What better scenario could there be than having all the suspects staying together in one place? A pang of excitement finally accompanied me to sleep towards dreams of an Agatha Christie ending.

The next morning, I slept late, which was unusual. I'd planned on an early surf but when I glanced over the balcony at 8.00 am, the beach was already busy with holidaymakers. *Bugger!*

The instructions from Alex, via Tyler, were that my partner and I were to be in Byron Bay at 12 noon. Jenny had arranged with Bradley for him to be at my place by mid-morning, and I guessed we'd be going down in his car. I needed to break the news to Elvis before he arrived, but instead of waking him; I showered loudly, clunked around in the kitchen, and packed my case not as quietly as I could have. When there was still no sign of him stirring, I knocked gently on his bedroom door and poked my head in. The bed was empty and made. Elvis' suitcase was packed and standing just inside the room. *Why hadn't I noticed the absence of snoring?*

At that moment, the front door to the apartment swung open and in swanned the man himself, carrying bags from the bakery and a newspaper. 'Hey bud.'

'Hey, mate. I thought you were still in bed.'

'Nah, I was up early.' He placed the bags on the kitchen counter and flicked on the jug. 'Went for a walk, got chatting with The Good Old Boys. You know what they're like. And then …' He lay two white bags side by side and ripped them open. In one were two Tradies Pies, and in the other was an apple turnover and a lamington. 'Thought we better get a last bit of substance down us. Protein and sugar. I'm guessing it might be vegetarian down there … or worse, vegan!' He thrust one of the pies in my hand. 'Here ya go, lad. Get that down ya.'

His cheeky grin was all that was required to prompt the next words from my mouth. It was a routine we'd perfected over the years since the old Four'N Twenty TV commercial. And our timing was still spot on. 'You bloody ripper.' Then together, we each took an enormous bite from our pies.

When the jug boiled, Elvis took charge of making the coffee, which came as a welcomed distraction, allowing me to duck away for a moment to gather my thoughts. *How the hell was I going to handle this?* I thought, looking into the bathroom mirror. Elvis was full of beans. After knowing him for so many years, I'd become accustomed to his ways. His level of excitement at that moment was on par with when Essendon won the premiership in 2000. And I was about to totally kill his mood by telling him he wouldn't be coming to Byron with me. No school camp for him, no rubbing shoulders with Phil Sexton and the band. And I needed to tell him now.

When I emerged from the bathroom, Elvis handed me a cup of coffee and grinned.

'Someone's on the way up.'

'Huh?'

'While you were in the bathroom, the intercom rang.' Just as he said that, there was a knock at the front door. Elvis bounded over and opened it.

My stomach bungeed to the floor. It was Bradley.

'Bradders,' Elvis cried, throwing his arms around him. 'It's great to see you, man. Come in, come in.' He ushered him into the tiny apartment.

Normally, I'd find his irritated expression after being called Bradders, comical. But not on this occasion. If there was a mirror handy, I'm pretty sure my complexion would have been a deadly shade of white.

'Hi Elvis. It's good to see you too.' His eyes met mine, and I was just about to jump in with a gob full of random words when he said. 'Sorry I'm early, Scott. I thought it might be a good idea if we got down there before everyone else.'

Elvis' face lit up to an even higher level. 'Awesome, are you coming too, Brad?' His eyes flicked from Bradley to me, back to Bradley, then back to me. Forgetting that he also knew me as much as I knew him, I realised he was reading my expression. The smile slowly sunk along with the happy lines in his face. 'What's happening, Scott?'

'I'm sorry, mate, I was just about to tell you.'

'Tell me what?' His voice had lowered to a whisper, and although he knew exactly what was happening, he needed to hear it from me.

'The Queensland Police asked me last night to take Bradley instead of you.'

'Last night? You mean when we were having a good time, laughing, being the old us?'

'Exactly. I didn't want to spoil that.'

Elvis looked at Bradley as if searching for sympathetic support. 'When you say the Queensland Police, Scott ... do you mean Jenny?'

'No, it's nothing like that, mate.'

Bradley interjected. 'This could be a potential police investigation. I'll need your assurance that you won't discuss this with anyone.'

For a moment, I thought Elvis was about to collapse. He steadied himself on the dining table, lowered into one of the chairs and directed his gaze towards the wall. 'But I've already told everyone. It was going to be great. Possibly one of the best times of my life.'

'I mean, about me going down there instead of you,' Bradley said. 'No one must know.'

Elvis didn't appear to hear him. His words were dissolving into a mutter. 'I was so looking forward to this. I—'

'Mate, I'm so sorry.' Kneeling by his side, I placed a hand on his arm. 'This is all fucked up, but I'll be back soon, and we can plan the next adventure.'

He wasn't hearing, so I shook him gently.

'You can stay here until I get back. I'll leave you the car. I shouldn't be away too long.'

'I guess this is just another chapter in the sad sorry life of Elvis, the fat Greek.'

'No, mate, no. I—' Rising to my feet, I turned my attention to Bradley and said, 'Fuck this. I'm not going!'

<h1 style="text-align:center">50</h1>

Thank goodness for Bradley. That boy never ceased to amaze me. Understanding the sensitivity of the situation, his social skills were undisputable when he sat down with Elvis at the table with a reassuring arm across his shoulder. 'This is all my fault, Elvis. It was me who insisted on accompanying Scott. He's as devastated as you are.'

'But I was looking forward to this so much.' He was gently rocking backwards and forwards now in his seat.

Leaning against the sliding door of the balcony, my heart was breaking.

'I know,' Bradley continued in a soft, sympathetic voice. 'And I'm so sorry. If this case wasn't so important, I would never have intervened, but there could be a killer present at the camp.'

Elvis nodded, but having known him for most of my life, I could tell things were far from all right.

Joining them at the table, I took the chair opposite. 'I'm sorry too, mate. Just say the word, buddy, and I won't go.'

Bradley shot me an icy glance, and I immediately saw the tougher side of the detective.

'No, no … you've got to go,' Elvis said without raising his eyes from the floor.

'That's right,' Bradley said. 'He's under contract.' The cold look lingered longer than a gaze, but his tone remained as warm as fresh muffins.

'As I said, you can stay in the apartment and use the car while I'm away.' I was trying not to sound patronising. 'And when I get back, we'll spend some serious time together. A trip maybe. Bali, Phuket …'

Elvis nodded. 'Yeah … yeah, that'll be good.'

We loaded Bradley's car out on the street in silence. When I looked up at the balcony to the apartment, Elvis was leaning against the balustrade. When our eyes met, he gave a pistol salute, nodded, then disappeared into the building.

'He'll be okay,' Bradley said as we buckled up our seatbelts.

'Will he?' Looking up at the balcony from the passenger window, I was hoping to get a last glimpse of my mate, but he wasn't there. A feeling of dread spread through my stomach when we pulled away from the kerb.

The instructions were simple and concise. Meet in the carpark at *The Farm Kitchen and Produce* establishment at mid-day. When we arrived thirty minutes early, the car park was full. In an attempt to find a parking space, Bradley was about to circumnavigate the rows of parked cars when there was a knock on the driver's side window. It was Mr Patel, the Indian gentleman from Phil's party—the butler, for want of a better term. The bling costume he'd worn on the previous occasion was replaced with a beige tunic, matching baggy trousers, and sandals.

'Hello. Are you here for Camp Sadie?'

He obviously didn't recognise me. Bradley and I nodded in unison.

The man produced a clipboard. 'Name please?'

'Stephens … Scotty Stephens.' The ever-present regulatory voice of Tetley whispered in my ear, "TWAT!"

'Ah, Mister Stephens, of course.' He ticked my name off the list with a dramatic flurry. 'And your guest?'

'Bradley Williams.'

Mr Patel wrote down Bradley's name. 'Okay. If you drive to the left of the building, you'll see an entrance with a 'No Entry' sign on it. Wait there and someone will let you in.'

'Thank you,' Bradley said politely.

During the forty-five-minute drive down from Kirra, we'd discussed Bradley's cover. His pseudonym was Bradley Williams, and he was my hairdresser. I had no doubts whatsoever he could pull it off.

When we approached the gate, a young Indian woman wearing an identical outfit to Mr Patel, met us. Gesturing for us to enter, she waved us on with a friendly smile.

After a short drive along a narrow track, we approached a gravelled area to find an American school bus but instead of the standard yellow, this one was painted in a colourful psychedelic design.

Margo and the camera crew were already there, set up and waiting. As well as Chris and Tim, there was another camera and sound duo—male and female.

Tyler appeared at the doorway of the bus, waving and smiling emphatically.

'Who's that?' Bradley asked.

'That's Tyler, Alex Mercedes' assistant.'

I noticed a definite twitch in the corners of Bradley's mouth.

'Steady on, tiger.'

'What?'

'You're working, remember?'

'What do you mean?' He fluffed up defensively, then looked towards Tyler. 'He's not gay, anyway. Look what's he's wearing.'

I had to admit, Tyler was looking vastly different from the previous occasions I'd seen him. Gone was the afro. Tightly braided hair made him appear smaller somehow. The colourful spectacles were also gone, replaced by gold John Lennon style frames. So too was the colourful outfit. In its place was that same beige pant suit. His feet were bare except for a pair of plain sandals.

As we climbed from the car, Tyler didn't move. Instead, he looked at Margo. She said something to him out of earshot. Tyler nodded and went back inside the bus.

Margo approached us. 'Hey Scott, you're nice and early.' Both camera crews shadowed her like minions. Her attention suddenly averted to Bradley. 'Oh, and who's this …? Wait … don't tell me.' She held out her hand warmly. 'You must be Jenny!'

'What? Don't be daft. This is Bradley. He's my … mate.'

'Bradley, it's so lovely to meet you.' As they shook hands, her gaze alternated between the two of us. 'I'm looking forward to getting to know you.'

Almost ploughing over her team, she backed away, and the small group returned to the bus. When they were in position, one pair in front of the door and the other to one side, she called out. 'Okay Tyler, action.'

Tyler reappeared and bounded towards me.

'Scotty, my man.' We shook hands LA gangster style. 'You're the first to arrive. Oh …' He noticed Bradley for the first time. 'And who's this?'

'This is Bradley. He's my … mate.' Introducing Bradley as my hairdresser seemed somewhat pretentious. I'd need to give this some thought.

'That sounds ominous.' He shook Bradley warmly by the hand. 'Hi Bradley, I'm Tyler.'

'Hello. It's nice to meet you.'

Yep, there was a definite blossoming across Bradley's cheeks. He caught me looking at him and frowned.

'Okay, do you have any luggage or—?' Tyler asked.

We unloaded two suitcases from the back of the car. Tyler instructed us to place them in a large shed that we hadn't noticed before, behind the bus. We did as we were asked.

'Okay, I'll need your mobile phones, keys, wallets, and any devices you might have,' Tyler said, handing us both an A4-size resealable bag.

Before I could get the word out, Bradley beat me to it. 'What?'

'Mobile phone, keys, wallets, and any—'

'I heard that,' Bradley said. 'But what's all this about taking our phones?'

'It's what you agreed to in the contract, remember? There's to be no contact with the outside world whatsoever. All devices and belongings will be temporarily removed.'

I did remember skimming through the pages and pages of terms and conditions until all the words morphed into *blah, blah, blah*. Bradley, on the other hand, who would have read every single word, and even understood it, hadn't seen or signed anything. It was Elvis' signature that adorned the document. I hoped this wouldn't be a problem.

'I can't give up my phone,' Bradley said, his chin rising to match his defiant stance.

'Then you can't come in, I'm afraid,' Tyler said, equally as defiant.

51

After a brief deliberation and a slight hissy fit from Bradley, we reluctantly agreed to place our belongings in the bags. Tyler put them in the shed with our suitcases, then returned carrying a pile of folded clothing, the same-coloured beige as his outfit.

All this time, Chris and Tim, camera crew #1, were slowly circumnavigating us with the camera rolling. Margo was leading the way.

'Here you go, two pairs each,' Tyler said, splitting the pile in two and handing one half to me and one to Bradley. 'One size fits all.'

'What are these for?' Bradley asked, the chin rising once more.

Tyler pointed to the shed. 'You can get changed in there.'

Bradley placed the bundle on the bonnet of his car, then opened out the top. 'You're not seriously expecting me to wear this?'

'Hey girlfriend, this is no time to be precious.' Tyler waved a hand down his body. 'Believe me, this is hurting me just as much, but if I can wear them, so can you.'

'But we've brought clothes in our suitcases.'

'They'll be staying here. No possessions, remember.' Then, with a cheeky grin, he added, 'Imagine that. It's easy if you try.'

'Come on, Bradley,' I said, holding up my new outfits. 'You never know, beige might be your colour.'

I went into the shed first and reappeared a few minutes later wearing an identical suit to the one Tyler wore.

'Very nice, Scotty. That looks good on you,' Tyler said.

Our attention moved to Bradley, who was clearly sulking. After a little huff, he stamped his feet and marched into the shed. When he reappeared, it was hard to know what all the fuss was about. Unlike me, who felt like a bag of spuds, he actually looked good.

'See. You look amazing,' I said, smiling.

'Just shut up.' He marched towards the bus and climbed onboard.

Over the next hour, we watched from the front of the bus as the guests arrived and were met with the same scenario that we had endured. Most were horrified when they learned they would be leaving their belongings behind.

Tommy Platt, the road manager; and his son, Lax, didn't have a problem. They simply did as they were asked and took their seats on the bus.

Although they'd changed a fair bit from their last photographs in public, I recognised the two women who arrived next right away. They were Bobby Sexton's ex-wives, Angel and Jo. Of interest, perhaps to me only, was that they arrived together and without other partners. *Were they friends?* Both girls nodded, winked and giggled slightly as they passed my seat. In contrast, Angel was wide shouldered and muscular while retaining a feminine beauty, whereas Jo was petite and waif like.

The band members, Mick Mantle, Jessie Flint and Zoey May, arrived together. There was no limousine for those guys, arriving in a dual-cab ute. Although I couldn't hear the words, it wasn't hard to lip read a barrage of expletives from Mick, the guitarist, when Tyler handed them their uniforms. It was down to Jessie the bass player to calm him down, while Zoey, the young drummer, stood silently blushing, as if to say, "What the hell am I doing here?"

When the matte black Range Rover with darkened windows pulled up, and Frank the bodyguard/driver jumped out and opened the rear passenger door, there was a collective gasp from everyone present on the bus. The guest who climbed from the back of the vehicle was the last person I would have expected to be present. It was Stella Morris.

There was no need for words between me and Bradley; our wide-eyed-gobs-ajar expressions said it all. A sentiment that was matched audibly by the ex-wives.

'What the hell is she doing here?'

After the now familiar ritual of defiance, followed by the acceptance of defeat and change of apparel in the shed, Stella headed towards the bus with her chin held high. I immediately noticed she was alone.

When she climbed the steps, she scanned the aisle hesitantly, but when her eyes met mine, I noticed a definite reaction, a physical jerk of the neck. Her expression was as easy to read as mine and Bradley's only moments earlier, "What the hell is he doing here?"

'Hi Stella. It's good to see you again,' I said, jumping to my feet.

'Hi Scott … yes … it's … it's good to see you too.'

'This is my friend, Bradley. He's my hairdresser.'

'Hi.' She shook Bradley's hand.

'Why don't you take a seat?' I offered, gesturing to the empty seats across the aisle.

After another quick scan of the unfriendly faces directed at her from farther along the bus, she accepted and took her seat.

'I'm surprised to see you here,' I whispered.

'Alex invited me.'

'Indeed.' The cunning old fox, excuse the cliché, but way to go putting the cat among the pigeons.

'But surely you're still in mourning for your son?'

'Yes, I need to address that.' Her eyes lowered to the floor. 'The police are refusing to release Jack's body, even though it seems the investigation is a foregone conclusion. So, I just needed to get away.'

I should have felt sorry for her if it weren't for the tiny insignificant detail that I believed she was full of shit. Her whole demeanour towards me had changed since our last meeting, and I suspected she was more here for herself than for anyone else.

Everyone on the list must have arrived because the camera crew, now also adorned in the same beige outfits, jumped aboard. I noticed Frank hadn't joined us, and that the Range Rover was no longer parked outside.

With the band sulking on the back seat. Tyler closed the door. There was no sign of the Sextons or the record executives. *Were they already at the destination, or would they be making a grand entrance later?*

Tap, tap, 'Uh, hum, if I could get your attention, please,' Tyler said, speaking into a microphone. 'First, I'd like to welcome you all this morning and thank you for your participation. We'll be travelling out into the hinterland now for just over an hour.'

'Bradley and I shared a quizzical glance that said, "I thought we were staying near Byron Bay?"

'Once we arrive, we'll be met by Phil and his family. So, sit back and enjoy the journey, turn off and just relax.'

Tyler, the jack of all trades, apparently, drove the large bus with competence, heading west through the narrow hinterland roads. Bradley and I remained quiet, but any hope of listening in on the conversations of the other passengers was dashed, as they all seemed to be in the same frame of mind, enjoying a bit of peace, perhaps. With the camera rolling, cameraman #2, who wasn't a man but a girl, wandered up and down the aisle with her sound person in tow, capturing us all in our thoughts.

After three quarters of an hour, the road became narrower until we eventually reached what at first appeared to be a dead end. Tyler slowed the bus but continued onto a dirt track. There were thick trees now on either side of the vehicle, blocking out the sunshine, branches scraping and clawing at the windows. As the old suspension bounced and squeaked over the uneven ground, the passengers bobbed up and down in their seats.

Around thirty minutes later, we approached a clearing and a large gate that reminded me of Jurassic Park. As the bus moved forward slowly, the gate opened and Frank, the security guard, reappeared. With no cheap uniform for him, he wore Levi jeans, Doc Martens boots, and a Fred Perry T-shirt.

When we passed through the gate, I noticed there was an equally high fence spreading out on either side.

Dense forest continued on the inside for about another ten minutes until the landscape thinned out. Soon I noticed the first building, a little stuccco bungalow with a flat concrete roof and iron-framed windows. It was the style of times gone by, but the rendering looked relatively new. Then there was another one, identical to the first, then another. Each was spaced about four metres apart, forming a curve. After passing number six, we arrived at a large, open-sided building that was basically a raised wooden deck under a wide expanse of thatched roof. On the other side of the structure were more bungalows completing a semi-circle of buildings.

Standing on the raised platform, and wearing the same outfits as us, was a group of people I recognised immediately. It was the entire Sexton family, including dad, Dhani; mum, Maeve; Bobby's widow, Sasha; Phil and Dee. Interestingly, none of the record executives were present.

When the bus pulled up, Phil approached it with open arms like an evangelist preacher.

52

Before we were allowed off the bus, it became apparent that reality TV was far from reality. Perching herself on the dashboard, Margo spoke to the group through the bus microphone. 'Okay peeps, before we disembark, I wanted to give you all a quick rundown of what's about to happen.'

I noticed the cameras weren't rolling. The crew stood quietly with their heads down, listening.

'First, Phil will welcome you all personally, then you'll each be met by a member of the Sexton family. Once you've all disembarked, you'll hear me cry, "Cut", and you'll be asked to wait while each of you is escorted to your bungalows. Do you understand?' Unenthusiastic nods met her question. 'One other thing, try not to look at the cameras. Once you get to your bungalow, you'll be asked to stay there and wait until we return to conduct your first interview.'

We watched as the two camera crews arranged themselves. Crew #2 remained inside the bus, while Chris and Tim, crew #1, waited at the bottom of the bus exit. Meanwhile, Tyler was handing out leather, plaited necklaces. 'These are microphones. You're to wear them at all times.'

Standing in the doorway, Margo spoke loud enough without the microphone for us all to hear, 'When I shout "Action", I want you all to get out of your seats and make your way off the bus in the order you are presently in. Got that?'

The group nodded in unison.

'And … action.'

Rising from our seats like aeroplane passengers after the seatbelt sign had gone off, and ever the politically incorrect gentleman, I gestured for Stella to go ahead of us. She held back, allowing Bradley and me to go first. Because we were the closest to the front, we made our way to the exit first. When we climbed down, I imagined the footage of us switching seamlessly from the interior shot to the exterior.

Phil greeted us as we stepped from the bus. He hugged me, then warmly shook Bradley by the hand. 'Welcome to Camp Sadie!'

'It's good to see you, Scotty,' Phil said.

'Good to see you too, mate.'

Minus the bumbling explanation, I introduced Bradley as my good mate.

It was that same what-the-fuck expression that appeared on each face of the Sexton family when Stella Morris stepped off the bus.

Phil offered a wane smile and a wary handshake. 'Stella … it's good to see you.'

Although my antenna was at full pitch, it wasn't hard to miss the shared glances between the family. It was obvious that no one except Alex knew that the wife of the man who killed their beloved son, brother and husband was invited without their knowledge. For some reason, it was a relief when Dhani stepped forward and offered to show her to her bungalow.

When the last member of the group stepped off the bus, to our surprise, Margo insisted we climb back aboard and do it again. For this shot, camera crew #2 set up at the main building by the side of the Sexton welcome party, while Chris and Tim filmed from farther back. Once again, I was visualising the footage but realised that if our every move were to be recorded this way; the days were going to be very long.

By the time we were shown to our accommodation, we'd already been there around an hour.

Phil's wife, Dee, was our chaperone for the short trip. 'It's good to see you again, Scotty,' Dee said, shaking my hand warmly. Her ebony skin, void of make-up, glistened with a light sheen of sweat, and her jet-black curly hair seemed to absorb the afternoon sunlight like dark matter. A sense of mischievous energy danced in her green eyes and that wide ivory smile. 'I'll be showing you to your bungalow.'

'Cool.' I introduced Bradley.

Dee grinned and winked.

The bungalows were identical, but there were no numbers on the doors, so we'd need to remember the location, which would be easy enough because ours was nearest to the main building on the left-hand side.

Before setting off on our little trek, Margo had instructed us to chat casually. With Chris, the cameraman in front, walking backwards while filming, Dee placed her arm in mine. Bradley dropped back behind us.

'Wow! I can't believe Stella is here.'

'Did you really not know she was coming?' I asked.

'No.'

'Phil?'

'No. He wouldn't have allowed it.'

'Awkward!'

'Yes. Why is she here?'

'To help prove her husband's innocence, I guess.' *Did I really believe that? I still wasn't sure about her motives.*

'Surely you don't believe Ray Morris is innocent?'

I suddenly realised just how weird this situation was. *Should I really be talking openly about the case?* A glance towards Margo and her reassuring nod told me that was exactly what was expected.

'What do *you* think?' It was a non-committal comeback, and I could tell by Margo's little fist pump that this was what she wanted.

'I try not to think about it anymore. It's done with.'

'Did you know Ray and Stella very well?'

'Back in the day, yeah. We were all mates.'

'Was Ray ever violent or …?'

'He killed my brother-in-law.'

'But what if *he* didn't kill Bobby? What if the real killer remains at large?'

'Ahh …' Dee grinned. 'I suppose that's why *you're* here?'

Her candid, casual approach to such a sensitive subject surprised me. She was grinning like a schoolgirl. *Was she high? Or was she just familiar with the television format?*

When we reached the bungalow. I wasn't sure if Margo was about to shout 'Cut' or not. She didn't.

Dee said, 'There are no locks. Relax for a bit. Dinner will be in the main building at the sound of the gong.' She kissed me on the cheek, then did the same to Bradley. While the camera remained, we watched as she returned to the main building.

There were no prompts from Margo, so while trying to act as normal as possible, and not looking into the camera, walking towards the door, I probably resembled Keanu Reeves in *Bill and Ted's Excellent Adventure.*

To say the inside of the bungalow was stark would be an understatement. Basically, it was an empty shell. There were two single beds, each with a beside dresser with one drawer—and that was it.

Chris, the cameraman, was a big bloke and with the tethered appendage behind him, who we knew as Tim the Soundman, the two skilfully negotiated the tiny space as they followed us into the building.

It wasn't until I looked at Bradley and saw his horrified expression that I lightened up. Poor bugger. I'd survive, but I didn't know if he would.

'And … cut.'

The camera crew disappeared instantly.

Margo instructed us to remain in the bungalow. Once all the guests were settled in, she'd return for our initial interview.

'What's the interview for?' I asked.

'It's something you'll need to get used to. You'll be pulled away regularly to fill us in with your thoughts.'

'Great … can't wait.' My sarcasm mirroring Bradley's expression.

53

Any feelings of grandeur were short-lived when I learned that the only reason I was being interviewed first was because the Sexton clan was having a private meeting in Phil's bungalow. For almost an hour, I sat on the ground by a little stream, with one camera in front, and another behind me. Before commencing, Margo explained that segments of the interview would be pasted in later during the editing stage and intertwined with the scenes. Then she asked a series of questions starting from the beginning. Why I'd agreed to take on the case. Did I believe that Ray Morris was innocent? If so, did I have any clues who the real killer might be? Could the killer be present at the camp? I couldn't help but notice an abruptness in her tone, as if she were in a hurry. When she'd compiled enough footage for the time being, she informed me that depending on the sequence of events, this could be a daily occurrence. *Whoopee-do*, I thought.

'Pack up and meet me outside Phil's bungalow in five minutes,' she barked at the camera crew, then marched away.

'What's up her arse?' I asked Chris as he lifted the tripod.

Chris grinned. 'You are aware of the situation, aren't you?'

'Situation?'

'You don't know about Margo and Sasha?'

'Sasha ... as in Bobby's widow?'

Chris nodded and threw the tripod over his shoulder.

'What about them?'

'Margo and Bobby had a thing going on.'

'They had an affair?'

'More than that. Bobby was going to leave Sasha for Margo, apparently.'

'You're kidding me.'

'Nope.'

'And this was just before Bobby's death?'

'Margo had originally pitched the idea of a documentary to Phil about filming the band recording a new album quite some time ago. Phil was interested, but the production company Margo worked for wasn't, so she quit her job and went it alone. Then, after spending some time with the brothers, she got smitten with Bobby and they had an affair.'

'Was he going to leave Sasha?'

'Apparently. Trouble is, Margo was still married.'

'Margo was married?'

'Still is.'

'Really?'

'Yep. Her husband is Dobie Mills!'

'Dobie Mills, as in, the gangster?'

'The one and only.'

Dobie Mills was a notorious and powerful underworld figure in Brisbane. As usual, my mind began to create and debate a possible scenario. *What if Margo was a reciprocate of one of Bobby's texts that night? Did part of his cleansing include confessing to his sins? Could he have threatened to tell Margo's husband about the affair? Or worse still, did he send a text to Dobie?* In the space of a casual conversation, two new suspects rose to the surface of the pale. Margo Mills and her husband, Dobie. I needed to share this information with Bradley as soon as possible, but a little more digging first wouldn't hurt.

'So, what happened to the documentary?'

'Rehab. Bobby's situation was getting serious. He was out of control, so he ended up in an LA private facility for six months.

At that point, they hadn't even shot any footage, and they put everything on hold.

'And Margo was out of a job.'

'This assignment is the first work she's had in all that time. I reckon Phil threw it to her as a lifeline.'

Hmm, it sounded more like a product of the calculating mind of Alex Mercedes.

'So, did Sasha find out about the affair?'

Chris shrugged. 'I guess.'

Wow, at last some new information to mull over.

'I've got to go, mate. Margo doesn't like to be kept waiting.'

'Yeah, no worries, thanks Chris.'

'You know about dinner?' he said over his shoulder.

I nodded. Dee had mentioned when showing us to our bungalow that there was to be a welcome dinner that evening in the main building. There was no time mentioned, which was understandable seeing as none of us had watches or phones, and so far, I hadn't seen a clock anywhere.

Trudging back to the bungalow, I took in a lung full of fresh air and listened while a whipbird called to his mate in the distant trees.

The interior of the tiny bungalow was dark and cool. The single layer brick walls were unfinished. The small windows on three of the walls let in little light, and there were crude curtains made of hessian hanging at the side of each. The floor was unpolished concrete. Bradley was sitting on one of the single beds, looking extremely glum.

'What's up, mate?'

'What's up? Are you kidding me?'

'What's happened?'

'This place, that's what's happened!' He waved a theatrical arm around the room. 'There's not just no running water or internet, Scott. There's no electricity even!'

'Of course, there's electricity.' I searched the walls for a light switch and sockets to find there were none. Then I realised there was no light fitting in the stone slab ceiling. 'Shit!'

'Yes, that's exactly what it is.'

'Lighten up, Bradley,' I said, sitting next to him on the bed. 'It might be fun.'

'Fun? This certainly isn't my idea of fun.'

Changing the subject, I shared the information with him about Margo and Bobby and Dobie Mills and the situation with the failed documentary.

'Dobie Mills? You think he's involved in this?'

'Maybe, but it also leaves Margo with a motive if her husband didn't know about the affair.'

'Could Bobby have sent her a text? Was he about to make the affair common knowledge?'

'That's what I'm thinking.'

'Would that be enough of a motive for Margo to kill Bobby?'

'Maybe. How would Dobie react if he found out his wife was having an affair?'

'She'd probably end up at the bottom of the Brisbane River!'

54

Assuming there was plenty of time before dinner, if Phil was yet to be interviewed, Bradley and I decided to take a walk around the place, to get to know the lay of the land. When we stepped out of our bungalow, I was amazed when we were immediately joined by camera crew #2.

'Hi, I'm Jill. And this is Toby. Just carry on as normal as if we're not here.' Hitching the camera onto her shoulder, the only cue that Jill had started filming was the red light above the lens.

The shared glance between Bradley and myself pretty much said, *this is what we signed up for. Better get used to it.* Thankfully, we'd had a moment before leaving the bungalow to discuss tactics. Divide and conquer would be the main objective. Speak to the guests separately, get to know them, win their confidence. My only concern was Bradley's cover. Could he maintain the ruse of a fake hairdresser? I guess the beauty of being cut off from the outside world was that nobody could check our alibi. That is, if we truly *were* cut off. Bradley also assured me that, if prompted, he could do a better cut than the one I presently had. *Cheeky bugger!*

Although there was no electricity in the bungalows, there had to be power in the recording studio, wherever that might be.

There were twelve bungalows in all, six on either side of the main building in a semi-circle, each being an identical grey rendered rectangle about the size of a single garage, with rounded, Art Deco style corners. The windows were white painted wrought iron made up of small square panes of glass. There was one on

244

each of the front and side walls. The front doors were plain timber behind wooden framed flyscreens. The roofs were flat poured concrete with coping around the perimeter edges.

'It's a strange design, not really Australian,' Bradley said as we strolled side by side.

'They're a recreation.'

'What do you mean?'

Since learning of the connection between Camp Sadie and The Beatles, I'd done some research online and learned all about the Indian ashram the Fab Four attended in 1968. Although their stay didn't involve recording any music, the seasoned songwriters had a very productive time, and many of the songs they wrote during that period ended up on *The White Album*. I quickly explained the concept to Bradley.

'Hmm, interesting,' Bradley said. 'So, you think Phil is trying to recreate the moment?'

'I think so, but I think Alex has other ideas.'

Our bungalow was the closest to the main building on the left-hand side. With only a few metres between them, each had a small yard out the front with two wooden outdoor chairs.

When we approached the bungalow next to ours, Dhani—aka Phil's dad, Dave Sexton, came skipping down the front path. 'It's great to see you again, brother.'

'Dhani, it's good to see you too.' We shook hands. 'This is my mate, Bradley.'

'Oh,' Dhani said, shaking Bradley's hand. 'I didn't realise.'

'Realise what?' I asked.

'That you were …' He twitched his head to one side. 'You know …'

Dee Sexton's wink and grin came to mind. 'I'm not gay, if that's what you mean!'

Bradley laughed out loud. 'He's still in the closet, but I'm working on it.'

'Hey, that's enough of that.'

'It's okay, Scott,' Dhani said, 'it's nothing to be ashamed of.'

'Aren't you supposed to be in a meeting with the family?'

'*Ahh,* I'm not interested in any of that.'

'Is it about Stella being here?'

'Probably. I don't care.'

'It doesn't bother you that her husband was convicted of killing your son?'

'Why should it? She's done nothing wrong.'

'I didn't see Harmony earlier,' I said, changing the subject.

'Oh gosh, no. She, uhm … this wouldn't be her thing.'

'She's not daft then.'

'No, she's not, but she might be a killer!'

'Huh?'

'My ex-wife. I think Harmony may have killed her, if she'd been here.' His grin was kind of reassuring that even though he was living the hippy lifestyle, he hadn't lost his sense of humour.

Bobby's ex-wives, Angel and Jo, were sitting outside the next bungalow. *Were they sharing?* Had they struck up a mutual friendship after their divorces? The Bobby Sexton Ex-wives Club perhaps, or maybe the Mutual Society of Bobby Sexton Haters?

'Hey Scotty,' Angel called out.

'Hey.'

Jo snuck towards us down the path as if she were on a secret mission. 'You wouldn't have any smokes, would you, mate?'

'No, sorry.'

'Bugger. I'm dying for a fag, eh!' Crestfallen, she sauntered back to her chair.

'Can I have a word with you girls when you're ready?'

They looked at each other and shrugged.

'Not right now though, Sonny,' Angel said.

'Yeah, no worries. Tomorrow perhaps?'

'Find some ciggies and I'm all yours,' Jo said.

At the next bungalow, Tommy Platt seemed to be snoozing in the late afternoon sun, while his son, Lax, strummed quietly on an acoustic guitar. His wave back to us was genuine and warm.

The front door of the next bungalow was open behind the flyscreen, so the occupants must have been inside, possibly the band members.

Unlike Lax's genuine greeting, the disinclined gesture from Zoey, the drummer, was merely an indifferent reaction to my wave as we passed the next bungalow. She also didn't appear to be sharing with anyone that I could see.

The next and last bungalow on that side appeared to be empty.

Retracing our steps, we headed back to the main building. Different to the bungalows, not only in size, but also in design, the entire front half and two sides were open to the elements, creating the impression of a communal meeting place. Across the back of the structure was a windowless block wall, behind which I suspected housed the studio, perhaps a kitchen, and hopefully a toilet and shower block. The front area was an expansive wooden deck. In the centre was a long, shin-high table with cushions, instead of chairs, on either side. The table was set for dinner and the smell of Indian food wafted out from the back of the building.

With camera crew #2 still filming us, we were keen to look around.

There were five steps leading up to the wooden platform. The settings on the table were basic: white plates, knives and forks, and crude porcelain mugs. 'Bloody hell,' I whispered. 'Were you ever in the Boy Scouts, Bradley?'

'Of course.'

'Of course.'

There was an entrance to the back of the building on the left-hand side. As suspected, when we opened the door, the heat and the aromas of a busy kitchen met us. Enormous pans bubbled on a large stove top, overseen by a short Indian lady. On a butcher's block, Mr Patel was rolling out what appeared to be batches of naan bread. The young woman from the gate was stirring a pot of rice. All three of them wore the same outfits as us.

'Namaste,' Mr Patel said, looking up as we entered.

'Namaste,' Bradley and I said in unison.

'Can I help you? Do you need the toilet?'

'The toilet. Yes, that's that we're looking for.'

The young woman glanced our way and smiled, and I guessed the older couple was her parents.

Mr Patel pointed towards the exit then rotated his arm, signalling around the back of the building.

Making our exit, we followed the outside wall to the back of the building, as instructed. Beyond the kitchen windows was another doorway. Before entering, I peered farther along the wall to see another entrance at the other end.

Inside the first door was exactly what I'd expected to find. Rows of sinks, toilet cubicles, a shower block, and a changing area.

'Are you going to be alright with this, Bradley?'

'Of course. Why wouldn't I be?' The defensive chin up told me he was far from alright with this. 'I used to love school camp.'

'School camp? Yeah? Where d'ya go?'

'Is that important?'

'Maybe.'

'Tangalooma.'

'Tangalooma? What, you mean the holiday resort on Morton Island? This is hardly the same.'

'I had to share a room with Katie Boswell.'

'Oh, heaven forbid.'

'You didn't know Katie Boswell. She was the school bully. No one else would room with her, so I was picked by the teacher.'

'How'd it go?'

'Okay, I suppose. I lost my virginity!'

'What?'

'I often wonder if that's what made me gay.' He was fucking with me. 'Of course I'm alright with this, Scott.'

Heading back outside, we made our way to the third door. Inside was what a pair of laymen, who knew nothing on the topic, would term as a state-of-the-art recording studio. We were standing in a small foyer. Through a glass wall was a dark room with a large recording console beneath a window. On the other side of the window was the studio where the musicians' instruments were set up: guitars, drums, a piano.

'Must be solar powered,' Bradley said.

I'd surmised the same conclusion; our minds were still working in unison.

'Come on, let's get back to the bungalows,' I said.

Stepping from the darkened room and into the sunlight caused us to shield our eyes momentarily. To the side of the building was a large shipping container, next to that was a small caravan. The door was open, but there was no one inside. Similar to the recording studio but portable, inside were monitors, recording equipment and a desk, which we assumed belonged to Margo. Jill and Toby, who were still in our wake, confirmed this.

After rounding the main building and emerging from the opposite side, we found Phil sitting outside the first bungalow. With an expression as sharp as an axe, it was safe to assume the family meeting hadn't gone too well.

Margo and camera crew #1 were backing away down the path.

'Hey Scotty,' Phil said wearily.

'Hey Phil.'

'What are you up to?' Perking up, he straightened his back.

'Just having a look around.'

'Good, good. Dinner shouldn't be too far away.'

'Cool.'

'Feel free to continue exploring. I need to get into the studio.'

'No worries. Listen, uhm … it must have been a shock when you saw Stella Morris getting off the bus.'

'It was.' He'd made his way out of the front yard and was standing next to us now.

'So, Alex didn't tell you she was coming?'

'No, she did not. But it's all good.'

'I notice there's no one here from the record company.'

'*Ahh*,' he waved a dismissive hand through the air. 'They just don't see the vision.'

'So, what …? They've pulled out and you're going it alone?'

'We're talking about INSEXT, Scott. We don't need them. Now if you'll excuse me.' He breezed past us, heading towards the studio.

Maeve Sexton sat in an outdoor chair in the little garden of the next building. Like her ex-husband, Dhani, she also greeted me warmly. 'Hello Scott.'

'Hi Maeve, this is my friend Bradley.'

'Oh, what happened to Elvis?'

'He couldn't come.'

'That's a shame. Well, it's nice to meet you, Bradley. No doubt you'll be spending some time with us girls while the boys play.'

Desperately trying not to laugh, I looked away.

'Can you believe that woman, Scott?' Maeve asked, lowering her voice.

'Stella, you mean?'

'Yes. Why on earth would she be here?'

'Don't know. Does it make you angry?'

'Angry, yes. But it's Sasha I worry about. She's got enough on her plate.'

'Because of Margo being here, you mean?' It was two years since her husband's death, so I doubted she was still in mourning.

'Margo? Who's Margo?'

'Margo Mills, the producer.'

'What's she got to do with anything?'

Didn't she know about the affair? 'Oh nothing. I just mean with all this reality TV stuff.'

'Oh gosh, no, she's used to all that. She was once one of the biggest models in the world, you know.'

'Yes, yes, of course.'

After a few minutes of idle chit chat, we made our excuses and continued on our way.

In the next bungalow was Sasha Coburn. When she saw us approaching, she stood from her outdoor chair and retreated into the building.

'Charming,' Bradley said.

The door to the next bungalow was open, but there didn't appear to be anyone inside. It wasn't hard to surmise that this belonged to Tyler.

When we approached the next building, Stella appeared on the doorstep. *Had Alex planned to put her so close to the Sextons?* Of course she had.

'Hi Stella.'

She marched down the path. 'What are you doing here, Scott?'

'I was invited.'

'Are you still thinking of investigating Bobby's death?'

'Maybe.'

I wasn't sure if she'd expected me to deny it, but as if suddenly remembering the camera crew, her demeanour changed. 'Well, I think that's great. Finally, we can prove Ray's innocence.'

Was she playing up to the camera? I wasn't about to let it go. 'You've changed your tune.'

'What do you mean?'

'Last time we spoke, you were quite hostile.'

'That's because, after everything that's happened, I'm not a very trusting person. Last I saw, you were in the news for accepting an award for being the Gold Coast's most eligible bachelor. That's hardly credible, Scott.'

Even though I didn't take the nomination seriously, she had a point.

'Are you truly serious about helping my husband?'

'Yes, of course.'

'Okay. Well … I'll help you in any way I can then.'

The dinner gong sounded.

55

Like Mayans, summoned to a sacrificial ceremony, or Christians following the church bells on a Sunday morning, we wandered towards the main building on mass. Stella placed her arm in mine.

When we ascended the steps, gentle Indian music drifting on an air of spicy aromas, met us. Camera crew #2 moved to the opposite side of the building while Chris filmed us approaching from the top of the steps, with Margo and Tim on either side of him.

Mr Patel bowed his head graciously and invited us to the table with a sweeping hand.

At one end of the table, Phil and Dee were already seated. Maeve and Sasha took the seats to their right. Dhani headed to the other end. Tyler sat to his left.

Hmm, which end should we sit at? Remaining diplomatic, I led Bradley to the centre of the table and dobbed down onto a cushion. Interestingly, Stella broke away and sat next to Dhani on his right.

Tommy Platt and Lax sat opposite us. The band took up the places on either side between Tommy and Maeve at Phil's end, while the ex-wives took up the remaining seats at Dhani's end. I didn't see Phil's bodyguard, Frank, anywhere.

When we were all seated, Phil rose from the table and cleared his throat to gain everyone's attention. Camera crew #2 moved stealthily around the table, focusing on the guests while Chris and Tim focused on Phil.

'First, I'd just like to say welcome everyone to Camp Sadie.' He paused for effect, and I wasn't sure if we were expected to

253

applaud. We didn't. 'The next few weeks are going to be very exciting.' Phil continued. 'The last time anything like this took place was in 1968, in a place called Rishikesh in India. He briefly explained the reason for the camp's name, and his expectation that the next INSEXT album would be as big as, if not bigger, than The Beatles' *The White Album*.'

Tyler, Dee, Tommy, and Lax were the only ones offering support with nods of encouragement, while the rest of the congregation's communal expression said, *Yeah, right!*

'For any of you who are Beatles fans,' Phil continued, 'you might recognise the compound that we have created as a homage to that famous camp.'

My speculation was confirmed: the architecture, the layout, the Indian theme.

'Before we get started, I'd like to introduce you to our hosts, Mr and Mrs Patel, and their lovely daughter, Jazmin.'

This time we applauded as Mum joined her husband and daughter in gracious bows of acknowledgement.

'They are here for your every need, but I'd ask you all to be realistic in your requests, please. We'll be undergoing a parsimonious lifestyle over the next few weeks, one of spiritual awakening, creativity and healthy living. All the food will be vegetarian. There will be no alcohol or drugs of any kind allowed in the compound.'

Ex-wife Jo Sexton's expression carried with it signs of desperation at this statement. Angel offered her a reassuring hand.

'There will also be no contact with the outside world and no means of transport back. The nearest property is around forty kilometres. Byron Bay is around seventy.'

Allowing my eyes to follow Phil's gaze as he slowly scanned each of the guests, there were mixed expressions, but none could be described as excited.

Phil continued, 'As our guests, I invite you all to relax and explore ways of expanding your limitations. Starting tomorrow morning at dawn, my father ...' Phil pointed to Dhani with an outstretched hand, '... will facilitate sessions in meditation and yoga. With the meditation, I encourage you to take part in as many sessions as possible. Our aim is to encourage the spiritual creativity that you all possess, and in light of this, there will be a wide range of activities available—music, art, sculpture, sports. Everything is here that you could possibly need.'

'Apart from a bar, internet, TV, a phone, and ...' Surprisingly, it was Zoey, the drummer, who spoke up. 'Is this all about control or what?'

'No, no, not at all. Your creative input will be welcome, sister. I'm merely trying to encourage and nurture an organic approach.'

Mick and Jessie shared a glance. Mick lowered his gaze, shaking his head.

'*The White Album* was a product of LSD. Everyone knows that.' Ex wife Jo said.

Dhani's nod offered support without conviction.

'Trust me, Jo. It was not. This is going to be a spiritual detox. Once we remove the toxins from your body through this spiritual detox, you're going to be amazed at the result.'

Jo's behaviour supported my earlier suspicions. She was craving much more than just a cigarette.

'Why is Stella Morris here?' The question came from Sasha Coburn, Bobby's widow.

Part of being a detective was watching and listening. Over the years, I'd honed the skill of people watching to a fine art. The glance between Phil and Dee was so quick it could easily have been missed, but interpreting its meaning was where the experience kicked in. 'That's what I want to know, Alex!' Phil screamed in silence.

The meal, albeit basic, served with rice, naan bread and poppadums, was a vegetarian curry made from lentils. This information came from Bradley when he noticed me scrutinising the little black beans.

'It's a dahl.'

'Eh?'

'A dahl, they're lentils.'

'Oh right.' I didn't mind spicy food as long as it wasn't too hot. This was just right.

During dinner, we chatted to the guests in our vicinity. While doing so, my peripheral antennae was scanning the rest of the table. Dhani chatted with Stella while Tyler listened in. Tommy Platt remained quiet. Lax was an interesting character, quite intelligent and confident in his conversation. Apart from training for the next Gold Coast marathon, he told us he was writing songs and hoped to record some of his stuff while at the camp.

The ex-wives remained quiet, but Jo's constant glances around the table gave the impression of paranoia, as if she were constantly checking to make sure no one was looking at her.

Conversations at the other end of the table were harder to hear, and I hoped Bradley, who was focusing his attention more that way, was taking inventory.

The evening was pleasant. When the food was cleared away, it was Margo who raised her voice and asked for hush.

'Just to let you know. The cameras are off now for the evening, so feel free to relax. But starting from sun-up tomorrow, they're going to be rolling pretty much 24/7, so you'll need to get used to it.' As if expecting opposition, she paused for a moment before continuing. 'The microphones must always remain around your necks. They're waterproof, so you can wear them in the shower and when swimming. Do you all understand?'

There were more reluctant nods.

'What about when we're in our bungalows?' Maeve asked.

'Of course. Your privacy will be maintained.' Margo's expression brought to mind the fable of the cunning fox.

56

There was a warning about the cockerel. What I hadn't expected was for it to be right outside our bloody window—or so it sounded. The old *cock-a-doodle-doo* would be our daily alarm clock. The only other measure of time would be the position of the sun throughout the day. Until this point, I'd had no interest in this kind of survival skill. Luckily for me, my roommate was taking things a little more seriously. When the cock crowed for the first time, I heard Bradley stir. On the second call, he was up, and I could hear him dressing in the dark.

'Scott, are you awake?'

'No.'

'It's time for the morning meditation.'

'You're not serious?'

'Yes.'

'What time is it?'

'Morning.'

Rolling over, I pulled the pillow over my head. 'The only thing getting me up this early, mate, is a Kirra Point offshore. Ain't no surf around here, bud.'

'We need to integrate.'

He was right. Normally I was a morning person, but for some reason, I didn't feel like getting out of bed that day.

'I'll see you over there.' When he opened the door, the first light of dawn spilled into the room, carrying with it a shiver of cool air.

I knew, of course, that there was no getting back to sleep. *Bugger.* I was wide awake now. So, like Bradley, I quickly threw on the pant suit that I'd discarded the night before, and headed out.

By the time I reached the main building, a cool orange hue was creeping through the trees and the random calls of stirring bird life echoed through the forest.

Seated cross-legged on the raised platform was a group in a semi-circle around Dhani. With their eyes closed and their backs straight, the collective focus was on the ageing hippies' gently spoken words that I couldn't quite hear from where I stood. Noting the participants, apart from Bradley, there were Phil and Dee Sexton, Sasha Coburn, Angel, Lax, the band members (minus the drummer, Zoey), and Tyler. There was no sign of Maeve, Stella, Jo, or Tommy.

Both camera crews were hovering slowly around the group while Margo was writing something on a clipboard.

A collective, *'Ohmmmmmmm,'* drifted and seemed to vibrate with the morning air like the gentle hum of an overladen fridge. After deciding it was too late to join the group, I headed back towards my bungalow. Margo, perhaps after deciding that tagging along with me was a better proposition, joined me. Chris and Tim followed.

'Good morning,' Margo said.

'Good morning.'

'Where are you headed now?'

'I'm just going back for a kip.' Seeing as no one else was stirring, and there was no sign of breakfast yet, I'd figured that was the only option available.

Directing her eyes beyond me, Margo added a gentle nod.

Following her gaze, I noticed the young drummer, Zoey, walking towards us. She was carrying what appeared to be her other set of clothing folded in her arms.

'Hey,' her greeting was typical mono Y-gen. 'Do you know where the laundry is?'

'Zoey, isn't it?'

She nodded impatiently, and I wasn't sure if her awkward disposition was from talking with an old geezer, or the camera crew filming us.

Today was to be all about getting to know everyone, to gain as much information regarding the case as possible, and although Zoey didn't really know Bobby, she knew the band, so standing over a coin-op washing machine for an hour was a chance of getting to know her. 'I haven't seen it, but it would have to be near the kitchen somewhere. Mind if I join you?' I hadn't considered until now that with only two changes of clothes, a daily wash would be necessary. I hoped there were plenty of washing machines.

Her shrug said, "If you must."

'Great, won't be a tick.' With only a few strides from my digs, I dashed back with Margo and the camera crew in my wake. They even followed me into the building.

'What are you thinking, Scotty?' Margo asked.

I spoke while pulling off the trouser suit and changing into the clean one. Normally, a shower would be the first activity, but the situation was far from normal. 'This will be a good chance to spend some time with one of the band members. I need to gather as much information as possible.'

'What do you think you can learn from Zoey?'

'Well, she's in the inner circle, and she was present at the meeting on the night of Bobby's death.'

'Right, I see.'

Unlike Zoey's, the little bundle under my arm wasn't folded neatly. We headed off, side by side, in silence. As if not digging the quiet, Margo prompted a conversation. 'You look a little uncomfortable, Zoey.'

Zoey shrugged.

'Is it the camera crew, or being with a detective that's making you uneasy?'

'This whole situation isn't actually normal, is it? I'm a session drummer, not a prima donna.' The glance in my direction qualified the statement with, "Not like some."

'Are you a prima donna, Scotty?' Margo asked with a smirk.

I stopped walking, lifted a hand, and sliced it across my throat. 'Can we cut for a moment?'

'Sure,' Margo said, nodding at the cameraman.

'Can you back off with the questions please, Margo? That's *my* job, remember?'

'Is that all you want to do?' Zoey said. 'Interrogate me?'

From the red light on the camera, I realised it was still running. Of course it was.

'Look, you know why I'm here,' I said to the young drummer. 'I'm sure you've all figured it out, but I *am* conducting an investigation, so I'll be speaking to you all.'

The shrug again. 'I don't know what I can say. That'll be of any help.'

We resumed walking.

'You know the band. You were present at the meeting that night. You know Phil.'

Noticing a slight grin when I mentioned Phil's name, I was about to follow up when we reached the main building. With the meditation session, albeit silent, still in progress, we made our way to the back of the structure. Poking my head in the kitchen to see the Patels preparing what I hoped was breakfast, I enquired about the whereabouts of the laundry. The young woman giggled. The older lady, her mother, didn't look up from stirring a large pot. Mr Patel followed us out of the building and pointed toward the trees at the back. 'You can wash your clothes down there.' He said, bowing his head graciously.

'Okay, thanks.'

We followed a track leading into the trees that I remembered from my interview the previous day. After a few minutes, the sound of running water attracted our attention.

'You've got to be kidding me,' I said when we reached the bank of the stream.

'What?' Zoey puzzled. 'Do we have to get to the other side? Is the laundry over there?'

With all eyes on Margo, she looked away, blushing.

'I'm afraid not. This *is* the laundry,' I said.

'But …? How can it be?'

'Watch.' Kneeling by the riverbank, I could clearly see the bottom. The depth was around a foot at the edges. Opening up the bundle from under my arm, I laid it in the water.

'This is a joke, right?' Zoey said.

'Nope. Come on.' There were shiny boulders just under the surface, which made the current flow a little faster. Picking up the top of my dirty outfit, I slapped it down on one of the rocks like we were on the banks of the Ganges.

'We're expected to wash our clothes in a river?'

I continued to slap the garments on the stone, then lifting a hand-sized boulder, I beat the fabric while dipping it in and out of the water. 'Like this. look,' I said, as if I knew what I was doing.

Zoey reluctantly joined me and mimicked my actions.

'That's it,' I offered with encouragement. 'It's quite therapeutic.'

'Is it?'

'So, what's it like being in the band?' I asked after she slowly came to grips with the process.

The shrug matched the vexed expression. 'It's alright.'

'Do you get on with Phil okay?'

'Kind of.'

'What's the new music like?'

It was the first time I'd seen her smile, but it wasn't a humorous gesture—more sarcastic. 'It's shit.'

'Really?' Industriously, we worked side by side, massaging the fabrics as we spoke. 'In what way?'

'Pathetic might be a better description. Phil's a good muso, but he's no writer.'

'But he's a very successful songwriter, surely?'

'No … it was Bobby who wrote the songs. Phil can't write shit.' Zoey seemed to have no problem sharing her views on camera.

'And you know this how?'

'Well, this is why Phil changes the band's line-up so regularly. He doesn't want the musicians getting too close, knowing the secret. But the original members know.'

'And they've told you this?'

'Didn't have to. I was there that night when Bobby threw us out of his house. Apparently, he was sober for the first time in years. In the past, he'd been banging out the songs while usually intoxicated—handwritten scribbles mostly, and a handful of chords, but masterpieces none the less.'

'So, then Phil would take them and produce them?'

'Yep, pull Bobby out of his box to lay down the vocals, then send him off with a bag of lollies.'

'Drugs?'

'Bobby had no problem with the arrangement as long as it financed his lifestyle.'

'Wow. So, what happened that night? At the meeting?'

'I think Phil was expecting to continue with the same arrangement, but although I'd never met Bobby before, I'd seen the footage, the interviews, read the magazines. But the man who met us at his home that night wasn't what I expected at all.'

'In what way?' I asked while ringing out my clothing in tight, twisted lengths.

'He was alert, articulate and stern. Phil tried to take charge, rambling on about a new album and a world tour, but Bobby was having none of it. Stopping his brother mid-flow, he just said, "It's over, Phil. I'm not going to live this charade a moment longer."'

'How did Phil react to that?'

'He went off big time. Called his brother a worthless piece of shit, who would have been dead years ago if it hadn't been for him bailing him out time after time.'

'Did Bobby fire back?'

'No, he just remained calm. This seemed to fire Phil up even more. He lunged at his brother and swung for him. Bobby stepped back and the band members intervened.'

'Really?'

'Yeah, he can be a nasty bugger, apparently.'

'What happened then?'

Zoey glanced at the camera as if she were considering her next words. 'Bobby said INSEXT was finished and that he would make sure the history of the band was rewritten. That's when Phil went nuts. It took Tommy, Mick and Jessie to hold him back. "I'll fucking kill you first, you ungrateful little bastard," he cried. "Just get out of my house," Bobby said, still calm and in control.'

'It took some doing to push Phil back, but when they got him to the front door, he suddenly relaxed, then left the building without looking back.'

'How come none of this came out at the trial?'

The shrug again as Zoey emulated my method of ringing out her wet clothes. 'Don't know. The police paid little attention to the band, and we didn't want the hassle, I guess. Plus, it was a forgone conclusion that Ray Morris did it.'

'Do you believe that?'

'Why wouldn't I?'

57

Chatting in the private darkness of our bungalow the night before, Bradley and I concluded it would be impossible for us to hide his identity from Margo and the film crew, so we decided to swear them to secrecy instead. It wasn't like Bradley was a regular undercover operative, so his identity wouldn't be compromised once the show was aired. In the meantime, we'd investigate, while conferring regularly without the knowledge of the other guests.

After returning to the bungalow from the stream and hanging out my clean outfit on a line behind the building, I asked to have a private word with Margo. Leaving the camera crew outside, we went into the bungalow. Bradley was just back from his first meditation session.

'No shit, Sherlock!' Margo said when I revealed Bradley's identity.

'You already knew?' Bradley asked.

'Of course. Sticks out like dog balls.'

'Does anyone else know?'

Margo shrugged. 'I don't know.'

'I'll need you to talk to your crew and swear them to secrecy.'

'Not a problem.'

'We'll be discussing sensitive material,' I said. 'You can film it, but you must share none of it until the investigation is complete.'

I could tell Margo's nonchalant attitude was pissing Bradley off by the slight blooming on his cheeks. 'It *will* be a problem if you disregard my instructions. Do I make myself clear?' he added.

'Perfectly.'

'Okay, now we've got that out of that way. How about we take this opportunity to have a little chat?' I said.

Margo frowned. 'About what?'

'About your motive for killing Bobby Sexton.'

Her eyes searched between us. 'Are you kidding me?'

'No.' I went to the front door and gestured for Chris and Tim to enter. 'If we're going to do this the way you want it to be for everyone else, it'll need to be on the record.'

'But I'm the producer. I'm not a part of the investigation, and I'm certainly not under suspicion.'

'You are now. Set up over here, guys. We'll be conducting an interview.'

'I'm in charge around here, not—'

'Sit down,' Bradley said, pointing to his bed.

With visible reluctance, Margo did as she was told.

As if rehearsed, Bradley took charge and spoke in front of the camera. 'I'm Detective Constable Bradley Foster. I'll be investigating the death of Bobby Sexton, while acting undercover with the assistance of Private Detective Scott Stephens.' Turning to Margo, he said. 'Would you like to state your name and occupation, please?'

As if recognising an opportunity to produce groundbreaking television, Margo suddenly perked up. 'My name is Margo Mills. I am an independent producer.'

I was more than happy to stand in the shadows and watch Bradley at work.

'Would you like to tell us how you knew Bobby Sexton?'

'We worked together ... well, sort of.'

'Sort of?'

She went into detail about the documentary she'd pitched to the brothers.

'And is it true you quit your job to work on the venture?'

'Yes ... I burned quite a few bridges.'

'So, what happened when Bobby pulled out?'

When she realised which way the conversation was going, Margo's complexion paled slightly. 'He didn't pull out. He just … went into rehab.'

'From what I'm hearing, the Bobby Sexton who returned was a completely different man to the bum who sought help.'

'How would I know? I didn't get a chance to see or talk to him when he got back.'

'Must have been a real shock when you received the text.' I couldn't help myself.

There was a definite flinch and Margo's eyes searched mine as if asking, "How the hell do you know about the text?" She quickly regained her composure. 'Text?'

'The one Bobby sent you just before he was killed.' Bradley took up the thread.

She shook her head warily. 'I don't know what you're talking about.'

'Margo … I think you do. Did Dobie receive one too?'

'Dobie? What's this got to do with my husband?'

'Did he know about the affair?'

She jumped to her feet. 'What the hell?'

Bradley continued. 'I'm guessing he didn't know. But Bobby was about to change all that, wasn't he?'

'I don't have to stay and listen to this. I won't be saying another word without my solicitor's presence.'

'No worries.' Bradley looked at me. 'I think we've got everything we need, don't you, Scott?'

'I do. For now.'

'Don't attempt to leave the camp, please. I'll need to know your whereabouts at all times.'

'Are you seriously treating me as a suspect?'

'I am. So far, apart from Ray Morris, you're the only other person with a motive.'

'This is ridiculous.' She headed for the door.

'One more thing, Margo, before you go,' I said.

The camera crew was inadvertently blocking her way.

'You live just across the canal from Bobby's house, don't you?'

'So?'

'I remember you said you're quite the paddle boarder.'

She pushed through the crew but paused at the door.

'Wouldn't take much effort to paddle across the canal to Bobby's private jetty.'

She swung open the door and marched out of the bungalow.

After ushering away the crew, Bradley and I stood in silence for a moment, our minds sifting through the information we'd just harvested. Although we hadn't received firm acknowledgement that Margo had received a text, I was 99% sure she had. *But had her husband, Dobie Mills, received one too?* I thought not. If he had, I doubt Margo would have walked away unscathed. As far as I knew, they were still together.

At times like this, when fresh evidence came to light or a new suspect entered the arena, I'd retreat to the whiteboard. An idea came to mind. 'You remember how Phil said he wanted to encourage our creativity?' I said, breaking the silence.

'Yes,' Bradley said.

'I've had an idea.'

Then the gong rang.

<h1 style="text-align:center">58</h1>

At the main building, the long, low table had been moved to the back wall. On it was a variety of fruit, cereals and juices. Angel was in the far corner doing a set of lunges. There was no sign of Jo. Seated cross-legged on cushions were Tyler and Dhani. They ate from wooden bowls as they chatted. The camera crews were buzzing slowly around the space.

To the side of the table stood Jazmin Patel. 'Namaste,' she greeted us, bowing slightly with her hands in prayer.

Under inspection, there was a choice of coconut yoghurt, fruit and cold porridge made with almond milk and local honey. Bradley ate only fruit. I was brave enough to try the porridge. To my surprise, it tasted pretty good, so I loaded up a bowl and filled a tumbler with juice. Then we grabbed a cushion each and joined Tyler and Dhani.

'How's it goin, boys?' I asked, after releasing the cushion from under my arm and negotiating a landing.

'Good …' Tyler hesitated, looking up at the camera hovering above.

'He's missing a few of the home comforts,' Dhani said.

'You and me both,' Bradley remarked, and the two young men's eyes met briefly.

'He'll be fine,' Dhani continued. 'He's moved into my bungalow. I'm the king of survival.'

'Can I join you guys?' It was Mick Mantle, the guitarist.

'Sure, mate.'

He sat down on a vacant cushion. In his hand was a mug of green tea.

'Not eating?'

'Nah. Don't do breakfast. Could do with a smoke, but.'

I didn't have a clue what time it was, early to mid-morning, perhaps. 'When do you start recording?' I asked.

'Already have. Jessie and Zoey are in the studio now. They'll be laying down the bass and drums this morning, so I'm not needed right now.'

'How's it going?'

Mick grinned and took a sip of his tea.

Although Bradley remained quiet, nibbling on his fruit like a gerbil, I knew he was mentally recording every word.

'What's with the grin?' I asked.

'It's going, okay. Well …?'

'What do you mean?'

'Half of the album is good. The half that Bobby wrote. Most of that's already down. Unfortunately, the rest of it is pure Phil Sexton crap.' His glance towards Dhani was the apologetic kind.

Dhani reacted with a knowing nod.

'That's what we're working on now.'

'So, Phil's got some of Bobby's songs?'

'Yeah. Without Bobby here to stop him, he can do what he likes with them. The ridiculous thing is, though, he reckons he might not use them.'

'Really? What, he's just going to work on his own stuff?'

'Apparently.'

'Does Alex know about this?'

'Don't know. It's probably the reason the record company pulled out, though.'

'They've pulled out completely?' This would explain the absence of the executives who we were introduced to at Phil's dinner party.

'Yep. Looks like Phil will be forming an independent label.'

Tyler and Dhani finished eating and excused themselves. Tyler headed towards the recording studio. Dhani went back to his bungalow.

'Can you tell me anything about that night?' I asked Mick. 'Anything that might have been missed in the investigation?'

Mick shook his head and inhaled loudly. A glance at the camera told me he was also contemplating the possible fall out from a candid response. 'Not really, only that Phil's anger was downplayed.' Like Zoey, I guess after realising he had little to lose, he decided to be up front. I hoped everyone here had the same attitude, but I also wondered if Margo had offered incentives for the juiciest information. It would be a clever ploy if she had.

'In what way?'

'Ah, he went apeshit, man. If we hadn't held him back, he would have done his brother some serious harm.'

'Is this something you'd witnessed before?'

'Heck yeah.'

I was trying to build a picture of Phil and Bobby's relationship. Apart from the wives and ex-wives, the band members probably knew them the most. 'Can you tell me what it was like when you were recording back in the day?'

'Sure. In the early days, we didn't have the luxury of home studios or flying out to record in the Bahamas or anything like that. Studios were rented, usually in Brisbane. Phil wasn't your typical rock-n-roller, staying in bed until the afternoon, then working through the night. He wanted us all there bright and early in the morning. Then we'd just work for however long it took. Bobby, however, he *was* a rock-n-roller.' Mick smiled as if he were recalling a certain episode in his mind. 'He'd rock up about two in the afternoon. He'd already be high, and Phil hated that.'

'How would Phil react?'

'He knew he was only going to get a certain amount of work from his brother each day. Once Bobby cracked open the flagon of bourbon, it was all over red rover. And it riled Phil that these small windows were the most productive times.'

'Did Phil write *any* of the songs?'

Mick threw his head back and laughed. 'Sure, but they rarely made the albums. He's a gifted musician, but he can't write.'

'How often did he get violent?'

'Daily. Once Bobby had reached that point where he was no longer coherent, Phil would go to a dark place.'

'Do you think Phil hoped that when Bobby came out of rehab, things would be different?'

'That's exactly what I think. You see, when Bobby was sober, he was a fucking genius, man. 'Passionate Ways'? He picked that song from the air while taking a crap. After humming the melody to Phil, they recorded it that afternoon.'

'You were telling me about that night?'

'Phil had had it all planned in his mind. He'd got the original band back together, apart from Ray, of course, and—'

'How come Ray wasn't invited?'

Mick's expression puckered as he shook his head slowly. 'Not sure, but Phil and Ray never got on. Ray was Bobby's mate, an ally if you like.'

'And Phil didn't like that?'

'No. Divide and conquer.'

'How come that didn't come out in court?'

'We, uhm, didn't really go into that much detail.'

'But if Ray was Bobby's mate, why would he kill him?' Understanding the importance of not breaking Bradley's cover, I purposely didn't look at him.

'*Was* his mate. I knew them both. When Ray was booted out of the band, he blamed Bobby for not backing him up.'

'Did Ray know Bobby was having an affair with his wife?'

Mick shrugged. 'Don't know about that, mate.'

'Did anyone else know?'

'Not that I know of.'

'What did it say in the text you got?'

'Text?' He frowned and shook his head. 'What text?'

'The one Bobby sent you not long after you left his house that night.'

'I didn't receive no text.' There was a definite quiver in his voice.

I wondered if Bradley had picked up on it, too. Mick was lying. 'That's odd because we know everyone else here received one.' *My* lie was of the white variety, of course.

'Not me, but.'

'You would have been present that night at the party when Jimmy Reggae died.'

His shrug harboured a defensive uncertainty. 'Earlier, yeah. But not when … you know …'

'Did Bobby kill Jimmy Reggae?'

'Of course he didn't.'

'Did you?'

59

After breakfast, and with camera crew #2 in tow, Bradley and I made our way to the supply cupboard Phil had mentioned at dinner the night before. It was the shipping container we'd noticed the previous day at the side of the main building. The doors were closed but not locked. The leaver latch sent a grinding grunt through the steel structure as I yanked it out and down. Friction laden hinges issued more complaints when I pulled open one side.

Inside there were art supplies: easels, brushes, paints, as well as a variety of musical instruments: guitars, bongo drums, tambourines, a trumpet, and even a mini harp. A folded table tennis table took up one side. On a shelf rack were a dozen or so old school typewriters and reams of paper.

Knowing what we needed and heading straight for the art supplies, Bradley grabbed a tin of white paint and a couple of smaller bottles of black, while I selected a wide brush and half a dozen finer ones.

Once back inside our bungalow, we set to work. After stirring the white paint with a stick, I painted a rectangle square on the breeze-block wall between the front door and the window. We'd chosen this wall because it wouldn't be visible from the outside when the door was open.

'What are you doing?' asked Jill from behind the camera.

'We're setting up a whiteboard,' Bradley said, placing the black paint and the finer brushes along the wall.

'And will this help with the investigation?'

'Yes, but your questions won't.' Bradley spoke with authority. 'We need you to remain quiet and, once again, everything Scott and I discuss must be of the utmost confidentiality. Do you understand?'

Jill and Toby nodded, but I realised there was an issue we had overlooked.

'Does Margo get to see everything you film?' I asked.

'Yes. She's the producer,' Toby said.

'Would it be possible to withhold any of the footage from her?'

The two young people looked at each other, then shrugged.

'I suppose,' Jill said.

'We need anything that we discuss regarding Margo to remain confidential.'

'I can store footage in a separate file. She wouldn't have to know of its existence.'

'Good. Once the investigation is over, all the footage will likely be examined by the Queensland Police before being released, anyway. Is that right, Bradley?'

'That's right, but there's a chance it might never be released.'

Although the high humidity was an unwelcome guest, it helped the paint dry. Tapping the wall with my fingertips after only a few minutes confirmed that we were ready to make our first list. 'What do you reckon? Main suspect?' I already knew whose name I wanted to place at the top, but Bradley's input was just as important.

'The only threatening behaviour towards Bobby on that night that we know of so far was from Phil!'

'Does that warrant putting him at the top of the list, though?'

'For now, and due to a lack of evidence, yes, I believe it does.'

My nod confirmed we were on the same page. Shaking one of the small black bottles, then twisting off the lid, I used one of the finer brushes to write Phil's name at the top of the board.

Normally, we would include photographs, but that wasn't possible. 'Was Bobby about to expose him as a fake? Was INSEXT really finished? How would it affect Phil if he realised his life's work was about to be pulled apart?'

'And could it be possible that Bobby had something else over him?'

'Zoey May told me that Phil controlled the purse strings and was happy to keep Bobby in an inebriated state, even though it pissed him off no end when they were working.'

'Did the sober Bobby feel cheated? Or was there more to it? Did Phil really have control over the money?'

'*Hmm*, the only way to find out is to keep digging. Next …' I glanced at the camera crew before continuing. 'Margo Mills?'

'Yes. This time yesterday, she wasn't even on the radar. It's only recently come to light that she'd had an affair with Bobby, and then there was the documentary,' Bradley said.

'Here's a likely scenario,' I said, stirring the fine brush in the black paint. 'Margo is set to produce and direct the docco. To do so she quits her job and breaks all ties with the people who mattered in her career. On top of this, she falls in love with Bobby Sexton and cheats on her husband, a powerful and ruthless man.'

'But then Bobby goes into rehab and Margo hears nothing from him until she receives a text the night he was killed.'

'So far, we only have proof that Ray and Dhani received texts,' Bradley interjected. 'The fact that anyone else may have is pure speculation.'

'That's right, but if we continue with the hypothesis that there were more texts sent, things might look a little different.'

'What would Margo's message have contained?' Bradley asked reflectively.

'If the exercise was part of Bobby's 12-point program, a therapeutic tool designed to rid himself of his conscience, confess his sins if you like, while seeking redemption, his text to Margo, killing the documentary and exposing their affair, would have had a disastrous effect on the girl.'

'She could easily have paddled over from her place across the canal, unnoticed in the dark.'

'That's right.' I wrote Margo's name under Phil's.

'What about Dobie, her husband? Could he have received a text also? If so, he could have had Bobby killed.'

'It would make sense, but I doubt Margo would have got away with having an affair behind his back. Remember who we're dealing with here. Legend has it that there are more bodies entombed in Gold Coast concrete than there are buried in Rookwood Cemetery.'

'Agreed. And I doubt Bobby would have his phone number. Next?'

The next name I wrote started with a capital S. 'Sasha Coburn.'

'Right. Bobby was going to divorce her. I did some digging yesterday and found a string of poor investments. Mostly fashion start-ups and cosmetics. A bit gullible, me thinks. When you realise also that her ex-employer sued her for pretty much every penny she'd ever earned, it's not hard to work out that if it wasn't for Bobby, she'd be broke!'

'There was a prenuptial in place, so if Bobby left her, he'd be taking his money with him. However, she was listed as joint benefactor with Maeve in Bobby's will, so the only way she'd get her hands on his money would be on his death.'

'Interesting. Next?'

'Do we know anything about Maeve?' Once again, my knowledge was limited to what I could find on the internet. Although unlikely, I wondered if Bradley had found anything on her.

'Only that she has no other source of income apart from a generous allowance from Bobby.'

'What about Phil? He'd be looking after his mum, surely,' I said.

'Apparently not. Not sure why, but the house, the Brisbane apartment, the cars and just about everything Maeve has belonged to Bobby. There is no record of Phil's input.'

'Dhani said she also received a text. This is what alerted me to the fact that there were likely more. If this was the case, did Bobby announce that he'd be taking everything back?'

'Let's suppose he did. How would she react to the fact that she was about to lose everything? Would she be capable of killing her son?'

'Hmm, dunno.' The M in Maeve's name fell on one of the mortared joints between the blocks and looked a little skewy.

'Next would have to be the ex-wives, I guess,' Bradley said.

'Did you find anything on them?'

'Jo was the first wife. She met Bobby while they were still at school, fell pregnant when they were in their late teens, got married, but then she miscarried. She was with Bobby through all the early years right up to the time of the Jimmy Reggae incident.'

'She was there that night?'

'Yes, but there were others there too, the band and a bevvy of girls, apparently. There are a couple of things that might be important, though. She received a substantial payout from the divorce, and she continues to draw a healthy allowance from Bobby's estate. However, she has been nicked on a couple of occasions for possession.'

'Is she an addict, do you think?'

'It's likely.'

'And Bobby's money is still funding it. How would an addict react if they suddenly learned their supply was about to be cut off?'

'Gee, I wish we had access to Bobby's phone,' Bradley said.

In order of age, I wrote Jo's name above Angel's.

'Angel seems like a nice person, and although she signed a prenuptial when she married Bobby, she seemed to come out of the marriage alright,' Bradley said.

I shared with Bradley what I'd learned about Angela's meteoritic rise in the fitness industry and how she'd amassed a not too shabby fortune.

'Could she have stolen from Bobby to get the business running?'

'Maybe. And if in Bobby's new era of sobriety, he decided to take legal action against her, would that give her the motive to kill him?'

'Before we move on,' Bradley said, 'it's interesting that the ex-wives have bonded.'

'Could they have acted together?'

'Possibly. We'll need to talk to them separately and then again together to see if their story changes. I'll get to know them too. Win their confidence and see if I can't prize any extra information from them.'

'My thoughts exactly. Next?'

'We can't rule out the fact that Jack Morris had possession of the knife.'

'True.' Although he was deceased, I wrote down his name anyway. 'What about Alex?'

'Motive?'

'If Bobby quit the band, she'd be losing her main cash cow.'

'Would that matter? She's super rich, anyway.'

'Not unless there's something we don't know. Like a lot of these people, perhaps Bobby had something over her. He was a different person when he came out of rehab.'

'Put her up, we'll dig deeper.'

'Who's next?'

'The band I guess.'

Although I wasn't convinced they had a motive, I included the names of Mick Mantle and Jessie Flint. My reasoning for being unsure was that if they had a beef with anyone, it would have been with Phil for treating them so badly. Their recollections of Bobby, it seems, were of the affectionate kind. However, I couldn't help feeling there was more to the Jimmy Reggae's death. Something, perhaps, that they weren't telling us.

'Everyone on this list had dealings with Bobby,' I said, 'so there's likely to be details we haven't unearthed yet. The only way we're going to find out is by talking with them.'

'I'm going to approach this as the caring confidant,' Bradley said. 'Get to know them all on a more personal level. Ask them how they feel about being a part of this ridiculous investigation, that sort of thing.'

'Yeah, and I'll adopt the pushy private detective persona. Get in their faces a bit. Throw around a few accusations and see what reactions we get.'

'Pushy persona?' Bradley grinned. 'That's not a persona.'

60

When we returned to the main building, the scene brought to mind a scenario somewhere between that of a typical youth club and my stay at 'The Door of Eden' health club in Tally Valley. Tyler and Lax were playing table tennis. Tommy seemed to be happy watching them. Dhani was giving Angel a massage. Maeve and Sasha, it seemed, had formed a knitting group. Stella sat alone, reading. There was no sign of Jo. At the back of the room, Mr Patel and his daughter, Jazmin, were tidying away the breakfast dishes. Margo, Chris and Tim must have been filming in the studio. Jill and Toby were recording the table tennis.

To divide and conquer was the course of action, mingle with the guests, talk to them, and listen. With a little more feminine sensibility than me, Bradley headed towards Maeve and Sasha.

While deciding who to talk to first, I made my way to the back table, hoping I could score some orange juice before it was too late.

Mr Patel had disappeared into the kitchen while, to my relief, his daughter was replenishing the jugs.

'Hi. Jazmin, right?'

From her quiet disposition and lack of eye contact, it wasn't difficult to suppose the young woman was shy, and although I hadn't heard her speak, I assumed she understood English. She nodded and smiled.

Thankfully, the camera crew hadn't noticed my arrival and continued to film the table tennis tournament. 'You seem to be working terribly hard.'

'Yeah, but it's all good. I don't mind.'

My assumption was way off; she didn't speak English nor was she shy. She spoke full-on Australian. My startled expression made her giggle.

'You're an Aussie?'

'Yeah. Lived here for most of my life.'

'Sorry, I didn't realise. I uhm—'

'It's okay.'

Unfortunately, my attempt to change the subject came out just as patronising. 'So, you work with your parents?'

'No, I'm a third-year medical student.' Once again, my reaction made her smile. 'I'm studying in the UK, but home for a short break. Thought it would be fun to help out the olds.'

'The UK. Wow!'

'Yes. Oxford.'

My next question wasn't meant to be rude or patronising, but it kind of was. 'Sounds expensive. How does a butler and a cook afford to send their daughter to Oxford?'

The smile again. 'Mr Sexton pays for my education. He's a very generous man.'

'Phil?'

'Yes.'

'So, you obviously know the Sextons very well.'

'Not that well, really. Even though we lived in their house, my sister and I were at boarding school in Victoria for most of our childhood. Mr Sexton was away touring. My father travelled everywhere with him, so did Mrs Sexton. For most of our school holidays, we had the house to ourselves with Mum.'

'You have a sister?'

The smile disappeared, replaced instead with an air of sadness. 'Had. She died.'

'Oh, I'm so sorry to hear that.'

'Thank you … I—'

Mr Patel reappeared, and when he saw me talking to his daughter, he politely intervened. 'Mr Stephens. Is there anything I can get you?'

'No thanks. I'm fine,' I said, holding up a glass of orange juice.

Jazmin slipped away, back to the kitchen.

'Mr Patel, could I have a word please?'

'Yes, of course. What can I do for you?' With only a hint of an Indian intonation, his accent was upper class English.

'How long have you worked for Mr Sexton?'

'I have worked for the Sexton family for just over twenty years now, sir.'

'Are you happy in your work?'

'Very.'

'What's Phil Sexton like to work for?'

'He is a very generous man. He has been extremely good to my family.'

'Did you work for Bobby too?'

'Yes.'

'And?'

'And?' He busied himself arranging the jugs and glasses as he spoke.

'What was he like to work for?'

'He needed someone to look after him.'

'And is that what you did?'

'Yes, sir.' Each time he spoke, he bowed his head slightly as if he were about to terminate the conversation and back away.

'What kind of things did you help him with?'

'Anything that was required.'

'Did you ever supply him with drugs?'

'What?' When he straightened up and puffed out his chest, he seemed to grow in height by at least a foot. 'How dare you ask me such a question?' He stepped towards me.

'I'm sorry, I didn't mean anything—'

Mr Patel's whole demeanour had instantly changed from one of gentle patience to intimidating anger. 'If I'd ever found out who was bringing drugs into this family, I would have killed them with my bare hands.' He held up his large hands and clenched his fists.

'You're very protective of the family.'

'Not *the* family, *my* family. I would protect them with my life!'

'I understand. I'm sorry if my questions upset you.'

'And I understand you have a job to do.' He took a deep breath, deflated somewhat and continued to rearrange the jugs that didn't need rearranging. 'I am sorry for my outburst.'

'I'm just trying to piece together a picture of the real lives of the Sexton brothers. How did you come to be working for them?'

'While working as a VIP butler at a prestigious hotel in Prague, I was assigned to work for a group of very important guests for one week. Until they arrived, I had no knowledge of the Sextons or the band, INSEXT.'

'What were they like then?'

'Mr Sexton was a businessman, very driven. We bonded because we shared a need for perfection.'

'Perfection as in?'

'Mr Sexton expected things to be how he wanted them, from his trousers pressed in a certain way to his orange juice served at a certain temperature.'

'And you were able to supply those things.'

'Correct. Mr Sexton had been searching for someone who understood him and who wouldn't let him down.'

'So, he employed you?'

'Yes, sir. And my wife.'

'And he helped you to come to Australia?'

'Yes, sir. He is a very generous man!'

'You testified in your court appearance that Phil Sexton was at home with Tommy Platt at the time of Bobby's death.'

'Yes, sir. That is true.'

'Could you have been mistaken?'

'No, sir. I remember because I served them brandy in Mr Sexton's study while my wife prepared a cold supper.'

'Was Mr Sexton angry?'

'Oh yes. Furious and upset.'

'Had you seen him like that before?'

'Yes, sir. Mr Sexton expected things to go his way at all times.'

'And when they didn't?'

'I'm afraid I must get back to the kitchen now, Mr Stephens.'

'Yeah, no worries. Thank you. You've been very helpful.'

'Hello, Scotty,' Maeve said as I approached the little knitting group.

Bradley seemed to have fitted right in and was busily concentrating on his purl loop. Sasha remained quiet, but seemed proficient enough in her knitting style to look away.

'I'm good, thanks, Maeve. How's the new bloke going?' I nodded towards Bradley.

'He's doing very well.'

'What ya knitting Bradders?' I asked, trying hard not to laugh.

'A gag for you.'

'Ouch, touchy.'

Stella Morris was keeping herself to herself, engrossed in a book. Dhani and Angel's massage, it seemed, had ended, and neither of them were longer present. The table tennis was of little interest, so there was only one place left to go.

Margo, Chris and Tim were already in the studio doing their thing. Margo's expression lifted from one of boredom to a welcome distraction when I entered the small reception area. Phil was seated with his hands spread out over the enormous console. The band was in the recording booth, visible through the window opposite.

'Okay, do it again.' Looking into the booth, Phil spoke through a microphone. 'But this time, for fuck's sake, try to do what you're being paid for.'

The band looked at each other with ashen faces while Phil counted them in. The song began with a crescendo of drums and a heart thudding bass line.

'How's it going?' I asked no one in particular.

'Like shit,' Margo whispered.

There was a glass partition wall between the reception and the studio. 'Should I go in?' I asked Margo.

'Heck yeah.'

'Will he mind?'

'Heck yeah.'

The mutual grin between us acknowledged a shared intent for stirring the pot.

Like a pressurised escape hatch, there was an audible *shlump* when I opened the door and the sound from within spewed out. 'Hey, Phil. How's it going, mate?' I asked, taking the vacant seat at the console. The room was tiny, but Margo and her crew still managed to cram themselves in.

'It's going awesome. Super busy at the moment, though. What can I do for you?'

'Ah, I just thought I might observe if that's okay. I've never been in a recording studio before.'

'Okay. Just keep quiet and don't get in the way, yeah?'

'No worries.'

He suddenly slammed his thumb onto a button on the console and yelled into the microphone. 'Stop, stop, stop. For fuck's sake.'

The band stopped playing, and I noticed the drummer hit the skins hard with frustration.

'Are you guys kidding me?'

'What's the problem now, Phil?' Mick, the guitarist, asked, his echoey voice coming through the speakers in the control room.

'The problem is, mate, I'd forgotten how shit you guys are. No wonder we gave you all the flick.'

Wow. I wasn't expecting that. To be honest—and what the hell did I know?—it sounded pretty good.

'Try it again. This time with my vocals.' After a count of four, the band began playing once more. Phil raised a sliding switch, and a voice integrated into the music. Fuck me, it was Saturday night at Tugun Surf Club. Karaoke at its worst, or as Tetley would say, Krappyoki.

This time, the band got through the entire song, and the look of relief on their faces matched mine. Although I hadn't listened to Phil's last solo album, I knew now why it flopped.

'What do you think, Scotty?' Phil asked with a smug expression that said, "I already know it's absolutely brilliant, but I just need to hear it!"

'Uhm … yeah …'

'What?' It was a question loaded with an intensity that appeared from nowhere.

'It's … different.'

'You don't like it?'

'Uhh … it's alright.' As well as the camera lens, I could feel Margo's stare burning into me. When I glanced her way, she gave me an encouraging nod that said, "Go on, give it to him."

'Not *my* cup of tea, but—'

'What the fuck do you know about music?' The intimidation that came with wealth and power was harnessed and delivered with perfection.

'I know what I like.' I wasn't about to back down like everyone else around him seemed to.

'Yeah right, pub rock, Acca Dacca, Sky Hooks and the fucking Angels.'

My wobbly nod was purposely nonchalant and annoying at the same time. 'I know good music when I hear it.'

'Oh right, okay, a connoisseur.' He looked around at Margo and the camera like a bully rallying support for an impending onslaught. Then he pressed another button and moved a couple of slides on the console. The sound of a beautiful acoustic guitar drifted from the speakers. 'So, tell me what you think of this.'

'Sounds good.' *Oops, I spoke too soon.* When the wailing vocal began, it killed the song dead in the water. 'Oh.'

My startled reaction caused Phil's fists to clench. 'What?'

Now it was my turn to rally the troops for support. The encouraging nod again from Margo prompted me on. 'It's shit, mate!'

61

Regardless of the fame, the power and the wealth, if the verbal abuse escalated into physical violence, I was ready to put Phil Sexton on his arse. The response to my honest critique was unexpected. The theme of his retaliation was pretty much, 'What the fuck do you know about music? Who the fuck are you, anyway? Why the fuck are you here?' Charming. When asked to leave the studio in no uncertain terms, I was happy to oblige. I'd got what I came for. I'd witnessed first-hand the infamous temper that I'd been told about. Interestingly, the camera crew following me out only seemed to make him worse. A tirade of abuse escorted us through the exit.

'I saw what you did there, Scott,' Margo said.

'Yeah? What was that then?' I was marching back around to the front of the main building with Margo and her crew racing to keep up.

'You purposely provoked him. I haven't seen anyone talk to him like that before. Why'd you do it?'

'To see if the reports of his erratic behaviour were accurate or not.'

'And your conclusion?'

'He's a firey bugger alright.'

'Could an anger like that escalate?'

'Absolutely.'

At the main building, Dhani was now sitting cross-legged on a cushion, playing chess with Tyler. The ex-wives had joined Maeve and Bradley's little knitting group. Stella was no longer present.

Tommy Platt and Lax sat opposite each other, strumming gently on acoustic guitars. There was a tambourine on the ground between them.

'Hey guys, mind if I join you?'

Tommy looked up, shrugged and nodded.

When Lax shuffled around on his backside, I grabbed a cushion and put it down in the space he'd created.

'I'm not much of a muso,' I said, picking up the tambourine.

Too engrossed in their guitars to listen, Tommy was finger picking while Lax gently strummed. So, picking up on the fourth beat, I tapped the tambourine across the heel of my hand. Lax's chord changes, alternating instinctively with Tommy's picking, sounded pretty good, while my mono beat may have lacked a little aptitude.

I needed to engage in conversation and if that meant ruffling a few feathers, then so be it. 'I was in the studio just now.'

No response.

'Jeez, Phil went right off, eh … I'm amazed the band puts up with that kind of behaviour …'

Lax looked up, but Tommy didn't meet his eyes.

'You guys would have been witness to a lot of that, I bet?'

Lax returned his attention to quite a tricky chord change.

'I'm wondering how much abuse Bobby had to endure.'

'Bobby could handle Phil,' Lax said.

'Did they fight much?'

'All the time.'

'That's the process,' Tommy said, still without looking up.

'What, Phil gets to bully everyone around?'

'No, he pushes hard and gets results. Everyone performs better when under a bit of pressure.'

'Physical violence though?'

'Nah, never. Phil can be aggressive, but he means well.'

Always watching, analysing, picking up on the tiniest reaction, Lax's frown told me he didn't agree with Tommy's assessment. 'You don't agree, Lax?'

'Phil can be a prick. I've seen him hit out on more than one occasion.' Lax spoke freely, as if the camera crew weren't there.

'Did you ever see him hit Bobby?'

'Yeah, all the time—'

Tommy strummed his guitar hard and stopped playing. 'Lax, shut the fuck up, eh?'

'What are you hiding, Tommy?' I asked.

'Mate, just leave it. Phil's a good bloke.'

'So far Phil is the only one who—' My attention was suddenly redirected when Zoey, the young drummer, stormed onto the platform. In her wake was Jessie, the bass player, followed by Mick, the guitarist.

Like flies heading for a juicier carcass, the camera crew left us. No one else was paying much attention, but my antenna was at full mast. Jessie reached for the young woman's shoulders and turned her around.

'Zoey, come on. It's all good.'

'All good? Are you serious?'

'It's okay, you'll get used to it. He's just—'

'He's just a bully, that's what he is.'

In my peripheral vision, I noticed Lax was also watching while Tommy continued with his finger picking.

'That's Phil. I did warn you about his temper,' Jessie said in a fatherly tone.

'I don't … *we* don't have to put up with that shit.'

The glance between Jessie and Mick said, "Well, actually we do."

When Zoey pulled away and headed to her bungalow, Mick sauntered back to the studio while Jessie followed Zoey.

62

Phil appeared and fixed himself a drink of water at the back of the room.

I was torn between following Zoey and Jessie, or approaching Phil to wind him up a little more to see how deep his anger really went. The latter option was too good to miss, so I wandered over to the water station. 'Hey Phil.'

Phil turned, and in place of the angry snarl, his expression was one of sorrow. 'Hey Scotty, listen man, I'm so sorry about back there.'

'You should be.'

'I know, I know.' He threw back a mouthful of water. 'I get like that.'

'So that happens a lot?' I wasn't about to let him off the hook.

'Only when things aren't going right. I get frustrated.'

'Is that how it was with Bobby?'

'Oh yeah. Bobby was … let's say … annoying.'

'But it was Bobby who was the musical *genius,* not you!' *Ouch.* That was a direct hit.

There was a gentle *whir* over my shoulder as the camera lens zoomed in on Phil's fractured facade.

'Are you trying to provoke me?'

'Is that what you think? If someone has a difference of opinion, they're a provocation?'

'Wow … why did we ask you here again?'

'To find the truth, remember? To find out what really happened to Bobby.'

'What, so you think I killed my brother?' His chuckle was void of humour.

'You're at the top of the list so far, mate.' I noticed Margo cringe, but I could tell from her intense expression that she was loving every moment.

'Are you serious?'

'If I was still a police detective, I'd be bringing you in for questioning.'

'Good job you're not then, eh? Thank God you're just a TV fake!'

I wasn't about to get sucked into a tit-for-tat slagging match. 'What really happened on that night?'

Phil shrugged nonchalantly. 'I'm sure you've read my police statement.'

'Yes.'

'So why are you asking?'

'Because I don't believe it.'

The fleeting frown told me I was slowly breaking through his armour, but I have to admit he was handling himself pretty well to say I was practically accusing him of killing his brother.

'And what is it that *you* think happened?'

'I *know* you received a text from Bobby shortly after leaving his place.'

His shocked expression was a dead giveaway. As on the other occasions when I'd claimed to know about the elusive texts, there had been subtle reactions. On this occasion, though, Phil's questioning eyes told me he definitely *had* received a text.

'Must have been a shock. You were already fired up when you left. Is that why you went back?'

'I don't have a clue what you're talking about.'

'I think you do. Not only was INSEXT finished, but Bobby was threatening to take back what belonged to him. The songs, the royalties.'

'That's all bullshit.' Phil's expression hardened but remained non-committal.

'Did you fly into another of your uncontrollable rages and kill him?'

Tommy Platt joined us. 'Is everything okay here?'

'Everything's good, Tommy,' Phil said. He finished his water then glanced at myself and Margo as if he were about to add a comment but then decided against it. Instead, he bowed his head and headed back towards the studio.

'So, Tommy.' I was in the groove. Directing my attention back to the road manager, I asked, 'Did you lie to cover up for him? Or was it you that went back to Bobby's?'

'What?'

Not sure if his reply was due to the deafness, I carried on, but spoke a little louder. 'You said you were with Phil at his home at the time of Bobby's death, but that wasn't true, was it?'

Unlike Phil's expression, Tommy's was easy to read. Anger blazed across his face like a caustic flame. I was purposely taunting him, and it was working.

'I went back to Phil's place, and we sat up late talking.'

'What if I could prove otherwise?' I was wandering into the realm of pure fiction again. There was no proof that Tommy had lied, and I certainly had no evidence to back the claim that either of them returned to Bobby's house. The only tool available to me at the moment was the stirring stick, which I was wielding with all my might.

Tommy grinned. 'You're full of shit.'

'I read the text you received from Bobby that night. Does Lax know Bobby was his father?'

The grin slipped away, and I got the impression he was about to grab me by the throat.

Regardless, I continued on. 'Is that why you killed him? To maintain the secret?'

Tommy leaned in and lowered his voice. 'You're way off, mate … Lax is *my* son, and I'm not a killer … but if one of the Sexton boys was, it wasn't Phil.'

Disengaging from my desperate little going-no-where performance, Tommy's words suddenly stole my attention. 'What does that mean?'

'You're the detective.' He walked away.

It's hard to think with a camera crew recording your every move, but I have to admit I was getting used to them being around and was gradually finding it easier to relax and be myself. In private, I had the habit of talking to myself out loud when pondering over a certain aspect of a case. 'What did he mean by that?' I asked, throwing out the question but not expecting a reply. 'Was he referring to the death of Jimmy Reggae?'

From where I was standing, I could see Jessie Flint standing outside Zoey's bungalow. I had yet to have a one-on-one chat with him, so decided to take the opportunity. It was only a short stroll.

'Hey Jessie, what's happening?' I asked, stepping into the small yard out front.

'Ahh, you know how it is, Scott. Phil can be hard to work with at times.'

'Zoey seemed pretty upset.'

Jessie nodded. 'She's not used to him like we are.'

'What happened?'

'Not a lot. That's the problem. The new stuff Phil's working on just isn't cutting it. You heard it.'

'I did.' There was no argument from me.

'Zoey suggested Phil listen to something she was working on.' He looked at the door affectionately in a parental way. 'Phil agreed to listen, but me and Mick knew exactly what was coming next.'

'Phil rejected it.'

'He never listened to ideas from the band, never mind a song, but she played what she had. And you know what? It was good. Bloody good. Mick and I fell in with it and started jamming.'

'How did Phil react?'

'While we played, he just sat there stewing. Kept checking the console or looking for other things to occupy his mind. But he was listening.'

'Then what?'

'After a while, he waved a hand for us to stop then said through the mic, "Okay, let's get back to the real music now." Zoey stood up and stormed out.'

'And you followed.'

'Yeah, she's a good kid. Talented you know.'

'So, what's going to happen to the album?'

'There is no album,' Jessie said. 'This is all just a joke. A television spectacle.'

'But you're going to continue recording?'

He smiled. 'That's what he's paying us for.'

With my antennae now permanently at full mast, I asked the inevitable question. 'Tell me about the text you received on the night of Bobby's death.' Surprisingly, employing the full resources of my focus on his reaction proved unwarranted.

'You know about that?'

At last, confirmation that the texts existed. 'I do, mate. Must have been a shock.'

'It was, but kind of cool too.'

'In what way?'

'To finally be acknowledged for all the work I'd done.'

'Is that what the text was?'

Jessie nodded, and his eyes squinted in that way when someone was reminiscing over a fond memory. 'He apologised for standing back while Phil made our lives hell. Said he was going to make it up to us.'

'Wow. Did Mick receive one too?'

'He did.'

'Why didn't you guys say anything about this in court?'

'We weren't asked. We weren't asked much at all, to be honest.'

'Do you think Ray killed Bobby?'

Jessie breathed in through his nose and straightened up. 'It was his knife. He had a motive after learning about the affair.'

'Ray's text also started out as an apology, but then moved into Bobby's confession and threat. Was there anything else in your text?'

'No. I still have it on my phone. I'll be happy to show it to you when we get back.'

'Okay, that will be helpful. You didn't answer my question, though.'

'Do I think Ray killed Bobby …? I do. The jury got it right!'

63

Refusing to speak, Zoey reluctantly joined Jessie and me as we headed back to the main building. However, as we ascended the platform, that all changed.

Phil, Dee, and Mick, the guitarist, were in deep discussion. When Phil saw us approaching, he greeted us warmly. 'Hey guys, I just wanted to apologise. You know how I get when I'm working.'

'Yes, you're an arsehole!' Zoey said.

As if predicting her husband's reaction at being spoken to this way, Dee placed a supportive hand on his shoulder.

Phil's glance at his wife was as sharp as a killer's knife.

'It's okay. Let them speak, remember?' Dee said.

Remaining quiet and observant, I was more than happy to let the conversation continue.

'The thing is, Phil,' Mick said, looking down at the floor. 'The stuff we're working on's not that good, mate.'

In an attempt to keep him calm, Dee's fingers massaged Phil's arm.

'And you think yours is better?' Phil asked, pulling his wife's hand away.

'It's something we've been working on. I think it's pretty good.'

'But you know I hate reggae. It's not gonna happen.'

'It's better than the rubbish we're working on.'

There were two different reactions to monitor during the exchange. Although Mick's opinion was delivered from an offensive point of view, it lacked confidence and commitment, while Phil's defensive scowl portrayed anger. Readying myself to intervene, my instincts told me he was about to hit out. But instead, and with Dee in his wake, he dismissed himself from the conversation and sauntered off to the other side of the room.

Tommy Platt, who had been listening in, joined us. 'Why did you have to go and say that?'

'Because it's true,' Mick replied.

'But why now? Why didn't you say something before?' Tommy demanded.

'We did, mate,' Mick said. 'Why do you think he replaced us?'

'But Bobby was doing all the writing back then.'

'He was, but Phil didn't like it. He wanted to use his own material even back then. It was only Alex who insisted we stick with Bobby's stuff.'

'So, you'd tried suggesting other music before?' Tommy was doing a great job inadvertently asking the questions on my behalf.

'Jimmy did,' Jessie piped in. 'And look what happened to him.'

Jimmy Reggae?

Tommy said, 'Jimmy Reggae was a bum—'

It was so unexpected and so quick that if I'd blinked, I would have missed it. Zoey, the drummer, lurched forward and smashed her fist into Tommy's nose. 'You don't talk about my father like that, you bastard!'

Tommy stumbled backwards, grasping his nose.

As if in the eye of a pub brawl, Zoey scanned the group with manic eyes, tensing her fists as if warning off anyone stupid enough to intervene.

Like a zookeeper in a tiger's pen, Jessie held up his hands and approached her. 'It's okay, Zoey. Tommy didn't mean anything.'

'Yes, he did.' Her vindictive eyes returned to those of the victim. 'He probably helped that bastard to kill him.'

Once again, ignoring the urge to intervene, I quickly checked the guests with a sweeping glance to find them frozen in silence. All eyes were on the young drummer.

Bradley rose slowly and came towards us.

'You're Jimmy Reggae's daughter?' Tommy asked through a bloodied hand.

It was a revelation indeed, but one thing I noticed was that Mick's expression, looking equally as shocked as the rest of the onlookers, was the opposite to Jessie's, and I realised Jessie already knew.

It was time for me to take charge. 'Zoey … it's okay. We're all friends here.'

'*Phff.*'

Stepping between her and Tommy, I eased the big man back with one hand.

Bradley steered him away and took his place.

'Relax, Zoey, no one is going to hurt you,' I continued.

'I can't relax. Not until I finish what I came here to do.'

'And what's that?'

'Revenge.'

'Do you think someone killed your father?'

'I know they did.'

'Who?'

'All of them. They all knew about it, covered it up.'

'So, you know who killed him?'

She looked beyond me at the group, and following her gaze, I noticed all eyes had lowered to the floor.

'Bobby Sexton killed my dad!'

There was a low gasp behind me.

Bradley remained silent, and I realised he was happy for me to take the lead.

'Did you kill Bobby?' The questions were lining up in my mind, ready for the asking. *Did she purchase the knife from Jack Morris?* She was present at the meeting with Bobby the night of his death. *Did she go back and kill him as revenge for her father's death?*

'No, of course I didn't.'

Jessie was gently stroking her shoulder now, and she lowered her fists.

'I think we need to speak to Zoey in private, do you?' I said, turning to Bradley.

Bradley nodded. 'How about we go back to your bungalow, Zoey?'

After a reassuring nod from Jessie, Zoey said, 'Okay, but not with you. Only Scott, and Jessie comes too.'

'That'll be fine,' Bradley said and took me to one side.

'Are you okay with this?' I asked.

'Yes, if Zoey's more comfortable talking to you, that's fine.'

Seated on her bed, the millennial disposition had all but disappeared, replaced instead with the angst of a worried child. There was no camera crew present.

'It's okay,' Jessie reassured her. 'You'll be fine. Just tell Scott what you know.'

'But I don't know anything. That's why I'm here.'

'How did you get into the band, Zoey?' I wasn't a hundred per cent sure why I asked the question.

Once again, a reassuring nod from Jessie seemed to be the permission Zoey needed to continue. 'Uncle Jessie put in a word with Phil.'

'Uncle Jessie?'

Jessie held up his hands as if to say, "You got me!"

'Were you related to Jimmy?'

'Not in the paternal way, but we were brothers.'

'Do you believe he died at the hands of Bobby?'

'I do!'

'But why? What did Bobby have against Jimmy?'

Now it was Zoey's turn to reciprocate the reassuring nod as if to say, "It's okay. You can tell them."

'He found out that Jimmy was having an affair with his wife, Jo.'

'Jo and Jimmy?'

'Yep.'

'Were you at the party that night?'

'I was, Mick and me, but I left early. It was getting too crazy, man.'

'I hear Jimmy was a wild one.'

'Out of control once he got on the piss.' He reached out and took Zoey's hand. 'But a great bloke nonetheless.'

'Why didn't Jo come forward after Jimmy's death?'

'Because life for her was just too good, I guess.'

'But there was no prenuptial. She could have divorced Bobby and taken half of everything he owned.'

'Not if it was proven that it was her who was having the affair.'

'Bobby was shagging anything that cast a shadow. It wouldn't have been hard for her to file for a divorce.'

'She was an addict and Bobby was her only source of income. I doubt she was thinking straight.'

'So, you reckon she kept quiet?'

'I know she did.'

'Was she there that night?'

'Yes, she was.' Once again, his eyes met Zoey's as he spoke, and a slight frown acted as an apology. 'Flaunting it with Jimmy.'

My attention returned to the young drummer. 'Did you memorise the security code?'

Zoey scrunched up her face into the universal what-are-you-talking-about expression.

'When you were at Bobby's house earlier? You watched Phil punch in the code and remembered it when you went back later.'

'I never went back. I went home.'

'Did you get the knife from Jack Morris?'

'No.' She glanced at Jessie.

Jessie took her hand and squeezed it.

'I didn't kill Bobby Sexton. I wanted revenge, but not that way.'

'What other way is there?'

'I was hoping to find proof he killed my dad so I could bring him to justice.'

'You'd be pretty cluey with a mobile phone, I bet. All them apps?'

She shrugged 'What's that got to do with it?'

'Whoever took Bobby's phone deactivated the security camera and deleted the footage for the last twenty-four hours.'

'I wouldn't have a clue how to do that.'

64

Zoey and Jessie returned with me to the main building. *Were they suspects?* Of course they were, but it's not like we could lock them up, so after a quick recap with Bradley, we agreed to monitor them at all times.

The whiteboard was in need of an urgent update, but with neither Bradley nor I feeling inclined to leave the main building, a cerebral upload would have to suffice. As often was the case, my mind offered up the facts, opening them to debate.

Although the positioning was now quite precarious, warranting a potential reshuffle, Phil was still at the top of the list, with Margo close behind him, and then Sasha and Maeve.

But if Zoey May believed Bobby had killed her father, would she have taken revenge? Without the usual vigilance of Mrs Kennedy across the street, she could easily have slipped back into the property. But this also applied to Tommy and the musos. She did, however, have an alibi and I'm sure, if checked, her housemate would testify to her being at home around the time of Bobby's death.

While pondering over my thoughts, a gentle voice brought me back to the present.

'How are you holding up, brother?' It was Dhani.

'I'm good, mate. What about you?'

'Strange times, Scotty, strange times. Listen …' He took me by the arm and led me over to an empty space where no one could hear. 'Did you ask Maeve about her text?'

'I did, but she didn't give me an answer.'

'Hmm, I wonder why.'

'Are you saying she definitely received one?'

'Shortly after receiving my text, I rang Bobby, but there was no answer. So, wondering if Maeve had also received one, I rang her.'

'And had she?'

'She did, and she was quite irate.'

Lowering my head was an invitation for him to continue.

'She said she was going straight over there to have it out with him.'

'Really?'

'Yes. I think I talked her out of it, though. She just needed to vent.'

'What did she say?'

Confirming our earlier theory, Dhani said, 'She was angry because Bobby was about to take everything back—the houses, the cars and everything else. He actually said she'd thank him for it later when she'd learned to stand on her own two feet.'

'When you say, angry …?'

Dhani flinched in an exaggerated expression of shock. 'You think Phil has a temper? Where do you think he gets it from? Certainly not me.'

'She wouldn't be capable of killing her son, though, surely?'

Dhani shrugged. 'Maybe not on her own!' He directed his eyes towards Maeve and Sasha, who were staring back at us.

The names on the list were switching like the arrivals board at Brisbane Airport. *Did the information Dhani just shared add strength to Maeve and Sasha's motives? Could they have worked together? Both would have had a lot to lose had Bobby still been alive. Both gained immensely after his death, allowing them to maintain the lifestyle they were accustomed to.*

There was one more name I needed to add to the list—Dhani. *What was the purpose of sharing this information now? And why didn't he say anything during the court case?* Boy, I'd gone from having no leads at all to a conundrum of possibilities, all within the space of twenty-four hours.

With the need to deliberate with Bradley, I was heading in his direction when

I noticed there was an exchange of confrontational whispers going on between Angel and Jo. Leaving Bradley with Tommy, I wandered in their direction with Margo, Chris and Tim in tow.

Holding back a little while remaining out of the women's eye lines, I focused in on their discussion.

'How dare you judge me?' Jo hissed.

'Nobody's judging anyone, Jo. I just can't understand where it all went.'

'Fuck you, Angel. At least I didn't steal from him!'

'I did what I had to do.'

'And how did he react when he realised just how much you'd fucked him over?'

'Okay, that's enough.' Angel looked away, as if hoping Jo would disappear.

'You started this, remember? Judging me ... my habit.'

'Alright, just let it g—' When Angel turned back to face Jo, she noticed me and the camera crew. Her eyes fell to the floor.

As if sensing something was wrong, Jo also turned and realised we were listening and recording. 'Do you mind? We're having a private discussion here.' The twitch was now quite prevalent. The pale complexion and dark shadows below her eyes brought to mind visions of a thirsty vampire.

'There isn't any privacy here, remember?' Margo said.

'Just fuck off, will you? We've all had enough of this now.'

'Angel ... can I have a word?' I said.

The two women looked at each other momentarily.

'Why?' Angel asked.

'I just need to ask you something. It won't take long.'

Reluctantly, she rose to her feet, and I led her to the steps of the platform. Taking a seat on the top step, I tapped the space by my side, inviting her to sit.

'I don't know anything,' she said, folding in the bottom of her tunic as she sat.

'Listen, there's no need denying it. We know you received a text from Bobby on the night of his death.' Knowing nothing of the kind, I was hoping my matter-of-fact manner would slip through unnoticed.

'Text?'

After listening in on the brief conversion she'd just had with Jo, my mind had automatically created a feasible scenario. 'We're talking millions, aren't we?'

Once again, Angel's eyes lowered. Now she was staring at the track at the base of the steps.

'And sober Bobby, fresh from rehab with a cleansed mind, was pissed off. Was he going to expose you, Angel? Get back what you had stolen from him?'

'It was *my* money as well,' Angel said. 'Jo got a payout, so why shouldn't I have?'

'Because you signed a prenuptial.' I was silently celebrating a breakthrough. She hadn't denied there was a text.

'I had to put up with his shit for five years—the drugs, the women, the abuse.'

'How did it make you feel when you realised you were about to lose everything you owned, or worse, be arrested and tried for theft?'

'It made me physically sick. That's how it made me feel.'

For confirmation, I needed to hear her say it. 'Did you keep the text?'

'Of course I didn't. I deleted it right away.'

Yesss. Get in! 'And then you went to Bobby's house!'

'No ... no. I never went ... what are you ...? Wait ... Surely you don't think I killed Bobby?'

'You had the motive. You probably knew the lock code to get into the house. Knew how to wipe the security camera.

I'm suggesting you went around there to talk to him, beg his forgiveness perhaps, but you ended up killing him.'

'That's crazy talk. I was at my mother's house. She'll tell you I was there all night.'

'That's right. I read your statement. It never ceases to amaze me what lengths a parent would stretch to protect their children.'

'My mother's a good woman. She wouldn't lie.'

'Shame her daughter turned out to be a lying thief, and possibly a murderer.' Harsh words, I know, but if there were any cracks in Angel's alibi, I needed to prize them open.

'I didn't kill my ex-husband. A part of me still loved him. Yes, I used our money to invest in my business, and yes, he probably could have gone to the authorities, but I didn't even take the text seriously. It was just one of many I'd received over the years. Usually when he was on a downer with the need to blame someone for his misery, that was usually me.'

While I had her attention, I changed the direction of my questioning. 'I heard Jo say you were judging her.'

'I'm sure you've guessed by now that she's an addict.'

'Yes. And I know she also received a text with the news that her allowance was about to be stopped.'

'She was devastated.'

'Sounds like you both were!'

From my peripheral vision, I suddenly noticed a figure emerge from the trees farther down the track. As I squinted into the afternoon sunlight, my surprise turned to shock when I realised the person emerging from the trees farther down the track wasn't one of the guests.

Rising from the steps and leaving Angel sitting there, I marched purposely towards the new arrival.

65

'Kea Chapman? What are *you* doing here?' I should have known better than to think I was alone. Both camera crews were close behind me and quickly took up their positions around us.

'Hello Scott. It's good to see you again. I was invited.' The little psychic medium held out a heavily ringed hand.

Reluctantly, I shook it.

With an unexpected strength, she pulled me close. 'The killer is here. I can sense them.'

'But how did you get here?' I asked, ignoring the theatrics and gently pulling away my hand.

'Why Frank—' She turned. 'Oh, where did he go?'

'Frank brought you?'

'Yes. He was right here,' she said, peering back along the track. When she realised she was alone, she lowered her voice. 'I need to talk to you about him, Scott. There's something you need to know.'

'I appreciate that and all but—'

'Bobby is here too.'

'Right … of course he is.'

Tyler appeared, running through the humid day, his tunic dappled with spots of sweat. 'Miss Chapman. You decided to come.'

'You must be Tyler.'

'Yes. We didn't expect you to—'

'I had to come. My friend, Scott Stephens, needs my help.' After glancing at the cameras, she theatrically directed her to

308

attention to Tyler, and grasped his hand. 'Ronny says to stop worrying. It wasn't your fault, and he's okay!'

'What?' Tyler's eyes opened wide like he'd just witnessed a miracle.

'He said you need to get on with your life.'

'But …' His eyes welled and his bottom lip trembled. 'How could you …?'

'Why don't we show Kea to her bungalow?' I intervened, taking Tyler's arm and gently breaking him away from the strange little woman.

'Yes … yes, of course.'

'I don't want to be alone,' Kea said. 'Perhaps I can share with you, Scott?'

'Uhh, sorry, would love to,' *not,* 'but I already have a roommate.'

'Then who can I share with?' She returned her attention to Tyler.

'You can share with Mrs Morris,' Tyler said. 'I'm sure she won't mind.'

'Good. Lead the way. Can you come too please, Scott?'

'Sure.'

After a quick confab with Margo, Tyler ran off toward Stella's bungalow.

Kea insisted on taking my arm as we strolled in the same direction.

'There's an almighty storm coming,' Kea said, looking up into the clear blue sky.

'You reckon it's gonna rain?'

'I wasn't referring to the weather.'

'Rightio …'

Margo, Chris and Tim took over us and assumed the usual position in front.

Dressed in the obligatory tunic, any hopes of Kea having her mobile phone were dashed when I realised her belongings back in Byron.

'Listen, uhm, Detective Bradley Foster is here.'

'Oh, how lovely.'

'The thing is, no one here knows he's a copper, and we need to keep it that way.'

'Ahh, under cover. How exciting,' Kea said.

'Hardly, not the most glamourous of jobs.'

'This will be a turning point in his life, just like the one you're facing, Scott.'

'You don't give up, do you?'

Ignoring me, she continued. 'Not only will he be the detective to bring the real killer of Bobby Sexton to justice, but he will find love here.'

'For the purpose of the case, Bradley is just a friend of mine, okay?' She nodded.

When we approached Stella's bungalow, Margo insisted we wait while Chris and Todd entered first to film our entrance from inside.

Tyler and Stella appeared at the door.

Margo approached them, and out of earshot, she appeared to be giving them instructions. They both nodded, then Tyler broke away, and without making eye contact, he marched past us.

'Okay, I'll leave you to get acquainted with your new housemate,' I said.

I was about to leave when Kea tightened her grip on my arm. 'Don't keep her waiting too long, Scott.'

Tyler was standing under a tree, waiting. We were getting used to having the cameras following us around.

'Alright, mate?'

'Yes.'

There was a question I'd been meaning to ask. 'Who is actually funding all this? Alex or Phil?'

'Technically, Alex is because she's got the most money behind it, but she's showing no interest at all in the music. They're both the executive producers of the show, but since the record company pulled out, Phil is funding the album.' He leaned in and lowered his voice. 'Between you and me, Alex was about to pull out, too.'

'Really? What changed her mind?'

I was glad to see the smile return, but not so happy with its connotation.

'You did. Alex realised that having you here investigating Bobby's death would save the project and make it a worthy investment.' Then the smile disappeared. 'The old lady?' He lowered his voice once more, as if forgetting about the camera crew.

'Kea?'

He nodded and his expression cooled.

'She's a clever old bugger, mate. I'm guessing the person she mentioned was someone you once knew?'

Nodding once more, moisture appeared at the corners of his eyes.

'She will have done her research. Read up all about you.'

'But nobody knows about Ronnie.'

'Did something happen to him?'

The nod again, but more guarded.

'Would it have been in the news?'

'No. Ronnie was my dog when I was a child. I let him off his leash. He ran in front of a car and was killed. I was nine years old.'

'Was there any local record of the incident?'

'Nope!'

Hmm, 'She must have got the information from somewhere.'

'I've never told a soul! The guilt still haunts me. Only my mum knows and she's in San Diego. Surely, she wouldn't go to all that trouble to track her down. And even if she did, my mum has dementia, Scott.'

As with my experiences with Kea Chapman, I couldn't explain or pretend to understand how she did what she did. Perhaps I didn't want to. 'Like I said, mate, she's a clever old bugger.'

'I better let Phil know she's here,' Tyler said.

66

Returning to the main building, my silence prompted a reaction from the ever-considerate Bradley. 'Is there something on your mind, Scott?'

'Kea Chapman's here.'

'What? The psychic?'

'The very same.'

'How?'

'Apparently, Frank dropped her off.'

'Is he still here?'

'Dunno. I don't think so.'

With Tyler in his wake, Phil rushed from the platform towards Stella Morris' bungalow.

'Could Kea being here hinder the investigation?' Bradley asked.

Taking a moment to ponder over the question, something occurred to me. 'Perhaps not ... perhaps her presence could help us.'

'How so?'

We'd moved to the edge of the platform where no one could hear us, apart from camera crew #2, that is. 'You've seen how good she is. I mean, I don't know how she does it, but she has an effect.'

'Are you thinking she could provoke the killer?'

'Exactly. What if he or she falls for the act and decides this little old medium is a threat?'

'Believing she could reveal their identity?'

'Right.'

'That could put her in danger.'

Although I didn't relish the idea, keeping close to Kea Chapman for her own safety would seem to be the right course of action. Reluctantly, I realised the task should fall on me, and I was about to head off towards the bungalows when I noticed Phil returning with Kea and the camera crew.

After sounding the gong, Phil and Kea stood against the back wall waiting for everyone to arrive. When all were present, Phil raised his hands and, like a preacher quietening his flock, he gestured for us to be seated. Taking random positions around the floor, we sat down on the cushions and crossed our legs like infant schoolkids. Margo was present, standing in the shadows. The camera crews were filming from either side of the platform.

'Friends, it gives me the utmost pleasure to introduce to you our friend, Kea.'

A smattering of applause followed the announcement.

Quickly scanning the reactions, I noted that Maeve and Sasha Coburn shared the same enquiring expression. Dhani, with his eyes closed, seemed to be meditating. The ex-wives whispered among themselves, and I was glad to see that Jo had perked up slightly since I last saw her. Tommy and Lax remained indifferent, while the band members looked on like passive observers.

Kea stepped forward. 'Hi all, my name is Kea Chapman. Some of you already know me.'

Maeve quickly looked down, avoiding eye contact with the little woman.

'For those who don't, I am a psychic medium.' Her eyes met mine, and she winked. 'I come here today with a message,' she continued. 'A message from Bobby Sexton.'

Oh, God. Here we go again.

'Tonight, I Invite you all to join me in a mass séance. Because tonight …' Now she was looking directly into the lens of Chris's camera. 'Tonight, Bobby Sexton will reveal the name of the *real* killer.'

Kea would have been disappointed if she was expecting a sensational reaction to her statement. The guests, turning inwards in their little groups, whispered among themselves.

With the need to poke the hornets' nest rising within me, I called out, 'Kea …' and the audience hushed immediately.

'Scotty.' Her smile was warm, but I wouldn't say genuine.

'Are you saying the killer is here?' I asked while still gauging the reactions in the group.

'That's exactly what I'm saying.' She paused for effect. 'Bobby is here too … and he's not alone!' She was in top form, skilfully displaying her carnival skills.

'Who else is here?' Maeve's whisper carried through the acoustic rafters enough for everyone to hear.

Kea squinted as if trying to focus her vision. Lifting her hands to either side of her head, she rested her fingertips on her temples. 'I hear music. Caribbean perhaps.'

'Reggae?' Jessie said.

'Jimmy?' Maeve asked with great interest.

'I see water,' Kea continued. 'So blue. A man is floating face down. There is a figure above him.'

Although I was buying none of this, the details of Jimmy Reggae's death were in the public domain, so Kea could have … no … *would* have, easily done her research.

'The poor soul died at the hands of another,' Kea added. She, too, now was scanning the crowd with wide-open eyes.

'Okay, okay, that's enough.' I said, raising the palms of my hands. 'Let's wrap this up.'

'Let her continue, Scott,' It was young Zoey who spoke up.

'Later, my child,' Kea said. 'Tonight, at the séance, all will be revealed!'

Then, just like that, she marched from the platform and back to her bungalow. To my relief, Stella and Tyler followed her.

67

Apart from the knitting group, the rest of the guests returned to their bungalows. My intention was to rejoin the ladies. I had had little chance to talk to Maeve and Sasha, yet, so interacting as a group might be of benefit. Bradley, it seemed, had had the same idea and already taken up the task, and from where I stood, his knitting skills had improved to a level suitable for the group. While contemplating how I too could interact, someone took me by the arm. Turning, I was surprised to see it was Stella Morris.

'Can we talk …? In private.'

My immediate concern was for Kea. 'Is Kea with Tyler?'

'Yes, when I left them they were talking about a dog or something like that … but I need to talk to you.'

Surrounded by a camera crew meant privacy was impossible. She knew that as well as I did, and I wondered if the worried expression she wore was sincere or purely for the cameras. *Gosh, I was being judgemental.* I hardly knew this lady. 'What can I do for you?'

'Not here.' She glanced at the group and I'd be willing to bet a few stitches were dropped.

'Sure, how about we go back to my bungalow?'

Stella nodded and led the way off the platform.

With our heads down, we walked in silence, allowing Chris, the cameraman, to take up his usual position in front. Margo and Tim were guiding him from behind. When we reached my bungalow, I directed Stella through the gate, and the crew skilfully

315

circled us and followed. Once inside the tiny building, they seemed to blend in with the walls. Keeping the door open allowed me to conceal the whiteboard on the wall behind it.

'I'd like to ask if I could I get you anything, but there's nothing to offer.'

'I know. It's a joke, isn't it?' It was the first time Stella had spoken to me without a defensive tone. 'Listen, I uhm … I wanted to apologise.'

'For what?'

'For being a cow. I was very rude to you before and I'm sorry.'

'That's okay.'

'It's not. I want to explain, but that's not why I asked to speak with you.'

My adoption of a casual, no worries, demeanour was natural and offered as a way of helping her relax. 'I understand.'

'Ray and I, although living in the same house, hadn't lived as man and wife for quite some time.'

'Did he kill Bobby?'

'Of course he didn't.'

'So, you were covering for your son, Jack?'

'No!' Her forehead creased into a frown. '*Jack* had nothing to do with any of this.'

'He stole the knife.'

'No, he didn't. Jack was an opportunist. An addict. He was always desperate for money.'

'I'm sorry for your loss.'

'Don't be. It's a horrible thing to say, but it comes as a relief that he's finally free.'

'So, who do you think killed Bobby?'

'I don't know, but I think I might be able to assist with the case.'

'Yeah?'

'I thought it might be helpful if I filled in a few of the spaces for you.'

'Spaces? Such as …?'

'I know how hard it is to get anything out of these lot. They're a tight-knit group led by King Phil.'

'What have you got?'

'I'm guessing you already know that Lax is also Bobby's illegitimate son?'

'What?' I'm not sure why, but I didn't let on that I'd already worked it out. 'Bobby was Lax's father?'

'Yep. Beverly Johnson was an early groupie who fell pregnant at fifteen. Alex and Maeve covered it up, sent Beverly down to Mildura to have the baby, and paid for the child's upkeep under the agreement that Beverly would never tell her story. But when the boy became inquisitive in his teenage years and started asking questions about his father, it was Tommy who stepped in. He was paid to admit that he was the father. Having no family of his own, I think he actually took to the idea, especially when he met the boy.'

'Did Bobby know?'

'Of course. Everyone did. Bobby didn't care.'

My mind was working overtime. Tommy Platt was some employee if he'd openly agreed to take the boy on, but I think Stella was right. To Tommy, Lax *was* his son. A couple of scenarios played out in my mind. *In his new sober state, could Bobby, realising he had another son, have had a change of mind? Could he have threatened to ruin everything for Tommy by stepping forward? Would this give Tommy a motive for killing Bobby to protect the life he'd created with Lax?*

Or did Lax find out that Bobby was his father? How would he have reacted when he learned that one of the richest families in Australia had herded away his mother? Was there a motive there? Perhaps.

Stella didn't hide that fact that she was happy to share this information and the way she kept looking at Margo and the camera made me wonder if she was enjoying the attention.

There was a knock on the flyscreen door.

'Come in.'

Tyler bounded into the tiny, already overcrowded, space.

'Hey, mate. Aren't you supposed to be with Kea?'

'Am I?'

Shit. We obviously hadn't shared with anyone our concerns towards Kea's safety. 'Where is she?'

'She's at her bungalow. She said she needed to be alone to rest and prepare for the séance tonight.'

'How long ago did you leave her?'

Tyler shrugged. 'Fifteen, twenty minutes.'

'Okay, if you don't mind, we'll head over there.'

'Is there something wrong?' Stella asked.

'No … it's all good.'

We headed back to the main building, and I instructed Stella and Tyler to stay there.

Bradley didn't need too much coaxing to leave the knitting group. 'What's up?' he asked as we descended the platform.

'Kea's alone in her bungalow.'

68

Call it a detective's instinct or maybe even a sixth sense, but the image of what awaited us flashed through my mind before we even entered the property.

There was no mistaking the cause of death. Kea lay face up on the floor between the two single beds. Her opaque, wide-open eyes were locked on a point on the ceiling. In contrast to her sickly white complexion, her neck was a shade of scarlet, with deep crimson welts like the fingers of a glove.

While Bradley carefully checked the body for signs of life, I blocked the doorway with my frame. 'Get back, please,' I ordered Chris, the cameraman, who was trying to film over my shoulder. 'I'll need you to step back outside the gate, guys.' The duo did as I asked.

With a grave shake of the head, Bradley rejoined me at the fresh hold of the bungalow. 'I have to be honest, Scott. I'm way out of my depth here.'

'I know you are, mate. You and me both.'

'But you've had much more experience in matters like this.'

'I have. What are you suggesting?'

'Do we leave the scene as is and raise the alarm? Or do we have a look around first?'

'I'm not sure how we're going to raise the alarm. We'll need to figure that out, but it wouldn't hurt to have a look as long as we don't disturb anything.'

'Then you do it. I'll go back to the main building and summon the guests. It looks like we've got a killer among us.'

It made sense. If Bradley could round everyone up in the one place, it meant we could keep account of them all. Safety in numbers.

I went about my business in silence, only commenting mentally when something of note caught my attention. A hair, a fingerprint. Of course, both were likely to belong to Kea or Stella. Without the resources of forensic science, I had no way of knowing, but my intention at this point was purely to observe, not touch.

The indented finger marks around Kea's neck were a darker shade of scarlet. 'Strong hands,' I commented, looking closely at the bruised flesh.

My mind automatically sorted through the guests, categorising those who matched the description of being strong: Phil, Tommy, Lax, Angel, Dhani, the musicians, were all to be considered, but I couldn't rule out any of the other guests. Kea, although spritely, was small and frail. It wouldn't have taken much to overpower her.

I wanted to close Kea's eyes, but I knew the importance of leaving the scene exactly how we found it until the coroner arrived. As an automatic response, I checked my wrist for the watch that wasn't there.

'I told you the killer was here.'

'You did.'

'And now look what's happened. You should have listened. Just like you should have listened to your mum.'

My imagination often got the better of me. I sometimes feared for my sanity.

'Do you like reggae, Scott?'

Reggae again. What's with the reggae? Bob Marley came to mind. *Were there clues to be found in the lyrics of the Rasta legend?*

'I tried to warn you, but you can be awfully slow on the uptake sometimes.'

I wasn't about to have a conversation with a dead person, and that's not what this was. It was my subconscious searching for clues that I may have missed. 'How's that, Kea? How did you try to warn me?'

There was no answer.

When I returned to the main building, I was glad to see everyone was present and seated in their little groups. Apart from Phil, that is. He was confronting Bradley at the head of the platform.

'I demand to know what's happened.'

Bradley forcefully pushed him backwards. 'I need you to step back, please.'

'Who the fuck are you?' Phil spat.

'I'm Detective Constable Bradley Foster. Return to your seat, please.'

Margo approached me. 'What's happened, Scott? Is Kea okay?'

The last time Bradley and I had stood side by side like this in front of a group of people was when we were in the crime incident room #1 of Surfers Paradise Police Headquarters. I was the detective inspector in charge of the *X* case. Bradley was my assistant. On that occasion, we fronted over 100 detectives and uniformed police officers flown in from around the country to assist us with Australia's biggest murder investigation. Now, wearing identical beige tunics, baggy trousers and biblical sandals, we looked more like Bing Crosby and Bob Hope in the *Road to* movies.

The guests whispered and confided in their groups, while the camera crews moved around us, filming every moment.

Bradley, with only limited experience during his short career so far as a detective, took control of the situation like a seasoned pro. 'Ladies and gentlemen, if we could have some hush, please.'

The guests fell quiet.

'First, I'd just like to inform you that I am not actually a hairdresser, I'm Detective Constable Bradley Foster of the

Queensland Police. My apologies for not being entirely honest with you all.'

'What's happened to Kea?' It was Stella Morris who spoke up.

'I'm afraid I have some bad news.' Bradley turned to me momentarily, as if checking to see I was still by his side. 'Miss Chapman has passed away.'

Stella released a wailing shriek like an African widow. Tyler comforted her.

'We can't be sure of the cause of death at this point but …' Of course this wasn't true, but the guests didn't need to know the finer details. 'But we can't rule out foul play.'

Maeve, speaking loud enough for everyone to hear, said, 'Is it the killer? Is it the killer who killed my Bobby? Is the killer here?'

Ignoring the question, Bradley tried to continue, but Maeve was on a nervous roll.

'Kea knew who it was.' Her eyes desperately scanned the crowd as if rallying for support. 'And she was going to tell us tonight at the séance.'

There was no argument with the logic. Earlier, Kea the psychic, had announced to the group that she would reveal the identity of the real killer at the séance that evening. *Did I believe her?* No. But it looked like someone did. I couldn't help feeling angry at myself and Bradley for allowing her to be left alone. We'd actually discussed this as a scenario but didn't act on it.

'I'm afraid this is all the information we have at the moment,' Bradley continued, 'but for now, I'll ask you all to remain in the main building, please.'

While keeping a close eye on the reactions and responses of everyone present, my mind was going over the case and the current events. *Apparently, Jack Morris was killed by his girlfriend, who then killed herself, but what if they had both died at the hands of Bobby Sexton's killer?* Prior to the discovery of Kea's body, I would have dismissed the evidence as inconclusive, but now we could no longer rule out the fact that we didn't just have a killer in our presence, we had a serial killer!

The information was passing between myself and Bradley telepathically. I'm not saying we were psychic or anything like that, just that the same questions, scenarios and conclusions were going through our minds at the same time. I noticed Bradley was looking a little pale though, and I realised the enormity of the task that lay ahead of him. The similarity of our situations wasn't lost on me either. Here he was, a rookie detective constable, suddenly thrust in charge of a possible multiple murder investigation. Sound familiar?

Jo Sexton sat with Angel. Although no longer exhibiting the withdrawal symptoms of earlier, she sat with her head down, as if not wanting to be noticed.

'Hey guys,' I said, joining them.

Jo fidgeted and frowned while her eyes remained fixed on the ground.

'You're looking a lot better, Jo.'

'Thanks, I'm … feeling better.' She glanced at Angel for support.

'She was just a little tired this morning,' Angel said.

'Oh, she was more than that.'

'What's that supposed to mean?' Angel took on the role of spokesperson.

'How did you manage to score out here, Jo? There's nothing for miles around.'

'I was run down, that's all,' Jo said.

'You were in the early stages of withdrawal; we both know that. But now look at you. Positively spritely.'

'I'm not an addict,' she snapped.

Grabbing her arm, I turned it to reveal a graveyard of track marks on the underside. 'Oh, I think you might be.'

'Leave her alone, can't you?' Angel demanded.

'I'm afraid I can't do that.'

'I'm in recovery, okay. You happy now? When I get run down, I suffer from fatigue. Not that this has got anything to do with you.'

Although I couldn't hear what was being said, it looked like Bradley was receiving a grilling from Phil and Tommy. My instinct told me to intervene, but my conscience was telling me not to leave Jo. 'I'll need to talk to you, Jo.'

'Why?' It was Angel who answered.

'This is police business. We need to speak with Jo.'

Angel leaned in and lowered her voice. 'You're not a copper, so how about you fuck off?' Like a mother cat protecting her kitten, she pulled Jo close to her bosom.

69

While searching Kea's bungalow earlier, I was also pondering over what to do next. Obviously, we needed to contact the authorities, but how when there were no phones, and no human contact for at least forty kilometres? We'd considered one of us taking off on foot and raising the alarm at the nearest farm, but we quickly concluded that either of us leaving, with the killer among the group, was out of the question. While searching our minds for an alternative plan, I remembered my first meeting with Tommy Platt and his son. Lax, the experienced marathon runner, had run all the way from Broadbeach to Coolangatta, a good 30 kilometres, while hardly breaking into a sweat. Without the aid of a simple timepiece, but estimating it to be around 4:00 pm, if we sent Lax for help, could he reach the nearest farm by sundown? It would mean running almost a full marathon on an uneven track for most of the way.

'Could he do it?' Bradley asked after I explained the idea.

'I reckon he could. He'd need to go right away, though.'

'I can't see another option.'

As usual, Tommy and Lax Platt sat together, and away from the other groups.

'Hey guys, can I have a quick word?' I asked, joining them.

'Sure,' Tommy said.

Listening intently, the father and son remained quiet while I suggested the plan.

'You expect me to run a marathon through the bush—and in these?' Lax lifted his sandalled feet.

'It would be a massive help, mate. At the moment, we have a dead body in the camp—and in this heat.'

The father and son looked at each other for a silent moment, as if reading each other's thoughts.

'Could you do it?' Tommy asked, finally breaking the silence.

'I'd need to go now if I'm going to get there before nightfall. But yeah … I reckon I can.'

It was impossible to break away from the group with no one noticing, so after a quick discussion with Bradley, we decided to keep everyone informed on what was happening.

'That would be one hell of a run,' Angel said, eyeing Lax with admiration.

'It will indeed,' Bradley said.

Lax was already warming up.

'If anyone can do this, it's my boy,' Tommy explained proudly.

'Lax, are you sure you're okay with this?' Phil asked, approaching the young man.

'Yes, I'll be fine.'

When Maeve rushed over and threw her arms around Lax, I couldn't help but notice Tommy's concerned expression. *Obviously, he was worried about his son, but did contact and affection from the woman who, unbeknown to the boy, was his grandmother, place Tommy in a vulnerable position?* There was a definite cringe when Maeve spoke.

'You take very good care of yourself, my boy. We need you to come back in one piece. Do you hear me?'

Lax looked at his father. The coy expression and the blooming cheeks suggested this was more than just an old lady's concern. *Bugger me.* I reckon he knew she was his grandmother.

'Okay,' I intervened. 'We better get you away, mate.'

Stepping down from the platform of the main building en masse, the guests followed the young man, who danced like a boxer approaching the ring. When we reached the last of the bungalows, he turned and hugged his father. 'It'll be okay, Dad. She'll be right.'

'I'm so proud of you, son.'

'I know.' Breaking away from his father's embrace, he lifted an arm and saluted the small crowd before heading off along the track and disappearing into the trees.

Tommy turned and faced me. 'If anything happens to him, this is on you, Stephens.'

'I understand mate,' I said, placing a reassuring hand on his shoulder. 'He won't let us down, I'm sure of it.'

The guests had dispersed, and I suddenly realised that for the first time since finding Kea's body, we couldn't account for everyone's whereabouts. This was a dangerous situation. One of them was a killer, so it was important to keep them all together and accounted for.

Bradley, as if reading my expression, said, 'We need to get everyone back to the main building.'

'My oath. Let's go.'

It was probably less than a minute until we were climbing the steps to the platform, but to our horror, there was no one present. Bradley rushed over to the gong and gave it an almighty whack. Within minutes, the guests began to reappear from their bungalows.

70

'Fuck that,' Phil said when I blocked his path to the studio. 'We've got an album to finish. That's why we're really here, remember?'

'I'm afraid I can't let you do that, Phil. You need to remain here with everyone else.'

'You're not a cop. You can't tell me what to do.'

'No, but I am,' Bradley intervened. 'I'll arrest you and confine you to your bungalow if you try to leave this building.'

Deflated, Phil returned to where his wife and mother sat.

After a brief meeting, Bradley and I agreed that questioning each of the guests privately could have some merit, so taking two cushions to the far end of the platform, we set up a little area.

'What are you doing?' Margo asked as we worked in silence with the camera crews filming us from different angles.

The plan was for Bradley to conduct the interviews, while I watched over and monitored the rest of the guests. Glancing towards the ex-wives, I noticed Jo was positively blooming now, with a cheerful disposition.

'Jo, can we have a word, please?' I asked, startling her when I approached from behind.

'Sure, what's up?'

'She's not talking without me being present,' Angel said.

'Can you stay out of this please, Angel?'

'It's okay,' Jo said, taking her friend's hand. 'I've got nothing to hide.'

The over reactive response, the slight twitch and the dilated pupils told me differently.

When she sat on the cushion facing Bradley, the young detective's compassionate smile seemed to relax her a little.

'Hi Jo, how are you holding up?'

'I'm good … never felt better.'

Scanning the room, I realised, not surprisingly, all eyes were on us. Apart from Dhani, who sat with Stella, the Sexton family had formed a group, while the musicians sat with Tommy Platt on the other side of the space. Tommy was speaking while Zoey listened, and I wondered if he were apologising for the things he said about her father. Tyler was sitting alone with his back against the rear wall.

'So, we know about the affair, Jo,' Bradley said.

Jo suddenly sat up straight. Her startled expression begged, "Who told you?"

'How long did it go on for?'

It was of interest that Jo glanced towards the musicians, but what I found compelling was that it was Mick Mantle who reacted by quickly averting his eyes.

Jo shrugged and shook her head at the same time.

'Did Bobby find out?'

'No.'

'Are you sure about that? Isn't that why Bobby killed him?'

'What?' Her horrified expression was as ambiguous as her tone.

'We know Bobby killed Jimmy Reggae. How did he find out about you two?'

'Jimmy? What, you think—?' The glance again, only this time it was directed solely at Mick. 'Jimmy and I weren't having an affair.'

'Yes, you were. And Bobby found out, didn't he?' Bradley asked.

'I was not in a relationship with Jimmy Reggae.'

I was listening, but my attention remained on the guitarist. Mick briefly met my gaze and once again looked away. It was a punt, but I threw it. 'What Detective Foster means is, how did *Jimmy* find out about you two?'

Now it was Bradley's turn to adopt the same questioning expression.

'Did he threaten to tell Bobby?'

Realising I was onto something, but not knowing what, Bradley fell in line. 'Answer the question, please?'

'Jimmy was a loud-mouthed idiot. He was crazy that night. Just pissing everyone off. Punchy, and the more intoxicated he got, the more aggressive he was.'

'What happened?' I asked, taking over the questioning.

'He'd been taunting us all night. "Does Bobby know about you two?" and things like, "Geez, Jo. Where you gonna get your next hit without Bobby's money?"'

'Is that why you killed him?'

'That's ridiculous. I didn't kill Jimmy. He was as strong as a horse.' The twitch was increasing in intensity.

'You could easily have held him under the water later when he was off his face.'

Bradley was watching me closely, and I could imagine his mind putting the pieces together. There was still one piece of the jigsaw, though, that he didn't have yet.

I'd only just found it myself, and here it was. 'Or did Mick do it?' Although this theory contradicted the scenario that Jessie had put forward earlier, *was the bass player lying to cover for his friend? Or didn't he know about the affair between Mick and Jo? Assuming instead, or misinformed, that it was Bobby who killed the drummer.*

Jo lowered her gaze. Mick was watching us now with an intense interest.

'Mick killed Jimmy because he was threatening to expose his affair with you. Isn't that right?'

'I was asleep in bed by midnight. So was Bobby.'

'Together?'

'Yes.'

Remembering that the time of Jimmy's death was around 2:00 am, if Jo was telling the truth, she and Bobby had already left the pool area at that time. 'Who remained? The musos?'

'I'm not saying another word.' She looked at Angel with pleading eyes.

Angel launched to her feet and rushed over. 'What's happening?'

'Are we done here?' Jo asked.

The unified shrug and nod between the DC and the PI were enough to end the interview.

'We'll be talking to you again, Jo,' Bradley said.

Jo rose to her feet and, with the help of Angel, she ambled back to her cushion.

There was no need for verbal communication. Bradley waited as I approached the group of musicians. 'Mick, can we have a word please, mate?'

Mick glanced at Jessie.

Jessie held his stare but then nodded slightly, as if he were giving his permission.

Mick looked me in the eye. 'What for?'

'Just a chat. We're going to be talking to everyone.'

The guitarist dragged himself warily to his feet and followed me to where Bradley was waiting.

Bradley's raised eyebrows told me he was happy for me to start the questioning.

I cut straight to the chase. 'So, why did you kill Jimmy Reggae, Mick?'

As if overhearing, Jo's eyes remained firmly fixed on the floor and didn't meet Mick's questioning gaze.

'It's okay. Jo told us everything.'

Mick frowned and sat forward.

'About the affair. About Jimmy threatening to tell Bobby. Was he going to blackmail you?'

'Blackmail? What the fucking hell are you talking about?'

'Come on, Mick, we know you were having an affair with Jo, and we know what happened that night.'

'You don't know shit!'

'Then enlighten us.'

'Okay, Jo and I was …' He raised his shoulders and held out his hands. 'So what? Everyone knew. Including Bobby.'

'Bobby already knew?'

'Of course he did. I was doing him a favour.'

'In what way?'

'Mate, Bobby was a serial shagger, not really your loving husband type.' He lowered his voice. 'He was happy with our little arrangement.'

'Then why was Jimmy threatening to expose you?'

Mick chuckled. 'Like Tommy said earlier, Jimmy was a fucking idiot. A loud-mouthed crazy man. He didn't know that Bobby already knew.'

'So, who killed him?'

'Who said anything about anyone killing him? The verdict was misadventure, I seem to recall.'

He was right, of course. Jimmy's official cause of death was drowning while intoxicated with a cocktail of drugs and alcohol. I had one more question. 'Did you receive a text from Bobby on the night of his death?'

In opposition to Jessie's claim earlier that they both had, Mick's answer was a solid, 'No.'

71

There was one person in the group who we'd hardly shared more than a few words with—Sasha Coburn.

'Sasha, do you mind if we have a word?' I asked after approaching the Sexton group.

'What's this about?' Phil asked.

'Nothing for you to worry about, Phil. We just need a chat with Sasha.'

Sasha sat firm and shook her head. 'I've got nothing to say to you.'

'Why the animosity?' I asked. 'You've been nothing but defensive since we met. Why is that?'

'She's very private, Scott,' Maeve said. 'That's all.'

Reading the situation from across the room, Bradley joined us. 'I'm afraid this isn't a request, Miss Coburn. I'm going to have to insist you join us.'

Maeve took Sasha's hand and reassured her. 'It's okay, Sash, you've got nothing to hide. Just tell them what you know.'

Reluctantly, the tall ex-model rose to her feet. 'That's easy. I don't know anything.'

When we approached the cushions that we'd set up, Sasha refused to sit. 'Let's just get this over with, eh? What do you want to know?'

It was obvious from the defensive body language that the usual preamble and pleasantries would to be a waste of time, so I got straight to the point. 'Did you kill your husband?'

Sasha threw back her head and laughed. 'That's ridiculous.'

'Is it?'

'Why would I kill Bobby?'

'How much did Chanel sue you for again?' I already knew the sum but wanted to hear it from her.

'That's irrelevant.'

'Is it? Sixty million dollars, I heard. Is that irrelevant?'

'You heard wrong.'

'And you haven't worked since the action was filed. How many years?'

'I had other streams of income.'

'Oh, that's right. Of course. The business ventures: the clothing label, the fragrance line. How did they go …?'

She shook her head and looked away.

'But I guess at least you had the appearances: *Celebrity Big Brother* and *I'm a Celebrity Get Me Out of Here*, and whatever else you could get. They didn't actually go that well for you, though, did they? I have to say you were very brave, allowing the public to see the real Sasha Coburn.'

'Just like this, those situations weren't real.' It was that same arrogant attitude which turned a television audience against her that encouraged me to dig deeper.

'How much did you lose from the business start-ups?'

Her impatience was turning to anger. 'You obviously already know. What are you trying to do?'

'I'm trying to find out your motive for killing your husband.'

'I didn't kill Bobby, you idiot. I loved him.'

'It must have hurt then to learn your marriage over was from a text.'

'Our marriage wasn't over. It was just beginning.'

With no acknowledgement of the text, Bradley intervened. 'Would you be willing to share with us what was in the text?'

'What fucking text?'

'The one that changed your life!'

'I don't know what the hell you're talking about.'

'What were you and Bobby arguing about?' I asked.

'I'm sorry?'

'The afternoon before Bobby's death, you were having an argument.'

'No, we weren't.'

'Bobby said he was going to divorce you. And what was it you said …? That's right, "I'll kill you first!" Did you say that, Sasha?'

'That's pure fiction. Just like your pathetic life.'

As the interviews continued through the evening, and the sun was setting in the west, Dee at first had very little to share. The doting wife of the rock superstar. She did briefly mention her sadness at not having children, but assured us she was happy nonetheless. Even when I quizzed her about the alleged affair with Bobby, she laughed it off as if I were making a joke. 'There was never anything going on between Bobby and me.'

'Did Phil know?'

The smile remained, but the eyes narrowed just a little. 'Are you not listening, Scott?'

'We know about the text.'

'Text?'

'Bobby was going to tell Phil, wasn't he?'

Dee laughed. 'Tell him what?'

The interview was cut short when Tommy Platt approached us in a state of anxiety. 'Scott. I'm worried about Lax. He should have reached the farm by now.'

'Agreed.'

'I'm going to look for him.'

'I'm afraid I can't let you do that, Tommy.'

He puffed up his chest. 'You can't stop me.'

'Nobody's going anywhere,' Bradley said.

'But my boy's out there somewhere.'

'What would be the point, Tommy? If Lax has reached the farm and raised the alarm, it'll still be some time before anyone gets out here.'

'But—?'

'He could be back anytime now,' Bradley added.

'He'll be right, Tommy,' I offered.

'If there's no sign of anyone soon, I'm going,' Tommy growled. 'You ain't gonna stop me. Neither of you.'

Bradley placed a reassuring but forceful hand on the big man's shoulder. 'Just have patience, sir. We have faith in your son.'

Continuing with the interviews, Angel was in full defence mode and had little to add when we once again quizzed her about her financial situation. 'Arrest me then if you don't believe me!' were her final words.

Although it may have seemed inconceivable to provoke a kind old lady, there was a need to test Dhani's accusations that Maeve, one, had a temper, and two, that she received a text. 'How would you have coped when Bobby cut your allowance and took back everything you owned, Maeve?'

'I'm not sure what you mean, dear.'

'Dhani told us about the texts you guys received.'

'Texts?'

'Yes, the night Bobby died. You received a text from him.'

'Oh, that was just my Bobby being silly.'

'You didn't take it seriously, then?'

'No, of course not.'

The meeting of eyes was equal to a fist pump between Bradley and me. We had confirmation of another text.

'So, you weren't worried that your life was about to change?'

Her chuckle was as jolly as a village pub. 'I'm Maeve Sexton.'

'What does that mean?'

She leaned forward and lowered her voice. 'Who do you think has kept this family together? Not David. Not Phil.'

'You.'

'That's right. Bobby, God bless his heart, had no idea about his finances or of the business. I took care of all that.'

'But he was going to take it all back. That must have made you angry after all the years you'd looked after him.'

Her smile was as warm as winter slippers. 'You obviously don't know me, Scotty. I never get angry.'

'That's not what Dhani told us.'

The chuckle again. 'Dhani? You mean my ex-husband, David? You're listening to a man who walked out on his family. Did he tell you about that?'

Maeve Sexton was either a genuine, kind, and loving mother, or a brilliant manipulator. I hadn't made my mind up of which yet.

'I reckon it'd be quite expensive living in Byron Bay these days?' I asked Dhani as he joined us for his interview.

'Yes, it is. The old place isn't the same.'

'Be hard to carve out a living.'

'Not necessarily.'

'The market store's that lucrative?'

Dhani chuckled. 'Not on its own, no. The yoga is my main source of income.'

'Two or three times a week?'

'Six. Then there's the meditation classes twice a day, and I have a regular clientele for my massage services.'

'Sounds like you're a very busy man,' Bradley piped in.

'Yes, sir, I like to keep myself active.'

'Not so great having to work so hard at your age, though, surely,' I said.

'It's not work, Scott. I love what I do.'

'How old are you now, Dhani?'

'I'm seventy-eight.'

'Wow. Does it piss you off knowing how wealthy your ex-wife is, and that she doesn't have to lift a finger?'

Usually, at this point, the interviewee would become ruffled and ask, "What are you trying to say?" But not Dhani. My subtle attempts at provoking a reaction were so far getting me nowhere, which in itself was interesting because normal protocol would see a person at least beginning to defend themself at this stage.

'It depends on your definition of wealth, Scott. I'm actually one of the wealthiest people in Byron Bay.'

'Yeah? How do you work that out?'

'Health is wealth, Brother.'

And who was I to argue? Taking this lean figure at face value, I saw a tanned, healthy individual void of worry lines and signs of age. His soothing voice could easily be described as heavenly, and his whole relaxed demeanour was captivating and calming. If it was all a charade, then Dhani Sexton was a bloody good actor.

'So how come you didn't speak to your boys for so long? Years, wasn't it?' Bradley asked.

'Very unfortunate. My sons blamed me for the marriage break-up, which I guess was warranted. I couldn't be a part of that lifestyle.'

'The drugs, the money?' Bradley had taken over the questioning.

'Yes.'

'But Maeve did?'

The smile was the non-committal kind that said, "Yes", without speaking.

'I bet it was a shock when you received the text from Bobby after all those years.'

'A very pleasant one, yes.'

'And you claim it was an apology?'

'That's right. In his sobriety, he'd realised that I wasn't the cause of the problems in the family at all.'

'Was there anything else in the text?'

I understood where Bradley was leading the questioning to. Of what we'd learned of the texts so far, they seemed to have been two-fold, beginning with an apology, then ending with a sting.

'He was sorry for what had happened and wanted to make it up to me,' Dhani replied.

'In what way?'

'He didn't say.'

72

Now we knew for sure that Maeve, Angel, Dhani, Jessie, and Ray Morris had received texts from Bobby shortly before his death. It was feasible to believe that, apart from Zoey May and the Patels, everyone else here had as well. Even Tommy. And now, in most cases, it was easy to work out the substance of those personal messages. An educated guess told me that Tommy's text would have read something like this:

> *I am indebted to you, mate, for taking care of Lax for all these years and bringing him up as your own. But it is time for me to take responsibility now. I need to be a part of my son's life.*

Would this be enough to cause a confrontation between the two men? Tommy was a physically powerful figure. *Would he be capable of killing Bobby if he were pushed?* Maybe. We decided to speak with him next, but after looking around the main building; we realised he was no longer there.

'I'll check the toilets and anywhere else he may have gone,' I said, but I was pretty sure that Bradley, like me, already knew he wasn't to be found.

Mr Patel confirmed Tommy was in the kitchen earlier, as if looking for something, but he hadn't stayed long.

After returning to the main building, I wasn't surprised that Bradley hadn't found him either. We came to the same conclusion. He'd gone after Lax.

'Surely he wouldn't be planning on walking all that way?' Bradley said.

'I don't know, but we can't do much about it now.'

'So, what *do* we do?'

'Do you mind if I try something?' I said, placing a hand on the young detective's shoulder.

'Like what?'

'A bit of a group session.' I glanced around the area.

Bradley understood right away and nodded.

After making my way to the centre of the platform, I raised my voice so everyone could hear. 'Can I get your attention please, people?'

The immediate hush carried with it a communal wave of identical expressions in the narrative of concern.

'Can you all bring your cushions and form a circle around me, please?'

Bradley was the first to make a move, followed by Dhani. The rest of the group reluctantly obeyed by simply expanding their little circles and shuffling around.

When everyone was in place, Dhani stuck up his hand. 'Where's Tommy?'

'I was hoping someone could tell me that,' I said. 'Does anyone know where Tommy went?'

'It's obvious, surely.' Phil's tone was like that of a militant shop steward's during a meeting with management. 'He's gone to find Lax.'

'Did he tell you that?'

'Yes, he did.'

'And you let him go?'

'I couldn't stop him. Everyone knows they're free to leave here at any time.'

'That's not true,' Bradley said. 'Not anymore. Camp Sadie is a crime scene. No one is allowed to leave.'

'Did he say anything else, Phil?' I asked.

'No, just that he was going.'

'Okay …' I didn't have a clue where I was going with this. No longer having Tommy here meant we no longer had everyone in the one place. *What if Tommy was the killer? What if he was still here watching us?* 'First, I just want to assure you all that you are safe, as long as we stay together. Lax will have raised the alarm by now. The authorities will be here anytime soon.'

'But?' it was Dhani who spoke up once more. 'But …? There's a killer among us?' His eyes scanned the group.

'That's right. One of you here killed Kea Chapman.'

Jessie, the bass player, lifted his hand. 'What if it was Tommy?'

The catalyse for forming the circle was courtesy of a middle school memory when Mr Talbot, my PE teacher, got the Grade 6 footy team to form a circle in the centre of the oval, and asked each of us to share our thoughts on how we could improve the team after a string of defeats. 'How about we do a bit of group brainstorming?'

The cameras were once again set up opposite each other, but Chris's lens was focused solely on me.

'What do you mean?' Phil asked.

'Well, unless more than one of you were involved with Kea's death, it means you're all innocent apart from one person. Which means you're sickened and scared about what's happened here.'

Everyone nodded.

'We know that each of you received a text from Bobby on the night of his death.'

Eyes averted en masse, but there were no denials.

'And we know what each of those texts contained.' Watching and listening as I spoke, I noted the glances between Sasha and Maeve, Angel and Jo, or the two musos, Mick and Jessie. but I *was* surprised when Phil and Stella shared a look. Zoey May had remained quiet and pretty much inanimate all this time, so too had Tyler. Dhani seemed to be analysing the proceedings as much as I was. 'If anyone can tell us anything that will help shed light on the case, tell us. Tell us now, please. You're all safe.'

There were no takers. In the interest of sharing, would going around each member of the group and openly sharing why I thought they had a motive to kill Bobby have some merit? I was mulling over the pros and cons of the idea when my attention was drawn to the ex-wives.

Jo, noticeably twitchy again, raised her hand. 'I need to go back to my bungalow, please.'

'Are you okay, Jo?'

'She's fine,' Angel snapped, massaging Jo's arm.

'I don't think she is. Is there something back at your bungalow that you need?'

'I'm fine. Just tired, need a lie down.'

'Where's Frank when you need him, eh, Jo?' Jessie, the bass player, quipped.

'Frank? What's he got to do with this?' Before I'd finished asking the question, the answer exploded in my mind with a *WOOF*, like igniting the first barbeque of the season. *Was Frank also the band's drug runner?* When my eyes met Bradley's, I imagined the same scenario running through his mind. *Had he continued with the role, even after Bobby's death? Supplying Jo, perhaps? And did Bobby send him a text denouncing him as the vehicle that had ruined his life?* This theory would certainly resolve a lot of unanswered questions. *Was Jimmy Reggae also threatening to grass him up? Did Frank get the knife from Jack Morris? And fit Ray up? Billy the Bong said Jack was visited by someone just before he was killed. Was that Frank?* My mind was racing until it suddenly hit a roadblock. *How could Frank have killed Kea? He wasn't at Camp Sadie at the time of her death. Or was he? Shit!* Frank had dropped Kea off at the camp but then disappeared. *Did he leave then? Or did he stick around? Did he have a rendezvous with Jo and supply her with a fresh shipment? Could he still be here?*

Although I was sure our minds were working in tandem, I desperately needed to speak with Bradley to see if our theories tallied. But that wasn't going to happen soon, because the attention of the group switched from me instantly when Phil suddenly jumped to his feet. With a sense of desperation, he pointed into the darkness outside.

When everyone, including the cameras, followed his gaze, the women cried out in anguish.

Drenched with sweat, Tommy Platt staggered up the steps of the platform, his red, swollen eyes raging with desperate disbelief. In his arms was the body of his son, Lax.

73

It was Maeve who raced to meet Tommy at the top of the steps. In a distraught fit of desperation, she shook the lifeless body as if trying to wake it. 'No, no, not Larry, not my Larry!'

Tommy turned his back on her and snarled over a protective shoulder. 'Get away from him.'

Everyone was on their feet now and had moved towards the grieving father. Sasha comforted Maeve while Phil stepped forward.

'What happened, Tommy?'

Tommy ploughed backwards through the group, almost knocking Phil over. Like a colony of hungry Ibis, the camera crews circled while Tommy navigated until he reached us. Then he turned, looked me in the eye and growled through quivering teeth. 'Why did you allow this to happen?'

I was lost for words.

Bradley took over. 'I'm so sorry, Mr Platt. Where was he?'

'He barely got a few hundred metres.' He turned back to the group. 'Which one of you evil bastards did this?'

Like mourners at a funeral, all heads and eyes were low, as if avoiding eye contact at all costs.

'TELL ME NOW!' Tommy's yell echoed under the eaves of the open building.

Bradley spoke up. 'Mr Platt. I know this is difficult but, I'm going to have to look at the body.'

Surprisingly, Tommy nodded. 'Yes.'

'Can we take him to your bungalow?' Bradley asked quietly.

Tommy released a heartbreaking sob, nodded, then turned purposely once more and headed back in the direction from which he'd come. Bradley followed.

Moving everyone to the back of the building, I asked them to take a seat, which they all did without complaint.

'Who would do this, Scott? Who?' Maeve asked through her own tears.

'I don't know, Maeve, but we're going to find out.' The group had moved closer together, and I was warmed to see them comforting each other.

A short time later, Bradley returned alone.

Leaving the group, I met him at the top of the steps. 'How's Tommy?'

'Distraught, angry, dangerous maybe.'

'What was the cause of death?'

'A blow to the back of the head with a blunt instrument.'

'Did Tommy say anything about how and where he found him?'

'No, he's shut down. Won't speak to me. Maybe you could go over there, see if he'll open up to you?'

'Yeah sure.'

It was a heartbreaking scene. The deceased young man lay in his bed as if he were sleeping. Tommy sat by his side, holding his hand. 'I always used to tell him a bedtime story when he was a kid. Even when we were touring, I'd put aside that special time each night.' He lifted a hand to his face in an unsuccessful attempt to suppress the sobs. 'Why the hell did I allow this to happen?'

Gently, I placed a hand on his shoulder. 'I'm so sorry this has happened, Tommy.'

Tommy's attention remained on his son.

'Where exactly did you find him?'

'He was probably halfway between here and the gate. Looks like he was hit from behind and dragged into the trees.'

'Were there any signs of a struggle? Footprints perhaps?'

'No, the ground's rock hard.'

'It's probably a stupid question, but you didn't see anyone else out there?'

'No. Who?'

'Frank maybe?'

Tommy squinted as his mind considered the question. 'Frank? Didn't he go back to Byron?'

'That's what we were all led to believe.'

'You think he stuck around?'

'Maybe.' I was consciously speaking quietly and slowly, remaining careful to avoid an interrogation. 'You would know Frank pretty well, Tommy?'

'Not really. He's been around a lot of years, but he's a private man.' He gently stroked his son's hand as he spoke. 'Never really mixed with the band.'

'But he supplied the band with drugs.'

'That's right. He could get anything at any time. I always used to think him working for INSEXT was just a front. He must have been making massive money just from Bobby and Jo, but apparently, he was and still is, supplying most of the bands on the Coast—sports stars, pollies, you name it.'

'Did Phil know?'

'No. I tried to tell him a few times, but he wouldn't have it. Frank was his right-hand man. Still is.'

'Is he violent?'

'Hell yes. He's a quiet bloke but you don't mess with him. Claims to be ex-Special Services, but how many of those blokes do you know who goes off the rails?'

'Do you think he could have killed Bobby?'

'Oh look, I don't know.'

'What if Bobby had sent him a text threatening to expose him?'

'Well yeah, I guess.'

Mentally, I braced myself before asking the next question. 'Could he have killed Lax?'

I could tell by his puzzled expression that this was something he hadn't contemplated. 'You think he's been hanging around?'

'It looks that way.' At that moment, something dawned on me that I hadn't thought of before. As an addict, I'd struggled to understand why Jo would sign up for Camp Sadie knowing that there were no drugs allowed, and although she could have smuggled some in, not knowing how long we were going to be here, meant she could easily have run out. But not if her supplier had arranged to deliver a fresh batch.

When I thanked Tommy for answering my questions, the tears returned. 'I'll be staying here with him.'

'That's okay,' I said.

It was a simple answer in a complex situation and one that probably should have been up for deliberation, especially knowing that we still had a killer among us, but I understood his reasoning. Tommy was suffering from grief. Letting him spend time with his deceased son was the right thing to do.

On my return to the main building, Bradley broke away from the solemn group and met me at the steps. 'How did you go?'

'Not much to tell, really. He found the body off the track and didn't see anyone else or anything.'

'Hmm. Where is he?'

'He's staying back at the bungalow. I wasn't about to argue.'

Bradley told me more about the fatal blow. There was no blood, but the area at the back of Lax's head was heavily bruised. 'He was hit hard around the occipital region. Would likely have died instantly.'

'A precise strike? Someone who knew what they were doing, perhaps?'

'It's hard to know. Could have, or might have just been an opportune hit.'

I shared with Bradley my growing concerns as to Frank's whereabouts and my theory of him supplying Jo with a fresh batch of drugs. We both agreed on the next course of action.

'Jo, can we have a word, please?' I asked, kneeling down beside the two ex-wives who had moved away from the rest of the group.

It was hard to tell if the animated body language was a shrug, a nod or a shake of the head. A prolonged pause prompted a response. 'You can say what you've got to say in front of Angel.'

Because the group now was still quite close by, it wouldn't just be Angel who was privy to the conversation, but that was okay. During the time between arriving at the camp until Kea's arrival, Jo had noticeably changed both physically and mentally. Her skin was pale and almost translucent, her hair whispery and dull. The slurred words delivered with a gravelly wheeze made her sound like a three-pack-a-day smoker. To an experienced copper, this was the sign of an addict desperate for another hit. But then, as soon as Kea arrived, Jo miraculously showed instant signs of recovery. Now she was relapsing once more. 'So, Frank finally came through with the gear, eh?'

I'd seen the expression many times before. Confusion, uncertainty, the desperate eyes, searching as if deciding whether to continue with the pretence or give it up. She glanced at Angel, who offered some support with a gentle nod.

'He was supposed to give it to me after we got off the bus.'

'But in all the commotion, it didn't happen?'

'No, he didn't have it.' She was speaking freely now, as if deciding to abandon the pretence. 'Said he'd be back as soon as he got it.'

'And he did come back, didn't he?'

The glance again towards Angel. This time, Angel looked away. 'He did.'

'And he had the gear?'

'Not all of it. He's been getting greedy lately. Price is going up, but the quantity is going down.'

Through my peripheral vision, I could see Phil shaking his head with contempt.

'Is Frank still here, Jo?'

There was a low gasp among the group, as if they hadn't thought of this.

'No, he left. Said he had to get back to the Coast.'

Stepping away from the group momentarily, Bradley I conferred in whispers.

'It's all pointing to Frank, isn't it?' Bradley said.

'I'm guessing the agreement he had with Jo suffered relegation when he realised that Kea may have had something on him.'

'So, he killed her, and killed Lax to prevent him from raising the alarm. Do you think he killed Bobby? And maybe Jack Morris too?'

'It certainly looks that way, but I'm still not buying this 100%, mate.'

'I know what you mean. Let's keep an open mind. But what the hell do we do now?'

'We need to check the murder scene.'

'Of course. I should have thought of that,' Bradley said.

'Well, only one of us should go and I know it's breaking police protocol, but I'd like to go and take a look around.'

'No worries, that's fine. You go. I'll stay here and keep an eye on the group.'

Phil was obviously listening because he rose from his cushion and approached us. 'Frank didn't do this. He's a good man.'

'Surely you knew he was the band's drug runner. Or did you turn a blind eye? Were you monitoring Bobby's substance intake? Controlling it, perhaps?'

'Are you serious? Who have you been talking to?'

'That's not important.'

'I'll come with you to the murder scene. I'll die of boredom here if I don't do something soon.'

'No, we need you here, I'm afraid, Mr Sexton,' Bradley said.

'But why?'

'Because you are a suspect in a murder case.' Bradley's words were firm and final.

It wasn't difficult to see the anger in Phil's body language when he marched back to Dee and the group with his fists clenched.

'Scott, can we come with you?' It was Margo.

Bloody hell, I'd got so used to her and the crews following us around, they'd almost become invisible.

Bradley answered for me. 'Yes, that's fine. Take Chris and Tim. It will be good to have four of you together.'

'Safety in numbers,' Margo said.

74

By the time I headed off with my little entourage, the first glimmers of dawn illuminated a thick humid mist that hung around the trees like the set of a Hammer Horror movie. Bradley and I had agreed that rather than just travelling to the spot where Lax was killed, after doing a thorough examination of the area, we would continue to the gate to see if there was anything of interest there.

'So, it looks like congratulations are in hand, Scotty?' Margo said as we made our way through the cleared track.

'Why's that then?'

'Frank's got to be the prime suspect now, surely?'

'No … no more than you are?'

'Really? You still think I killed Bobby Sexton?'

'Unless you can prove otherwise.'

'That's just silly.'

I half agreed with her. She was no longer one of the main suspects, but it didn't hurt to keep her on her toes. 'Can I have a look at your hands?'

'Why?'

I reached out and took her right hand. 'Wow, you've got some power in them mitts. Is that from the paddle boarding?'

'I guess.'

As usual, Chris and Tim walked skilfully backwards while recording. Interestingly, Margo, seemingly no longer concerned about being caught on film, walked by my side.

The problem with keeping everyone together in the main building meant Bradley and I had little chance to discuss our findings in private, and even when we moved away from the group to engage in a quick discussion, I got the impression Margo somehow managed to overhear what was said. I guess this was how she made her living.

Apart from the fallen Stringybark that Tommy told us to look out for, he was right when he'd said there was little to see at the spot where Lax was killed. Although the ground was hard, there were some disturbances to the undergrowth. Unfortunately, there were no signs of a murder weapon.

'What do you see, Scotty?' Margo asked. She had moved back to her usual position behind the camera, and the threesome stood over me as I knelt, examining the ground.

'Apart from this area where the body was dumped ...' I was pointing at the indent in the layer of bracken, and the channel through which Lax's body had been dragged. '... it's clear that he was attacked from behind on the track then moved over to here.'

'Who do you think's responsible?'

Ignoring the question, I carefully retraced my steps back to the track.

It took about an hour to reach the gate. I was surprised to find it open.

'Why would this be open?' It was a question to self.

Margo remained quiet, as if she'd grown used to my strange ways.

There was very little to see on either side of the tall fence. The only tracks were hard, baked from past traffic.

The sun was slowly rising above the trees now and as its pink rays spread across the ground, something suddenly caught my eye. A reflection in the trees not far outside the gate, a glint from something shiny.

The ever-alert Margo saw it too. 'What's that?' she said, pointing in the direction of the flash.

Without the need to reply, I headed towards the spot with the crew close behind me. A black Range Rover was parked under the trees and would have been impossible to see if it weren't for the morning sunlight bouncing off the only non-stealth surface—the headlights.

'I've seen this vehicle before,' Margo said.

'Yes, it belongs to Phil.' I'd seen it a couple of times, but more recently, when Frank dropped Stella Morris off at the pickup point.

'But Frank uses it, right?'

'Right.'

Trying the handle on the driver's side, it was of no surprise to find it was locked.

'So, Frank's still here,' Margo said.

'We need to get back to the camp immediately.'

75

During the walk back to Camp Sadie, Margo was firing questions like bullets from a World War II Spitfire. Fortunately, my impenetrable shields were high, protecting a safe harbour, where I could think.

'So, Frank's obviously the killer. What do you do now, Scotty?'

'If he's here, is he watching us right now?'

'Will he strike again?'

'Who will he kill next?'

'Will he kill us all?'

'Oh, my God. What if he's already killed everyone back at the camp?'

My thought process was analysing the same questions as the TV producers, while adding my own. But the ripostes were just as illusive because there were more questions than answers. *How long had Frank been back at the camp? Had he been there since dropping off Kea? Or had he left and returned?* I found myself discussing these points in my head with Bradley.

"Do you think Frank killed Bobby?" Bradley asked.

"Let's suppose, like everyone else, he received a text from Bobby on the night of his death."

"A threat to expose him as a drug dealer?"

"That's the thing. I don't think any of these texts were idle threats. They were intentions. Bobby had made his mind up and he was going to follow through with a course of action to liberate himself."

"So, Frank killed him and framed Ray Morris."

"Possibly. Perhaps he got the knife from Jack Morris in exchange for drugs."

"Then he killed Jack when he thought the addict was about to squeal."

"It makes sense."

As we drew closer to the camp, my senses were suddenly alerted to the unmistakable aroma of fried bacon. The delightful smell of a proper breakfast intensified, greeting us when we approached the main building.

'Scott, how did you go?' Bradley asked, meeting us at the steps.

'Good. We need to talk.'

While in eyeshot of everyone on the raised platform, Bradley and I stepped away from the main building and into the shade of a tree across the track.

'What did you find?'

'Frank's still here!'

'What?'

'We found Phil's Range Rover parked outside the gate.'

'Can we be sure Frank was driving it?'

'Who else?' Camera crew #2 had joined us and were filming us from the opposite side of Chris and Tim. Margo, remaining out of shot, coordinated them with silent hand gestures.

While I filled Bradley in on what I'd found at the gate, I was eyeing the people on the raised platform of the main building. The small groups had reformed, and most of them were active. Dhani was giving Stella a massage and I remembered his strong fingers around my throat that evening when he gave me a neck massage at the Byron Bay markets. Mick, the guitarist, and Jessie, the bass player, were strumming guitars, while Zoey tapped the wooden floor with a pair of drumsticks. Tyler, sitting with them was hitting the tambourine in time.

Maeve and Dee sat together knitting. Phil was pacing backwards and forwards across the back wall, and I wasn't sure if this was a product of nervous energy or just the need for a feed.

Then I realised there were two people missing. Understandably, one of them was Tommy. We'd just passed him sitting outside his bungalow. Interestingly, he was smoking a cigarette. *Where did he get the smokes? Frank?* The other person missing was Sasha. Perhaps she'd slipped away to the toilet or to grab a shower. It was Angel, however, who caught my eye. Stripped down to her waist, wearing only a sports bra and the tunic bottoms, her muscular torso gleamed with a thin layer of sweat while she shadow-boxed a combination of martial arts offensive moves.

'Can I join in?' I asked after returning to the platform.

Lunging forward, Angel suddenly threw a punch, pulling it only millimetres from my face.

Reaching for the fist that remained locked in position, I drew it towards me. 'That's a powerful weapon you have there, Angel.'

'Better believe it, fucker.' Withdrawing her fist, she nestled it into her left hand, which was just as big.

My new fixation with hands resulted from the conclusion that whoever strangled Kea and killed Lax must have been reasonably strong. Dhani the masseur? The string musicians, Phil, Mick, and Jessie? The drummer, Zoey? And of course, the martial arts expert, Angel.

'Have you ever strangled anyone, Angel?'

'What kind of question is that?'

'A straightforward one.'

'No, I haven't. You?'

'You'd know where all the pressure points are. Wouldn't be hard to kill someone with your knowledge.'

Mr Patel was laying out the table with eggs, bacon, sausage, and all the ingredients of a full Aussie breakfast.

'Fuck that vegetarian shit!' It was Phil who approached the table first, grabbing a plate and shovelling as much animal protein onto it as he could. To the relief of the vegos, Miss Patel was loading the other side of the table with plant-based food.

'Can we have a chat, Phil?' I asked.

'As long as you don't mind doing it while I eat. I'm starving.'

'No worries.'

Once again, I was happy to let Bradley take control as the three of us sat down on the nearest cushions.

'Does anyone apart from Frank get to drive the Range Rover?'

'No … why?'

'It's parked outside the gates.'

His eyes searched mine for an answer.

'We think Frank's here.'

'Where?'

'Don't know, but we reckon he's been here for at least twelve hours.'

From the corner of my eye, I watched as Angel and the musos lined up at the carnivorous side of the buffet, while Tyler and Dhani were at the opposite end of the table. Maeve and Jo didn't appear too interested in the food. Dee joined us. She also wasn't eating.

'Hey, Dee. How are you holding up?'

'Good … not hungry, but.'

'You haven't seen anyone else hanging around here, have you, Dee?'

'What do you mean? Who would be?'

'Frank perhaps.'

'Frank? No. He's not here, is he?'

Phil excused himself and wandered over to the nearest cushion with a fully laden plate. Dee followed him.

Leaving Bradley to mingle in the breakfast line, I headed over to Stella, who was sitting on her own.

'Hey Stella, how's it going?'

'Good.'

'I noticed when you arrived. You came with Frank?'

'Yes.' She ate muesli as she spoke. 'Alex arranged that. It was a last-minute thing. I only agreed to come the night before.'

'Did Frank say anything on the trip down?'

After a sip of orange juice, she spooned in more cereal before answering. 'No, he never said a word after showing me into the back of the car.'

'Do you know him? Ever met him before?'

'No. He arrived on the scene after Ray's departure from the band.'

'Did he know Ray?'

'I don't think so.'

Along with everyone else present, Stella and I flinched and instinctively ducked our heads when a loud scream slashed through the morning air. Sasha Coburn came belting onto the platform from the back of the building.

Instinctively, Bradley and I rushed to her aid.

The ex-supermodel threw herself into my arms and, burying her face into my chest, her sobs reverberated through my body.

'What is it, Sasha? What's happened?' Bradley asked.

With her face still hidden, Sasha pointed towards the back of the building.

Gently, I prized her away from my chest and held her at arm's length. 'What's happened, Sash?'

'The stream ... at the stream ... it's ...' The sobs took control once more.

As before, Maeve, the matriarch, appeared and placed an arm around the woman's shoulder. 'What is it, dear?'

Shaking free of my grip, Sasha transferred to the welcome bosom of the older lady. 'The stream ... at the stream ... Oh God ...!'

Before we could protest, Phil was on his feet and rushing towards the back of the building. Everyone except Sasha and Maeve followed in hot pursuit.

By the time Bradley and I reached the stream, the group was already there, standing in a semi-circle in silence with their heads lowered. Ironically, they reminded me of mourners at a funeral.

76

It was the highly polished, cherry Doc Marten boots that first caught my eye as Bradley and I pushed through the small group. The blue Levi jeans, and the black Harrington jacket reminded me of Tetley's dad, Col, who'd been a bit of a skinhead back in the day. The shaved head and the large frame made it easy to identify the body, even though he was lying face down in the stream. It was Frank Mallard.

'Okay, I want everybody back over there please,' Bradley instructed, taking charge. 'And nobody leaves.'

Scanning the faces, I noticed Tommy had rejoined us after obviously hearing Sasha's screams, as too had the Patels. Under Phil's guidance, the group remained quiet and did as they were told. I wasn't completely surprised when Bradley allowed Margo and the camera crew to remain. They really had become shadows, which was a testament to Margo's skill as a producer.

The big man hadn't merely been stabbed; the laceration across his neck spread from ear to ear, and although his head was half submerged in the shallow stream, there was no need to move the body to determine the cause of death. The gaping wound had been washed clean from the flow of water and there was no blood around the scene, which lead us to believe the killing took place sometime ago. Touching the body confirmed that rigor mortis had set in.

'Once again, Scott, I'm out of my depth,' Bradley whispered as we knelt by the body. 'Do we follow procedure and leave the scene undisturbed? Or should we move him?'

We checked the banks on either side of the stream. The familiar tread of the other boots was prevalent in the damper ground on the far edge. Frank had approached from the other side. Interestingly, the footprint closest to the water's edge was deeper and elongated, as if the big man had launched himself across the narrow expanse. Unfortunately, any tracks that might have been present on this side of the stream had been annihilated by the group. However, on reflection, the only thing we would have learned was that the perpetrator was likely wearing the one-size-fits all sandals like the rest of us.

A thought came to mind. Submerging a hand in the water, I felt around the body. As suspected, I found a mobile phone crammed tightly into the right front pocket of his jeans. Carefully prizing it out, I handed it to Bradley. Then, checking the other side, I retrieved the Range Rover key.

Due to being submerged in the water, the phone was inactive, and even if we dried it out, no doubt it was password locked. Hopefully, the car key would dry out and still work.

'I'm making the call,' Bradley said. 'We leave him here and one of us goes back to Byron to raise the alarm.'

'I'm not sure that's such a good idea, mate.'

'Let's get everyone back and together.'

There were no objections when we shepherded the group back to the main building. On our return, Bradley took charge. 'Okay, I'd like everyone to grab a cushion and take a seat, please,' he instructed. 'Close in please, no stragglers.'

'How are you holding up?' I asked, crouching next to Sasha.

'I'm okay.'

Maeve was still comforting her.

'What were you doing at the stream?'

'My clothes. I needed to wash them. I can't stand dirt.'

'She *is* a clean freak. I can attest to that,' Maeve said.

'And you just found him there?'

'Yes.'

'Did you see anyone else?'

'No.' With a gentle shake of her head, she closed her eyes.

'Can I have a word please, Scott?' Bradley said.

'Sure.' We wandered over to the opposite side of the platform. This time, Margo and her crew were instructed to stay with the group.

'So …' The dark patches beneath Bradley's eyes told me he was struggling with the situation. And why wouldn't he be? A young, newly appointed detective constable with little experience. This case would be taxing, even for the most seasoned detectives. 'I still think one of us should head back to Byron.'

'We can't do that Bradley … think about it. The killer's here and they've got a knife.'

'What if we sent one of the others?'

'Like we did? Lax, you mean?'

'Fair point.'

'Who would likely have been the last person to see Frank alive?'

'Jo perhaps. Did she rendezvous with him at the stream after he'd dropped Kea off?'

'It's possible.'

'We need to talk to her again.'

'We do, but I've got an idea first,' I said. 'We've got everyone here. I think it's time we flushed out the killer.'

'What are you suggesting?'

As he listened to my suggestion, the reluctance in Bradley's response was matched by my own uncertainty.

'You'll need to do it in an official capacity.'

Bradley nodded. 'Yes, makes sense.'

We returned to the group.

'Can I have your attention, please?' It was a pointless request. He already had everyone's attention. 'We have reason to believe there is a weapon present in the camp.'

The only notable reaction apart from the nervous glances was a gasp from Maeve.

'I'm going to ask each of you, one at a time, to approach me,' Bradley continued, 'and you will be hand searched.'

Glances were replaced with frowns.

'I'd like you to step up first, please Mr Sexton,' Bradley said, directing his attention to Phil.

'You're going to search me like a criminal?'

'Not like a criminal, sir. More like an innocent person who has nothing to hide, perhaps?'

I was only half surprised at the reluctance in Phil's manner as he approached Bradley with his arms out wide. After all, he was once one of the biggest rock stars in the world, but could his imposition be down to that or the fear of being caught out?

While Bradley patted him down textbook style, I checked the cushion he'd been sitting on to make sure he had concealed nothing there, which he hadn't. When he returned to his seat, he remained quiet, as did the rest of the group while they went through the same procedure. Of course, we weren't really expecting to find the knife concealed on someone's person. If the killer was smart, they would have hidden it somewhere. The only estimation we could make of Frank's time of death was that it was sometime after he'd dropped off Kea. And at that time, everyone was still free to come and go as they pleased.

Apart from Dhani, I wouldn't say the rest of the guests obliged willingly. After everyone was searched, only the Patels were left. They had drawn closer together.

'Mr Patel, would you like to go first?' Bradley asked politely.

'I cannot allow you to touch my family, sir.'

'This is just procedure. It won't take a minute.'

'No, sir. I cannot allow it.'

'It's okay, Baba,' Jazmin said, standing up. 'We have nothing to hide. I will go first.'

'NO!' Mr Patel launched himself to his feet. 'Not one of these heathens will touch you.'

'But it's fine, Baba—'

'No. Never!'

'Mr Patel, I'm afraid I insist,' Bradley said.

'Just let him pat you down, Amir.' It was Phil who spoke up. It means nothing. Let's get it over with, eh?'

'No, sir. I cannot allow this.'

'Amir, as your employer, just do it, please.'

When Bradley stepped forward, the defensive demeanour of a proud, protective father instantly morphed into that of a cornered Bengal tiger. With wild, blazing eyes, Mr Patel lunged forward. I wasn't sure if what happened next took place in my head milliseconds before the actual event, or if it was my natural intuition kicking in, but I'd grabbed Bradley by the shoulder and yanked him backwards just as the blade swung through the air, missing his throat by millimetres.

Totally bewildered, Bradley stumbled backwards and landed on his butt.

There was no time for words. The manic Indian gentleman was coming for me now. Maintaining the momentum of his speed, he pounced forward with the large kitchen knife aimed at my stomach.

I'd like to say I'd lost none of my own speed and precision over the years since giving up the footy, but in reality I'd hardly even picked up a ball since I was fourteen, let alone kicked one. But if the media were to report on what happened next, after similar incidents during the *X* and *Tallebudgera* cases, they would likely coin it as my signature move. Without thought or commitment, the right leg of that promising fourteen year old shot out to deliver the perfect fifty-metre goal. Although the sandals gave little assistance as my toes made contact with the hand clutching the knife, those adrenalin-filled extremities felt nothing as they made contact, forcing the hand to release the knife, and sending the blade spinning up into the ceiling where it embedded in one of the rafters.

Bradley and Tommy Platt were on their feet and the three of us dived onto Mr Patel at the same time. But the man was unnaturally strong. It took the three of us to eventually wrestle him to the floor.

77

Was Mr Patel a killer or just an overprotective family man?

'Calm down please, sir,' Bradley said, as the three of us remained on top of the heaving mutation. 'Nobody is going to hurt you or your family.'

Mrs Patel cried out something in Indian.

Responding in his native tongue, the tension in his body diminished slightly at the sound of his wife's voice.

'Your family is safe, and you have my word. No one will touch them,' Bradley continued.

The muscles in the man's body relaxed.

'We won't need to search them, sir.' Proving to be the young professional he was, Bradley remained calm and respectful, even though he'd literally just been a whisker from losing his life.

Mr Patel nodded.

While maintaining a measure of restraint, we allowed the Indian gentleman to rise to his feet. As we did so, Bradley was gently whispering instructions. 'We're going to take you back to our bungalow.' Anticipating the reaction, he quickly added, 'It's okay, your wife and daughter will come with us.'

'It okay, Baba, we are here,' Jazmin reassured.

Mrs Patel stepped forward and placed her hand on her husband's shoulder. The Indian words she used seemed to synchronise with her daughter's reassuring tone.

'She says she is proud of him and that she will stand by him no matter what,' Jazmin said, translating her mother's words.

Mr Patel nodded once more, and the last remnants of strength drained from his arms.

'Do we need to restrain you, sir?' Bradley asked as we entered the bungalow.

After a fleeting glance towards his wife and daughter, Mr Patel shook his head solemnly.

I was the last to enter the building after briefly swatting away Margo and her minions and ordering them back to the main building. Also, trying to stay one step ahead, after realising there was no other form of seating apart from the two single beds, I carried in one of the outside chairs.

Mr Patel quietly took his seat as Bradley cautioned him, while I gestured for his wife and daughter to sit by his side on Bradley's bed. Tommy was still present, standing by the door.

'You can leave us now, Tommy,' I said without the need to deliberate with Bradley. 'We can handle it from here.'

'Yes, thank you for your help,' Bradley said.

Tommy momentarily scanned the room, then left.

Careful not to make any sudden movements or gestures, I asked the women if they were okay. Jazmin nodded, as too did Mrs Patel after her daughter had translated.

'Mr Patel, can you explain to me what just happened?' Bradley asked, taking a seat at the end of my bed.

'I was protecting my family.'

'Do you always carry a knife with you?'

'There is a killer in the camp.'

'And that isn't you?'

Mr Patel glanced at his wife once more before answering. 'I am an avenger, sir.'

'What does that mean, exactly?' Bradley asked, tinged with a questioning frown.

'I will not speak now without a solicitor present.'

'Did you kill Frank Mallard? And Kea Chapman and Lax Platt?'

Mr Patel sat silently, staring into his wife's eyes.

Although Bradley's method was admirable, it was textbook all the same. Meanwhile, my mind was delving outside the parameters of the information we had so far, searching for answers from unasked questions. It was time for the Scotty Stephens' approach. Something Jazmin had said earlier was turning in my mind like an orbiting satellite. 'I was sorry to hear about your eldest daughter, Mr Patel.'

It was apparent from Jazmin's earlier translations that Mrs Patel couldn't understand English, which meant I only had two pairs of eyes to analyse. A brief squint from Mr Patel asked, "How did you know about my eldest daughter?" while Jazmin's startled reaction asked, "Where are you going with this?"

'How did she die?' It was a pure hunch, but none the less feasible to assume that there was a reason for the overprotective behaviour.

Mr Patel remained firm in his silent conviction, so I directed the question to Jazmin.

'Two young girls living in the house of a rock star. Did something happen? Did something happen to your sister, Jazmin?'

There were two expressions shifting over the young woman's face. One was pleading for protection from her father, while the other begged him to remain calm.

'Answer the question please, Miss Patel,' Bradley said.

'My sister got caught up with it all. She …' Her eyes filled with apologetic tears as she remained looking directly at her father. 'She died from a drug overdose.'

Mr Patel inhaled loudly through his nose, and I feared he was preparing another offensive defence.

'It's okay, sir.' I spoke in a quiet, reassuring tone. 'We're here to help. If your daughter was harmed, we can help bring the perpetrators to justice.'

Mr Patel turned and looked at me directly through determined, bloodshot eyes. 'Justice has already been served.'

'Mallard?' My thoughts were working in real time with my mouth now, instantly translating into words. 'Frank Mallard supplied the drugs that killed your daughter?'

It was of no consequence that Mr Patel didn't answer. My mind was answering the questions as quickly as it could ask them. 'So, you killed him in revenge for your daughter's death?'

'He was an evil man. My actions avenged the many lives he took.'

'Why now?'

'I did not know who gave the drugs to my daughter until I saw that demon handing a package to Miss Sexton.'

'Jo Sexton, you mean?' I asked.

Mr Patel nodded.

'So, you killed him?'

'Avenged!'

'Have you … avenged before?'

Taking his wife's hand, he gently squeezed it. 'Only when needed.'

Mr Patel's nonchalant attitude towards taking a life in the name of revenge not only showed a disregard for the seriousness of his actions, but suggested he could justify them. He was gradually opening up, so I continued with the course of questioning. 'Was there anyone else?'

'The drummer!'

Bradley's glance in my direction said, "Whoa! Now we're getting somewhere."

'Jimmy Reggae?'

'The devil himself.'

'What did Jimmy Reggae do to offend you?'

When Mr Patel looked at his daughter, I could tell from her shocked expression that we'd headed into territory she knew nothing about. 'He raped my Senita.'

Once again, Bradley seemed happy to allow me to continue with the questioning.

'At the party?'

'Yes.'

'So, you went there and drowned Jimmy in the pool when no one else was around?' I was asking and answering my questions at the same time now.

'I didn't have to. He was lying face down in the water. There was no one else around. I wanted to make him pay, but even though I held him under, he was already dead.'

Speculation maybe, but the pieces automatically transformed into words as they fell into place. 'And Bobby saw you.'

'I didn't know that at the time.' He was speaking freely now, as if the information was common knowledge.

'Not until you received the text.'

'Yes.'

'So, he had to die.'

'There was still work to be done.'

'Right. If Bobby reported you to the police for killing Jimmy Reggae, as he promised in his text, you would never find out who was responsible for Senita's death and fulfill your vow of revenge.'

'I am an honourable man, Mr Stephens.'

I wanted to say, "You're a cold-blooded killer!" but resisted the urge in favour of maintaining calm. Instead, I asked, 'How did you get hold of Ray Morris' knife?'

'I did not.'

'But you used it to stab Bobby Sexton.'

'I did not.'

Bradley piped in, 'Are you saying you *didn't* kill Bobby?'

'I am not.'

'Then what *are* you saying, Mr Patel?' In contrast to the Indian gentleman's cool demeanour, my wavering patience was wearing thin. But when his eyes prompted a response to my question, the answer was there. 'You didn't use Ray's knife.'

Mr Patel narrowed his eyes.

Bradley remained quiet, no doubt realising I was onto something.

'You used *your* knife. The one that Bobby gave you.'

'There were two knives?' Bradley said.

'Two identical knives. I'd be willing to bet that Bobby had them made at the same time.'

<h1 style="text-align:center">78</h1>

While an army of uniformed police officers erected a makeshift control centre in the main building, the rumble of a diesel-powered generator created a carnival atmosphere.

After the interview with Mr Patel, it was obvious that someone needed to drive the Range Rover to the nearest farm and raise the alarm. Because Bradley was in charge, it was right that he remained at the camp with the guests. And seeing as Tommy Platt had taken on the role of his unofficial assistant since he helped us to overcome Mr Patel, the task fell on me.

With the detainee and his family under guard in our bungalow, and the guests briefed and ordered to remain in the main building, I hastily left the compound alone on foot until I reached the vehicle beyond the gate. Within the hour, I arrived at a farm called Boggers Way. Interestingly, it wasn't the case that occupied my mind during the drive. It was the situation with Jenny.

Although Jenny wasn't the detective in charge—that had fallen to our NSW associate and newly promoted DI Kelly Blake—she was very much the figure of authority.

There were words, but little comprehension. All I had was the visual. Blue eyes flicking between Bradley and me. The short hair—a little longer now. The charcoal grey business suit. Tanned skin after a week in the Whitsundays.

Jenny nodded as Bradley spoke, and I found my head was inadvertently following each nod.

'How about you walk me through this, eh?' She was talking to me now. 'Scott. Hello? Are you okay?'

'I fucking love you, Jenny Radford!'

Jenny frowned, but I noticed a slight blush. She glanced at Bradley, but he was staring at me wide eyed.

'That Dorian idiot's not the bloke for you.'

Jenny raised a hand, indicating me to stop. 'This is hardly the place, Scott.'

What the hell was I doing? I may as well have been standing there stark naked for everyone to see. The self-inflicted slap was a mental one.

'Do we have motives?'

'We have more than that,' Bradley said, before reciting an abridged version of Mr Patel's confession.

'Why didn't you call earlier?' Jenny asked.

'We didn't have a phone,' Bradley said. He explained how we'd had to give up all our possessions.

'You're a police detective. You came in here without a phone?'

'I was an undercover operative. I had to blend in.'

'You should have kept your phone, Bradley.'

Bradley lowered his head like a scorned child.

'I'll need you guys to make statements.'

'Of course.'

'Go back to one of the vacant bungalows for now. Try to get some rest.'

Reluctantly, we did as we were told.

'There's something I still don't understand, Scott,' Bradley said as we lay on our beds.

'What's that, mate?'

'Why did Mr Patel kill Jack Morris?'

'He didn't.'

'Then who did?'

'Frank Mallard, I'm guessing.'

'So, you think his death was unrelated?'

'I do. If it wasn't for Billy the Bong who said he saw a big man leaving Jack's unit not long before we found his body, I would have dismissed his death as just another drug-related incident.'

'But Jack had his father's knife.'

'No, he didn't. Never did. He was a desperate addict who was always looking for an angle to make money.'

'He thought he could sell us the information.'

'Yep. That's why he asked us to meet him at his unit.'

'But why did Frank kill him?'

'I'm guessing Jack's desperation prompted him to threaten the dealer with blackmail. Bad move.'

79

It was early evening when Bradley dropped me outside the X building in Kirra. Looking up towards my apartment, I noticed the lights were on.

Elvis must have stuck around, and although I was grateful for it, I was also anxious as to what state of mind I'd find him in. There were some bridges to mend, and I'd be doing my best to rebuild our fractured relationship.

After bidding Bradley good night, I trudged through the foyer towards the lifts, still wearing my Indian tunic. The short distance to the second floor didn't give me enough time to gather my thoughts. *What kind of mood would Elvis be in? Had he sunken back into depression? What kind of a mate was I to leave him when he was so down?*

The elevator pinged, the door slid open, and I stepped out onto my floor. The apartment was directly across the hall. Approaching it, I stood for a moment, listening. The faint sound of music filtered through the heavy fire door. *Was that laughter?* Like a hotel room, the lock whined and illuminated green when I swiped the key card across it. Opening the door, intense light spewed out into the corridor, carrying with it a wave of rock'n'roll music—Little Richard, if I wasn't mistaken.

With intense concentration, Elvis, wearing only his underpants, was jitterbugging with his chin up and his eyes closed. Facing him, and with her back to me, was his dance partner, wearing only a bra and panties.

They didn't hear me until I allowed the self-closing door to swing shut behind me, which always sent a shudder through the walls.

Startled, Elvis' eyes opened wide, then his face broke into an enormous smile. 'Scotty!'

The girl turned. 'Oh … Scott.' Blushing, she tried to cover herself with her arms.

Momentarily rendered silent with shock, this was the last thing I'd expected to see, but when my old mate bounded towards me, threw his arms around my shoulders, and lifted me off the ground in a bear hug, I realised I was almost in tears.

'You're back, mate!' Elvis said, squeezing me tightly.

'I am, yeah.'

'It's bloody great to see you, bud.'

'It's good to see you too.' And it was. It was more than good. When he put me back down and I had time to look into his eyes, there I saw the old Elvis that I knew and loved: the mischievous energy in full flow.

The dance partner had disappeared. She'd obviously ducked into the bedroom while I'd been distracted. The music was off.

'Is that really …?' I asked, knowing full well who it was but not really believing it.

She reappeared, buttoning up a bright summer dress. I'd never seen her like this before. Normally she wore trousers and a blouse. 'Hey, Scott.' She offered again, still embarrassed.

'Cassie.' I was as embarrassed as she was. It's not every day you see your architect dancing with your best mate in her underwear.

'We, uhm …' She looked at Elvis for support.

'We're getting fucking married, Scott. Can you believe it?'

'What?'

'Come in, come in.' Elvis beckoned me into the heart of the apartment as if he owned the place. 'What the hell's that you're wearing?'

'It's a long story.'

'Well, get showered because you stink. I'll fix you a beer.' Yes, the old Elvis was definitely back, bossy and in control. 'You can tell us all about what happened on your camp, and we can tell you what we've been up to.' A mutual glance caused Cassie to blush some more.

'You obviously haven't seen the news then?'

'No, why? What's happened?'

'I reckon it'll be on every channel,' I said, sauntering towards my bedroom carrying my suitcase.

Before stepping into the shower, I heard the unmistakable monotone voice of a news reporter blaring out from the TV. At least I wouldn't have to waste time telling them about the case. They even aired a brief interview with me at the camp.

Purposely taking my time in the shower, it was good to feel a proper flow of hot water on my body. When I eventually emerged feeling clean and relaxed, I slipped on a beloved T-shirt and a pair of shorts, then returned to the living room.

Elvis and Cassie, both dressed now, were seated side by side on the sofa, watching the TV.

'Bloody hell, mate,' Elvis said. 'We haven't seen any TV or even been out, so we didn't know.'

Cassie stood and offered me her place on the sofa. Elvis turned down the volume on the TV and also stood.

'That's okay,' I said, gesturing for them to sit.

'But are you alright, mate?' Elvis asked, remaining standing.

'Yeah, I'm good. It's all over and done with.'

'So, Ray Morris really is innocent?'

'Yep, looks like it.' The investigation was pending, so there was little more I could tell them than what was reported on the news. Turning to the TV, in a 'Breaking News' box at the bottom of the screen, I read the headline, "Three killings on remote Northern NSW farm!"

'And what about Phil? How did …? What did—'

'Forget about all that for now,' I said, stopping him in full flow. 'I want to know about this.' Smiling, I waved a finger between the two of them.

'Well,' Elvis said. 'Where to begin.' He looked at Cassie.

'At the beginning, perhaps,' Cassie said, taking his arm. 'It's all your fault, Scott.'

'My fault? Why?'

'We had an appointment to discuss the house plans, remember?'

'Did we? Oh shit, that's right, we did. Sorry.'

'You were obviously distracted. Anyway, not knowing you weren't here, I turned up with the plans.'

Now it was Elvis's turn to blush, which was something I'd only witnessed on a couple of occasions in all the years I'd known him. 'When she buzzed the intercom, and I told her you weren't here, I suggested she bring up the plans anyway and leave them here.'

'Which I did, and uhm ...' As she spoke, her eyes didn't venture away from Elvis'.

'Uhm ...' Elvis took up the thread, 'One thing led to another and ... and here we are!'

Overwhelmed with emotion at seeing my best friend happy once more, I dismissed the obvious nagging question: "Marriage?" No, for now, I was happy to bask in their happiness.

We shared a couple of beers out on the balcony, and Cassie eventually relaxed.

'So, remind me why we needed to meet about the plans? I thought everything was finalised.'

'Hmm, so did I,' Cassie said. 'Until that pig stuck his oar in.'

'Pig?'

'Dorian Malloy.'

'Ahh, Dorian, that's right.'

'He's trying to take over the build. Force me out.'

'Well, that's not going to happen.'

'I haven't met him, Scotty,' Elvis said, 'but from what Cassie tells me, he sounds like a right dick.

'He is.'

'You can't let Jenny get involved with him.'

'Sounds like she already is.'

'No, it's not too late. You need to meet up with her, tell her how you really feel and apologise for being a twat.'

'Hang on a minute.'

'Just do it, mate!'

80

Elvis had some secret business in Surfers Paradise that he refused to divulge and had already asked if he could use my car. He didn't have a problem, though, dropping me off at the Police Headquarters the next morning.

As I watched the VW Golf move away on Ferny Avenue, I realised how much I missed the old Dub. Sure, the Golf GTI had all the bells and whistles, but what it gained in comfort, it lacked in character. The Dub, on the other hand, was old, slow, a bit smelly, but bursting with character, and appreciating with age. A bit like me, perhaps.

Once again, Jenny was all about business. Her greeting was dispassionately official. That she was wearing the same clothes as the previous day may have explained this in part. She'd obviously done an all-nighter. From the dark bags under his eyes, so too had Bradley, by the looks of him. Far from his usual immaculate self, hair somewhat dishevelled, the casual clothes were the ones he'd worn on the way down to Byron Bay two days earlier.

We went straight to one of the interview rooms. When the three of us were alone, the atmosphere remained a little tense for the next hour as Jenny quizzed me over the events of the last couple of days. When my official statement was finally signed, Jenny sat back in her chair and quietly delivered one of those infectious yawns that prompted first Bradley, and then myself to follow suit.

'So, do we have any more information about Mr Patel?' I asked.

'We do,' Bradley said. 'He's highly decorated ex MARCOS—'

'What's that?'

'The Marine Commando Force. It's one of India's top Special Forces units.'

'An ex-marine? Wow! What else do we know?'

'There's very little else to know about his personal life. He's worked as a high-profile majordomo since—'

'Layman's terms, Bradley, remember?'

'A household steward, or a butler, at some of the most esteemed hotels around the world. He's also worked privately for several wealthy families.'

'Does he have a rap sheet?'

'Not a thing. Squeaky clean.'

Jenny was sitting back in her chair, happy, it seemed, to let Bradley answer my questions. I couldn't help noticing, though, how she diverted her eyes every time I looked at her.

'What do we know about the eldest daughter?' I asked.

'Senita Patel dropped out of law school while in her third year. Twelve months later, she died from an overdose of Fentanyl.'

'Was there any report of a rape?'

Bradley shook his head. 'No. Interestingly, though, she passed only three months after Jimmy Reggae's death.'

'Do we have proof that she was at the party that night?'

'No.'

'So, what happens now?'

Jenny sat forward. 'Mr Patel has confessed to the murders of Bobby Sexton, Kea Chapman, Larry Platt, and Frank Mallard.'

'What about Jimmy Reggae and Jack Morris?'

'He claims Jimmy was already dead when he arrived after the party. He flatly denies killing Jack Morris.'

'I'll speak with Billy the Bong again,' Bradley said. 'See if I can't get him to elaborate on his recollection of the person he saw leaving Jack's unit around the time of his death.'

'Frank Mallard?'

'Maybe. But we might never know.'

Jenny and Bradley rose to their feet at the same time, and I realised the interview was over.

Shaking their hands warmly, I congratulated them on a great job. 'Now go home and get some sleep,' I ordered.

Outside the building on Ferny Avenue, I was about to call Elvis to come get me when my phone rang. It was Phil Sexton.

'Hey Scotty, is there any chance you can drop by my place?'

'Sure. Now?'

'If you can.'

'No worries. I'll see you soon.'

After a short Uber ride, I arrived at Phil's house. When I pressed the intercom at the side of the gates, Phil answered almost immediately.

'Scotty, come right in, mate.' He buzzed me in, and the gates parted slowly.

Within a minute, he arrived in a golf buggy.

We shook hands warmly.

'Hey buddy, thanks for coming around.'

'No worries.'

'So, it's all over the news, but they haven't released any details yet. What's happening? Did Amir really kill Bobby and Frank and …?' he asked as we drove towards the house.

'It's an ongoing investigation, but I'm sure the Queensland Police will release a statement to the press soon. What did you know of him before you brought him to Australia?'

'Very little. Just that he was a highly recommended house manager. An honourable man, by all accounts.'

'And Frank Mallard?'

'Ah, now that was Bobby who originally hired Frank.'

'But you kept him on?'

'He was quiet, but very reliable and efficient.'

'Efficient in what way?'

'He managed our security. Kept us safe.'

'So, you knew nothing about the drugs?'

'No, not at all. I would have dismissed him years ago had I known.'

I found this hard to believe, but was willing to give Phil the benefit of the doubt.

'I've got something for you,' Phil said, changing the subject.

Uh, a cheque perhaps? Although it was Alex who hired me, the contract between us was a legal document, unlike the agreement with Phil. When he'd said he'd match my fee, it was on a handshake. Legally, there was no contract, so I wouldn't be pushing it.

As we approached the garage, Phil pressed the button on a handheld fob and the wide door opened. His timing was perfect, and we drove straight inside.

Like diamonds in a jewellery shop, the row of gleaming toys glistened beneath strategically placed LED lights in the ceiling. Leading the way, Phil moved to the farthest end where, nestled between a vintage Porsche 911 and a Ferrari Dino, was the 1967 VW Beetle. Exactly the same as my much beloved, and much missed girl, except showroom pristine in appearance, the sight of her brought a lump to my throat.

'As a sign of my appreciation, I wanted to give you a gift.' He held up a key.

'What?'

'It's the least I can do, Scott.'

Well, not really. You could pay the million bucks that you owe me, but the sentiment wasn't lost on me. 'You're giving me your Beetle?'

Phil frowned. 'Huh …? Oh, shit no … that's the first car I ever owned. *She's* not going anywhere.' Then I noticed the Porsche emblem on the key dangling in his hand.

'The Porsche?' I almost squealed, quickly forgetting about the VW.

'Yep!' He threw me the key. 'It's all yours, mate.'

'But I can't accept this.' The last time I'd been here, Phil had enjoyed sharing his knowledge of his cars. When describing the Porsche, he'd taken great pride in telling us how rare it was and how much it was worth. About $450k.

'I insist.'

'But …'

'Don't worry, this isn't payment, this is a gift between mates. The balance of your fee will be transferred into your account. Congratulations. You're a wealthy man!'

I was still in shock as Phil spent the next hour retelling me all about the car and going through the service history before skilfully manoeuvring it out of the garage. 'Just keep it serviced twice a year. She'll last forever and probably be worth a million dollars in the next five years.'

'Thank you.' I didn't know what else to say.

'No, mate. Thank *you*!'

A smouldering red sunset filtering through the Norfolk pines cast a pink hue over Burleigh Beach. Mowbray Park was alive with the nightly *chirpy-cheep* cacophony, as the local flock of rainbow lorikeets skittered from branch to branch, before bedding down for the night. The surf lifeguards had packed away the flags and headed home. Only a few swimmers remained, while a row of surfers sat bobbing out the back, waiting for the next set of waves.

To a Philistine such as myself, driving the Porsche wasn't that much different to the Dub, a lot faster of course, but more of a squashed down version. Being only two years' difference in age, the Porsche, a 1969 model, meant my preference for the classics was restored. As I strolled across

Mowbray Park towards the surf club, I couldn't resist turning for a look at her in the car park.

I'd arranged to meet Jenny in the bar, but when I arrived, she was standing alone outside the entrance. Seeing me, she smiled and waved.

'Hey.' I leaned in and kissed her on the cheek.

'Hey.'

Feeling a little awkward, I gestured towards the entrance. 'Shall we go up?'

'No, not yet.' Jenny took my arm. 'Let's go for a walk.'

We strolled arm in arm towards the beach. There'd been a high tide that afternoon, so the sand was firm when we stepped onto it. At the water's edge, we turned and continued to stroll north. An awkward silence pursued for some time, until Jenny asked, 'So, how have you been?'

'Good.'

'It's good to hear Elvis is back.'

'You've spoken to him?'

She shrugged. 'Maybe.'

'Right. And how's Dorian?'

'Dorian?'

'Yeah, you know, the bloke that whisked you off your feet?'

Jenny laughed out loud. 'Is that what you think?'

'What else is there to think after you disappear to the Whitsundays on his yacht?'

This brought on more laughter. 'You can be such a dick sometimes.'

'What do you mean?'

'Scott, Dorian is as gay as a picnic.'

'What? No …'

'Yep. I'm surprised at you for not picking it.'

'But he …? He's moving in with you?'

'Yeah, I'll need help to pay the mortgage, so he was going to be my flat mate.'

As always, my mind picked up on the finer details. 'Was?'

Jenny stopped and turned to face me. 'That's what I wanted to talk to you about.' She took my hands. 'I've decided I'm not going to buy the house.'

'What? Why?'

'It just wouldn't work—me living next door to you.'

A mixture of anxiety, fear and desperation overwhelmed me. 'Yes, it will. It'll be awesome—'

She put a finger on my lips. 'No, it's too late, I'm afraid. I've already sold it.'

'No.'

'Shh, listen to me.' She put her hands in her jacket pockets. 'I've sold it to Elvis and Cassie.'

I was stunned into silence.

'It's perfect for them.'

'I thought it was perfect for you.'

'No … there's a reason I can't live next door to you, Scott.'

Although Elvis had said nothing to me, planning the news as a surprise no doubt, on the one hand, I should have been happy for him and Cassie, but where did this leave Jenny and me?

Jenny produced something from her pocket—a small red box. She lowered to one knee and opened the box. 'The reason I can't live in the house next door, Scott, is because I need to live in the same house as you!'

I wasn't slow or anything like that, but an overwhelming ball of confusion swallowed up any words.

'Scott Stephens. Will you marry me?'

81

According to Jenny, the Quilpie opal, set into a silver signet ring, was 80 million years old and unique to Queensland. After a midnight swim at Burleigh Beach, the tiny gem flexed red, green and blue, under a moonlit sky. We spent the night at Jenny's, and although she had to be away early the next morning for work, we slept very little. I'd cried when she proposed. A group of walkers, recognising us first then realising what was happening when Jenny dropped to one knee, crowded around us.

'Will you marry me, Scotty?'

Lost for words and not really sure what was going on, I'd stood there, gob wide open, eyes searching the amazing blue orbs blazing back at me.

'Say yes, ya goose,' a voice from the growing crowd called out.

'Uh … yeah.' *Shit, what was I doing?* 'YES. Bloody yes!'

The crowd cheered when Jenny sprung to her feet and flung herself into my arms.

Lying in bed at Jenny's apartment on Goodwin Terrace, we were still chatting as the first rays of morning seeped over the horizon. The morning sex was even better than when we'd abandoned the idea of eating at the surf club the night before and gone straight back to Jenny's place. Making love to Jenny was more than just sex, and I hoped it would remain that way for the rest of our lives.

Unfortunately, Jenny had to leave for work quite early, but there was still time for a quick breakfast at the beach kiosk. Of all the topics we'd approached through the course of the night—the future, our careers, travel, and kids—we'd avoided the issue of Dorian Malloy.

'So, this Dorian bloke?' I asked with a mouth full of egg and bacon roll. 'What's the story?'

Jenny smirked, and I knew that look. There was mischief in the air.

We took a seat at a picnic bench on Mowbray Park. It was a perfect Queensland morning. The tumble of a gentle surf, the chatter of lorikeets, and the hum of early morning traffic carried on a warm summer breeze.

'Dorian?'

'Yeah, was he really going to move in with you?'

'Nah, not for a moment.'

'Then what was all that about?'

The smirk again, before she also took a huge bite from her roll.

'Was you playing me, ya bugger?'

She nodded, and the smirk graduated to a grin.

'You thought you could make me jealous?'

'Yep,' she put down the half-eaten roll, and wiped the corner of her mouth with a paper napkin. 'It worked, didn't it?'

'You scheming little sod.'

'I just figured it would never happen without a bit of help. You needed to see what you were missing out on.'

Although she was half joking, she was right. If it had been left to me, our relationship would have continued going nowhere.

My phone rang. As always, the jolly face on the screen made me smile. 'Good morning, Bradley.'

'Scott. How are you?'

'I'm good, mate—' I was about to qualify this by upgrading my status to, "really good in fact," when he interrupted me.

'Right. Is Jenny there?' I sensed caution in his tone.

'She is.'

'Is there anything I should know?'

'Nah, not really, mate. Just having some breaky.'

As if she could hear the other side of the conversation, Jenny jabbed me with a finger and giggled.

'Oh yeah, sorry. There is one thing, Bradders ... we're only getting fucking married!' I switched the phone to speaker so Jenny could hear Bradley's ecstatic cry. Then we both frowned abruptly when we heard another voice—a deep, familiar one.

'Congratulations!'

'Tyler? Is that you?'

There was a silent pause on the other end, before, 'It is ...'

Staring at each other, our faces locked in mirrored surprise, our eyes asking the same question, "Bradley and Tyler?"

Bradley spoke up. 'You're not the only happy people. Got to go, love you both, catch up soon.'

'Bloody fucking hell. Bradley and Tyler?' The words blurted from my mouth after the call.

'Good for them,' Jenny said.

'My oath.'

'Unfortunately, I've got to go,' Jenny said, after checking her watch and standing.

We arranged to meet at my place after work. During our long night, we'd discussed wedding plans and decided to tie the knot in three months' time, around completion day of the build. Until then, we'd flit between each other's apartments.

'See you tonight, Mrs Stephens,' I said after kissing Jenny passionately.

'You will.'

I didn't have a problem finishing Jenny's half-eaten roll as well as my own. Sitting alone at the picnic table and enjoying the morning sun, my phone rang for the second time that morning.

This time, the scrawny arse picture on the screen did more than make me smile.

'Tetley! Bloody hell, mate, it's great to hear from you.'

He was calling from the UK. 'Hey, Scott.'

The despondent tone immediately told me something was wrong. The absence of the cheeky, high-pitched greeting was foreign to me. Plus, he'd usually playfully address me as dick splash, or shit breath, or something like that. Never Scott. 'What's up, mate?'

There was silence on the other end.

'Has something happened? Are you okay?' I wanted to tell him about my engagement to Jenny and all the amazing things that were happening in my life at that moment, but I couldn't. Instead, I felt the need to listen.

'Yeah, I'm … alright, but …'

'But?'

'I'm not alright.'

Standing from the picnic table, I placed my other hand over the phone so I could hear better. 'Tell me what's happened.'

'It's Dad.'

'Colin?' A stupid question. He only had one dad.

'Yeah, he's in a bit of trouble.'

'What kind of trouble?'

The pause again, and I realised the guy on the other end, choosing his words carefully, wasn't Tetley. It was Sean Webster. 'He's been arrested!'

'Arrested? What for?'

'Murder!'

'What?'

'I can't speak about it too much at the moment, but they've opened up a cold case. They reckon Dad killed someone back in the eighties.'

'Bullshit. Not Colin.' I was pacing now across the park. Collin Webster had been like a second father to me since I'd arrived in

Queensland at the age of fourteen. An English migrant, he'd brought his family over from the UK in the late eighties. He was gentle, kind and considerate, with a subtle sense of humour.

'I know, it's crazy. The thing is, mate, we don't know what to do. Mum's beside herself with worry.'

'I bet. Have you got a brief?'

'We do, but I'm not very confident in him. It's not looking good, mate.'

There were a million questions I wanted to ask, but only one rose to the surface. 'What can I do to help?'

'Mum wondered if there was anything you can do.'

'Ah, mate. I'm not sure what I can do from here.'

'We realise that …' This time the pause lasted a little longer, and I was just about to ask if he were still there when he said, 'Mum said she'll pay for your return flights. You can stay with us and—'

'Come to the UK?'

'Yep. To Nottingham. I hate to ask, but we're desperate, Scotty. Will you come?'

I should have paused, took a moment to think, perhaps even discussed it with Jenny first, but I didn't. 'Of course, I bloody will!'

How would you rate
this book?

I hope you enjoyed reading *INSEXT*. If so, I would be truly grateful if you would consider writing a review.

Reviews are a very important way of enabling me to reach a wider audience and bringing my stories to more readers just like you.

If you have an Amazon account, you can rate this title and leave a customer review by scanning the QR code below or logging into you KDP account.

Or, alternatively, if you purchased your book from one of the online stores, you can login to your account and leave a review there.

Or if you have a Goodreads account you can post your review at:

Thanks in advance, I really appreciate your support!
Andrew

ACKNOWLEDGEMENTS

As a proud Queenslander, I'd like to begin by acknowledging the traditional custodians of this land which we inhabit, and pay my respects to the Elders past and present.

Thank you to my editor, Julie Guthrie, for your concise edits that force me to work a little harder, of which I am grateful. And a big thank you to the best beta readers ever, Carole Phillips, and Jane McDermott.

ABOUT THE AUTHOR

Andrew McDermott was born in Nottingham, England. A naturalised Aussie he has lived on the Gold Coast Australia since 1989 with his wife, Jane. He is a patron of the Gold Coast Writers Association, and currently resides at Kirra Beach.

Other books by this author...

Scotty Stephens Gold Coast Detective - Book 1

X

The eyes of the world are on Australia's Gold Coast, but for all the wrong reasons. Seven young women have been killed over a two-week period. The cause of death on each occasion was a slash to the throat in the shape of an X.

Detective Constable Scott Stephens is inexplicably plucked from obscurity, promoted to Detective Inspector, and placed in charge of the investigation.

Gold Coast Mayor, ex-AFL star, and billionaire property developer, Julian Monroe, has a lot to lose. Along with his involvement in various multi-million-dollar projects, his long-anticipated cruise ship terminal and casino resort is at a sensitive stage with potential investors.

Scott unearths withheld CCTV footage of the killer fleeing the scene of the last murder. The face of the offender is unmistakable - it's the mayor's son. The only problem is, he has an identical twin.

Scott not only needs to determine which twin is the killer - the brash, up-and-coming AFL star of the Gold Coast Suns, Dillon Monroe, or his brother, Troy - but he also faces a backlash from his employees when he suspects there's been a cover-up.

An explosive climax ensues, around the vibrant streets of the Gold Coast, when the killer's attention shifts, catapulting Scott's plight in a new direction - a fight for his life.

Also by ANREW M^cDERMOTT

FLIRTING WITH THE MOON

High-profile LAPD detective, Joe Dean, loses his career, his family, and his sanity when the twelfth victim of the serial killer – The Moon – is taken from right under his nose.

Twenty-five years later and Joe is a reformed character operating as a private detective. While working on a case, he comes across a book called *Flirting with The Moon*. Each of the twelve entries is a precise description of The Moon murders, which could only have been written by the killer.

The publisher is tracked down to Sydney, Australia but the only details they have of the author is a pseudonym and a post box number in a Far North Queensland town called, Candle Stick Bay.

Obsessed with the possibility of finally bringing The Moon to justice, Joe flies out to Australia and travels to the remote tropical North to find a tiny picturesque town overlooking the Coral Sea.

While posing as an American tourist, he secretly digs for clues and unearths some surprising secrets about the town and its inhabitants. But as his investigation twists and turns, the murders begin once more, and Joe is forced to confront the demons of his past.

Purchase your copy from all good online book stores or at:
www.andrewmcdermott.com.au

Download the prequel, Hidden Moon, for free at:
www.andrewmcdermott.com.au

Also by ANDREW M^cDERMOTT

THE TIGER CHASE

Dr Elizabeth Smith brings a rare Chinese tiger to the La Zoo, but the tiger is stolen on its arrival. Detective John Dean of the LAPD hates two things in life, strong willed woman, and cats. His worst nightmare is realised when he is ordered to retrieve the tiger with Dr Smith and travel back 2000 miles across America in a station wagon, with the tiger in the back, and a gang of crooks in hot pursuit.

The Tiger Chase is an action-packed story that incorporates drama and humour with a wealth of information about one of the most precious, yet most endangered, species on earth the South China tiger.

An entertaining story about the fight for survival which is sure to raise awareness about the very real threat of extinction facing the mystical and majestic South China Tiger.

Nick Rhodes, Duran Duran

For the first time in history, this most ancient tiger – the South China Tiger, is brought to the consciousness of the western public through story telling. The Tiger Chase has captured the spirit of the Chinese tiger, ancestral to all other subspecies, as well as the culture associated with it. I hope that the awareness it raises would encourage the reader to join us in our fight to save this cultural symbol and protector of nature from the fate of extinction.

Li Quan, Save China's Tigers (Charity)
www.savechinastigers.org

Purchase your copy from all good online book stores or at:
www.andrewmcdermott.com.au

Sign up at the link below to join Andrew's mailing list and receive your free ebooks, his bi-annual newsletter, be the first to know about up and coming titles, and have direct contact with the author.

"I would love for you to be part of my writing community. Your opinion is dear to me and I hope you will enjoy the books in my catalogue and all future releases."

Andrew

X'posé (X prequel)
Hidden Moon (Flirting with The Moon prequel)
Download your free ebooks here:
www.andrewmcdermott.com.au

You can also follow Andrew at:
Facebook: https://www.facebook.com/andrewmcdermottauthor/
Instagram: https://www.instagram.com/andrewmcdermottauthor/
X (Twitter): https://x.com/andymcdauthor